ARC RIDERS
THE
FOURTH ROME

DAVID DRAKE &
JANET MORRIS

ASPECT®

WARNER BOOKS

A Time Warner Company

WARNER BOOKS EDITION

Copyright © 1996 by David Drake and Janet Morris
All rights reserved.

Aspect® is a registered trademark of Warner Books, Inc.

Cover design by Don Puckey
Cover illustration by Jean Targete

Warner Books, Inc.
1271 Avenue of the Americas
New York, NY 10020

Ⓦ A Time Warner Company

Printed in the United States of America

First Printing: July, 1996

10 9 8 7 6 5 4 3 2 1

LET THE GAMES—END!

⇨ ⇨ ⇨

The tunnel acted as a wave guide, channeling the blast. Tiberius turned. Gray smoke puffed from the archway behind his chair.

A second grenade burst with a red flash. The guards went down like bowling pins.

Spectators screamed, surging like the tide.

"*Pauli*," Beckie Carnes said in a tone of quiet desperation, *"I can't get to the tunnel. There's too many people."*

The shock wave had knocked Tiberius down. His two surviving guards tried to carry him out of the way. The shouting mob blocked them.

One of the guards crumbled slowly to his knees. The other bellowed. He dropped his sword, clutched at his face, and collapsed onto the body of his fellow.

Kyril Svetlanov stepped out of the tunnel, reloading his submachine gun. His face was cheerfully pink, framed by its flowing white hair and beard. He looked like a 19th-century Santa Claus as he aimed the Skorpion at the future Emperor . . .

⇨ ⇨ ⇨

"FAST- MOVING AND EXCITING."
—*Kliatt* on *Arc Riders*

Also by David Drake and Janet Morris

Arc Riders

PUBLISHED BY
WARNER BOOKS

Acknowledgments

I asked Sandra Miesel for some research help on this one. She responded, as usual, with a stack of material which turned out to be crucial not only to the project's accuracy but to the way the story developed. Many thanks—also as usual.

—David Drake

The Russian characters in this book are fictional. Beyond the known deeds of historical figures on the public record, any resemblance to actual serving officials of the US or Russian Federation governments is coincidental and unintentional.

The Russian portions of this book are dedicated, on the American side, to Lt. Gen. Jerry Granrud, USA (Ret.), Gen. Dennis Reimer, USA, and John Thomas, whose vision and commitment made the real trips to Moscow during the winter of 1991-92 possible.

And on the Russian side, to Oleg, Sasha, Egor, Boris, Viktor, and Big George: may your hopes for your country come true.

Some of the places, events, and technology in the Russian portions are actual, some fictional. FILI did house SS-N-25s during the time period indicated. Whether they were armed is anyone's guess. Obninsk had no known temporal displacement project. To my knowledge, its real mayor and all its people are alive and well.

—Janet Morris

ARC RIDERS
THE FOURTH ROME

ARC Central

Out of the Temporal Universe

The six ARC Riders laughed and chatted in low voices as they walked into the briefing room together. Sure, you always looked forward to leave at the end of a mission; but you wouldn't be an ARC Rider if the missions and the people who shared them with you weren't the most important things in your life. Team 79 was glad to be back on the job again.

"Central's background material covers 1992 Russia where the revisionists come from and early 1st century AD Europe where they're operating," Nan Roebeck told her Anti-Revision Command field team. "Just so we know, though, I asked Gerd to predict the result if the revisionists succeeded in carrying out their plan."

The excellent holographic projectors of the ARC Central briefing room created solid-looking images with no fuzz or fade. A huge war machine hung in the air above the projector, appearing to trundle across a rolling plain. Black smoke spewed from four stacks. The turtle-backed monster rolled on pairs of iron-shod wooden wheels ten feet in diameter.

"For normal transit the machine is pulled by teams of oxen," explained Gerd Barthuli, the team's analyst. "In battle, as now, it's operating on its own steam engines. The boilers can use any solid fuel, but on the plains they're normally heated by a mixture of hay and horse dung."

He cleared his throat. "This is the most advanced military weapon of its day," he added.

Gerd wore a slightly quizzical expression, as though he wasn't quite sure what he was doing here. That was how the analyst usually looked. And felt, Nan assumed, which she regretted even though it didn't harm Gerd's performance. Gerd was the best field analyst in the Anti-Revision Command. He had his quirks, maybe even more quirks than other ARC Riders did, but Nan wouldn't have traded him for a pair of people who took her orders better.

"What period?" asked Tim Grainger, leaning forward slightly as if that would give him a better view of the puffing tank. A squadron of horse cavalry cantered past the vehicle. Half the riders carried a matchlock musket and a pair of long bamboo poles tied so they hinged into a bipod shooting rest. The rest had composite bows. "First century?"

Tim was thirty years old, little more than half Gerd's age. He was thin, intense, and an outsider like the analyst despite Nan's attempts to make him welcome. Grainger had been recruited from the beginning of the 21st century, a paranoid age of technologically literate "Haves" living in enclaves among a huge underclass of "Have-Nots."

Tim was of the former class. He was smart by any standards and comfortable with the technology of time displacement, but he was first and foremost a shooter. Tim Grainger had none of his 26th-century colleagues' horror of killing other human beings. That was both a benefit to the team and a constant worry to Nan as team leader.

"This is an extrapolation to 1992," Gerd said with a smile. "The same location in western Russia as well, though the city of Moscow doesn't exist in the timeline the revisionists' actions would create."

Gerd Barthuli could have been running a bureau in ARC Central instead of being part of one of the action teams tasked to eliminate revisions of the space-time continuum. He chose to be an ARC Rider because he was under a medical death sentence. Gerd had a genetic propensity to Alzheimer's disease and a protein allergy to the vaccine that had protected the general populace from the condition for centuries.

Gerd knew that at some indeterminate time his splendid mind was going to dissolve into static and psychotic rage. Until then he intended to experience as much of human existence as possible. There was no better way to do that than be an ARC Rider whose field was all history and prehistory.

"Is the background briefing right about this being a deliberate revision?" Pauli Weigand asked. "Not just Russian time tourists screwing things up by accident? Because that sure doesn't look like much of an improvement over where they came from."

Pauli was a big man with blond hair and Nordic features. From the outside he gave the impression of being solid to the point of stupidity. Inside he was so full of self-doubt that he was *never* sure what he was doing was correct. He acted anyway, with speed and resolution; the fears harmed only himself.

Pauli was Nan's assistant team leader. She couldn't have asked for a better one.

"The revisionists intend to make specific changes," Gerd explained. "They simply don't understand the real effect of those changes—which is scarcely surprising since the data-processing power to compute such complex models won't be available for five centuries after their period."

The display continued to move while the team talked. For a moment Nan thought the tank had exploded. Dense white smoke spewed from the bow, obscuring the front half of the vehicle. The cloud spat a glowing spark that sailed downrange in a high curve: the tank had fired a bombshell from a short-barreled cannon or mortar. The vehicle wobbled forward.

Musket barrels projected from ports around the tank's sides. A mast rose from the dorsal spine to hold a basket of archers and musketeers sixty feet in the air. No matter which way the wind blew, one or more of the stacks bathed the basket in smoke. The tank's interior must have been even more uncomfortable, an oven filled with smoke from the fireboxes and steam leaking through every joint and seam of the boilers.

Gerd allowed himself a smile. "There are those of us who believe there's an art to analysis beyond mere computation. This group fails on both counts. They'd be as horrified as anyone else to learn what their meddling with time had achieved."

"I'll still bet they don't thank us for dropping them back in 50K," Pauli said. "Well, I suppose I can live with that."

"First we have to catch them," Chun Quo said. Though her face and tone were impassive, the words made clear her mild disapproval of taking anything for granted.

Grainger was a shooter who could do tech in a pinch. Chun—family name first in Oriental idiom—handled the controls and understood the systems of a temporal transportation capsule superbly, but she was almost useless in direct confrontation. Quo's unwillingness to harm another human being made her hesitate to use even the nonlethal devices that were the ARC Riders' weapons of choice.

Nobody was perfect; a six-person field team was large enough to allow for a degree of specialization. As leader, though, Nan Roebeck made it her object to be able to do each job on the team almost as well as the expert.

She'd never be the analyst Gerd was, but she could do his job as ably as anybody else Central might assign to the slot. She was fast and accurate with the team's weaponry: microwave pistols, gas guns, electromagnetic pulse generators; needs must, with fléchette guns and plasma dischargers, too. Nan didn't like to kill, but she'd killed before and would kill again if that was the only way to save the mission or her team.

She didn't have Quo's intellectual understanding of TC 779's systems, but her own control of the transportation capsule was instinctively light and precise. Above all she knew her people, their weaknesses and their strengths. Central had made Nan Roebeck leader of Team 79, but her teammates followed her by their own decision.

"It's pretty straightforward, isn't it?" Tim Grainger said. "We eliminate the revisionists in 9 AD, then take out the laboratory in 1992."

He gave Quo a quirky grin. "And the population of 50,000 BC goes up by a dozen or so."

The Anti-Revision Command didn't kill—except as a last resort—those who tampered with time, nor did it exactly imprison revisionists. The ARC Riders took their captives to North America in the case of males, Australia for women, and released them in 50,000 BC, 50K, before human beings had reached those continents in the course of history. Each group of revisionists was separated from others by a century.

Though unharmed, the naked captives were of no further danger to the temporal continuum. They'd have to be both lucky and skillful to survive their first winter in their new environment. Those running the Anti-Revision Command might choose not to kill, but they were sufficiently ruthless in carrying out their mandate.

"I'm concerned that they use a psychic technique for temporal displacement," Quo explained. "It's not particularly subtle or flexible, but just because it's unique—that's correct, isn't it, Gerd?"

The analyst nodded agreement.

"Because it's out of our—out of Central's—previous experience," Quo continued, "there may be something to trip us up. I can understand any of the mechanical displacement methods we've run into, but this notion of mentally projecting people into the past is—"

Quo was small without being slight. She couldn't compete in peak strength with the team's males or even with Nan's own rangy body, but her stamina—mental as well as physical—was remarkable. She fluttered her stubby, capable fingers. She used wands for choice to control electronics; her hands were the most expressive part of her body.

"—magic. Fantasy. To me."

" 'Nevertheless it moves,' " Gerd said, quoting Galileo. "We can expect to increase the sum of our experience on this mission, indeed. And Central's experience as well."

He smiled again. There was always something sad behind Gerd's humor. It seemed to Nan that the analyst was really laughing at himself and his own vain hopes.

"Speaking of experience," Nan said, "have any of us worked in this sector before? I haven't. Early Roman Empire, I mean. Soviet breakup period we've done as a team."

"I did when I was in training," Pauli said. "But that was 3d century BC Sicily, and this is the Rhine area three hundred years later, right?"

Gerd nodded again. "Two hundred and sixty-four years after you were in saving Hamilcar Barca, Pauli," he said. "Effectively a different world. And none of the rest of us have been involved with the region at all. I'm looking forward to the experience."

"Gerd, you looked forward to the Black Death," Tim said. "Believe me, *I* didn't trust Central's vaccination that far."

"At least we don't have to worry about our timing at the early locus," Nan said after the general chuckle. "On the other end, we'll be upstream of our 1991 insertion, so that's safe enough."

Tim grinned at Quo. "Unless these psychic Slavs are making time run backward," he said. "Then we're in deep trouble."

Two versions of the same entity couldn't exist in the same continuum. An ARC Rider vanished if he visited a timeline for the second time. Maybe she was ejected into another lifetime, maybe he was dead. Maybe she drifted for all eternity in a timeless gray limbo.

In any case the duplicated Rider was no longer able to carry out the directives of the Anti-Revision Command, so the internal database prevented a transportation capsule from displacing to a timeline where any of the Riders had been before. That didn't keep somebody from displacing to a time before his previous visit and staying too long, though Nan had never heard of that happening.

Individual displacement suits didn't have all the safety features of a capsule. At least two Riders *had* managed to eliminate themselves temporally by getting hasty in their suits.

"Speaking of fantasy," said Rebecca Carnes, "that's what the revisionists' whole plan looks like to me. Did they really think changing history is so simple?"

She gestured toward the display. Beyond the steam-powered tank, teams of oxen hitched to poles were pushing forward a pair of wheeled bulwarks. Musketeers sauntered along behind the loopholed bulwarks. Tendrils of smoke drifted from their broad-brimmed hats. They carried spare matches in their hatbands in case the one burning in the gunlock went out.

"Permit me to introduce Trainee Rebecca Carnes," Roebeck said dryly. "Late of the 20th century, late of Team 79. She'll be with us while Jalouse is on leave."

"Hey, Beckie," Weigand said. "Good to have you back."

"I put in for you guys but I wasn't sure they'd let me," Rebecca said. "I'm glad they did."

Beckie Carnes was smart though not brilliant. Technology didn't scare her, but she wasn't technically oriented. She was in good physical condition for a woman of forty, but that wouldn't have earned her a slot in the ARC Riders either.

Beckie didn't panic, and she didn't quit. As a combat nurse in Vietnam she'd been in the middle of situations as bad as any in Anti-Revision Command's scope. She'd come through them—and come through still human, still able to care.

Besides, Nan was glad to have somebody on the team who thought her primary job was to help people.

"If we've got a trainee along, then Central thinks it's a milk run," Tim said. "Not that you're really a trainee, Beckie."

"If Central were perfect," Nan said before Quo could respond, "then you and I wouldn't have as many scars as we do, Tim. But we are all pleased at the assignment, Beckie."

Team 79 had snatched Carnes from a timeline that had to be destroyed. They'd needed her local knowledge to understand a period that didn't exist in the continuum in which their database was set.

After that operation was completed, Beckie had the choice of a comfortable existence in the 26th century—to which she was completely alien; or joining the ARC Riders herself. She'd taken the second option, just as Tim Grainger had done on an earlier mission. She was an asset to the organization and to Team 79.

Gerd nodded. "Rebecca," he said, "you're correct that the revisionists' concept is more a religious myth than a historical paradigm. That's unfortunately common in political discourse. After Constantinople fell to the Turks in 1453, Russian clerics invented the notion that as secular power had passed from Rome to Constantinople when the emperor created the new capital in 330 AD, so power had passed from Constantinople to Moscow in 1472 when the czar married the last Byzantine princess."

"It makes as little objective sense as Manifest Destiny or the Divine Right of Kings," Chun Quo said. "But those were good enough reasons in their times, too. Reasons to kill."

"The monk Philotheus of Pskov said, 'Two Romes have fallen and the third stands,' " Gerd quoted. " 'There will never be a fourth.' "

He looked at his display and added, "Of course, that's what the revisionists want to change. *Their* Moscow has fallen. They want to create a continuum in which a new Moscow rules the world, a Fourth Rome. The display shows what they would have achieved."

The tank had come to a halt. One of its eight bogeys sank to the wheel hubs in soft ground. Officers in carriages shouted abuse at one another and at the stolid footmen nearby. Sparks from a smokestack had started a grass fire. It was likely to spread out of control if everyone continued to ignore it.

"These revisionists were the scientific elite of a superpower," Pauli said. "With the collapse of the Soviet Union, they became the detritus of a Third World country that couldn't even feed itself. No wonder they're willing to grasp at straws."

He'd crossed one ankle over the other knee; his hands rested lightly on his thighs. Somebody who didn't know Pauli would think he was relaxed. Nobody really relaxed before a mission, and nobody with any experience trusted that a mission was going to be as simple as it looked in ARC Central.

"This is the revised timeline's military technology," Nan said. "What do their cities look like?"

"About what you'd expect," Gerd said. He adjusted the flat

gray device he was using to control the display at the moment. It was a multifunction sensor, display, and processing unit in its own right. Nan knew the analyst would sooner lose his right arm than give the device up. "Mud, hovels, and churches."

The display shifted to a village of round-topped huts, each in its own fenced yard. Pigs and chickens wandered through the unpaved streets, picking at the garbage. The onion-domed church was the only building constructed of stone rather than wood or wattle and daub.

"The revisionists' concept was rather clever," Gerd said. "Though the Romans began to exercise administrative control over all Germany during the reign of Augustus, their power effectively stopped at the Rhine after Quinctilius Varus was defeated in 9 AD. To Romans the frontier was a zone rather than a line in the sense that later ages thought of boundaries between states. By trade and military contacts—raiding on both sides, and from German mercenary service in the imperial armies—the German elite became aligned with the Roman elite. They had more in common with each other than either did with its own rural population."

"And when central authority in the West collapsed," Quo said, "the German elites were ready to replace Rome."

"Exactly," Gerd agreed. "What Central—and I—predict our revisionists intend is to permit the Roman Empire to continue expanding eastward to the Vistula River. That way the zone of assimilation will be among Slavs, not Germans, and the successor state will be a Slavic Fourth Rome instead of a Germanic Holy Roman Empire."

"They should have looked at what resulted when Moscow really did replace Constantinople as the power in the Balkans after 1453," Tim said. "Why would they expect the result to be any better if it included Central Europe as well?"

"Because they were desperate, Tim," Beckie Carnes said softly. "You and I don't have to look any farther than the worlds we grew up in to know what kind of bad decisions desperate people make."

She'd been a nurse in an Asian war her United States fought for thirty years, until war and nation ended with Amer-

ican warlords slinging nuclear weapons at enemies both at
home and abroad. Oh, yes, she understood desperation.

Nan stood up. Gerd switched off the image of squalor.

Nan looked her team over one by one and smiled. "Revisionist proposes, ARC Central disposes," she said. "Let's go
shift a little population back to 50K, people."

ARC Central

Out of the temporal universe

Carrying his personal kit in a cylindrical bag no bigger than his muscular upper arm, Pauli Weigand followed the rest of the team down the narrow red-outlined walkway. There were eight transportation capsules in a docking bay that could hold twenty. If you stepped outside the markings there was always the chance that you'd be standing in the spot another capsule transferred into.

A technician in the cab of a robotic workstation had removed a section of outer hull from TC 754, baring the ceramic core. Three members of Team 54 watched with studied unconcern. They had no part in dockyard maintenance like this, but they were well aware that the hull matrix held the electronics that displaced their capsule in time and space. Pauli understood why you might want to watch even if that was all you could do. He'd been there himself.

The hatch in the middle of TC 779's port hull bulged and opened as Nan reached it. The vehicle was a cylinder with rounded ends, a little under three meters in diameter and almost nine meters long. Now with its systems off, TC 779 looked gray and was mottled with marks of stress and repaired damage. A chameleon program would give the outer skin whatever color and pattern the operator chose, though it couldn't change the hull's basic shape.

Voroshilov turned from 754 and waved. He shouted, "Timothy, come see me when you get back." The bay's volume drank his booming voice. "I've got some schnapps you must try. Not vodka, schnapps!"

Grainger paused in 779's entrance lock. "Wish us luck, Klimenti," he called back.

Tim and Voroshilov had trained together. Both had been born in earlier centuries, giving them a bond of sorts in an organization largely recruited in the 26th century. They probably thought of themselves as outsiders; which was true, but *any* ARC Rider was an outsider. Even ARC Central itself, though located "in" the 26th century, was slightly out of temporal phase with the sidereal universe.

The only way to enter or leave ARC Central was by time machine. The psychic distance separating ARC Riders from their contemporaries was as complete as Central's separation from the continuum.

Voroshilov came from a period in which nationalism was still a powerful force. How would he react if this mission had gone to his team instead of 79?

You had to assume Voroshilov wouldn't have gotten through ARC screening if that was going to be a problem he couldn't overcome. Besides, no Russian nationalist would want the result these revisionists had achieved, whatever he might think of the idea in the abstract.

Gerd walked just ahead of Pauli. Instead of entering the vehicle, the analyst started around the blunt bow. Pauli caught him by the elbow and guided him back across the line. "I thought you were coming with us, Gerd," he said mildly.

You got used to Gerd wandering off. At least here Pauli was in a position to stop him. That hadn't always been the case.

"I wanted to see if TC 712 was in one of the berths on the other side of us," Gerd explained. "I like to keep track of the movements of other capsules."

"I talked to Metcalf yesterday in the canteen," Pauli said. "712's in the synchronous dock. She's been losing eight minutes every displacement, no big thing, but this past mission she started to gain instead. That's got them looking for the problem."

"Ah," Gerd said, nodding in appreciation. Pauli didn't

bother wondering *why* he wanted the information. For all he knew, Gerd might chart the movement of clouds every time he was under an open sky. The analyst did his job and then some. If he was weirder than the norm even for Anti-Revision Command, well, then he was weird.

"Pauli," Gerd said, "do you ever wonder who we're preserving the continuum for?"

Pauli blinked. The rest of the team was in the vehicle, but it'd take a few minutes for them to stow their kit and check on-board gear like weapons and displacement suits. Besides, an ARC Rider had all the time in the world.

Grinning faintly at his unvoiced joke, Pauli said, "Well, for everybody, I guess. I mean, people in the past as well as the folks Up The Line."

"Sometimes I wonder if we work for human beings at all," Gerd said. "Our century didn't create the Anti-Revision Command, you know. We just staff it. And there's no reason that the persons who made ARC Central and the capsules and the suits—the folks Up The Line, in the future we can't reach with their equipment—"

He smiled. On anybody else it would have been a sad expression, but with Gerd you could never be sure.

"There's no reason they have to be related to us," the analyst went on. "Whoever succeeds man on Earth would have an equally good reason for not wanting the continuum revised."

Pauli felt his guts go cold for a moment, then he laughed.

"Gerd," he said, "my job is to make sure that my parents get born the way they were supposed to, and all my friends' parents get born, and all my nieces and nephews and everybody else. That's a job I'm proud to do. I wish I were better at it, maybe, but I'll keep doing it as long as they let me. And if I'm working for cockroaches three million years Up The Line—well, that's all right. It's still a job worth doing, and they're welcome to the place after we've left it."

"Pauli?" Rebecca Carnes called from the hatch. "I can't carry you so you better come yourself. Gerd, you I can carry so you'd *damned* well better come."

"Sorry, Beckie," Pauli said. His arm shepherded the analyst forward. He didn't actually touch the smaller man. "We're having a discussion about the human condition."

"I don't think cockroaches are the most probable successors," Gerd murmured, "though it's an interesting concept. And you're quite right, of course, that it doesn't really matter."

He stepped aboard TC 779. "Measured against the heat death of the universe, at any rate," he added.

TC 779

Rebecca Carnes waited, feeling a little awkward. She was starting her first operational deployment as an ARC Rider and she didn't really have a job.

Nan was at the capsule's console, though for the moment the software controlled their displacement. The main screen turned the curving forward bulkhead into either a display or an apparently clear window to what was outside TC 779. While the capsule displaced, the exterior was a gray blur.

Quo sat with her back to the team leader, watching her personal display with a short wand in either hand. She would take over if something happened to Nan and the primary system.

The Riders' ordinary uniform was a body stocking with multiple pockets and the ability to change color as the user desired. The stocking and soft boots acted as undergarments for the rigid-walled displacement suits that Tim and Pauli wore as they faced the hatchway with weapons ready. The suits had integral time travel capacity, but for the moment the two men used them as armor against a possible threat outside the vehicle.

Tim held a fléchette gun with an electromagnetic pulse generator clipped beneath the barrel. The Anti-Revision Command didn't like its personnel to kill, but sometimes lethal force was the only practical option. High-velocity osmium fléchettes could penetrate armor or a vehicle, while the EMP generator fried electronics without damaging people or structures.

Pauli had an EMP generator also, but his was attached to a shoulder-stocked gas gun that could also fire acoustic grenades. A gas bomb paralyzed everyone in an area of two hundred square meters for up to three hours, while the sudden pulse of an acoustic grenade stunned people instantly over a similar area. Between them the two shooters could expect to handle any problem that arose.

Gerd Barthuli sat beside Nan at the bow controls, but his eyes were on an air-formed holographic display that from any other angle quivered like a heat refraction. The analyst's job was to browse the datastream TC 779's sensors would encounter as soon as the capsule reached a temporal location. Until then he was probably reviewing background materials downloaded for this mission.

Rebecca was backup for all the other team members. She sat before a flip-down console from which she could pilot TC 779 or direct its sensors. In her lap was a light plastic microwave pistol that would knock a man flat at fifty paces or give him a headache at twice that distance. Its twin barrels projected pulses of high-frequency energy that converged on the target to produce an 8-Hertz difference tone of very high amplitude. The effect was much like the kick of a mule.

There was almost no chance Rebecca would be called on to use any of those capabilities, but she noticed with some inner amusement she wasn't concerned that she'd screw up if she had to act. She'd had lots of experience dealing with extremely complex devices—human beings—in circumstances where there were a lot more ways to go fatally wrong than be right and there wasn't any time to think about it. That's what nurses do.

"Ten seconds," Quo murmured. Displacement—in time or space—took a perceived eighty-nine seconds irrespective of the distance involved. From inside, the only indication that a transportation capsule was displacing was the unnatural silence and the gray emptiness of the main screen.

Displacement suits supposedly had the same temporal engines as a capsule did, but Rebecca had never been able to believe the process was identical. Displacing in a suit was a taste of purgatory that missed being hell only because it ended. She was never sure the enveloping limbo *would* end.

Nan was as still as a wax image at the console. Her hands were spread above the keyboard controls. The pilot of a capsule on preset commands had nothing to do unless something went wrong. In that case she'd better do it right.

"Engagement," Quo said. The cabin brightened as if TC 779's hull had vanished and the crew stood in a marshy clearing. The main screen could again display the sidereal universe. There was no human being in sight. A long-eared squirrel chattered angrily at something in the branches above it.

"I have the controls," Nan said. Her hands now rested on the keyboard. Light shimmered before her, displays projected for her eyes alone instead of as sidebars to the main screen.

"Accuracy to within one meter and three minutes," Quo reported. She tried to keep the statement neutral, but there was obvious pleasure in her voice. Everything was going as smoothly as a training exercise.

"There are no revisionists on this time horizon," Gerd announced without emphasis.

Time travel affected the continuum the same way a tossed pebble affects the ocean. Even ARC transportation capsules left wakes, and the cruder techniques of revisionists experimenting with techniques new to them were more disruptive by orders of magnitude.

Instruments in ARC Central registered the disturbances, plotted them, and vectored a field team to readjust space-time to its original pattern. A capsule's own sensors were only marginally less capable than those at the base. Gerd had used them to cross-check the original tasking. This time the check contradicted Central.

Rebecca stood up for a better look at the main screen. To keep the pistol out of the way she thrust it into the cargo pocket on her right thigh. The problem wasn't one that she could help by shooting something.

"Temporal parameters check," Nan said. Her voice was calm but sounded thin.

"Sensors check!" said Quo.

Gerd Barthuli's fingers moved on the flat surface before him. Rather than a keyboard, the analyst used an unmarked plate to achieve greater flexibility of control. His face was still and he didn't speak: he'd said all he had to say at this moment.

Tim Grainger looked toward the bow. It was easier to switch the display within a suit's featureless helmet than it was to turn since the helmet was rigidly locked to the shoulder piece, but in a crisis Tim was likely to fall back on old reflexes. He preferred the speed and flexibility of the bodysock and wore armor only when he was ordered to.

"It's the phase lock!" he said, his voice booming through the suit's external speaker. "Drop us straight in. We'll be all right!"

As initially calibrated, TC 779 hadn't quite reentered the continuum. It hovered a fraction of a millisecond out of temporal phase, invisible—nonexistent—to eyes in the sidereal universe but still able to observe that universe through its sensors. Sound waves and the electro-optical spectrum were shifted a few angstroms, but the capsule's AI could adjust that in the rare instance it made any difference.

Tim was saying that the capsule's being out of phase was causing the sensors to miss the presence of temporal anomalies. Rebecca couldn't imagine why that would be, but she didn't have a better notion.

Apparently neither did Nan Roebeck. "We're going in," she said and touched a control. TC 779 wobbled minutely as it settled into boggy soil.

The squirrel vanished to the other side of the trunk. Its furious chattering resumed a moment later.

"There are still no revisionists on this horizon," Gerd said. "This isn't a sensor failure. All the background readings show proper variation. The indications that Central noted are not present *on* the horizon."

"They spotted us and displaced," Pauli said. He remained

poised by the hatch; as good a place as any and the one he'd been given before the problem occurred. Solid as a tree, Pauli was.

"If they had been here, there'd be traces in the continuum," Quo said in a brittle tone. Her wands moved in short, sharp arcs like the tapping of a bird's beak. She scowled at whatever her display showed. "They're not here!"

Rebecca had a sudden vision of TC 779's presence buffeting naked figures aside like flotsam caught in a speedboat's bow wave. The revisionists' displacement technique was radically different from the bubbles of separate space-time generated by ARC transportation capsules. Different, and on the evidence incompatible.

"They didn't run," she said. "We pushed them away. They can't exist where we do."

"Right," said Nan Roebeck without particular emphasis. "I'm going to displace us out of phase to the revisionists' predicted location."

"I've set those parameters," Quo said tightly.

"So have I," Nan replied as her fingers moved on the controls. "So have I, Quo, but I'm going to take us in manually."

Rebecca felt the capsule's floor grow vaguely unstable. The display blurred as if they were driving through the trees and occasionally the ground itself. Because the vehicle was again outside the sidereal universe, there could be no actual contact.

"Rebecca's suggestion would explain the anomaly," Gerd said. "I don't believe that Central was completely in error."

"Right or wrong," Tim Grainger said, "how do we nail them if we can't get into the same time horizon? They're going to land somewhere. The chances are they'll do just as much harm in the year 10 as they would 9."

The viewpoint feeding the display swept forward. Nan had programmed TC 779 to arrive at an uninhabited spot so that they could check calibration without risk of being seen. The capsule was supposed to be out of phase, but no machine is perfect. Now they were moving to the place where Central believed the revisionists had entered this time horizon.

"I can take a team forward in suits," said Pauli Weigand without turning. "We can store them out of phase and go after the revisionists with minimal equipment."

"First," said Nan from the controls, "we gather information so long as we're here. We learn where here *is.*"

The terrain was wooded, rolling, and initially without any sign of human habitation. The capsule came out of the woods onto a road built up slightly from the ground and paved with split logs laid flat side up. The forest had been cleared for a hundred feet to either side of the roadway.

Three wagons, each drawn by a pair of mules, and a dozen soldiers under an officer on horseback proceeded east on the road. The troops wore mail shirts and carried spears, but their helmets were slung from their right shoulders. Any other baggage must be in the wagons. They were headed toward the walled encampment in the near distance.

"This is where the revisionists appeared," Nan said softly. "Should have appeared. And there's where they were going unless I miss my bet."

The capsule surged ahead under her direction. "Aliso," Gerd said with satisfaction. "Varus' summer camp on the Lippe River. Three days before he decided to change base to the mouth of the Weser to bring the benefits of Roman justice to the barbarians there . . ."

Nan adjusted the controls, lifting the capsule's viewpoint a hundred feet in the air. Moments later she brought them to a hovering halt above the fortress.

"But that's huge," said Chun Quo. "That's a city."

"It's like going back to Fort Bragg," Rebecca said, staring at the camp. "How many troops are here?"

The rectangular camp stretched over a mile along the river and nearly half a mile back from the bank. A turf rampart with wooden battlements bounded the exterior. Outside the wall was a V-sided ditch set at the bottom with sharp stakes. Within were hundreds of neat timber buildings, roofed with thatch or—in the case of a few of the larger courtyard houses—baked tile.

"Three legions plus auxiliary units from conquered peoples, armed and equipped in Roman fashion," Gerd said. The team's mission was with revisionists, not Romans; the Riders didn't have to know much about the local situation. But Gerd of course did.

"Thirty thousand men," Pauli said, showing that he'd gone beyond the required brief, too. "If they were all present."

"And their servants," Gerd agreed. "Varus has sent nearly half his force out in small units on policing duties as if Germany were already conquered, but the housing has to be available for them anyway. The buildings outside the walls are the civilian settlement."

"That's as big as the camp," Tim said; an exaggeration, but only a slight one.

"Coke girls and hooch maids," Rebecca said with a grim smile. "There's never been an army base without a strip outside it. That'd be like an army without mud."

"Wives and taverns and laundries," Gerd said. "Remember, this is a long-service army. It's all the home these men have for twenty years or even longer. When they move their base, they move their whole lives with it."

"Merchants here to trade with the army," said Tim Grainger. "More merchants to trade with the local population because the army's here to protect them. Rich locals come to buy all the civilized goodies their own people can't make. Poor locals come to work for the outsiders. Come to sell their sisters or themselves because they're poor and they don't have anything else to sell."

Tim continued to face the hatch, watching the scene on the display within the opaque helmet of his displacement suit. His voice rasped. He was seeing the enclave in which he grew up and which he almost died defending from an underclass just as dangerous as the Free Germans surrounding this bastion of armed civilization.

Rebecca wanted to reach out and touch Tim's arm, but it was encased in armor. He wouldn't have noticed; and anyway, Tim's Sunrise Towers hadn't been the last time mankind repeated mistakes of the past.

"That will be the governor's palace," Gerd said. Rebecca

didn't see his fingers move, but a red circle haloed a large courtyard building in the center of the camp. "Next to it is the army headquarters"—a similar complex of structures—"and the housing for the governor's personal staff."

"What's the high building right in the middle?" Pauli asked. "A citadel?"

"It's an ornamental gateway built where the camp's two central roads cross," Gerd said. "Brick and stucco rather than stone, I suspect, but still impressive from a distance."

The square tower expanded to fill half the main display. Each side had an archway twenty feet high flanked by a pair of smaller openings like the entrance to a cathedral. Two higher bands of statues and pillared windows gave the impression of upper floors, but in fact the structure was a hollow shell.

"But what does it do?" Rebecca asked. "Is it just there to impress the locals?"

Gerd smiled at her. "That isn't 'just,' Rebecca," he said. "It was the only thing that Varus was interested in doing—convincing the Germans that they were already conquered, rather than expending the effort to conquer them."

His grin grew broader. "Winning hearts and minds," he said.

Rebecca felt her guts tighten. The analyst loved to use idioms from ages not his own. He always used them correctly, but he couldn't possibly understand the horror that particular phrase awoke in someone who remembered it on the lips of liars in uniform.

" 'Get them by the balls and their hearts and minds will follow,' " she quoted. "But that didn't work either, Gerd. Nothing worked. Nothing."

"We work, Beckie," Nan Roebeck said, looking back with enough hard-edged concern to snap Rebecca out of memories of a world from which she'd escaped. "Pauli, you're team leader for the 9 AD locus."

"I've been planning cover stories," Gerd said, "since we'll have to operate in the local ambience if we separate from the capsule."

He cleared his throat with a tiny cough. "For the same reason I'll have to be present. This—"

He patted his sensor pack.

"—isn't as broad-ranging as the capsule's capabilities, but in my hands it should be sufficient."

"I'll go," Rebecca said. "One member of the team should be a woman."

"You're in training," said Chun. "I'll go."

"Quo, you're Oriental," Rebecca said. "You'd stand out like a sore thumb."

Also you might not be able to pull a trigger fast enough when the situation demanded it. Beckie Carnes knew she wasn't the best choice for that ability either, but at least her conditioning was five centuries less intense.

Nan looked at her with a cold glare, then a smile. "Right, you'll do," she said. "The rest of us will deal with Moscow and pick you up on the other side. Will a week be enough time?"

"I would suggest a minimum of three weeks," Gerd said. "We'll be limited to local transport. Now, as background for the three of us . . ."

Aliso, Free Germany

August 23, 9 AD

Pauli Weigand liked horses and his job had given him plenty of opportunity to use the riding skills that were part of ARC training. Right now, though, as he rode toward the fort he was glad that he was unlikely to need to move faster than his mount's comfortable walk. The horse he'd bought the previous evening had a decent enough canter, but its trot was a stiff-legged wracking pace that Pauli would never be able to manage without stirrups.

The ten men guarding the gate at ground level were relaxed without being blasé. One of them picked up the pair of lead-weighted javelins he'd leaned against the wall beside him, though there was nothing threatening in his posture. The gateway was divided into eight-foot halves by a log wall down the middle. The heavy timber panel across the left side remained closed.

The noncom in charge was younger than most of the legionaries. He'd probably gotten his rank for being fully literate. His face showed no expression as he eyed Pauli, Gerd leading the pack mule, and Beckie walking between the two men.

The animals' shod hooves clopped on the wooden road. Two artillerymen watched from the platform above the rampart over the gate.

"There are six with the catapult on the upper deck," said

Gerd in the English-based Standard language. "They're arguing over a dice throw."

The analyst spoke in a muted voice, as though he were talking to himself. The teams' headbands were communications devices set at the moment for continuous operation. When the band's faceshield was pulled down, it also provided the user with thermal viewing, light intensification, and air filtration.

"Guys, they don't think the three of us are much threat to their camp," Beckie said.

She sounded calm, not that Pauli had really been concerned about her performance. Beckie knew her guise as a female slave in this milieu had significant risks, but she'd accepted Gerd's plan without comment. Of course, she might correctly believe that the risks were no greater than they'd been when she served in the army of her own time horizon.

Pauli drew up two strides short of the gate. "Courier from Rome," he growled. His Latin, though perfectly grammatical, had a distinct North German clip to it.

He snapped the fingers of his right hand. The horse whickered softly as Beckie ran forward with the orders. The noncom stepped forward to take the tablet from her. He undid the twine and slanted the boards so that light shadowed the writing on the waxed inner surfaces.

"You're a Batavian, then?" one of the older legionaries said to Pauli.

"That's right," he replied, neither hostile nor friendly. "One of Augustus Caesar's horse guard, here on Augustus Caesar's business."

"These look to be in order," the noncom said as he handed the documents back. He looked sharply at Pauli and said, "Gaius Julius Clovis, do you want to bathe and change clothes before you attend the governor?"

"I do not," Pauli said. "My comfort can wait until I've delivered my commission from the emperor."

The noncom grinned. "I think you'll find Governor Varus considers it more to *his* comfort that he not have to deal with anybody travel-stained," he said, "and a soldier besides. But I daresay he'll make an exception in your case."

He looked at his men. "Flaccus," he said to the man holding the javelins, "take Gaius Clovis to the forum and see that the bailiffs inform the governor of his arrival. Crispus, you take the gentleman's servants to headquarters. When they're assigned billets, you go to the forum and guide Gaius Clovis to them after he's finished his business with the governor."

"Forum?" Pauli said.

"The governor is a great one for the law's civilizing effect," the noncom said dryly. "He's so convinced of that that he's spent most of this campaigning season holding court and settling disputes between our benighted German subjects . . . at a nice profit to himself."

"He might think about first making sure the Fritzes *were* our subjects," Flaccus said. "In the course of which there might be some profit for a poor legionary, too, you know."

"Put a spear up the backside of enough of them," another soldier agreed, "the rest get subject real quick—for a while. Thing is, you got to keep applying the treatment to make sure it's taken."

Pauli laughed. The legionaries knew—thought—he was a Free German himself. They clearly assumed that as a fellow soldier he would understand and sympathize with their complaints about a civilian commander who didn't know his ass from a hole in the ground.

"I don't know anything about that," he said. "I'm like you. I just carry out my orders."

Pauli dismounted, careful not to fall and make the troops wonder at his clumsiness. He was riding with just a blanket rather than a saddle. The facilities in TC 779 could have produced a four-horned military saddle along with the other articles of clothing and equipment. Bareback was the more likely riding style for a Free German even in Roman service, and Pauli had enough experience with the technique that he thought he was safer than if he used an unusual saddle for the first time.

He handed Gerd the reins. "See that she's properly stabled and fed on the imperial account," he ordered. "I don't want her being fobbed off with the baggage mules' chaff and moldy hay."

"Master," Gerd said, bowing without a trace of sarcasm. Part of the mission prep had been hypnotically implanted languages. Gerd spoke upper-class Latin and Greek—as well as several dialects of German that he didn't expect to use. The microprocessor in each headband could translate virtually any language the team might encounter, but that wouldn't permit the team members to reply to the speaker.

Pauli checked the flat document safe on the left side of his belt where it counterbalanced the weight of his long cavalry sword. "All right," he said to Flaccus. "Let's go see the governor."

He strode through the long gateway with the swaggering arrogance of a man in the emperor's personal service. Augustus used foreigners, mainly Germans, for his bodyguard. He knew they'd be loyal because if something happened to the emperor, the guards were friendless in a hostile city. Augustus' adopted father, Julius Caesar, had dismissed his foreign guards when he returned to Rome in 44 BC since he didn't think he needed barbarians to protect him from his fellow citizens.

Caesar's confidence in Roman loyalty was an error that none of his successors repeated; and it was clear to all that a man who guarded the emperor's life was a man whom only the emperor could discipline.

"So," Pauli said to his guide as they walked down the log street. "How does the governor get along with Germans, then?"

"Oh, he's close as this with some of them," Flaccus said sourly. He held up his middle and index fingers twined. "Sigimer and Arminius, now, I shouldn't wonder if they were asshole buddies to our noble Varus."

The Roman was walking at a military pace but quick-stepping to keep abreast of the much taller man. He looked up at Pauli. "Arminius was a horse guard, too," he said. "Guess you probably knew him. Maybe you're even related?"

Pauli snorted. "Hermann, that's Arminius if you want to make a Roman of him, wasn't a real guard," he said. "He's a prince, you see. Tiberius brought him back to keep around Rome for a few years. If you called him a hostage you wouldn't be far wrong. I'm no fucking prince."

He spat into a rut wagon wheels had worn in the roadway. The logs would have to be replaced soon. "Besides," he added, "I'm an Ubian and Hermann's Cheruscan. A bunch of cowboys wandering around with the seat out of their britches, that what the Cherusci are."

"Well, he's good enough to have dinner every day with our noble governor," Flaccus said. "Varus doesn't know the name of a Roman citizen in this camp below the rank of tribune. It wasn't like this under Tiberius, you can bet your life."

The combined headquarters of the three legions was in line with the gate on the camp's main north–south street. Flaccus had turned left instead and was leading Pauli past officers' housing to an open area near the west rampart. About a hundred people were present, most of them standing. A file of ten soldiers guarded a dais under a purple awning. Everyone else was either German or wore a toga, the uncomfortable formal garment whose use was limited to Roman citizens only.

"Hell of a thing to see in the middle of Fritz country, isn't it?" Flaccus said, voicing Pauli's thought.

It was one thing to know that Varus took a disastrously civilian view of administering a region that hadn't been fully conquered, much less pacified. It was another thing to see the governor holding court just as he would have done if he'd been assigned to the administration of Athens or Marseilles.

A thought made Pauli stumble. "We're going to have to repave these streets pretty quick," Flaccus said apologetically. "This time Varus is going to want stone, and tell me *that's* not going to be a bitch on soil this weak."

You're not going to have to repave the camp, Pauli thought. *In a few days you're all going to be dead.*

An ARC Rider knew that everyone on the horizons he visited would die before he was born, but he didn't often look around himself and realize that tens of thousands of people in his immediate vicinity would die almost at once. There'd been a team in Nagasaki on August 8, 1945. Pauli had heard that two members had retired shortly after they returned to ARC Central.

"Wait here," Flaccus said when they reached the back of the crowd. He pushed through to the chief lictor and spoke urgently, gesturing toward Pauli.

The lictors were attendants whose bundles of rods and an ax indicated the magistrate they attended had the authority to beat or behead. In court sessions they were his bailiffs as well as symbols of power. Nowadays the rough work of flogging was probably delegated to a slave, and the execution of a Roman citizen required imperial approval, but you could never tell.

A lawyer was in full cry, making broad gestures and speaking in sonorous Latin about the inalienable rights of free peoples. His clients were a group of German nobles wearing dyed woolen cloaks, leather trousers, and long swords. Their dirty blond hair was knotted above the right temple; the tassel of horsehair worked into the bun was probably a clan marking, because none of their otherwise similar opponents had it.

The Germans looked puzzled or bored. One of them was picking his nose. The groups glared at one another, and the way their hands patted their sword hilts looked to Pauli like more than mere posturing.

Publius Quinctilius Varus sat on the dais in a folding ivory chair. He was a balding man in his mid-fifties, heavy enough that Pauli wondered how he got a breastplate that fit. As he listened he picked at grapes from a silver dish held by a handsome slave boy.

Standing on the dais with Varus were a group of toga-wearing Roman citizens, including one who was obviously German by birth: Arminius, a powerfully built man in his late twenties. The German's gaze swept the crowd and lingered for a moment on Pauli, obvious for his height and mail shirt.

Pauli met the prince's eyes with equal staring arrogance. Not only was the ARC Rider staying in character, it was the way he instinctively responded to a challenge. He'd never been quite civilized enough for 26th-century society. That was why he'd become an ARC Rider.

Flaccus made his way back to where Pauli stood. The lawyer spoke, the Germans fidgeted; the folk on the dais chattered among themselves, ignoring the proceedings. Varus ate his grapes.

"There'll be a recess in a minute or two and you can speak your piece to his nobility then," Flaccus said. He nodded scornfully in the direction of the orator. "Them Fritzes don't have a clue what he's talking about."

"He's not talking about anything," Pauli said. "He's telling a creation myth that I suspect he's just invented. What's this all about, anyway?"

"Making money for the governor's friends," Flaccus said, lowering his voice slightly so that he could at least claim he'd been misunderstood by the nearest civilian onlookers. "It's a cattle-stealing case, the usual barb sort of problem. Instead of letting the Fritzes knock each other's heads in, which is what they'd do if we weren't here. And instead of *us* knocking some heads in—"

He spat in the dirt beside his heavy ankle-laced sandals.

"—which is what we'd be doing if Tiberius were still here in command," the soldier continued, "why, they have to hire lawyers to sue it out in court. Wonder of wonders, the governor brought a bunch of lawyer friends with him, and *don't* they charge dear. Somebody might guess that part of the fees migrate to the governor's strongbox."

A water clock stood beside the dais, watched by a slave. Water dripping from the reservoir above filled the fourth bowl, which promptly overturned. The slave struck a tubular gong with a wood block. Its musical tone cut through the whispers and shuffling feet.

The lawyer held his pose for a moment, hand raised and finger pointing to heaven. Then he turned and bowed to the dais before walking off to where servants held beakers and a drinking cup ready.

"What a twat," Flaccus muttered. "What a *mob* of twats!"

A lictor pushed through the crowd. "Gaius Julius Clovis?" he called. "Attend me, please, I'm taking you to his excellency!"

Flaccus patted one javelin against his chest, a half-mocking salute before he walked away.

A pretty good soldier, Flaccus. So was his noncom, whose name Pauli would probably never learn. They'd be dust scattered evenly across the surface of the globe in 2,500 years whether or not they'd had the particular misfortune to be commanded by a man without a clue about his situation.

But still . . . a pretty good guy.

Varus was talking with the civilians on the dais. The lawyers for both parties had joined the group and were laughing at a joke one of them had made. The military guards watched Pauli's approach attentively though without concern; and Arminius watched also.

"Your Excellency!" the lictor said. "I present Gaius Julius Clovis, the messenger of Augustus Caesar, First Speaker of the Senate, Tribune for Life, and Father of his Country."

Varus turned and eyed Pauli coolly. "The words of our father in Rome are always welcome," he said. If he spoke without enthusiasm, there was at least nothing sarcastic in his tone. Varus owed his position to the emperor's favor. He wasn't the sort of man to get worked up about political issues like restoration of the republic when there was money to be made under the current system.

Pauli unlocked his iron belt safe and handed the parchment scroll to the lictor, who passed it in turn to the governor. Varus checked the signet impression on the wax seal, then broke the thread and read the document.

"This just says you're to accompany me and report at the end of the summer on the conduct of the campaign," he said. As the governor spoke, he lowered the scroll. One of the lawyers took it from his hand and read it in a circle of other staff members squeezing close to see it themselves.

Pauli nodded agreement. "Yes, Your Excellency," he said. He closed the belt safe. Its thin iron sheets wouldn't keep out a thief with a cold chisel, but they were proof against casual pilferage.

"Well, whatever Caesar wants, of course," Varus said. "You're German, aren't you? Why don't you dine with me tonight. You'll have some of your fellows to chat with, won't he, Arminius?"

"It's always a pleasure to meet another of my fellows who realizes the future is with Rome," the big German said.

"I'm giving a dinner for the chiefs who'll be aiding us in the coming campaign," the governor continued to Pauli in a conversational voice. "If Augustus wants to know how we conduct things in Germany, I'll be glad to oblige him. You'll make nine at the table, Clovis. 'Not fewer than the three Graces nor more than the nine Muses,' that's the rule for dinner."

He looked suddenly concerned. "You do have proper garments, don't you?" he asked. "That sort of thing may be well enough in a legionary tent, but we of the better classes try to keep decent standards even here in the wilds."

Pauli brought his heels together with a hobnailed click, then bowed. "As do we who serve the emperor in Rome, Your Excellency," he said.

"Fine, then go get yourself cleaned up," Varus said. "We'll recline in my quarters at the tenth hour"—late afternoon—"since I don't think we're going to be through this case before then. Are we, Gallus?"

The second of the lawyers involved in the action had passed Pauli's perfectly counterfeited orders on to another civilian. "I'm very much afraid not, Your Excellency," he said. "I've already told my clients that they must be prepared to recompense my services for another two days still."

"How many daughters do you have to provide dowries for, Gallus?" the first lawyer asked. Everyone laughed.

"Well, if it takes that long, it'll have to stand over until I've handled this business with the Chauci," Varus said. "Though I shouldn't think that will take long either."

He looked at Pauli. Seated on the dais, the governor's eyes were on a level with the ARC Rider's. He frowned. "Till dinner then," he said.

Pauli made a crisp about-face and strode away. Crispus, the soldier who'd gone with Gerd and Beckie, was waiting to guide him.

Varus had a very capable army here. Pity the troops didn't have a capable commander, but Pauli couldn't worry about that. It was Team 79's job to make sure they all died . . .

Rebecca Carnes carried the three-gallon ewer of water on her right shoulder, her right hand lifted to the handle to balance it. It was her job to see that her master's washstand was prepared for him. The well serving this group of barracks was on the far end of the building.

The barracks block was intended for a company of eighty troops, but almost half of Varus' army was on detached assignment. The building was empty except for two legionaries just out of the hospital, and now the three ARC Riders.

An anteroom divided the legionary quarters on one end from the suites for the centurion and the two junior noncoms. Rebecca walked through the outer doorway and found a pair of well-groomed civilians lounging on either side of the door to the officers' quarters. They were obviously waiting for her.

"Do you speak Latin, girlie?" the older man asked. His outer tunic was of fine wool. Its border was embroidered in saffron thread that matched the dyed leather of his sandals.

"Bit long in the tooth, isn't she?" said the younger man to his companion in Greek. He wore an undertunic cut higher and with longer sleeves than the outer tunic so that everyone could see that it was of expensive violet silk.

"I speak Latin," Rebecca said. Her pronunciation was thickened to fit her guise as a slave from Caria in Asia Minor. Switching to a better grade of Greek she went on, "My master, being a man, has no need of perfumed boys like you."

The younger man tossed his curly head; his nostrils flared in anger.

Rebecca stood hipshot. Because of the society in which the team had to blend for this operation, their weapons were limited to microwave pistols. She wasn't carrying even a pistol at the moment because there wasn't a place to conceal it in a pocketless tunic and shift. A three-gallon bronze bucket would make a decent club if she needed it, though.

The older man laughed. "She's a spunky one, Nestor," he said. "Sometimes an old mare gives the best ride."

He turned to Rebecca and continued, "We're all friends here, girlie. We just came to let you know that our master, Lucius Silius Gallus, is a very generous man."

"I can see he keeps you well fed," Rebecca said. She'd been called worse than "girlie," but it wasn't the way to get on her good side. Whatever this pair had in mind, it didn't affect the team's mission. Rebecca had no reason to pretend friendliness.

"Spunky indeed," the man said with a chuckle. "You know, I wouldn't mind running you through your paces myself."

Rebecca's expression was hard enough to break stones. The man raised his hand and said, "Peace, peace. I didn't mean to offend a lady of such high standards. The point is, the noble Gallus would be very interested to learn what the emperor's spy is thinking."

He mimed pouring coins from one hand to the other. "Very profitably interested, if you catch my drift."

"Then I suggest," Rebecca said carefully, "that you talk to an imperial spy. If you know one."

The younger man, Nestor, said, "This wouldn't have to affect your master's mission, you see. Gallus is on the governor's staff, but if something were going to happen abruptly to the governor, important business might call Gallus home ahead of time to avoid mistaken impressions. You could come out of it well enough to not only buy yourself free but also to buy yourself some companionship."

Rebecca smiled. Gerd had planned that Varus and those around him would assume the imperial guard was being sent to spy on the governor's personal life as well as to observe the conduct of his campaign. Fear of Clovis' secret agenda provided cover for anything he or his servants did that didn't fit with their public duties.

"My master may not be as generous as yours," she said. "But he has a very strong arm with a whip. If there's something about his business that you or your master think you need to know, you can ask him yourself. But I don't recommend it."

"Girlie," the older man said with a trace of frustration—the first honest emotion he'd displayed during the interview. "This isn't idle curiosity. If the noble Gallus is prosecuted for having the wrong friends, that's his lookout. But if it happens *here,* in this wart on the hide of the empire—who's going to buy his estate? Some hairy centurion whose idea of the good life is to drink till he pukes? A German princeling who hasn't bathed since the last time he fell in the river? It's important to us to know if the ax is about to fall!"

"And we'll pay," Nestor said. Desperation tightened the lines of his face, making it less handsome but far more human. "Just give us the chance to get back to civilization before it happens."

Rebecca realized that she was talking to slaves, not men. Under Roman law they were furniture. Their apparent wealth couldn't change that unless their master chose to sell them back their freedom . . . which Gallus hadn't done, or they hadn't asked him to do until now when the arrival of the emperor's agent made them think it might be too late.

"I don't need your money," Rebecca said, lowering her voice. "But I don't think your master has anything to fear from the emperor."

The older slave nodded. "Come along, Nestor," he said. "We won't forget this."

No, you won't, Rebecca thought. *But at least the Germans will treat you the same as they do free men when they sweep over the army.*

The slaves closed the outer door behind them. Before Rebecca could touch the latch of the suite's entrance, Barthuli pulled it open from inside. He held a microwave pistol.

"I thought we could give them an overdose of sedative and hide the bodies in the storage room," he said. "No one would notice the smell until long after we've left the horizon."

Gerd had come to terms with mortality, his own and others', when his condition was diagnosed as incurable. He was a gentle man, as kind as he was intelligent; but he was also as ruthless as a cobra.

Rebecca entered the suite and set the ewer on the triangular table. "Close the door," she said. She felt drained She knelt and rested her forehead against the cool bronze container. "Gerd," she added, "slavery is evil."

"Umm," the analyst said, a noncommittal syllable with a vaguely positive lilt. "The most likely place for our revisionists is the settlement outside the camp, Rebecca. I thought I'd go check it over."

Rebecca stood and managed a smile. "We'll both go," she said, "because I don't trust you alone, Gerd. But we'll wait till Pauli gets back and discuss it with him before we act."

She didn't want to call Pauli unless there was an emergency. Interrupting a busy teammate was a good way to screw up both him and the operation.

Gerd nodded. "All right, Rebecca," he said. He projected a shimmering display on his multifunction sensor and seemed to be concentrating on it. In a tone of mild interest he added, "I've always wished I could understand the concept of evil in a meaningful way."

TC 779

Displacing to 1992 AD

Nan Roebeck had her issue weapons spread out before her on her command station's console. The team in TC 779 was about to go operational.

Everybody was rechecking their equipment one last time before insertion. Her people were nervous. She understood that. She listened with one ear to them as she repacked her own weapons carefully in the black nylon gearbag she'd be taking into Russia on 9 March, 1992. She checked the weaponry she had in front of her against Central's manifest.

Then she went through the nonweapons essentials her team had been issued. If these items weren't perfect, all weapons could do was get you out of a disintegrating situation alive. Entry documents: invitation, visa, passport. Local currency: a roll of Russian roubles. Venue-correct clothing: suit, shirt, underwear. She hoped she'd pass for a middle-aged American bureaucrat. She was probably a little too tall, a little too straight in bearing to really look the part. Her brown hair was a little too short, her skin a little too tanned, her muscle tone a little too good. Maybe she'd look like a US bureaucrat who happened to lift weights. Oh, well. She rubbed her fingers through her brush-cut hair. This was the age of women's liberation they were displacing into.

Roebeck added the little extras she always took along, things that were never on any manifest: a half-dozen redundantly spare power packs, an assortment of replacement circuits. You never knew what was going to go wrong. But something always did. You didn't join the operational arm of the ARC in order to spend life in an error-free environment.

Grainger was saying, "Can't you print us some US dollars, Chun? Forget about these roubles Central gave us. They're nearly worthless. And these plastic credit cards won't be good for anything but ID. Another typical ARC screw-up."

Before Chun could answer, the temporal capsule around them hummed, shivered, and stabilized with a slight whining sound. It didn't sound right to Roebeck. Her hands froze on the quaint metal zipper of her gearbag.

It didn't sound good to her ops specialists, either.

The three ARC Riders exchanged glances. Chun's control wands knitted and purled a systems check. Chun gave the ARC Riders' thumbs-up hand sign. "Just a little boundary turbulence. Nothing to worry about."

Everybody relaxed. In the close confines of the TC, Nan Roebeck could smell the shock and fear leaking from her team's bodies as acrid perspiration. The air circulator hummed comfortingly. The waft of nervousness was quickly replaced by machine-cooled air, tainted only by hot, thrumming components.

If your temporal capsule malfunctioned coming out of phase, nobody ever found your remains. Time travel was relatively safe. The dicey moments were during displacement phase-in and phase-out. If you were hashed during either one, nothing rematerialized for an investigation team to find. That was why they called it "hashed." You were static. Forever.

Nan Roebeck had no interest in becoming a bit of cosmic background noise. None whatsoever. She dragged the gearbag across her console and dropped it onto the deck, by her feet.

The technology that powered the TC wasn't something any ARC Rider understood very well. It was from too far Up The Line. But after a few missions, you understood what was survivable and what wasn't. The longer they stayed out of phase, the harder the TC had to work. The harder the TC had to work, the more chance there'd be a malfunction during displacement.

It didn't happen often. But it did happen.

As team leader, Roebeck was responsible for everybody's safety. She'd given the order to hang out of phase. If she wanted to sit here for any number of elapsed-time hours, that was up to her. The maneuver should be well within TC 779's tolerances. The funny whine was just that: a funny whine. An artifact. That was all.

Chun's control wands tapped again, summoning an exterior view to the bow screen of the temporal capsule. TC 779 was now hovering placidly out of phase over the Moscow River, a little downstream from the Russian White House. The night around them was starless and a deep, pollution-browned black. They'd phase-locked the TC at a 30-millisecond offset for safety's sake in an urban, post-industrial venue. The capsule was not only invisible from the river or its banks but also from above or below.

In its current state, TC 779 provided no resistance to local matter, making it sensor-proof in every domain Russians could monitor. All sensors from this period, active or passive, utilized a surface from which to generate a return, a measurable perturbation, or a change in state.

Grainger pursued his earlier point from where he'd broken off when the TC's whine stopped unrelated conversation cold. "My grandpa's friends used to tell stories about this period— March of '92," he reminded the others. He was talking to hide his jitters. Or to forget them. "Russia was the Wild West and the Klondike all rolled into one. And the dollar was king. With dollars, you could buy anything: fissionable materials, weapons systems, scientific patents, whole government departments. The rouble's in a hyper-inflationary spiral. The average Russian barely had enough food to get through the winter. That food went to people with dollars. Factions of the fledgling government here are fighting internally for control. Those factions want dollars like everybody else. And Russians want new-looking dollars. They don't like shabby-looking money."

"Okay, Tim, you've made your point," Roebeck decided. "If plastic is virtually useless except as ID and the local currency isn't worth anything, then we'll take dollars onto the local economy—if Chun thinks making some is doable." Roebeck looked at Chun for a feasibility estimate.

"Counterfeit money that *looks new* in '92? At least *old*-looking counterfeit is easy. That means fabricating high-quality currency on the fly." Chun's almond eyes narrowed. Heavy black hair shimmered as she bent her head to study her desktop display. Her control wands tapped again.

The capsule's wraparound bow screen split. One half showed a US ten-dollar bill circa 1992 as Chun analyzed its constituents. The other half began detailing the fall of a great totalitarian empire and the stumble from its wreckage of an uncertain, defiant democracy.

Chun's bowed head raised. "Okay. We can do it. If dollars are what you want, Nan, dollars are what you'll get. Plan to hover out of phase a few hours longer while we make up reasonable facsimiles of this fancy currency."

"Oh, great," Grainger groaned and glowered at Chun. A 21st-century primitive, Tim Grainger was both claustrophobic and leery of temporal travel. The weird whine that TC 779 had made coming out of displacement hadn't helped.

"By the way, how many dollars are we talking about, exactly, Nan?" Chun wanted to know.

"So how much money *do* we take, Tim?" Right now, Roebeck was willing to capitalize on the tension between her team members. Some of that tension was an echo of their last mission. Last time out, the ARC Riders' targets had been Oriental revisionists. Grainger's own primitive cultural prejudices had transmuted Chun's lineage into a reason to question her allegiance to the team and the mission at hand. But then, killers were always racists, and Grainger was a shooter, a killer from one of the most primitive times in Earth's history: the 21st century. One hundred sixty million souls had been killed in conflict during the 20th century. The 21st doubled that number before it was done—all in the name of freedom, democracy, humanitarian relief, and peacekeeping.

"How much money do we need?" Tim Grainger pursed thin

lips and scratched his stubbled, angular jaw. "Maybe thirty thousand dollars. We've got places to go and people to bribe."

It was Chun's turn to groan. Grainger swiveled in his seat. He looked long at her, then at Roebeck. "Just make sure the bills are new-looking and none are higher than hundred-dollar denominations. In those days, the US dollar bought something worldwide. In Russia then, it was the only stable currency."

"All this money isn't going to raise suspicions?" Chun, the senior analyst on this mission, tapped her control wands once more. The screen displayed a photo of a stocky, florid man with a shock of white hair. He was standing on a tank, mouth open and fist clenched. "The US didn't recognize this man Yeltsin's government until Christmas Day, 1991. And then only after flagrant diplomatic maneuvers by the US meant to unseat him and reinstate Gorbachev despite Yeltsin's popularity. Americans can't be too welcome, currency or not."

"*Au contraire, mon ami,*" Grainger said, "1992 Russia is full of *Americanskis*. And other foreigners. Entrepreneurs, spies, scientists, officials from the Koreas, Japan, India, the Arab world, and the NATO countries are crawling all over Moscow buying or stealing technology." Grainger grinned thinly.

"So you think we can just *buy* our way to the revisionists?" Chun scoffed. Her control wands were now tapping constantly. A window appeared in the datastream and began running Russia-related 1992 US State Department message traffic.

"Maybe. Or at least to the technology," Grainger answered.

"Okay, you two," Roebeck said at last. "That's enough. This team is about to be up to our hips in end-game 20th-century alligators, whether we like it or not. Chun, get started counterfeiting the currency. I want a final logistical plan by thirteen hundred hours—everything, including where we're going to stash the capsule safely while we all go sightseeing. I need a safe place to park TC 779 that's round-the-clock accessible, if we're *all* going anywhere. Otherwise I'll have to leave one of you with the capsule. Right now I'm not sure who I can spare."

Chun and Grainger just stared at her. Both specialists were in hot competition for the lead on this mission. It had never occurred to them that all three ARC Riders might not go downrange. Each had all the equipment, all the documentation necessary to be tasked with the field action. Each was uniquely qualified. Neither wanted to be left behind.

Chun, with her 26th-century double doctorate, was indisputably their technical expert. If the ARC Riders found some new, unknown technology, Chun was their best-qualified evaluator. Leaving her with TC 779 was unthinkable when unknown technology was in question and access windows might be fatally short. But Chun was their least experienced field operator.

Grainger had an inherent feel for the venue. In his native 21st century, he'd been an expert on Techno *Fin de Siècle*. His grandfather had been an old Soviet hand, a Cold Warrior. His savvy and his closeness to the period's cultural mechanics made him the perfect field operator in a venue where human intelligence collection and evaluation on the fly could be the make or break.

Let them sweat it. She wasn't going to designate a lead. Not yet. Maybe not at all.

The only problem with taking them both onto the local horizon was that there'd be nobody on board TC 779. For the duration of their recon, the ARC Riders would have no viable link to ARC Central's terraflops of archival data. Or to an easy emergency extraction, if it came to cut and run. It was a calculated risk that Roebeck was willing to take, if she heard the right answers from her ops team.

"I'm waiting," said Nan Roebeck, "for that real good plan for stashing the TC where it'll be safe and snug and ready whenever we want it." Setting the capsule to autophase in and out of the space-time continuum on a schedule was an easy matter when the local horizon was populated by techno-primitives on earlier horizons. But here and now, among Russians, discovery of a temporal capsule might lead to technological exposure. Even to reverse engineering. The Russian science community was arguably the best educated and most forward-thinking group of its time. She couldn't risk even one Russian scientist getting a good look at TC 779. Especially since Russians were already fooling around with the space-time continuum. She wished to hell somebody on her team had even a half-baked theory about how the Russians were doing it.

But nobody did. And neither of her ARC Riders seemed to have a ready answer as to how to secure TC 779 for the duration, either.

"Make it an idiot-proof scenario," Roebeck prodded. "And make it quick. I don't want to wait too long out of phase here in what, despite all we think we know, might be plain sight. Especially if the revisionists we're chasing are using different space-time mechanics."

Nan Roebeck drummed her nails on the padded bumper of the ship's command console while, behind the ARC Riders' heads, the text window faded and the fate of the former Soviet Union unrolled in graphic detail.

Civil Aliso, Free Germany

T he alloys used in twentieth-century tools differ from their first-century equivalents," Gerd explained.

Rebecca Carnes grabbed his arm and kept him from taking the next step. The whip of the teamster standing on the seat of his bogged cart whistled back to where it would have taken off the analyst's nose if he'd continued.

The whip popped. The bullocks grunted against their yoke and started the cart lurching forward again. The street between the line of civilian settlements and the river wasn't paved, though a few shopkeepers had placed logs to corduroy the stretch immediately in front of their establishment.

"Ah!" said Gerd. "Thank you, Rebecca. As I was saying, the alloys are different, so when they're moved through the Earth's magnetic field they resonate in identifiable fashions that we can locate."

He patted the slung pouch where he kept his sensor. He was linked to the unit by a receiver in the mastoid bone at the base of his ear.

Three barges full of grain in huge jars proceeded up the river toward the landing on the fort's northern side. Their masts were stepped, but the breeze was fitful and none had set their sails. The leading barge was drawn by a team of mules plodding in line up the outer edge of the road. Slave gangs pulled the other two.

"The objects don't have to be, well, pulsed by an electric

current for that to work?" Rebecca said. She'd heard of the technique, but it hadn't seemed that simple.

"Oh, no," Gerd replied. "In your day, yes, because your equipment lacked discrimination."

"Oh, right," Rebecca said. She felt a wash of gloom.

People hadn't changed in the five centuries between her time horizon and Gerd's, not really. Language had, but she'd been adjusted to that as easily as she now spoke dialectical Latin. The 26th century's state-of-the-art technology was at least as accessible as that of her own day. She could handle a transportation capsule in an adequate if not brilliant fashion; better, at least, than she'd been at the controls of a helicopter the times a pilot had brought her onto the seat beside him when things were slack.

The *reality* underlying that technology was still magic whenever her nose got pressed up against it. To Rebecca's teammates, she was a caveman who'd learned to flick a light switch.

"Have you ever considered what we mean by knowledge, Rebecca?" Gerd said. She reached for his arm again, but this time the analyst had seen the danger himself. They paused.

A hulking German bouncer hurled a man out the door of a brothel. He splashed in the mud squarely in front of the Riders. A red-haired woman, naked to the waist, came to the doorway and began screaming abuse.

Rebecca and Gerd stepped around the victim and walked on. "I understand the use of sensor technology," the analyst continued, "but I could never build a device like this myself." He patted his pouch. "And while I could provide a detailed plan of the body of the man lying in the street back there, I wouldn't know what to do to help his condition."

Rebecca smiled. "Pressure cut to the scalp from the bouncer's club," she said. "Not serious but it ought to be bandaged. Possible concussion. Keep him quiet and at least get him out of the road so the next wagon doesn't drive over him. Probable gonorrhea, at least that was the girl's diagnosis. Unlikely to be a resistant strain since back now there's no antibiotics."

She looked at the companion who'd just proved she *wasn't* an ignorant barbarian. "Thanks, Gerd," she added.

"I'm not a social person, Rebecca," Gerd said. "I'm very fortunate that this team provides me with a society despite myself."

In the same mild voice he continued, "It's the next building, the upper floor, I believe. Ah—from the quantities and types of alloy, particularly the tool steel and chrome in pure form, I would guess the objects I located were pistols with plated bores."

"Somehow I didn't expect these revisionists were here to take pictures," Rebecca said.

Buildings in the strip outside Aliso were of two distinct types, local and imported Mediterranean styles. The inn Gerd had identified was a Germanic longhouse with stables at one end and living quarters including a loft beneath a high-peaked roof at the other.

A dozen toughs squatted against the outer wall. There wasn't a paved stoop, but the overhanging thatch kept rain from turning the ground to mud like the street proper was.

The men were armed with swords or clubs. They held wooden drinking cups but most of them were empty. Rebecca's hypnotically implanted language training indicated a broad mix of dialects when they spoke German to one another and to the servant girl entering with a wicker basket of produce.

These weren't tribesmen. They were bits various tribes had spat out, men who'd lost their homelands. There were people like them in every war zone. If you were lucky, you could avoid them.

Rebecca kept wide of the building front to stay clear of the loungers, but one of them squatted beside the narrow doorway. She sent Gerd through ahead of her. As she started to follow, the German stuck his leg across the opening.

"Not so fast, honey," he said. He wore a greasy cowhide jerkin, hair side out. His boots were hide cut and strapped over his feet without any real attempt at shaping. "You haven't paid the toll."

The German reached for Rebecca's crotch. It might have stopped there, but it might not. She wasn't in a mood to learn, so she kicked the knee of his outstretched leg hard enough that her hobnails bit bone.

The German bellowed and lurched upright. He grabbed the long sword leaning against the wall, then went slack as a silent pulse from Gerd's pistol hit the back of his skull like a battering ram.

The German pitched onto his face in the mud. The half-drawn sword fell beside him. It was rusty and of crude local workmanship.

Rebecca skipped into the inn's dim interior.

She was afraid, for the mission and for herself. As soon as they arrived, the three of them had sent their suits three weeks forward in time so that their displacement mechanisms wouldn't block the revisionists' arrival. The empty suits would appear in a grove outside Aliso for a few seconds every three weeks. She, Gerd, and Pauli were on their own until then.

The upper sections of the longhouse walls pivoted down to provide ventilation and some light, but the openings were largely shaded by the overhang. The straw on the floor hadn't been changed in a week or more; the remains barely gave texture to the mud. The odor of the animals stabled in the other half of the building was heavy but less unpleasant than the sour smell of the humans on this end.

Gerd's left hand held the front of his cape closed over the microwave pistol in the other. Rebecca gripped her own pistol beneath a similar short traveling cape, but using it openly might cause the very sort of anomalies ARC Riders were tasked to prevent.

"Landlord!" she shouted as she strode toward the counter separating private from public areas of the single room. "There's a man hit his head on your door beam!"

Germans crushed into the inn behind the two Riders. Their angry hurry made the doorposts creak and delayed them while Rebecca and Gerd joined the heavyset man coming out from behind the counter.

"Hold it right there, Osric!" he shouted to the leading thug in German with a Rhenish accent. His hands were beneath his leather apron.

"Fuck off, Lothar!" Osric replied. He raised a knobbed club, thumping one of the beams that supported the loft. Rebecca prepared to shoot him and worry about the consequences later.

Lothar stepped forward, bringing his right hand out in a straight punch to the club-wielder's face. His fist was wrapped in a bronze-studded leather strap, a professional boxer's cestus that added several pounds to a punch. He broke the thug's nose and cheekbone, flinging him backward.

Other members of the inn staff appeared. A woman advanced with a grinding pin and a pair of cook boys carried turnspits from the central hearth.

"Which of you dog turds is next?" Lothar said, breathing hard. "Which fucking one?"

Rebecca guessed the innkeeper was in his late forties; obviously a gladiator who'd retired on his earnings. He might not be the man he once was, but that punch proved he was still a man *once*.

"Hey," muttered one of the thugs. "They knifed Hilderic. You can't let them—"

"Well it's about time somebody knifed him!" cried the woman, waving the stone grinder under the thug's nose. "All of you out! Out now and stay out. We don't need your sort in this inn!"

Two men came down the ladder from the better class of sleeping accommodations in the loft. The first was a big, graying fellow who could possibly have been born on this time horizon. His slight blond companion was certainly a revisionist. Rebecca didn't need Gerd's confirming nod as he glanced—even now!—at the sensor in his palm.

"What's this?" the gray man demanded. He spoke German but his accent must have been almost unintelligible to the others. The Russians had prepared themselves as carefully as possible in their time, but they wouldn't have been able to study the actual dialects in use on this horizon.

"They knifed Hilderic, Master Hannes," said the same thug who'd spoken before. "We was just—"

"Wha happen?" Hilderic demanded muzzily, supporting himself on a doorpost. His head must be solid bone. A point-blank microwave pulse could easily be fatal.

"Get your trash out of here, Hannes," the innkeeper said in a low growl. His hairy left hand massaged the muscles of his right shoulder. His loaded fist twitched sideways. "Get them out or you'll go with them!"

"Tomorrow we will go, brother," the slight Russian said. "When the army leaves."

"You know we need bodyguards and handlers for the slaves we will buy," the older man added. He threw back the right flap of an embroidered cloak. "Come, Lothar, how much to settle this?"

"What the hell happened?" Hilderic repeated, still hugging the door frame. "Osric, have I been drinking?"

"I said I didn't want you!" Lothar said. "Get your trash out or get out with them!"

"And if we don't choose to do that?" the younger Russian asked coolly. Both his hands were under his cloak, and Rebecca didn't figure they were on his purse. She moved to the side so that she wouldn't be hit by bullets aimed at the innkeeper.

Lothar looked around the big room and smiled with real humor. "So," he said, "there's twice as many of you as there is us, Istvan? That's what you're counting on? Sure, you all can stay. Until my daughter—that's her at the window—"

Rebecca glanced toward the street. Sure enough, a moon-faced girl whose braids were woven on top of her head watched the events from the street.

"—tells the soldiers it's free ale for the whole company whose men bring me all your heads. I don't even think they'll wait till dark to finish the business, Istvan."

Hannes turned to the bodyguards. "Go on, then," he snarled. "You act like pigs, you can sleep like pigs in the street tonight. Go on!"

"Hey, that's not right," said the thug who'd been sure Hilderic was stabbed. He looked in puzzlement from his employer to Hilderic standing in the doorway. "We got a right to a roof. What if it rains?"

"Find a roof, then!" Hannes said. He shook three gold coins from his purse and tossed them at the man. "Go on, get out!"

The guards moved toward the door with a good deal of mumbling and groping for the coins—enough to pay the wages of all of them for a week. Rebecca suspected they'd wind up sleeping in the street anyway after getting pig drunk on the unexpected windfall.

"Master Istvan," she said to the blond Russian in Latin. "Our master Gaius Clovis sent us to see what stock you had on hand. He'll be returning to Rome in a few weeks and thought he'd take some slaves back with him if the price was right."

"What?" said Istvan. His Latin was slightly better than his German, but the revisionists' accents probably had the locals wondering if they came from Hyperborea. "We don't have any slaves. We won't have slaves till the governor puts down the barbarians who are causing trouble."

Hannes turned his attention to the discussion also, but he didn't seem unduly concerned. Both Russians had taken their hands away from the weapons that were apparently hung from their belts.

"Well, till later, then," Rebecca said. "You'll accompany Varus tomorrow, then?"

"Yes," Hannes said curtly. "Come, Istvan, our goods are in the loft."

"Have a drink with us, masters?" Rebecca offered. Gerd was manipulating the sensor concealed in his left palm. It was her job to give the analyst time to gather as much information as possible. "Wine, perhaps?"

The Russians ignored her. Istvan preceded his companion up the ladder.

Lothar and his wife looked at Rebecca without warmth. The innkeeper didn't know exactly what had happened, but it was clear Rebecca was somehow involved in it. Now that the adrenaline rush had worn off, the strain Lothar had put on age-stiffened muscles was probably making itself felt.

"Rebecca," Gerd said in Latin, "our master won't be back

from dinner with the governor for many hours yet. I'm glad we'll have the opportunity to eat and drink here in this inn."

Rebecca looked at him. The analyst was dead serious. He really was happy for the chance to eat on the economy in this horizon. It was an experience he never would have had if the operation had been a quick in and out by transport capsule as the team had intended.

"Sure, Gerd," she said, looking at the cauldron that was probably pork being boiled flavorless. God only knew what the beer would taste like. Still, they needed to eat somewhere and close to the revisionists might be a good choice. Their immune-system boosters were going to get a workout. "We sure are fortunate."

"A meal for each of us and a mug of your house ale," the analyst said to Lothar, beaming.

Rebecca sighed. *If you told Gerd you had to amputate his leg without anesthetic, he'd probably look forward to that experience, too . . .*

"You'll have to wait here," the majordomo said to Pauli Weigand in the dark reception room. "Someone will come to collect you, I'm sure."

It said something about Varus' attitudes that he'd changed the orientation of the governor's residence from an outward-facing villa to a town house with blank outer walls. The fort's residents were disciplined soldiers, not a city rabble. Varus simply didn't want to have to look at the men he commanded.

The reception room was intended to be lighted through the front colonnade, so oil lamps were the only illumination when Varus boarded up the windows. The open skylight of a Mediterranean-style atrium wasn't possible because there were rooms on the floor above. German winters would have made that a bad plan anyway, though Pauli couldn't be sure Varus, fresh from a profitable governorship in Syria, quite appreciated the differences in climate. A Roman aristocrat didn't trouble himself with details of geography.

The majordomo was having his nails buffed by a young boy. Three ushers lounged in the reception room, all of them

pointedly avoiding looking at Pauli; a fourth usher had been
sent off at his arrival.

The ten-man military guard outside the building had let
Pauli through without delay. They didn't see their job as requiring status games.

Pauli wasn't bored: he was listening to Beckie and Gerd
through the bone-conduction output of his headband. It worried him that the other two were operating without him,
though time contraints and common sense required it. He
worried more that they'd only located half the revisionists
Central briefed them to expect. He worried that he was going
to make a blunder at dinner and compromise the mission.

Oh, no, he wasn't bored. But still . . .

He smiled at the majordomo. "Do you visit Rome often?"
Pauli asked in a tone of mild interest.

The plump servant flicked his eyes sideways, caught
Pauli's smile, and jerked his hands away from the manicurist.
If this barbarian *did* chance to have the emperor's ear . . .

"Stupid donkey!" he shouted and slapped at the startled
boy. "Rufio!" he ordered an usher. "Take the gentleman's
cloak. Blaesus, conduct Master Clovis to the garden."

To Pauli the majordomo added, "I don't know what's become of the boy who was supposed to fetch you. It's so difficult to buy good help these days."

"I can imagine," Pauli said mildly as he unfastened the ornate gold pin that closed his knee-length military cloak. He
handed the garment to Rufio. Underneath he wore a dining
cape of cerise linen, tied at the throat with ribbons. Most of
the team's baggage consisted of Pauli's garments and equipment. His slaves could wear the same tunics and cloaks
throughout the operation without arousing curiosity.

Blaesus, a sad-looking man of Egyptian or Levantine ori-
gin, guided Pauli through the building. Varus had brought a
huge household; there were a number of slaves in every room.

The furnishings were sparse by the standards of later days,
but the bronze work, statuary, and ceramics on display were
obviously expensive. Slaves were packing many of the items
into traveling chests. Pauli almost walked into a wall as he re-

alized Varus intended to take the goods along to decorate the new camp to be built on the lower Weser.

Dinner was laid in the garden at the back of the building. Three benches were set against a round serving table; the fourth side was open to permit servants to change the dishes. Diners reclined on their left elbows in eight of the nine places; the lowest in status, the end place on the right arm of the U, waited for Pauli.

A quick glance convinced Pauli that the garden was converted from a section of the stables that were part of the building's original design. Trees stood in pots and roses had made a start on the trellis. Suncatchers of colored glass wobbled on threads from the branches.

The orange tree certainly wasn't going to survive its first German winter. On the other hand, its owner wasn't going to survive the remainder of this month . . .

"There you are, Clovis," Varus said. "We'd wondered what happened to you."

He took in Pauli's dining cape and added approvingly, "Ah, yes. Very urbane. Well, there's a few of us in this benighted bogland who try to keep up civilized standards."

Pauli eased himself onto the pillowed couch. Five of the governor's guests were civilian friends, including the lawyers from the afternoon's trial. Arminius reclined in the place of honor beside the host, next to another German. Based on the background briefing he must be Sigimer, another leader of the conspiracy. Sigimer was a little younger than Arminius; the Latin in which he demanded wine from a servant was much less fluent than his fellow's.

The other diners probably lived in the governor's residence as Varus' special friends. They had no need to twiddle their thumbs at the entrance, waiting for servants to pass them through.

"Tell me, Arminius," one of the lawyers said as he swallowed a sausage ball from the platter in the middle of the three benches, "do you think these Chauci rebels are going to fight? I'd like to have some stories to carry back to Rome."

"You'll carry back stories anyway, Gallus," another lawyer gibed. "The truth would just get in your way."

"Yes, I *am* your lesser in that fashion, Lentulus," Gallus agreed urbanely. "You've never let truth delay you in the slightest."

"Bah, the Chauci won't fight," Sigimer said in his heavy accent. "Anyway, it's just the Squirrel Clan if they did. Nothing to worry about."

He slurped down his wine and belched. He was drinking it unmixed and from the slurring of his voice this wasn't his first cup. The beer Sigimer had been brought up on wouldn't have anything like the wine's alcohol content.

"Some of the boys got drunk and killed a few traders, Gallus," Arminius said. He lifted a sausage ball between thumb and middle finger, aping the refined technique of the Romans around him. "You know how it is. When they sobered up in the morning it was too late. They decided they'd rather be rebels than be crucified alone."

"There's no profit in crucifixion," Varus said through a mouthful of honeyed sparrow.

"Oh, but you've got to crucify some of them, Publius," protested the lawyer beside Sigimer. "And after all, there's not a lot of profit to be made from bog-trotting Germans even when they're alive. Scarcely what milady's looking for in the way of a house slave, are they?"

"Depends on the lady, Cisius," the man on the far end said. "How do you suppose your wife's keeping warm while you're away?"

Cisius shuddered. "The same way she keeps warm when I'm in Rome, I trust," he said. "What a thought. But she brought three adjoining farms as a dowry."

"There'll be plenty of wealth!" Arminius said. "Sigimer and I will bring our folk to drive all the cattle out of the woods where they'll be hidden. Oh, yes, we'll have a fine time chasing animals in the woods!"

"Gentlemen, cups all round!" Varus ordered. He raised his own, a fine piece of silver. "To Arminius and Sigimer, and to the success of their enterprise!"

I'll drink to that, Pauli thought as he took a filled cup from a servant. *I came back twenty-five hundred years to make sure the Germans succeed.*

But for all that, thought of what success meant soured the Gallic wine in his mouth.

Moscow, Russia

March 9, 1992

Grainger hated enclosed spaces. They made his skin crawl. Usually he was happy to leave the confines of the temporal capsule for the wide-open spaces of any temporal horizon you could name. But not this time.

Inside the Kremlin's high brick walls were churches as well as government offices. Under one of them, the chapel of Ivan the Terrible, were catacombs, all but forgotten, long unused. Deep in those catacombs, the ARC Riders left TC 779. Grainger hated being underground more than anything but being sheathed in his ARC Rider's hard armor.

The temporal capsule's chameleon skin mimicked the rough-cut stone walls perfectly before TC 779 phased out of the continuum. Then the team was alone, committed—at least for nine minutes until the capsule phased back into reality. Looking at the empty space where the temporal capsule had been, Tim Grainger felt as if he'd lost his best friend.

Chun had found a hoary escape route leading from a priest-hole in the chapel through the catacombs to the riverbank. She was outdoing herself on this mission. Grainger was certain she'd chosen the underground hiding place for the TC just to torture him.

Theoretically, the ARC Riders could access TC 779 anytime of day or night in an emergency, whether or not they could get into the chapel from above ground. The escape route was so ancient that there was a distinct possibility no

Soviets were aware of it. It dated from Ivan the Terrible's time and hadn't been rediscovered until the 22nd century.

Of course Chun convinced Team Leader Roebeck that they'd better walk the course. Thanks, Chun. They traced the length of their underground escape route, going all the way to the river and back to where they'd started. Never could be too sure that Central hadn't missed something. A critical passage could have been blocked by natural or human caprice. Officially forgotten tunnels might have become some Russian splinter group's secret headquarters.

The ARC Riders remained silent as they wandered the catacombs, using Chun's handheld positioner to test Central's mapping, communicating only by hand sign until Roebeck was satisfied that plan and reality were compatible. That was good, because if Chun said one gloating thing about how Grainger was handling this spelunking, he was going to shoot her there and then. Claim an accidental discharge of his weapon. But she didn't. So he focused on keeping his multifunction command and control membrane's physio monitor from betraying any sign of his physical distress. You can control claustrophobia. You just have to concentrate.

Finding the priesthole exactly where Central said it would be, Roebeck gave them a thumbs-up. Through Grainger's multifunction control membrane, pulled down over his face, everything in the catacombs was as bright as day. The membrane filtered out the dust of centuries. Perhaps they could have chanced verbal communication via their membranes' communications link, but Roebeck was being careful. Grainger always respected careful.

Like wraiths, they stole into the chapel's known extent. Here, where they might encounter a custodian or a guard, they could no longer rely on their command and control membranes. Grainger and the two women rolled the C and C devices down around their necks, where the membranes looked enough like scarves to pass muster. Then the ARC Riders climbed single file up crumbling stairs. Their first priority was orientation—a walkabout. It seemed safe, even prudent.

But nothing on a new horizon is ever safe. And prudence would have meant leaving Chun behind with the craft, as far as Grainger was concerned. He'd argued. Roebeck had overruled him. She'd held firm, even knowing that anybody other than a white person was worth a second look in Moscow in '92. Twentieth-century Moscow had a vast reserve of white people in case the rest of the world ever ran out. In Grainger's timeline, that hadn't happened. In the timeline that the Russian revisionists were trying to institute, it might happen. Chun's presence set them apart. Their Oriental teammate marked them as touring foreigners or part of some official visiting delegation.

So be it. Grainger knew he could get himself out of whatever he got into. He'd memorized the bolt-hole routes and alternate access points around Moscow that could get him back to the catacombs. So he could get back to TC 779 whatever happened. From several places in town. With the women in tow, or alone if it came to it.

Each ARC Rider had a separate go-to-shit plan in addition to their joint plan. Their separate plans might be the only viable alternatives if one or more ARC Riders were caught and interrogated by any of a number of Russian security services. The Soviets were unparalleled interrogators. A change in government didn't mean that the apparatchiki—the functionaries—had lost their memories. Or their abilities. So you wanted to be redundantly prepared to ensure your own security. It was that kind of mission.

If it all went to shit, Tim Grainger would do whatever it took to survive. He was armed and more dangerous than anybody on this horizon had ever dreamed a single person could be. He'd made every contingency preparation personally. He'd brought along every weapon he could think of, wrapping them in the mission-correct clothing provided by Central. His 26th-century weaponry was heavy in the black ballistic nylon gearbag on his shoulder.

Less than half an hour into the recon, he was sure he was going to need every weapon he had.

They'd planned to use the state-run guided tours of the

Kremlin's historical monuments as a cover, posing as tourists to get out the Kremlin gates unchallenged with their black nylon gearbags. They found a tour group examining the jasper floors, the Botticelli oil lamps, and the priceless icons encrusted with precious stones. They tagged along.

The tour group was mostly Westerners. The default language of the tour guide was English. They hadn't been with the group for more than five minutes when a sharp-nosed Russian spotted them. This Russian, emaciated, waxy-skinned, and wearing eyeglasses held together with paper clips, sidled up to Grainger.

The Russian asked, sotto voce, "American?" His breath and body smelled of strange spices and raw garlic.

Grainger saw the frown on Roebeck's face before he answered, "Yes." Central had costumed them purposely to clearly mark them as Americans, for whatever protection easy identification with the world's single remaining superpower might afford. The ARC Riders wore white running shoes, blue jeans over regulation bodysuit, puffy quilted parkas complete with US flag patches on the arms.

"Ladies should wear coverings on their heads in this place." The Russian's hair was greasy, unwashed for far too long. Even soap was scarce here now, let alone shampoo.

Damn, of course. This was a church, after all. And newly won religious freedom was quickly leading to religious fervor. Central hadn't bothered to tell them they needed babushkas—head scarves—for the ladies.

Roebeck and Chun had heard. The team exchanged glances for an instant in silent evaluation of possible damage control measures.

Grainger said, "Custom dictates scarves, ladies," very quietly, and tugged at the comm membrane around his throat.

Chun rolled her almond eyes ceilingward as she and Roebeck pulled their comm membranes up over their faces and foreheads to cover their hair and ears—barely. To Grainger, the ARC Riders with comm membranes on their heads looked like high-tech washerwomen. The membranes were a mottled gray color when not in use. The material was like nothing from this century. But maybe they'd pass. Many things from the outside world were still alien to the cloistered populace of the former USSR. The Soviet empire's main preoccupation had been protecting its citizens from decadent, corrosive foreign influences.

The frail Russian sidled even closer to Grainger—disturbingly close. Grainger wanted to back up but remembered that this culture had a different set of criteria for personal space. So he held his ground. The indig looked at his feet, saying in a whisper: "Interested in icons? I have copper icon, 15th century, very waluable."

"Nan, Chun, let's move on." Grainger tried to ignore the solicitation. This Russian could be what he seemed: a black-market entrepreneur who'd sighted a rich American. Selling cultural items to outsiders was a serious infraction of current local law. This hungry-looking fellow might be so desperate he was willing to take nearly any risk to get hard currency. If Grainger had been stupid enough to buy such a thing, chances were probably fifty-fifty that this waxy-faced Russian had friends working in airport Customs. The friends would have seized the icon as a hapless American tried to leave the country with his prize. The Russians would have shared the money. Then they would have looked for another fool to fleece. That is, unless the Russian was part of the security apparatus, in which case the game was a bit more sordid: catch an American doing something wrong and shake him down or use him for diplomatic leverage.

Grainger moved away from the Russian, shaking his head. *"Nyet, nyet. Spacebo."* No, no. Thank you.

Central had missed the bit about covered heads in churches, so what else might it have missed? Now that Grainger was attuned to the cultural faux pas, he remembered the occasional disapproving look from other tour groups filing through the small stone chapel rooms. "Let's go, ladies. I'm getting real claustrophobic in here."

The truth always had a nice ring to it. And he couldn't very well say, *Got to get out of here before we do something else stupid.*

He left the would-be icon seller looking wistful, crestfallen, and disappointed. The "Evil Empire" of late 20th-century fame was staggering to a halt, but its traditions remained. *Blat,* or the black market trading of expropriated goods, was one of those traditions.

The ARC Riders wandered through several twisting corridors lit only by arrow slits, looking for a way out. They jostled past tourists who stopped unpredictably, craning their necks to stare at the ruined splendor marginally preserved. In the main chambers, scaffolding abandoned against high walls still supported a few working lights. The lights threw an intermittent, anachronistic glare that cut like knives through age-old shadows.

Down winding stone stairs and out the narrow arched door they went. Grainger had to stoop to pass. The team emerged from a covered portico, down three flights of broad steps into an early dusk laced with winter chill even in March.

Out in the air, Grainger started feeling much better almost immediately. Even polluted air beat the close confines of Ivan the Terrible's chapel. The cold reminded him how far north Moscow was. Zipping up his jacket, he felt the acoustic pistol in his hand-warmer pocket. A guard with a green uniform and red-piped cap eyed them curiously.

"Let's go *now!*" he muttered urgently, still working his cover. "I need a bathroom." Plausible.

Chun, Roebeck, and Grainger struck out for the Kremlin gates, past the huge bell commissioned by Catherine the Great and a cannon made for giants. They passed more guards. These soldiers were young men with cold-reddened cheeks. In tall fur hats they waited to twirl their rifles on their palms and march their stiff-legged march when the honor guard changed. The honor guard stared straight ahead, stubbornly unwilling to admit that anything that could change their traditional role in society had occurred. Ancient cobbles underfoot had been worn by peasants, sleighs, wheeled carriages, revolutionary mobs, automotive tires, obedient workers, missile trucks, disobedient workers, and tank treads in turn.

The colored onion domes of St. Basil's gleamed dully in sunset. Across Red Square, the state department store, Gum, sprawled Gothic and looming. Black government cars came by in a flag-fendered rush: Zils with chromed grills like sharks' teeth, Ladas full of spooks from Dzerzhinski Square. Before them, the gates to the working Kremlin opened and then closed. The red brick walls had swallowed them up.

Seeing unescorted Westerners, peddlers scuttled out from shadows toward the ARC Riders. Wan children and sparse-toothed old men, backed up by toughs in uniquely Russian gray leather jackets, approached like jackals from the bush. One blond boy came right up to Roebeck before Grainger could intervene.

"Hard Rock Cafe Moscow!" he proclaimed. His hands, blue with cold, held out a T-shirt with bilingual printing.

"Don't buy anything. They'll be all over us," Chun hissed. Behind her, already more than a dozen Russians with bags full of goods were watching whether Roebeck would buy.

"Where's Hard Rock Cafe Moscow?" Roebeck asked the boy, slowly, clearly. "We're hungry and we need a bathroom." Her breath streamed white out of her mouth.

The boy said, "We have only T-shirt, madam! Soon, if it is possible, we will have cafe. Now, buy T-shirt, okay? Twenty dollars, my first price to you."

"No, no," Roebeck said as peddlers began to encircle them. "That's too much."

"My first price, only first price to you." The boy moved closer, pushing the T-shirt at her.

Roebeck backed away. Grainger had a shoulder bag full of weapons that were totally useless in such a circumstance. He moved in, inserting himself between Roebeck, who was now walking swiftly backward, and the boy moving inexorably forward. All around, the encircling wall of peddlers grew thicker as it moved with them.

"You haven't heard my second price," said the boy plaintively.

"Forget it," Grainger growled at the boy as kindly but firmly as he could manage. "We're not buying anything, hear that? *Nyet, nyet.*" He stared around at the thickening ring of peddlers. Over their heads he could see green-uniformed Kremlin guards approaching to break up the crowd.

He really wished Roebeck had kept her mouth shut. He grabbed her roughly by the shoulder, saying, "Now look what you've done, honey," as if he were an angry husband. Russians understood angry husbands. And Russians understood the booted tread of guards approaching.

The peddlers dispersed as quickly as they'd massed, back into shadows and nothingness. In seconds, the three ARC Riders stood alone on the cobbles. The team was now the only source of amusement for the guards.

"Move," Chun said. "Come on! Now! Before those soldiers decide we're any more interesting."

"I told you not to try to buy anything!" Grainger said loudly, for the benefit of the oncoming guards, now close enough that the red trim on their hats could be seen. He took Roebeck's elbow, reached for Chun's arm.

Arms linked, just ahead of the booted guards, the ARC Riders strode three abreast toward the street beyond, making loud small talk in English to advertise their American cover.

Long after they'd passed out the Kremlin gates, Grainger held on to the two women. He was speechless with irritation and operational tension from the flub they'd made of a simple walkabout. As soon as he dared, he looked back. The guards had disappeared. He saw only the tomb where Lenin was supposedly buried, the square where so many missiles and mock missiles had been paraded before Politburo masters on ramparts while workers obediently thronged on cobbles below.

This might be the dead past to Roebeck and Chun, but it was very real to Grainger. The USSR had been the great threat of his grandfather's era. The very idea that a Russian-dominated Fourth Rome might plunge the world into the hopelessness of totalitarian misery terrified him. Tim Grainger knew too much about the former Soviet Union to ever believe that this mission was a cakewalk. He'd dealt with the aftershocks of the collapsed USSR for his entire adult life, until the ARC Riders had snatched him out of the jaws of death and history.

"Easy, Tim. Let me go. It's all right now," Roebeck said softly, and tried to step into the street to cross it.

"You can't do that, Nan," Grainger snapped. "You've got to cross underground." He pulled her back roughly, pointing at a set of concrete stairs leading down under the street. He wasn't going into another damned hole in the ground until and unless he absolutely had to. "I don't want to go down there. Too risky. Let's just walk along in plain sight until we find the hotel, okay? Stay above ground. And don't offer to buy anything. You see any stores here— apart from the Gum, I mean? Take a look. You won't find stores, not yet. Maybe next year. Now it's just semi-illegal card tables and people selling their family treasures from paper bags, plus a couple large open-air markets. You see a small state store, you see a line. Don't talk to anybody. Don't flash American money. You could still get people in trouble just by talking to them. For sure by handing them US dollars openly—"

"But you made such a fuss about bringing the dollars!" Chun said hotly. She stopped. Hands on hips, she seemed like a dragon breathing smoke in the cold air. The late-day Moscow light was nearly omnidirectional, giving everything an unreal quality. The streets seemed free of shadows, as if the shadows themselves were afraid to declare themselves or mass publicly.

"Just move along. This is still a real controlled society." It was all coming back to him, tales told to a wide-eyed child by a grandfather on Sunrise Terrace.

Police drove by in a dirty cruiser, followed by a green camouflage-painted van loaded with soldiers whose semiautomatic rifle barrels were sticking out every window.

Chun said, "I don't understand this. By March, 1992, you had privatization of industry. They'd been through the Winter of Discontent without a coup. The hard-liners were on the run . . ."

"Books are written by so-called authorities after the events. Records are what people want them to be," Nan Roebeck reminded her technical expert. "Remember, this was the era of 'political correctness.' Not just here, but in the West as well."

Good, at least Roebeck was processing ground truth. Nothing like a little reality to awaken people to how fragile the truth really is.

"Just let's go around this corner, ladies, and check into the damned hotel, okay? We're lucky Chun got us rooms at the Metropole. It's Westernized enough that we won't be constantly stumbling over ourselves. And on the surface it should seem only semicontrolled. Don't let that fool you." He was racking his brains for old memories of how things ought to be here and now. He'd heard dozens of war stories from his grandfather's cronies. But then it hadn't been important.

Now, those memories were all he had, besides Central's inadequate database. "They're going to ask to keep our passports and visas for a bit while they check out our credentials." This was a society with only rudimentary computerization. It hadn't been easy for Chun, even with Central's help, to falsify a paper trail simulating Russian visa processing. "Those visa checks are still standard procedure. Within a couple hours, we'll know how well we did at passport, invitation, and visa creation . . ."

Chun looked past him, to Roebeck on his far side. "Boss, is this the way it's going to be here?" She didn't like Grainger taking the lead.

Tough. He was too focused now to do any less.

Nan Roebeck didn't answer Chun directly. She was staring around at the red, yellow, and cream brick buildings dominating the streets. Empty plate-glass windows that might have held store displays in another culture here displayed only twisted crepe paper. Working people quietly moved toward subways, carrying bags held close. A man at curbside was using a foot pump to reinflate his auto's tires before heading into traffic in a small, dilapidated automobile. "It's amazing," Roebeck said, "that these people put up with this for so long."

"People will put up with a lot of repression if that repression promises security," Grainger replied. "Otherwise, the ARC Riders wouldn't exist. We're predicated, subsidized, and operated on that assumption."

Then Roebeck took her arm out of his. "Tim, just throttle back, will you? You're way too torqued."

Chun snorted her approval.

"Look," Grainger said, "we're going into a venue where all indoor conversations must be assumed to be monitored. Sort of like inside the TC." Grainger kept walking, head down. They'd come if they wanted. "So let's talk while we're out here and moving. This isn't a milk run. We've been sent chasing putative Russians who can travel temporally using some kind of nonstandard apparatus—I'm unwilling to credit 'psychic' force—which is sensitive to our TC's bow wave. That sensitivity obviates all of our standard working assumptions and methodologies. We can't catch these revisionists the easy way. Maybe we can't catch them the normal way. The folks Up The Line who sent us on this mission understand what's going on here. We don't. We don't even really know who sent us—*who* we work for. Don't forget that. Barthuli didn't bring it up for nothing."

"Where are you going with this, Tim?" Chun stepped toward him to avoid a hunched grandmother offering tins of caviar to passersby.

"I'm not going anywhere, Chun. I already am somewhere: '92 Russia. Let's say the Wise Ones Up The Line know what they're doing. Let's say Russians are using indigenous technology to defeat technology six centuries in advance of theirs. I guess it's possible."

"Tim," Roebeck cautioned, "if I wanted paranoid speculation on the motives of those Up The Line, I'd have brought Barthuli and left you slogging in the Roman mud with Carnes and Weigand."

"Okay, point taken. Look, these Russians were brilliant theoreticians. Don't let the dilapidated streets fool you. They didn't *care* about cosmetics. They didn't care about creature comfort. They cared about state supremacy, about military and ideological primacy. They gave up *everything* for scientific and technological excellence because they were told that such primacy was their only guarantee of security—and they believed they had it."

"That's a fallacy, Tim. Look around you," Chun objected. "This culture is falling apart. It's poor and getting poorer. According to Central, their military superiority was a sham. I can't—"

"Despite what Central says about this time horizon, the Soviet Union was not simply a Third World country that happened to have nukes. That's propaganda put out by the winners—my side. I ought to know. The Soviet Union was without peer educationally where technical subjects were concerned. For decades, they were twice as literate and twice as committed to intellectual superiority as any culture of their time. Their need to compete head-to-head with the West was what destroyed them. You couldn't win the technology race while protecting your people from corrupting influences. You had to learn about the other side's capabilities. As they learned about life in the West, the Russian people stopped believing that the price they were paying societally was worth it. Keep in mind that the West outspent them; it didn't outfight them. Russians may not make great-looking civilian trinkets yet, but their high-end space and military technology was kick-ass. Not sleek and pretty, but tough and effective. Their understanding of physics in many areas surpassed ours—may still, centuries later, surpass ours because so much was lost in the breakup."

"You think that's what we encountered in 9 AD?" Roebeck probed. "Forgotten Russian breakthrough technology?"

Grainger shrugged. It was exactly what he did think. There was no other answer that made sense. Much of Russia's more metaphysical or unconventional scientific explorations had been rejected as funding candidates by the West because of the "not invented here" syndrome and institutionalized hatreds.

To Roebeck, he said, "They had better metalurgical skills than the West. They had better algorithmists. When the US had a problem with a technology area, we added another supercomputer. If that didn't work, we dropped the problem and went on to something easier. These guys hunkered down and solved problems we'd discarded as insolvable. Often they picked up discarded US patent work and improved it. In a dozen key technology areas, they were well ahead of the West."

"Then how do you explain the societal failures? This city's infrastructure is in terrible shape," Chun demanded, her brow furrowed. "Everything's old, dirty, patched together. That guy pumping up his tires before he drove away . . ."

"They just never understood how to capitalize on what they had, that was all," Grainger replied. "To win in a capitalist world, they needed marketeers and couldn't produce them for ideological reasons. Once they lost the Cold War, the Western powers, led by US Deputy Secretary of Defense Donald Atwood, tried real hard to starve them back to the 18th century, so they'd never be a threat again. Meanwhile, the West, the Asians, and the Arabs were stealing them blind through both governmental and private initiatives. The entire technology curve—not just weapons proliferation—of the early 21st century was accelerated by Russian theoretical work exploited by unscrupulous commercializers."

He paused to rub the back of his neck and squint through the lowering haze at the city around him. Neither woman commented. Maybe he was getting through to them.

He hoped he was. "My era was a direct result of that epoch. My whole division was formed to protect the US from competition based on the proliferation of Russian technology to the Pacific Rim nations and the Muslim world. Don't think there's nothing here that's a threat to us just because we're from their future. And start asking what we're going to do about it when we find the technology center that's produced these revisionists. Whatever one group of Russians did, three more groups were also doing. That may hold true for revising the timeline, as well as for titanium alloys or directional acoustics or production of unobtanium."

"Unobtanium?" Chun asked archly.

Okay, so maybe he wasn't getting through to Chun. Yet. He still had to try. "Sorry. Idiomatic. Russians had so many exotic alloys and materials that certain myths got started about materials and technologies the Russians were withholding. At their poorest, they still funded twenty percent of their tech base. 'Unobtanium' meant literally substances which were so sensitive they couldn't be obtained by outsiders. Coming into the turn of the century, Western governments were near hysterical at the classified level about what the Russians had, who was getting it, and what it could do. Osmium 187, subatomic explosives, and red mercury were part of a category called unobtanium, along with cold fusion generators, offensive beam weapons, zero cavitation electrical coatings for submarines, psychotronic devices, and scalar wave projectors."

"Scalar wave projectors? You mean Tesla coils and all that silliness?" Chun was as deep as Grainger into this turf battle over whose knowledge base was relevant.

"I've seen ball lightning running around laboratory floors in my own time. I've seen some nasty magnetic weapons prototypes that came from Russian work. Don't laugh. Whatever this 'psychic' temporal generator is, it's more than somebody's grandmother moving frogs through time. It's real. It's hardware based. And it's a significant threat to us and what we do, if our failed attempt to stop these revisionists in 9 AD is any sample. If you asked me for an overview of this mission, Nan, which you carefully haven't done anywhere where we're on the record, I'd have to tell you . . ." Grainger stopped. Overviews were strictly Chun's job, not his. He'd gained a lot of ground with Roebeck today. Best not to push too far and lose it all.

"Okay, Tim," Roebeck said. "Let's have it. I'm asking for your overview."

Chun glared at him but said nothing. Russians passing on the sidewalk stared covertly at the Oriental in American clothes.

"This is our you-bet-your-job mission. If we can't stop these revisionists, we're out of business."

Nan was still walking, but not looking at the Moscow streets any longer. A truck went by billowing raw blue exhaust that smelled as if it contained all the pollutants of hell.

When the roar had passed, Chun said, "You know, Tim, I'm glad you're offering to do my job for me. But if you bothered to read my daily log, you'd see I have already covered the salient parts of that long speech you just gave us. As for the rest of it . . . Well, you're not objective, are you?" Chun Quo smiled sweetly. "This looks like the Metropole Hotel. Isn't that what it says?" she asked innocently. A fleet of small white hotel-owned Mercedes were parked outside, the first decently maintained vehicles they'd seen.

"Yep. Into the breach, troops." Roebeck, the ARC Riders' team leader, squared her shoulders. She took the broad steps in long strides, leading the way into a lobby full of polished brass and dark wood and carpet.

Up to the long registration desk they went, fake passports, plastic credit card ID, Central-processed visas, and counterfeit currency in hand.

Sure enough, their passports and visas were taken from them by one of the most beautiful blond girls that Tim Grainger had ever seen. She wore no makeup. Her skin was peaches and cream. Her hair was clean and shining. Lounging behind her was a huge security type with no neck and the build of a bull, watching them closely as they registered.

The girl dutifully told them in passable English, "Passporta and visa will be returned to you in couple hours. Please call later." She slid three small booklets across the desk toward them, plus three keys. "This is rooms, and *passporta* for hotel. You wish porter?"

Roebeck looked at Grainger. Grainger and the guard were busy recognizing each other as operators. Roebeck touched his arm.

"Huh? Oh, no. The airport will send our baggage later—if they find it."

"Ah," said the girl with a real but brief smile. "Often they do find these lost baggages. Do not worry. We will inform you if they arrive. Have a nice day."

In the lobby there was a giant arrangement of dried flowers, almost as tall as Chun. A live cellist was playing a Bach solo somewhere above their heads. At the elevators they piled into a narrow car whose buttons depressed with a loud snap when one pushed them to choose a floor.

The elevator stopped at the third floor and its door opened, revealing the cellist and the rest of a string quartet performing in an atrium.

No one got in, and the elevator closed.

"This isn't so bad," Chun said. "In fact, it's beautiful."

"Thank God," Roebeck muttered.

"That's because we're rich *Amerikanskis,*" Grainger reminded them.

The hallway of their floor had a reception area of its own, with several couches, tables with ashtrays, chairs. The acrid smell of Russian tobacco permeated the huge open space. Wood and glass double doors separated the hallways from the meeting space.

Walking through the halls, Grainger was struck by the sheer size of the place, a calculated opulence of scale. Maybe the hotel had been built by claustrophobics. Or giants.

His room was huge by any standard, and Russian enough to bring back more of his grandfather's tales of diplomatic derring-do. Beautiful brocade curtains were nailed carelessly to a board over a tall window. Twin platform beds were low, their mattresses thin. On each bed, blankets nearly as thick as the mattresses were covered with linen cases. The cases were pierced by large diamond-shaped holes revealing colored wool blankets inside. The decor was Diplomatic Conservative, to match the curtains. Vaguely 18th-century brocade chairs were arranged under a grand crystal chandelier that Grainger's security scan revealed to be loaded with rudimentary surveillance equipment. His room was completely bathed in radio frequencies.

The house phone had a dial, not push buttons. After a few moments of study, he called Roebeck's room with it. "I'm sitting in an RF bath. How about you?"

"Do we want to discuss it?" said Nan's voice, tiny and so full of static it sounded light-years away.

"Maybe it's standard and they'll quit it if they know we know," he suggested.

"Maybe. Let's get something to eat where there's music or general background noise."

They met downstairs in one of the most amazing rooms Grainger had seen anytime, anyplace. Rococo gold columns rose two stories to a backlit stained-glass ceiling of great beauty and complexity. A harpist played here. Businessmen were drinking Russian *chai*, a strong tea, and eating cakes. Various vodkas had already been ordered on several tables. Here, too, the waitresses were extraordinarily beautiful, and the waiters equally handsome in their white shirts and black ties and slacks.

"This country's not all bad," Chun said. "Do you think they all look like that—all the girls?" She touched her black, straight hair.

"They all look like the people you saw outside. The lucky, the prettiest, the handsomest, the most connected, get these jobs. There's relatively big money for these kids. Look at the prices on this menu."

Their menu was in English. The prices were fabulous—tea and cakes could cost them a hundred of their dollars.

"Tim was right about needing money," Roebeck muttered. You didn't want to have to go back to TC 779 for a reason as trivial as printing more counterfeit.

They ordered, ate, and tipped in cash, leaving dollar bills under their plates. As they left, the waitress who served them scurried over, lifted the plate, and made the dollars disappear. She saw Grainger watching and cast him a grateful, sunny smile.

Roebeck noticed. "Do you think we overtipped? She can probably live for a week on the economy on those dollars."

"Yeah, I think we did. Let's keep doing it," Chun said before Tim could answer. Her counterfeit US currency would be as good as gold here, undetectable by any current means. Only the most unlikely of circumstances—two bills with identical serial numbers falling into the hands of a single party—would reveal that one was counterfeit. Even in that case, determining which bill was fake would be impossible in the 20th century. For all intents and purposes, the currency they were passing was good. And the ARC Riders were putting too small a sum into circulation to damage the US economy. So it was a win/win situation, unless you were the

US Treasury, in which case the duplicate currency would be an embarrassing mystery best hushed up.

The team was heading toward the elevators when the beefy security guard intercepted them. Grainger's hand went reflexively to the acoustic pistol in his pocket.

"Sir," the guard said in heavily accented, guttural, and painstaking English. "Come, please."

Grainger just stared at him.

"Come where?" Roebeck asked when Tim didn't respond.

The guard, frustrated, put a hand on Grainger's elbow. He was about to shoot down the guard there and then when he saw the pretty desk clerk beckoning. "Passports!" he exclaimed, realizing what was afoot.

"*Da, da, da,*" said the guard, nodding vigorously. "*Passporta.*"

Grainger deftly disengaged the guard's grip, patting the big man's arm, twice the width of his own.

"*Passports,*" Grainger reiterated to Nan. "They still have our passports."

Under the guard's watchful eye, they went to reclaim their visas and passports.

The desk clerk handed each one back, but then she frowned. "Ah—there is—*problema.*"

A problem. Terrific. The guard was still watching them.

"Problem?" Nan and Chun said nearly together. "What kind of problem?"

"The baggages. *Nyet* baggages."

The ARC Riders exchanged glances.

"That's no problem. We'll make do with what's in our overnight bags," Chun assured her.

Grainger was too tense now to pay attention to the words. Turning his back on the desk clerk, he leaned both elbows on the reception desk, ready to draw on the guard and any number of comrades at the slightest additional provocation.

"*Nyet problema?*" said the desk clerk wonderingly.

"*Nyet problema,*" Nan assured her.

Tim Grainger's skin crawled all the way to the elevator. He looked at the passport he got back. There wasn't a stamp or mark that he could see. The blue-gray paper Russian visa with his picture, however, clearly had been processed.

As they waited for a car to take them to their floor, he said, "Well, you two are making real strides in the Russian language, anyway. When you find out how to say 'where's the bathroom,' there'll be no stopping you. I don't know about you, but I'm ready to try my share of Chun's phone numbers. How about it, Nan? Chun?"

Each of them had a group of phone numbers to try. Tim's were at 11 Gorki Street, where the current General Director for Foreign Relations held court in the Ministry of Science, Technology, and Education Policy. Nan had the Foreign Ministry. Chun had the Academy of Sciences. Central had narrowed the field for possible revisionists to those three government departments. But Central also didn't know whom within those bureaucracies to target. So you picked a number and you took your shot.

"Let's go do it. The first one to get somebody who'll let us buy him dinner, call the others."

Within half an hour, each ARC Rider had a dinner date.

"That's not good," Nan said. "I wanted one meeting for all three of us, not three meetings. What time is yours, Tim? Chun?"

No one had thought it would be so easy to access senior officials. When Tim had called to tell Nan he had a meeting with Alexander Matsak, Deputy Director for Privatization of the Science Ministry, her extension had been busy.

The same thing had happened when Nan had called Chun to say Nan had arranged a meeting with the Foreign Ministry's Special Assistant for Proliferation, a Sergey Orlov.

And Chun had gotten through to a Professor Viktor Etkin of the Academy of Sciences.

Tim's meeting was at 1730 hours. Chun's was at 1700. Nan's was at 1800.

"Unless they're real short meetings, we're each on our own," Nan said. "Let's check these names with Central's database." They were in Chun's room, a virtual double of Tim's, even to the pictures on the walls. Chun had set up a countermeasures suite that blocked ninety-five percent of EM surveillance and a sound cancellation program that made the area around the twin beds safe for conversation. It would have to do. A live Russian peeking through a pinhole might take verbatim transcript, but the ARC Riders were safe from primitive electronic surveillance. They ran the full names of their dinner companions, found the patronymics in Central's database, and read historical profiles and cross-references until it was time for Chun to meet her guest downstairs.

"Won't this Etkin ring your room?" Nan asked.

"Evidently not the custom. He asked me how he'd recognize me and gave a pretty good description of himself. He says he'll be carrying a red umbrella. He must keep it handy for meetings such as this. His English is better than mine."

"Ought to be. He's KGB or whatever they called it this week, if Central's right. Section 6—Technology. Hold on to your own technology, and don't leave the hotel without us for any reason," Roebeck said. Chun wasn't experienced as a field operator. "After five minutes, ask if we can join you and we'll come down. I've got to meet my guy downstairs, too."

Tim's man, Matsak, had made similar arrangements.

Chun began disassembling her portable secure facility, reeling antennae into a keeper that she replaced in her bag along with a handheld EM generator. "I'm ready, Nan."

Roebeck looked at her chronometer. "I have 1655 local time. Don't do anything I wouldn't do, Quo."

After Chun had left, counterfeit business cards in hand, Tim eyed Nan until the team leader spoke.

"Don't say anything, Tim, okay? Don't say a word. She'll do fine. Neither you nor I were going to cut it with some 'Doctor Professor.' Central says they have to believe they're talking to an expert of some parity before they'll open up."

"I don't think that can happen when a white Russian male meets an Oriental female, no matter how much more she knows than he knows," Tim said mildly. "But as long as Chun doesn't get mugged for her handheld, I don't care. Keeps her out of my way." Had to be careful what they said now that they had no countermeasures in place.

"And you'd like me out of your way as well?"

Last time they'd gone into the field together, Roebeck had behaved more like a woman and less like a superior officer toward Tim Grainger. This time, it wasn't happening. Or at least, not yet it wasn't.

"I'm going to go shower and change, assuming my readout shows insufficient toxins in the water to be more of a problem than not showering." Central had warned them about the water, the food, and the pollution-ridden atmosphere, and then loaded them up with vaccinations and a list of additional required immunizations that were circumstance dependent. Presumably, Chun and Roebeck had already complied with the immunization requirement.

Tim had yet to self-administer his shots. The exact immunization recommendations could only be finalized from site data added to previously stored data. He wasn't looking forward to it. He could put it off a few hours, but he couldn't skip it. First he had to take air and water samples to feed to his handheld. Once the handheld analyzed the samples, it would transmit directions to his pharmakit. He had to discharge his pharmakit's recommended load into his flesh during the first twelve hours of this mission. If he couldn't show that he'd taken his shots, he'd be quarantined and disciplined when he got back to Central.

"And take your shots, Grainger," Nan said as he left the room. "No cheating." She knew him too well.

When he got back to his room, he unpacked his handheld, then his pharmakit. He hooked up the sampler and fed samples to his handheld. The handheld transmitted its requirements to his pharmakit. He monitored the process using his comm membrane. His arm was going to hurt for a week. His pharmakit had decided that he needed not only immunization boosters against hepatitis B and C, cholera, and diphtheria, but an antiradiation shot as well. Usually, his standard immunization load was adequate for fieldwork. The antiradiation shot was going to limit his mental agility for at least twenty-four hours. The hepatitis boosters were going to make whichever arm he chose real sore. He dialed everything into one unpleasant cocktail and pressed the pharmakit against his left biceps with his right hand. Then he pulled the trigger and pretended he didn't mind the pain. He could feel the antiradiation drug burning its way into his system.

By the time he was done, he didn't want the real H_2O shower as much as he had before. He took it anyway.

When he came out, Nan had let herself into his room.

"Time to go down and meet Chun's blind date."

"Yeah, well, I want to be wearing clothes when I do that," he said, peeking around the Russian-style wardrobe at her. She looked downright accommodated to the venue in dark loose pants and shirt over her bodysuit and flat shoes. She'd worked on the color scheme of her comm membrane. It was now displaying something much more like paisley than cammo.

"Good enough," she said when he'd dressed in what Central had provided, a dark lightweight jacket and slacks. They'd made adequate padding for the weapons in his gearbag. He shouldered the bag. "I'm not leaving this. You didn't leave yours . . . ?"

You couldn't. Not here. A good investigation of empty guest rooms was part of the culture in Moscow. It would change later, at least on the surface. But not yet.

Roebeck's lips twitched. She pulled her own black bag from under the bed. "We're Americans. All women of this era carried tons of stuff. I'm way ahead of you, Grainger. Don't forget that."

"Yes, sir," he said. He understood the larger message. Keep your place. Don't cut the line. The addition of Chun to the ground team made this a much different, more formal mission format than their last outing.

They found Chun with her Academy of Sciences honcho/KGB agent, Viktor Etkin, who carried the promised red umbrella. Etkin was six feet tall, smooth as silk, handsome as a Russian TV commentator. He had a firm, dry handshake and a full blond head of hair. He was wearing impeccably tailored Western clothes. Lucky Chun. Maybe she'd get laid in the process. She looked impossibly diminutive beside him.

Grainger wasn't expecting anywhere near Etkin's level of polish from his guy, Matsak of the Ministry of Science, or from Nan's Mr. Orlov from the Foreign Ministry.

"Completely my pleasure to meet you, Mr. Grainger. And you, my dear lady official, Madam Roebeck. On behalf of the Academy of Sciences of the Russian Federation, let me welcome you to our beautiful capital. You have chosen one of my favorite hotels. This is a place that is truly Moscow, but not . . . truly Russia, not yet. If you understand me. I apologize for my sorry English."

Grainger said, "Nice to meet you, sir. And don't apologize. Your English is lots better than my Russian. I've got another meeting, but we'll sit for a moment with you." He put his hand in the small of Chun's back and pushed her toward the bar in the rear of the Metropole's lobby.

"Yes, let's have a drink and see what we can do to arrange for follow-on meetings before Tim and I have to dash," Nan suggested.

"It is sad you must be leaving us so soon . . ." Etkin looked disappointed in a polished, insincere way as he strode alongside them. The bureaucrat knew this place like the back of his hand, Grainger realized.

The bar, despite some uniquely Soviet artifacts still displayed, was comfortingly similar to bars everywhere and everywhen. Low lights gleamed on wineglasses hanging inverted over a long counter. So early, patrons were sparse. Etkin chose a table, seemingly at random. A white-shirted waiter scurried over. Before the ARC Riders could suggest anything, Etkin said, "You say this is first time in Moscow, yes? Then, Jack Daniel's for me, in your honor, of course. And for you a special wine—from Stalin's favorite vineyard." He spoke rapidly in dialectic Russian to the waiter, who melted away into the convivial dimness.

Etkin leaned forward. He had shooter's eyes that stared appraisingly at Grainger as if from a thousand miles away. "Tomorrow night, your party will be our guest at my club. This is private club. Very much unchanged since before ... the new government. *Concretne*—concrete business can be done there, has been done there for many years. Tonight, we get to know one another, Dr. Chun."

"Professor," Nan said, pulling out her "visit" card with English on one side and Russian on the obverse, "let me give you my card."

Everybody dove for their cards. The Russian put the ARC Riders' cards in front of him, professionally arranging them so that each card was closest to the person who'd given it to him.

The ARC Riders' cards all said, "US Department of Commerce, International Programs." Under Chun's and Nan's names were some likely titles. Nan's was Assistant Principal Deputy Undersecretary for Special Projects. Central's choices were savvy, considering the current state of the Russian security system. The titles were junior enough to not raise flags, senior enough to ensure access.

Chun's card dubbed her "Doctor," "Physical Engineer," and "Staff Specialist."

Tim's said nothing under his name. He wasn't trying to hide his intent here, just where he was from. It was a calculated risk meant to cut to the chase, through what otherwise might have been a lot of Ruskie hemming and hawing. There were guys with cards like Grainger's hunting technology all over Russia, and buying it for dollars.

You had to give a card to get a card. The three for one trade produced Etkin's "visit" card, with a lot more information on the Russian side than on the English side. The fact that the card was printed on both sides proved that visiting delegations were part of his everyday business. Grainger increasingly didn't like Chun's blind date. But he had his own coming up.

As the waiter brought the wine, the Academy of Sciences official looked at Grainger's card and then at Grainger again. "Ah, yes. I see." Etkin shifted his gaze to Nan Roebeck and said collegially, "Madam Roebeck, there are many things I already miss about the old days, and men like this are one of these things. I understand why you have him. And it makes me feel, umm, right at home."

Etkin turned to the waiter, who had poured some wine into one glass and was holding it out. His ring finger had a wide white swath on it, as if he'd removed a ring recently. Probably his KGB class ring, pocketed for the duration of this meeting. Etkin's suit had all the earmarks of a privileged class: real buttonholes on his cuffs, hand-stitched lapels, soft chalk stripes. Only a few prize-winning Russian scientists had the kind of cash it took to buy a suit like that. The ones that did were "show scientists," trusted party functionaries. KGB Department 6 senior personnel, especially, spent lots of time abroad under the cover of scientific exchanges.

Etkin tasted the wine, approved it, and pushed his glass aside to make room for two fingers of Jack Daniel's. "You may leave the bottle." This guy was not going to miss a free bottle of Western booze. Etkin addressed the ARC Riders as a group, formally:

"A toast. Today you are here seeing for yourselves how we have screwed up communism. Tomorrow, may you return to see how we will screw up capitalism!" His smile was dazzlingly white.

Nan Roebeck and Chun laughed out loud. Grainger forced a grin, but Etkin's toast chilled him. Too temporally focused. Was Etkin warning them? Acknowledging them for what they really were? Telling them he knew exactly why the ARC Riders were here and now? Volunteering his services? Or merely making amusing conversation?

"To capitalism," Nan said, taking a deep swallow of wine that made her eyes grow round in her head.

"To Russia," Chun added.

"And to absent friends," Grainger amended, picking up the blood-dark wine and looking at his wrist chronometer at the same time. His left arm already hurt when he raised it. The combined injections had made a sore lump that felt as big as a rat under his skin. Stalin's favorite wine was so dry it tasted like red dust. "Got to run. Please, Colonel, forgive us." Grainger didn't like being talked about in the third person, as a "thing" the way Etkin had talked about him to Roebeck. Nothing on Etkin's card had indicated a military rank or KGB affiliation, but it was time to call a spade a spade.

Etkin's pale shooter's eyes caught his and held him still for a moment. Not unfriendly, just acknowledging a kindred spirit. An amusement drifted in their depths that was colder than a winter wind. Etkin inclined his fine-featured *nomenclatura* head infinitesimally.

Okay, maybe Etkin wasn't a mere colonel, but someone of higher rank. Either way suited Grainger's mood. Tim Grainger wasn't Nan's guard dog, some expendable piece of well-conditioned flesh here to provide muscle in dicey moments.

On second thought, maybe he was. "Come on, Nan. I'll walk you. Tomorrow night at your club, then, Professor Etkin—it will be my pleasure to accept your hospitality." He stood and Nan followed suit.

"Whatever specifics Chun Quo arranges are fine with us," Nan Roebeck said. *"Das vedanya."*

There was no other way. They had to go meet their own contacts, leaving Chun in the silky smooth clutches of Academy of Sciences Professor Viktor Etkin, KGB.

Civil Aliso, Free Germany

August 23, 9 AD

The breeze had picked up slightly as the afternoon wore on. Occasionally a wave slapped the bank, though the river was low at this time of year. If Gerd fell from the stump on which he leaned outward, he'd land in mud without injury.

"We need to be inside the gates before sunset, Gerd," Rebecca Carnes called.

"Yes, I'm coming," the analyst said; and for a wonder, he did hop back to her across the trench trampled by the feet of the barge tows. He'd slipped his sensor into his purse for safety.

"I wanted to get a view of the barges," he explained. "There's too much activity at the dock inside the fort for me to record details from close by."

Rebecca grimaced. "I thought you were scanning for the other revisionists," she said.

"Of course, Rebecca," Gerd said with a faint smile. "I'm constantly scanning within my sensors' fifty-meter effective radius. From this angle of the river, I was able to view the barges as well. Did you realize that virtually all the army's supplies have to be brought in by water? There's no settled agriculture in this region, only a little gardening."

"But there's people, aren't there?" Rebecca said. "What do they live on?"

Evening had brought more traffic, mostly toward the fort.

With the army moving out in the morning there wouldn't be the usual number of overnight leaves.

"The Ubians and some other of the Rhenish tribes grow crops," Gerd said. "The Germans of this area and eastward herd cattle. Even if Varus conquered them, they couldn't support a Roman garrison. The troops' staple is bread, not meat. Changing the region's agriculture would take generations."

A soldier rode by on a mule, splashing mud. He was very drunk and singing at the top of his lungs about a girl named Lalage. He wasn't wearing armor, but he carried a javelin from whose tip streamed a woman's silk bandeau like a crimson flag.

"So there's really no risk?" Rebecca said as she tried to process what Gerd was telling her. "Even if we didn't prevent the revisionists from saving Varus and his army, the Roman Empire *couldn't* really expand to the Vistula?"

"It would make no administrative or economic sense to expand the empire to the east, Rebecca," the analyst said. "Overland communications with the central government would be a nightmare, and the combination of soil and climate make most of Germany of only marginal argicultural value compared to Gaul and the Rhine basin, which supported Rome's frontier garrisons in our timeline."

He looked at Rebecca with his frequent wistful smile. "But they could have done it, Rebecca," he said. "Without Varus losing ten percent of the empire's total army at the critical moment, Central projects that Roman generals *would* have marched and conquered as far perhaps as the Ukraine. Russian generals conquered Siberia in the 19th century, even though they brought down the czarist state behind them because of the resources they wasted in the effort."

"Thereby bringing into being the Soviet state the pair back at the inn wants to expand," Rebecca said. She laughed.

A woman coming from the fort looked at them. She led an eight-year-old by the hand and a four-year-old clutching his elder sibling's other hand. The woman had blond hair and

Germanic features, but the children's complexion was Mediterranean olive.

"I'm afraid that people don't often learn from history," Gerd said in an apologetic tone, as though it were somehow his fault.

"You're wrong, Gerd," Rebecca said. "We've learned a lot."

She grinned at him, feeling brighter than she had for most of the day. Maybe she'd gotten over the shock of brawling with the revisionists' bodyguards.

Gerd raised an eyebrow in question. They were approaching the gate. Both halves were open with outbound traffic on the left side. There was a short line of returnees being checked into the fort; a few civilians argued at their exclusion.

"We've learned that humanity can't afford to let idiots do idiotic things," Rebecca Carnes said. "They've got to be stopped. And you, me, and Pauli are going to do just that."

The garlic sauce had an interesting flavor, but the meat was tough even though it'd been boiled and Varus referred to it as "calf." Pauli Weigand had trained his palate in meals eaten across ten millennia. He guessed the donor hadn't been a calf for at least a year, and that it had been a pretty rough year besides.

As worried as he was about Beckie and Gerd, anything Pauli ate was going to taste like sawdust. His jaws moved stolidly on the bite he'd torn from the slice he held in his right hand.

"Wine!" Sigimer demanded. His mustache and much of his blond beard were purple with spillage from previous cups. A girl with a ladle of wine reached cautiously toward Sigimer's cup. Earlier the German had jerked the dress down from her bosom, though that had been several cupfuls before.

"Why don't you barbarians make wine yourselves, Arminius?" asked Silius Gallus. The lawyer'd been drinking also or he might have found a more tactful way to phrase the question. "I tried some of your *ale* when I arrived here and it was terrible. Why, I'd have believed a slave had pissed in my mouth!"

"Is that the sort of problem you often have, Gallus?" Cisius asked in false concern.

"Oh, good one, good one!" Varus bellowed. He mopped his lips. Like the governor's tunic, the napkin had a broad violet border to show that he was a member of the Senate. " 'Is that the sort of problem you often have?' "

"Ah, most of my poor people haven't had the experience I have of seeing Rome firsthand," Arminius said. He'd drunk his share during the meal, but he had a stronger head than Sigimer and, for that matter, many of the Romans. "Soon I'm sure all Germany will have a chance to see exactly what Roman power amounts to."

Pauli put the remainder of the meat into his mouth and resumed chewing. He licked his fingers, then wiped them on the napkin he'd brought with him. The linen was dyed to match his dining cape; sauce stains only darkened the fabric.

He hadn't been expected to take part in the conversation. The last place at table would probably have been filled by one of the governor's freedmen had not "the messenger of Augustus" arrived. Nobody thought Pauli's position gave him status to equal that of the nobles with whom he dined.

There was commotion in the hallway. The majordomo himself ran in. "Master!" he cried. Varus was looking over his shoulder to talk with the chief steward and didn't notice the intrusion for a moment. "I would have brought this to your attention properly, but—"

A big, middle-aged German strode into the garden. He was flanked but not prevented by two soldiers, one of them the centurion commanding the guards outside the residence. Besides his swagger stick, the centurion carried a long sword with an ornate hilt.

"Quinctilius Varus!" the German said in a voice raised nearly to a shout. "Listen to me, my prince!"

Sigimer looked up and said, almost sober, "Hey! What's Segestes doing here? Hermann, look who's here!"

Arminius got to his feet, hindered by the pillows and the couch coverlet that tangled with his short cape. Pauli rolled his knees under him though he didn't rise, not yet.

He didn't think things could get too badly out of hand. The carver slicing bits off the veal loin at a side table hopped back, taking the big knife with him. That was the only weapon in the garden besides those the legionaries carried—and the microwave pistol in the lining of Pauli's cape.

"Ah, Segestes," Varus said, pursing his lips in concern. "I had no idea that you'd be in Aliso today or I'd have invited you to dinner. As it is . . ."

"Sir, I thought I'd better let him through, being he's a king and an ally and all that," said the centurion. He looked relieved that the governor wasn't tearing a strip off him, at least not as a first thought. "We kept the folks riding with him outside, though."

Segestes had a dark red beard and mustache, while the shoulder-length hair of his scalp was blond and speckled with gray. The borders of his long blue cloak were worked with gold lace; the tip of the scabbard poking beneath the hem of the cloak was gold cut-work as well.

"I didn't come to eat!" Segestes said. He threw the right side of his cloak back over his shoulder as if to clear his sword arm, though the ornate scabbard was empty. Segestes wore a torque like a giant horseshoe around his neck. It must be made of tubing rather than solid metal or the weight would have bent him double. "I came to warn you that this Cheruscan viper is planning to murder you and all your army if you march against the Chauci tomorrow!"

Gallus burst out laughing. Cisius stifled a smile in his napkin and said, "The whole army? My goodness, that's a little extreme even for barbarian hyperbole, isn't it?"

Sigimer stood up, swaying noticeably. He looked in puzzlement at the cup in his hand, then cocked his arm back. The chief steward snatched the cup from his hand before he could hurl it at Segestes.

"That's a damned lie," Arminius said. "Segestes, you're a damned liar!"

The Cheruscan prince turned to Varus. "The Ubians are cowards who grub in the dirt and forget how a man lives," he said. Under stress his Latin had become more guttural, though it was still more intelligible than Segestes'. "This king of cowards can't raise his men to march with you, so he tries to frighten you into not marching at all. He doesn't want anybody to get loot and glory because he has no chance of that for himself!"

Segestes started for his younger rival. His knees bumped the serving table before the young legionary put an arm around his throat from behind and started to choke him. The centurion dropped the sword to help. Segestes might be a king, but to Roman soldiers he was still a member of an inferior race.

"Now, now, friends," Varus said. He found it awkward to look up at Arminius standing behind him, particularly when he wanted to keep an eye simultaneously on the Ubian whom his guards were wrestling back on the other side of the benches. "Why don't we all sit down and have a friendly drink together?"

He twisted his head in the opposite direction and said to the steward, "Grommus? There's a jar of Falernian still sealed in the storehouse. Have it brought in immediately."

Segestes relaxed. The soldiers let him go, though they braced themselves to crush the German between their armored shoulders if he tried violence again.

"My prince," Segestes said a little hoarsely. "This whole business is a conspiracy, and there—"

He pointed at Arminius with his full arm.

"—is the one who planned it. This so-called Chauci rebellion is just a ruse to draw you into the middle of nowhere so you can all be massacred!"

"Liar!" Arminius repeated. He sounded angry, but Pauli could hear an undertone of concern. The Cheruscan was trying to goad his rival into a physical attack that would get him ejected before he could argue his case.

"Your chief of engineers did seem to think the roads to the

Weser were difficult, Publius," a lawyer said. His eyes drifted toward Arminius with dawning suspicion.

"What he said was that there *aren't* any roads," Cisius added. "Just a track Tiberius cut five years ago, with corduroy on the low spots. The logs will have rotted away."

He looked at Arminius also.

Sigimer's flushed face went pale. He grabbed the small figure of a faun standing in a wall niche beside him. For a moment Pauli thought the German meant to use the statuette as a missile, but he was merely reaching for support.

The faun came away in his hand. Sigimer leaned forward and vomited across the bench on which he'd been lying. Because Arminius had risen also, only Cisius was in the target area.

Sigimer had eaten more than Pauli thought between cups of wine, but he hadn't wasted much effort on chewing. Spasms ejected slices of meat the size of a man's hand in the midst of the vividly purple wine.

Cisius leaped to his feet with a cry of horror. The bench drapery tangled the lawyer's ankles and sent him pitching backward into a rosebush.

Sigimer straightened. He had a dazed expression. His eyes rolled and he toppled face-first onto the dripping bench.

The servants who'd been keeping their distance when it looked like a brawl between German chiefs now rushed from all sides. Some tried to rescue the yelping lawyer without damaging the rose, while others gathered the snoring Sigimer. The chief steward gave high-pitched orders, raising the hem of his expensive tunic for fear it might get stained.

Pauli stood and moved to the shelter of a Lombardy poplar where he could watch but also avoid wild blows or missiles.

"Oh, Hercules!" Varus said, scrambling to his feet. The other diners were getting up as well.

"This is all very entertaining, Publius," Gallus said. "But before we go off to make our wills in anticipation of the wild barbarians slaughtering us, I think we ought to recall that King Segestes and Prince Arminius here have a long history of disliking each other. Eh?"

Gallus and Cisius had been sticking verbal pins in one another throughout dinner. The present comment seemed to be Gallus' way of showing appreciation to the Germans who'd discomfited Cisius so thoroughly.

"Segestes claims he's a friend of the Romans," Arminius said. "I've proved a hundred times that I'm *your* friend, Publius, haven't I? What do vague words count against real deeds and gifts?"

"Faugh!" Segestes shouted. The centurion waggled his swagger stick in the king's face, but Segestes didn't try to lunge forward. "Are you going to sell your army and your life because this Cheruscan dirt finds blond boys to warm your bed? Don't be such a fool!"

Varus' face went chilly. He stiffened, gaining a certain hard dignity that Pauli hadn't previously thought the governor was capable of. "Thank you for your concern, King Segestes," he said. "You and I can discuss the matter further when I return from putting down the rebellion among the Chauci as my duty requires."

"Even so," said a lawyer who'd kept out of the discussion to that point, "if there's some question about the business, it'd be common prudence to investigate before we sashay off into the boggy asshole of the continent. After all, the Fritzes only killed a few traders—and most of them lower-class types besides. Nothing much is going to happen if we take our time on this."

Gallus pointed at Pauli. "The emperor's courier is an Ubian, too," he said. "What does he think?"

Segestes turned, really looking at Pauli for the first time. "Who's this?" he demanded. "I don't know him!"

"I'm Clovis, Ludwig's son, of the Robin Clan," Pauli lied. "The Emperor Augustus' man now, not yours, King."

His cover was as complete as possible. There was an Ubian of the assumed name in the emperor's guard, and there were more than twenty thousand men of military age in the tribe. Segestes couldn't possibly know every male born in the scattered farms and hamlets that he ruled in theory.

This still wasn't a situation Pauli would have picked if there'd been a choice.

Segestes was angry. That anger was the card Pauli needed to play, just as Arminius had done. He turned to Varus and said, "Everybody knows why Segestes hates Hermann. Hermann's been poking Segestes' daughter Thusnelda ever since she was old enough to bleed. She's like a mare in season, Thusnelda is, and Hermann's the stallion she twitches her rump for!"

"*You—*" the king bellowed as he lunged for the ARC Rider. The legionary stepped into his way and held him for the centurion to get a chokehold with his vinewood swagger stick. Pauli folded his arms across his chest and sneered.

Four slaves lifted Sigimer to carry him out of the garden, holding him by wrists and ankles. He was facedown and still snoring. His beard dragged in the dirt.

"Thank you, Gaius Julius Clovis," Varus said formally. "Your remarks are in line with my own thinking." He turned to Segestes and continued in a cold, clear voice, "King Segestes, I think it would be as well if you rested after what I'm sure was a hard ride."

"You fat fool!" Segestes shouted. "Do you think I'm going to sleep under the same roof as these vermin?"

"Barbarians usually wait for me to offer them hospitality before they refuse it," Varus said. His tone by now was icy. "Centurion, see to it that the king is escorted out of the fort. At once!"

"Come on, old boy," the centurion said as he tugged Segestes backward with the swagger stick. "You've outstayed your welcome."

Segestes swung an angry fist. His knuckles thudded on the centurion's mailed breast. "Temper, temper," the Roman murmured and tightened his grip. The legionary picked up the king's sword and followed his superior out of the garden.

"Well, I certainly have to go change, don't I?" Cisius said, looking in theatrical dismay at his splashed garments. "Publius, your cook could be improved on, but your dinners are always so *entertaining.*"

"Segestes is a fool," Arminius said to the governor. "He belongs back on his farm, threshing grain."

He was still tense, though everyone but Pauli would blame the Cheruscan's concern on the scene that had just occurred. By the standards of German drinking parties, this fracas had been pretty mild. Arminius couldn't believe that his planned victims would completely disregard the warning they'd just received.

The majordomo had a rancorous discussion with the chief steward and three lesser slaves carrying buckets and towels. Finally the trio carried off the bench as well as their cleaning equipment. "There'll be a slight delay, Your Excellency, while we prepare other seating arrangements," the steward explained. "Some of the furniture has been packed."

Pauli blinked. Varus was taking dining benches on a punitive expedition? But of course he was.

"My, that was an impressive piece of barbarian candor, Clovis," Silius Gallus said to Pauli. "I don't suppose you intend to return to Ubian territory until there's a new king, hey?"

"We are a free people," Pauli said. To stay in character he glared at Arminius and added, "Even though we don't chase cattle through the marsh the way some tribes do."

"I have no quarrel with the Ubians," Arminius growled. "Only with their fool of a king. Here, my hand to seal our friendship!"

He stepped forward and reached across the serving table. Pauli hesitated for a moment, then clasped the Cheruscan forearm to forearm, each gripping the other at the elbow. Arminius' muscles were firm though there was a layer of fat over them.

Servants were coming out with rushlights, tallow-soaked slips of pine that burned with smoky, yellow flames. The sun had well set, though the sky was still pale.

"Excellency," Pauli said to the governor, "I thank you for your hospitality. I must return to my quarters now."

"Oh, surely not," said Cisius, returning from the interior of the house in fresh garments. "Why, the meal's not over."

"And the drinking has scarcely begun for most of us," Gallus said. Isn't that so, Cisius?"

"My master expects me to keep a daily log," Pauli said. "I want to dictate it to my secretary while there's still light."

He needed to know what Beckie and Gerd had found, and there wasn't anything more to be gained by staying here. Though he didn't have a sensor pack as discriminating as the analyst's, Pauli's headband had swept the electro-optical spectrum as he was guided through the governor's residence.

He hadn't found anything out of place. He'd thought the revisionists might have planted a device to frighten Varus out of the expedition by "ghostly voices" or other faked omens. That didn't appear to be the plan, or at any rate the revisionists hadn't managed to execute it.

"Well, as you please," Varus said, frowning in irritation at the replacement bench. It was a settee with a flat seat instead of a proper dining bench that sloped up toward the serving table. "Chresimus, lead the emperor's man to the door. Grommus, can't we do better than this bench?"

The majordomo, Chresimus, looked shocked at being directed to so menial a task but he didn't argue with his owner in a peevish mood. He bowed, led Pauli into the large meeting room just inside, and there passed him off to a boy carrying an armful of pillows toward the garden.

For several minutes nobody seemed to know where Pauli's cloak had been deposited. He found it himself in a side cubicle, serving as a pad for a sleeping slave.

"Oh, by my fortune!" the usher with Pauli said. "Carus!"

"I'll wake him," Pauli said.

Pauli gripped the embroidered hem with both hands and jerked the cloak out from under the man. Carus spun into the wall with a startled squeal.

Pauli pinned his cloak over his right shoulder as the slaves watched in concern. He was nervous and angry. He was controlled as well, but he hoped nobody was going to push him very far. His barbarian persona suited his present mood a little too well.

The guard detachment had changed at sunset. There were

only six men, under a junior noncom rather than a centurion. Pauli nodded to them and walked down the building's columned facade in the direction of the barracks he'd been assigned.

A trumpet blew *Stand Down* from the roof of the headquarters building. The long curved horns of each cohort repeated the signal. The garrison's whole strength was supposed to stand to for half an hour at dawn and sunset, the most likely hours for surprise attacks. At Aliso the command stood for the action, though perhaps the process of preparing for a change of base had made troops less scrupulous than they'd otherwise have been.

There seemed to be the full thirty horns, though many of the cohorts were only skeleton formations with their strength dispersed in small detachments throughout Free Germany. The scattered forces were Varus' way of preventing raids and banditry. A general revolt would sweep them away like sand castles before the tide.

Pauli sighed. Humanity had by the 26th century achieved a unified society bound by common standards of ethics and justice, in balance with itself and with the remainder of the Earth's life-forms. Pauli understood that if history changed, it would change for the worse . . . but there'd been a lot of nasty spots before that balance was achieved, and an ARC Rider got to see most of them.

"With hindsight," said Gerd Barthuli from the shadows beyond the range of the glass-windowed lantern above the residence door, "it would be possible to change things for the better in the very short term. Our duty is to stop folk who would change them for the worse."

"You had some excitement," Beckie said. She deliberately let the concern show in her voice.

A column of wagons jingled past, heading for the warehouses on the fort's river side. Slaves drove the teams, overseen by a dour-looking soldier in tunic and hobnailed sandals.

"The problems with this mission seem to be more the local circumstances than the revisionists," Pauli said. The colonnade of the governor's residence was as safe a place in the bustling camp as any for the team to plan. "Of course that may change if we ever learn what the revisionists are planning to do. Gerd?"

"The two men we've located, Hannes and Istvan as they call themselves, carry short-range radios and submachine guns," the analyst said. "I've dusted their cloaks and footgear with finely divided rubidium. It's not an active emitter, but because the element is so rare I can set my sensors to extreme sensitivity and locate the subjects at a distance of over a hundred kilometers now."

He gave Beckie a tight grin and said, "One hundred *klicks,*" using the military terminology of her own day.

"The weapons are significant, Pauli," Beckie said. "They're carrying Czechoslovak M61 Skorpions. Not Soviet products, so they didn't grab what was closest. The guns fire a very light subsonic cartridge, the 7.65 by 17 millimeter round, and they're fitted with sound suppressors."

"Assassination weapons," Pauli said, nodding in agreement with her unstated conclusions. "No other equipment?"

"Night-vision goggles and short-range radios," Gerd said. "And gold."

"The two we haven't found may be waiting to use tactical nukes on the Germans," Beckie said. "But this pair can't be planning to fight off the barbarian attack themselves. It looks to me as if they hope to kill Hermann."

"Or Varus," Pauli said. "That'd stop the expedition. Probably. And heaven knows, any general who replaced Varus would be an improvement."

"You should study Roman generalship, Pauli," Gerd said dryly. "There was more incompetence than you might think in the Roman high command."

"Judging from what I saw in Viet Nam," Beckie Carnes said in a distant tone, "you needn't limit that statement to the Roman high command, Gerd."

"All right," Pauli said. The phrase was a placeholder to take charge of the conversation; a placeholder borrowed from Nan Roebeck, and *how* he wished Nan were here to run the opera-

THE FOURTH ROME   95

tion. He felt as though he were diving through muddy water, unable to see either his goal or the sharks he knew shared the darkness with him.

"I don't want to eliminate the two revisionists we've found until we locate the other pair," Pauli said. He didn't know if that was the right decision or not. He *had* to decide; it was his responsibility to decide. "We'll observe the pair we've got unless they force our hand with some overt action or until they bring us to the others. I'm aware that we might be able to find the others faster by interrogating one of these two."

"The radios Hannes and Istvan have in their luggage are short range, no more than ten kilometers or so," Gerd said. "I believe the equipment's intended for the pair of them to coordinate, not to communicate with the other pair."

The analyst looked at Beckie and added, "I'd be able to locate a nuclear weapon at a considerable distance, Rebecca; at least two hundred kilometers. Though nerve gas or biological weapons wouldn't be nearly as easy to detect before employment."

"The target's too dispersed for area weapons," Pauli said with a brusque shake of his head. "Until the Germans come in contact with the Roman army, at least; though the revisionists may not realize that. Well, we're still going to wait a few days."

"Hannes and Istvan have a gang of local goons around them," Beckie said. "It'd be risky to try to snatch them with the equipment we've got. If we wait till they're deep in their own operation, then the chances are a lot better."

Pauli looked at her and grinned broadly. What she said was about half true. You could just as easily claim that hitting the revisionists before they got keyed up to act themselves greatly increased the chances of success. Beckie was supporting his decision because that's the sort of person she was: supportive.

Pauli put a big arm around each of his teammates, hoping the darkness would disguise the hug he gave them. "Come, faithful slaves," he said as he broke away. "Back to the barracks. Gerd, I want to see all the imagery you've got of this pair and their local talent. And I also want to get a night's sleep, because I think we're going to need it in the next few days."

A group of two-wheeled mule carts carrying light catapults trotted down the road. The soldiers driving the vehicles laughed and sang. They were looking forward to loot and a chance to kill people they didn't really think were human.

They'd soon find that the Germans felt exactly the same way.

Moscow, Russia

March 9, 1992

As soon as Grainger met his target, Matsak, in the lobby, sparks began to fly.

"Your Western standard of living has made your people lazy and complacent, sapped your creativity. Our lower standard of living gives us the great competitive advantage. We will soon outdo you in all forms of capitalism!" Alexander Matsak of the Science Ministry told Grainger flatly through chapped lips. "Help us now, and you will be our great friend. We wish alliances with our peers in the US, rather than with our inferiors from lesser powers. On the American side, your country should either keep its promises of assistance or stop proclaiming them publicly. The Russian people think we in the new government are getting all these dollars you are not sending and keeping these fairy-tale dollars for ourselves. On our side, it damages our government's credibility to proclaim that the mighty US talks of assistance but does not deliver. Other nations are already doing, while the US is still talking. Soon we will not need you. And we will not forget."

Nan Roebeck was pretending to examine black pottery for sale to tourists inside the hotel entryway. When she heard Matsak's words she turned, mouth already opening.

Grainger forestalled whatever she might have said: "Nan, I didn't see you. Let me introduce you to Deputy Director Matsak, of the Privatization Committee of the Ministry of Science, Technology, and Educational Policy. Mr. Matsak, this is my boss, Nan Roebeck, Assistant Principal Deputy Undersecretary for Special Projects for the US Department of Commerce."

Nan strode over to shake hands with Matsak. The lanky Russian grasped her outstretched right hand in his and raised it firmly to his lips, stopping her cold and completely short-circuiting her game plan.

Grainger sympathized with Roebeck but couldn't help giving Matsak credit for sizing up the enemy and moving in fast to neutralize any possible threat. Roebeck was even more confused by the gallant gesture than a woman of the nineties might have been. She stuttered. She didn't seem to know what to do with her hand when Matsak released control of it.

The work modalities for this sort of mission were coming back to Grainger fast. It felt as natural as breathing to tick off bureaucratic protocols, track the infinitesimal wins and losses that added up to success or failure. Play the old game, the old way.

To give Roebeck time to recover, Grainger handed her Matsak's visit card. The obverse, in Russian, said that Matsak was a general officer.

Roebeck frowned, studying the Cyrillic. "An army general? Good to meet you, sir."

"In these days, Ms. Roebeck, I use my Ministry titles only. Everything before the new regime is long ago and far away. Are you directing Mr. Grainger in his search for unique Russian technology? Perhaps I can be of service. My Ministry has the charter for privatizing the best of Russian science. Russian scientists need hard currency. We have created a semi State organization to facilitate interaction with the West and to protect our scientists' know-how. No matter what you wish to see from the former military-industrial complex, we can help you find the best of it."

Having given his pitch, Matsak waited for Roebeck to answer.

Grainger was praying that Nan could handle this tough, seasoned, turn-of-the-century bureaucrat. *Just say something nice* and get *out* of here, he thought, wishing he could use his comm membrane to alert her.

Matsak was drawn and pale. His translucent skin had a greenish cast from exhaustion or poor nutrition or both. He had a receding hairline and a full beard beneath an aquiline nose and long-lashed, burning eyes. Around those eyes were dark circles like bruises. His suit was domestic. His shoes were gray Russian leather. They seemed at first to be orthopedic. His shoulders were flecked with dandruff. His tie was silver-gray silk, slubbed from wear. He carried a battered briefcase.

This was a man staggering under a workload beyond anyone's ability to manage. Grainger had recognized Matsak the moment the man had stepped through the door, without having to reference the gray tie or the briefcase. Commitment burned in Matsak like fire. The intensity of it radiated like physical heat from his person.

This was one of the people who would make this revolution work or die trying.

Nan Roebeck, regaining her composure, said, "Mr. Matsak, we've just been meeting with the Academy of Sciences about accessing some of your unique technology. I think the meeting was very—"

"Stupid," Matsak interrupted. "You Americans *still* do not understand, I suppose? Or you just wish to exhibit the appearance of action? Which is it? You meet with this official, that functionary, what do you think happens? Each Russian wants the contact to be his alone, go through his channels, no one else's. Then what happens? They fight among themselves. They argue about who will get what. *Aahb-so-lute-ly,* the difficulty of access increases. The price to you goes up with each ministry or department involved. In our new Russia, your officials can no longer deal through their old channels. You must accept this."

"But—" Nan began.

"No excuses, please." Matsak shook his head dolefully. "We have told your side this repeatedly. Now, if you wish to deal with the Academy, then go deal with them." The Ministry man took two steps backward. "In my opinion, they cannot get you what you want. They have to come to us for permission to make any deal. We are the signature authority. Yeltsin has signed a paper saying this. So what have you accomplished?" His voice was very low and sibilant. His cheeks were flushed. He had no time for amateurs.

Nan said archly, "Tim . . . I have another meeting." She looked at her watch huffily. "Mr. Grainger has my full authority to bring to bear on our joint interests . . . I'm sure we'll meet again, if you and Mr. Grainger can determine a specific area of—fruitful—discussion."

Matsak was incredulous that she hadn't responded placatingly to his accusations. He watched disbelievingly as Roebeck turned her back on him and climbed the stairs into the bowels of the Metropole.

"Perhaps this meeting is over? Perhaps we are wasting our time. This woman is your superior?"

"She's a senior official," Grainger said dryly. "I'm my own authority."

Matsak peered sharply at him for a moment, and then began to laugh. He came up to Grainger in two quick strides and clapped him on the back. *"Bolshoi privyet, tovarisch."* A big hello, comrade. "I have been waiting a long time to meet an American with authority, like myself. We who get things done are in constant conflict with those whose life is dedicated to avoiding action. Now, say me what you want. *Concretne stoh?"* Concretely, what? "And do not be shy."

"Here?" In a hotel lobby?

"I have a driver outside, a car. We may go wherever you wish."

"I wish, Deputy Matsak," Grainger said, taking his cue from the other man's candid style, "to meet scientists in the area of geochronometry and spacetime physics, who may be working on temporal realignment programs. I have such a program of my own and money to spend on anything that may accelerate it."

"Ah, a real deal. So. This is well. Mr. Grainger, we will be working together very hard. Call me Sasha. And I will call you . . . ?"

"Tim. I'd like to meet whomever you suggest, in any discipline, who might be working on concrete programs in this technology area." He felt light-headed, maybe from the anti-radiation shot in combination with everything else he'd injected into himself. Maybe from elation. He'd hit pay dirt.

"Then, Tim, we must go to a house phone. I will make some calls. It is late, you must realize. I suppose some scientists may be available here, but the most important ones are not in this city, in any case. Will you go with me tonight—just a short drive from Moscow—to meet such scientists? See an enterprise? A laboratory demonstration?"

"I'd love to get out of this city, Sasha," Grainger said honestly, aware of the privilege of using the diminutive. "If I see what I want, I can buy it, cash on the spot—hardware, technical report, whatever meets my criteria. I can give you technical detail in your car."

Matsak was nodding. "To the phones then. Lead the way. And *spacebo*, keep your woman official from complicating my job by involving too many other officials. What we do must stay between us, Tim, until we're sure we can make a contract. Specifically, until we have permissions of my senior officials. Perhaps even after that, depending on what is involved."

"You're saying she's not invited?"

"I say you that only principals need attend. I also say you that I suppose prudence is advisable. I have all the contacts, all the friends I need to make a contract. Different friendship networks cannot be included, or nothing will come of our labor. How many days are you staying in Moscow?"

They were walking toward the house phones. Grainger could feel how real this Matsak was. Roebeck had made a bad mistake, perhaps a critical one. "I've got maybe a week." If they found any technology to buy, they'd better buy it quick. If they could steal what they needed or destroy the revisionists' program out of hand, so much the better, but time was still an issue. Time, in Grainger's line of work, was always *the* issue.

"Not much time for complex negotiations," Matsak said as if reading Grainger's mind, "but let me see what I can do. Our only option may be to undertake some visits which will take place quite late tonight. Is it possible for you?"

"It is possible for me," Tim Grainger affirmed as they reached the phones. He was feeling hot, flushed. Probably a mild fever reaction from the shots.

Matsak pulled a worn black leather folder from his breast pocket and thumbed through it.

The Russian's tone as he talked on the phone was nowhere as gentle as he'd been with Roebeck. Grainger caught a few phrases, including *voyenna technologie,* which roughly translated meant "military technology," followed by growled colloquial and scatological orders.

Grainger picked out, *Yop t'voyu robotnicki,* and then stopped trying. "Fuck your workers" was an indicator of intensity but not substance.

This hotshot Matsak was capable of rousting people out of their homes, or beds, and opening up some sort of laboratory or facility after hours. That was all Grainger could glean, and all he needed to know. He'd gotten to somebody with juice. If he could hold on to the momentum building here, he'd see whatever Matsak had to sell. He could only hope that the Ministry of Science official had access to what ARC was trying to find.

If Tim Grainger believed in luck, he'd have thanked his lucky stars that he, and not Roebeck or Chun, had drawn Matsak's number from the contact list that Central had established. This general had plenty of use for women, but not as peers. If Grainger's card had contained any ranking data, Matsak probably would have decided that Grainger was too junior to be worth his time. As it was, Grainger hoped he could maintain the fiction of parity in this culture where friendship networks and parity were just about all that mattered anymore.

When Matsak was finished on the phone, he patted his

pockets ostentatiously. "Do you have American cigarettes, Tim? I have left mine in the car."

Right. The game begins. "I have to buy some anyway. Can I get Marlboros here?"

"Certainly, I suppose." Off they went to get cigarettes. Tim bought two cartons for twice what he expected to pay, and gave one carton to Matsak. "Please accept these as a personal—not state to state—token of appreciation."

Matsak's lips twitched and he flipped open his briefcase with a practiced gesture, balancing the case against his hip as he stashed the carton within.

"Have one of mine," Grainger said, seeing that Matsak wasn't going to crack that carton in public. He hadn't smoked since he was a kid on Sunrise Terrace. He held out the pack.

Matsak said, "Let us get a coffee to go with it."

"An espresso would be great, if we can find a place to serve it."

"Express? I suppose they will serve it wherever you want," Matsak said and, lighting his cigarette in hands cupped against a nonexistent wind, led the way to the front restaurant. There, dinner was being served in elegant style with pink linens and crystal. Matsak strode up to the maître d', spoke quietly, and personnel scrambled to accommodate them.

When they were seated, a tray was wheeled up containing a teapot, coffeepot, chocolate pot, condiments, and cakes.

"Express?" Matsak said with a wicked gleam in his eyes.

"Espresso? Sure, please," Tim Grainger replied. He was absolutely sure now that Matsak was wired like a radar trawler. "What about your driver? And the scientists? They're waiting for us."

Matsak sprawled back in long, spidery indolence, cigarette in one hand, espresso cup in the other. *"Express* without a cigarette is like sex with a condom." He sighed, puffed, and sipped. "As for who waits . . . The driver—is a driver. So what if he waits? Only Americans worry about these things. My scientists, they have been waiting for years to talk to someone who could even *ask* such questions as you are asking. I suppose they will wait until we are ready. Tell me more about what you wish to find." At the other end of the room, a violinist began to play softly.

Tim Grainger knew he'd now pierced the veil. This was the real Russia. As Churchill had said, Russia was like dogs fighting under a blanket. Maybe Matsak was going to pull off the blanket, maybe not. But he knew each dog beneath it by name and fighting form.

"Concretne stoh?" Concretely, what? Tim's long unused Russian was beginning to stir. "There's a problem we're facing which we can't solve with US technology. We've heard that some Russian scientists are working on temporal alignment. Maybe it's involving scalar waves and Maxwell's field equations. Maybe it's using psychotronic research somehow. I'm not a technology snob. We'll crack this nut any way we can, conventionally or unconventionally. And I'm not the technical expert on this trip. That's our other team member, an Oriental-American named Chun Quo. She's at another meeting right now but I'll get her if you wish."

"Nyet, nyet, nyet. Don't get her. If you say me she is meeting with other Russians, let her pursue that path independently." His flat, angry coldness returned. "In my opinion, I suppose she will not find this group of scientists through any other channel. But it is unfortunate that she is asking. It draws unhelpful attention."

"I thought," said Grainger, putting his pack of opened cigarettes on the table so that Matsak could chain-smoke if he wished, "that whatever problem one group was working, others were also working, as a methodology here."

"Maybe this is so in some parts of our technical establishment. But I am not so sure about such a method with this technology. This is closed city technology. A closed city is a science city. No one there is . . . average. The closed city network will outlast all upheavals of our state's shape and form. It still spans the former Soviet Union. And in it, our best scientists are working in concentrated groups and secluded situations on . . . special projects."

"Working for how long? What I'm looking for is relatively mature. At the stage of fieldable systems, or at least hardened prototypes." If what Grainger was looking for was really in a closed city, as Central had predicted, that didn't necessarily mean that only one group was working on it, but might mean that a relatively mature project was ongoing. Whatever project Matsak had in mind might just be advanced enough to cause the kind of problem Central was trying to preempt.

Matsak's answer was evasive. "Working for lifetimes, I suppose. They raise their children there. They go to school there. If your intelligence is great enough to allow you to reside in a closed city, life is . . . still good." He waved his hand and a long ash spilled to the floor. "We may go to one. Tonight if you wish. I have already arranged for the official invitation for your visit. It is a few hours drive from Moscow, nothing more. Do you wish it?"

"Hell, yes," Grainger said. Without an official invitation, even Matsak probably couldn't have arranged this visit. Without an invitation, any visit would have to be kept too far off the record to be sustainable.

Matsak took another cigarette. "You are not smoking," he observed.

Anything for God and continuum. Grainger picked up a Marlboro and lit it, dragging cautiously. His head spun. Every hair on his body stood on end. Years of abstinence hadn't diminished old desires. He knew after that one drag that he was lost, that he'd be happy to match Matsak cigarette for cigarette, despite the fact that Central would put him in detox as soon as he got back there.

Grainger must have closed his eyes. When he focused again, Matsak was signing the check.

"You're my guest," Grainger protested. The waiter with the initialed check scurried away.

"Please, do you see currency changing hands here? When I am in your milieu, you will be my host. Here, it is my duty. Now you will tell me just whom your colleagues have contacted. I must assess the damage."

Only then did Grainger remember that Nan Roebeck was alone in a meeting with Orlov. "Sergey Orlov of the Foreign Ministry . . ."

Matsak winced elaborately and shook his head. "So sorry, Tim Grainger. This is a bad miscalculation. Now that your friend is in the hands of the Foreign Ministry, we should leave her there. No one trusts them from the Yeltsin government. They are outsiders, Gorbachev holdovers, trying to use foreigners to secure their jobs and regain lost power. If Yeltsin were stronger, he would fire them all in one day, call them back to Moscow, and have them shot. But, of course, we don't do such things anymore. Not since we have new senior officials who were just yesterday boys standing on top of tanks waving flags." He waved his cigarette to illustrate. "In my opinion, these Foreign Ministry officials are the enemies of revolution. You should tell your friend not to trust the hardliners. All that has changed with them is the names of their jobs, not their offices, not their tactics, not their hearts."

"Great. I'll be sure to tell her."

"Say me who else you have contacted."

Matsak might be planning a little coup against possible rivals, but you had to play along. None of the locals meant anything to Grainger. And he had to go with his instinct. "Viktor Etkin, of the Min—"

"Ha! Etkin!" Now Matsak looked at Grainger pityingly and stroked his beard. "KGB. Very good. Very smart. Typical American efficiency. How do you say, spook to spook cultural exchange? The security service will take care of problems from the Foreign Ministry, at least. You will go ask your friends not to mention in their meetings that you are meeting with us as well, or else to conclude those meetings by telling other Russians you will meet only with us henceforth. I will wait here for you. I have everything I need." He shook another cigarette from the pack although he had one lit and burning in the ashtray. "Confer with your colleagues. When you have a decision on how to proceed, we will go see the technology."

Quid pro quo. Lucky that Russians were hive-mind sort of folks, who expected decisions to be at least ratified by groups.

"I'll go talk to my people, then." Grainger stood to go. "Should I get some roubles, for the trip?"

"Roubles? You want roubles?" Matsak's bearded upper lip curled. "I have thousand of millions of roubles. I need this many to pay for lunch. I have a man who follows me around with a briefcase full of roubles and stays behind to count them out to pay the luncheon bill. Sometimes it takes half an hour to count the total." He reached into his pocket and pulled out a wad of roubles. On top was a thousand-rouble note. "Here. Take it. You can tip the chambermaids with it."

Grainger was embarrassed. And despite himself, he was impressed by Matsak's candor, his wry sense of humor, and his pragmatic approach to his country's problems. Grainger took the roubles. He dared not offend this proud man.

"Spacebo." Thank you. And: "I'm sorry," he said softly. "I'll be right back with that decision."

He found Chun where he'd left her, bleary-eyed and drunker than he'd have liked. Etkin was holding her hand in his. Classical balalaika music was playing somewhere and a few couples were dancing slowly, hardly moving, swaying in place.

"Chun, I need to see you alone for a minute," Grainger said without ceremony.

"Viktor Ivanovitch, you must excuse me," she muttered thickly, stumbling over her gearbag as she rose.

"Seen Roebeck?" he asked. His eyeballs felt as if they were pulsing. His mouth was dry. His arm hurt. Damned shots. He grabbed Chun's gearbag from the floor by her chair and thrust it at her.

"Not since you two left us," Chun said, slinging the bag over her shoulder insouciantly.

Grainger took her by the hand and pulled her a short distance away. "Ditch that guy. We've got an invitation to a closed city to see relevant technology. And my guy doesn't want you dealing with anybody else."

"No Russian wants you dealing with anybody else," Chun said, brushing black hair out of her eyes. "I'm making good progress. Tell your friend we'll deal with whomever we choose. And as for a closed city trip—that's fine with me. Just check with Nan. What time tomorrow?"

"You don't get it. Now. Bus is leaving. Be on it or stay behind. As a matter of fact, given that you're not exactly sober,
maybe you ought to stay behind and sleep it off with Son of
Ivan over there."

"Tim, stuff it. You need me for any serious evaluation and
you know it."

"My guy won't take you if you're interacting with the
KGB, there."

"Okay, fine. Whatever Nan decides. But I think I'm onto
something here."

Grainger was exasperated. "We brought you to evaluate
critical technology, not seduction techniques of a vanished
civilization. Russians like parity, remember. You're our best
technologist."

"You said it—vanished civilization. I didn't. Your grasp of
technology's good enough for this closed city junket, as far as
I'm concerned. Anyway, it's up to Roebeck. Not to either of us."

"Great. Good. You stay right here, then, until I find her."

"I had no intention of going anywhere," Chun said sweetly.

Grainger slapped left-handed at a plastered column, hard,
on his way out of the bar. His whole arm pulsed from the concussion and the injection he'd taken.

Where the hell could Nan Roebeck be?

He checked everywhere: the lobby, the beautiful main dining room where the harpist had played, even—against all protocols of the era—the ladies' toilet.

She wasn't anywhere.

Don't leave the hotel without us for any reason, Roebeck
had decreed during the planning session.

Only then did he think to call her room.

He hoped to hell she wasn't up in her room with Orlov,
beating Chun to the punch. Then he hoped she didn't answer
the house phone.

But she did.

"What the hell are you doing up there?" he nearly snarled
at her when she said hello.

"What the hell do you mean, talking to me like that, mister?
I'm having a meeting."

"With your shoes on, I hope."

"Excuse me? I'll forget I heard that. What's the problem, Tim?"

"Permission to leave the hotel requested on a priority basis." He didn't feel well. Roebeck was really angry at him now. He couldn't cope with Chun and Roebeck and the Russians as well. He didn't want to take either woman along. They'd second-guess him all night long and blow his rapport with his target. "By myself if possible. With you if necessary. Not with Chun."

"Why? And it better be a damned good reason. Nothing justifies your behavior tonight, mister!"

"I need to talk to you, now. In person. Not on any phone. And I don't want to come to your room if you've got company. This can't wait."

"Where's Chun? We're just getting started here."

"She's pretty far along with lover boy in the bar and doesn't intend to take direction from me. I have a proposition from my guy for you. And I need clear direction about who does what in the next few hours."

"I'll be right down." Roebeck slammed the phone down.

Grainger waited by the elevators. When she came out, he grabbed her by the strap on her gearbag and pushed her back against the wall.

Leaning over her, one hand on the wall beside her head, he made as if to nuzzle her neck. "We've got an offer to go technology shopping in a closed city tonight—now. Chun doesn't want to go. The offer's contingent upon our choice of two options. Option one is breaking off other meetings with alternate technology channels and saying we're using my guy exclusively—then everybody who's up to it goes to the closed city tonight. Option two is you both keep meeting with your guys, don't mention anything about my guy, and only I go to the closed city tonight. What's your pleasure, boss?"

"What's Chun want to do?"

"Chun's falling in love. She wants to sleep with the poster boy. Or she's too drunk to know what she wants. She says I don't need her to look at this primitive tech base, but she'll do what you say. So she's not blind drunk. Just drunker than I like."

Roebeck closed her eyes and blew out a deep breath. Then she opened them and looked at him analytically. "How come all these demands?"

"Maybe I've got the right tiger by the tail. He got people out of bed. I listened while he kicked ass. I didn't get all the words but I got enough. He says he's the only channel to what we want. He says mixing other channels will just make it harder—maybe impossible—to cut a deal. They'll start fighting among themselves. He says you especially don't want to be involved with the Foreign Ministry—the Yeltsin government hates them and distrusts them. The distrust extends to anybody dealing with them. They're all Gorbachev hold-overs, hard-liners, due for early retirement. I think he doesn't need to lie to me. I think I want to go with him. You're the boss, but I'm asking that you at least protect my association with him and let me go. If you want everybody to go, that's fine, too—under his rules. But I don't want to fuck with this guy. It's his ball, his court. If we play his game, we've got to play it his way." Stripping proper names from targets was second nature to them both at a time like this.

"I don't know, Tim. My guy talks a good game, too."

"Did he offer to show you anything tonight? Mine did. And I'm worried that Chun's professor already knows just exactly what we're looking for—maybe who we are and why we're looking for it. You heard that toast. If he knows, he's got to be involved with the revisionists."

"That's your assessment?"

"You bet."

"And Chun wants to stay with him?"

"Seems like."

"Then let her stay with him. It'll raise the ante if we pull her out. If he's what you think, we can't tell him who else we're working with, so option one is out. Option two may fly, but I'd like to go with you. Can't I meet with your guy again and see if we can reach a compromise?"

"You can meet with anybody you want. You're the team

leader. It's your mission. But you and my guy didn't exactly get off to a flying start. He'll take you anyway. He just doesn't want a KGB escort. And neither do I, frankly. You'd have to ditch your guy, fast."

"I can't—it would look funny. Okay. I'll tell Chun not to mention anything about your channel. I haven't mentioned your guy, but I think I already told Chun's guy about mine."

"You *think?*" If Nan had done that, there was no use in referring to Etkin as "Chun's guy" and Orlov as hers.

"It's been a long night."

"With all due respect," Grainger said, "if that's so, then you might as well take Orlov down and introduce him to Etkin. Give Orlov a chance to defend himself. My guy says they'll cancel each other out. Could be. Who knows how it really works here, this far through the looking glass? And please, *please* give Chun some amended marching orders. She wasn't taking any advice from me, that's for sure. She'll put my initiative at risk without meaning to."

"I've decided. You go downrange. Go on. Get out of here. I'll stay in the hotel until I hear from you tonight. Ask me how I'm feeling if you're in trouble and need help. Then maybe Etkin will come in handy. Otherwise, ask me how Chun's doing. No matter what happens, be back here by nineteen hundred hours tomorrow for Etkin's dinner party."

"I will. You have my word on it."

"Just where is it you're going?"

"I don't know. He wouldn't tell me. I'll call. Got my gear with me. Don't worry." Grainger was so relieved he was nearly babbling. "I sure hope you'll trim Chun's jets. I don't know why we brought her if we can't use her for this excursion . . ."

"Let me worry about Chun." Roebeck slid out from under his aching left arm. "Get out of here. Go play in your sandbox. We'll say you were called away to the Embassy. Don't trip us up."

"I won't." He turned and started down the hall.

"Tim," Roebeck called after him. "Good luck."

"I don't need luck," he said over his shoulder. "I just need time."

But it wasn't true on this occasion, and he knew it. He was already straining the Bell curve of probability. Tim Grainger, ARC Rider, had gotten too lucky, too fast. Now all he could do was let himself be swept along and hope his luck would last.

Three Kilometers East of the Ems River, Free Germany

August 25, 9 AD

A bat fluttered about Pauli Weigand's head, then twisted into the evening sky. The little animal's movements were quick and the track of its flight as complex as that of a lace-maker's needle. A number of them were out, drawn to the insects put up by the feet of thousands of men and animals. Pickings must usually be slim for bats this deep in the forest.

"Pauli, Hannes and the other six bodyguards are leaving the camp also and proceeding up the old road," Gerd's voice cheeped from Pauli's headband. "They're on foot. I'm following them."

From where he sat on horseback near Varus and the German chiefs, Pauli could see Hannes and half the thugs continuing up the overgrown track. They vanished into the brush and shadows, ignored in the milling chaos of tent-raising, cookfires, and attempts to corral the baggage animals and cattle driven as meat on the hoof.

The troops had laid out a camp, but the march had gone too long into the afternoon for them to raise a proper palisade. The first day had been through open country, but today the army was in forest that had virtually reclaimed the roadway Tiberius cut on his expedition five years before.

The need to bridge gullies and pave the low spots with logs had slowed the column as a whole, but the troops in the lead still moved faster than the mass of wagons and litters that followed over the crude surface. If this were a real military expedition, the minimal baggage would be carried on pack mules. Half the personnel in this column were noncombatants, and at least a third of the latter were women.

"My governor," said Arminius. He leaned from the Roman-style saddle of his horse to speak to Varus who'd gotten out of a litter carried by eight slaves. "Sigimer and I will return in one day or two after we've gathered our people. The Chauci rebels won't be able to hide from us, any more than they can stand against you."

"Pauli, Istvan and his gang have moved off the road to hide in the brush two hundred meters from the camp," Beckie's voice said. She was following the blond revisionist who'd gone on ahead with six bodyguards when the army halted to encamp. "I've stopped ten meters from them."

She paused, then added, "Pauli, I can see them on infrared from here, but I won't have a shot unless they come out of the bushes."

The microwave pistols had no effect on the other side of a solid object, no matter how flimsy a barrier it was. The weapons formed a difference tone at the intersection of two beams focused precisely by a laser rangefinder. Anything that reflected modulated light would take the full force of the pulse. Unlike a bullet, the pulse couldn't penetrate a screen of leaves to stun the man behind.

"Well, be sure you hurry back, Arminius," the governor said, resting on his left hand on the couch. It had a lacquered roof and side curtains. "Otherwise your people won't get their share of loot."

"Oh, there'll be plenty of loot for all!" Sigimer boomed. Laughter fluffed his blond mustache.

Sigimer rode with only a saddle blanket, as did most of the score of retainers attending the two princes. The Germans all carried long swords, though a number of them had lances also. They wore metal helmets and slung round shields on their backs. Without saddles they couldn't hang the weight directly on their mounts. Medals dangled across the chest of Arminius and several others, but none of the Germans wore body armor.

"Till I see you again," Varus said. "And I hope we'll be out of this damned wilderness by then."

"Oh, you'll forget the trees soon enough," Arminius said. He straightened; his legs tensed to prod his horse forward with his heels.

"I'll ride with you for a little way, Prince," Pauli said. "I want to take a look at the road farther on."

"What?" said Sigimer. He glared at Pauli. Arminius kept his composure better, but there was no warmth in his expression. He muttered a warning to his retainers. Several of them reached reflexively for their swords, but a sharper order stopped them.

Pauli rode alongside the chief. "I won't go far. Just enough to eye the route."

"There's nothing to be seen different from what's around us now," Arminius said. "But come along, my Ubian friend. The emperor's man is welcome to ride with us as far as my homestead if he wishes."

Yes, but returning might not prove so easy, Pauli thought as he prodded his mount into motion with the Germans. The road was dangerous at anything faster than a walk. Logs laid in a corduroy by Tiberius' engineers were a bumpy surface when new. Five years on the damp ground left some of them so rotten that they disintegrated underfoot. The horses stumbled frequently, making even experienced riders jerk and curse.

One way or the other, he wouldn't be going far. The revisionists were about to make their play and Pauli Weigand had to be close by. Beckie and Gerd could slip through the undergrowth covered by their dull capes, but a big imperial bodyguard in armor wasn't going to sneak along unnoticed by those he followed.

It was already too dark under the trees to see colors. The conspirators must expect to pick up a familiar trail nearby if they were going to ride any distance tonight. The military road didn't appear to have been used since Tiberius returned to the Rhine along it.

The troop of mounted men rode past Hannes. The revisionist's guards pressed to the side of the track to keep out of the nobles' way. The man Gerd had stunned in Aliso the previous day, Hilderic, hadn't gotten far enough clear. A rider kicked at him. The thug cowered back, but he glared at the horsemen beneath the shelter of his raised arms.

"Who's that lot?" Sigimer growled.

"He claimed he's a slave dealer," Pauli said. He spoke in German to warn all the retainers, not just those who'd learned Latin. "He has a partner who left the camp this way earlier. Could they be enemies planning to ambush you, Prince Hermann?"

"I don't have any quarrels with worms, Ubian," Arminius said.

"Hannes is putting on a set of night-vision goggles," Gerd's voice warned.

"I think Istvan is doing the same," Becky said. "I'm going to move closer."

Pauli felt his guts tighten. His teammates were using the faceshields to enhance their vision. Thermal viewing let Beckie see forms but not details through the screen of leaves. Pauli didn't think she could safely close in on the revisionist, but he couldn't order her to keep clear because Arminius was right beside him.

"Hannes has radioed his partner that you're approaching," Gerd said. "I—oh!"

"Take them!" Pauli shouted, drawing the pistol from beneath his cloak. Still holding the reins in his left hand, he pulled down the faceshield to improve his view of events. What Arminius and his fellows thought of ARC equipment was of secondary importance for the moment.

Bellowing thugs with swords and clubs rushed the front of

the mounted Germans. In the darkness there could have been ten times the real number.

A figure twenty-five meters in the background braced himself against a giant pine as he sighted a weapon. It was a bad angle for Pauli but he snapped a shot anyway. Pulverized bark flew from the tree trunk. The revisionist went down.

Horsemen and their attackers on foot mixed in shouting confusion. Several retainers jumped or fell to the ground when their mounts stumbled. Sigimer chopped at a thug's head, then tried to ride over the wounded man. He stabbed up into the horse's belly. The animal screamed and tried to corkscrew away stiff-legged. Sigimer came off his back, yelling even louder when a hawthorn broke his fall.

Pauli wheeled his horse. Hannes' gang had attacked the rear of the column when their fellows hit the front. Gold alone couldn't make men fight at odds so long. Perhaps these clanless folk wanted revenge on nobles of the society that had cast them out, but Pauli suspected there was more to it. The revisionists must have demonstrated a submachine gun on a dog, a sheep . . . or, most likely, on a man.

Hannes and Istvan were raised as elite members of a culture that had never concerned itself overmuch with the sanctity of human life. They'd have made sure to convince their hirelings that they were magicians: powerful enough to overwhelm the troop of horsemen and far too dangerous to cross.

"Gerd!" Pauli called. "Where's the other man?"

His light-enhancing faceshield made a flaring torch of what was really a foxfire quiver: powder gases burning at the submachine gun's muzzle. Hannes was firing from an elderberry thicket.

Three mounted retainers howled in surprise. One of them touched his chest, stared at the blood on his fingers, and slid off his horse.

Pauli hosed his microwave pistol across the thicket, stripping patches of bark. The pulses shook individual finger-thick stems without affecting the revisionist at the heart of the clump. Hannes knelt, replacing the magazine he'd emptied without hitting his intended target.

Arminius cut right and left over his mount's neck. He wore his shield on his left arm and used the sword with his right, guiding the horse expertly with his heels. All of the footmen were down. The German chief shouted exultantly and brandished his sword. Blood spattered from the back edge of the blade.

Pauli drove through the melee. His horse tripped on a squirming body but didn't fall and didn't, for a wonder, throw its rider. Noise and the smell of blood had maddened the beast. It was ready to bolt, but there was nowhere to run on the narrow road.

Hannes straightened. He was only twenty feet away. Pauli pulled his reins with both hands to put himself between the revisionist and the leader of the German revolt. He tried to aim the pistol but Hannes' muzzle flash filled the whole world with red-orange fire.

Pauli felt the blows to his chest. His horse tossed its head, then fell as if boneless. There was froth on its jaws and a fleck of dark blood on the skull between the bulging, empty eyes.

From his viewpoint in the air above the suddenly silent battlefield, Pauli Weigand watched his body topple backward over the haunches of his dead horse.

The revisionists' guards burst from ambush twenty feet from where Rebecca Carnes concealed herself. Screaming murder, they launched themselves toward the band of riders.

"Take them!" Pauli ordered. Rebecca's headband chirped each syllable fractionally before air transmitted the shout, syncopating the radio transmission.

She was already aiming at the head of the blond revisionist. As she pulled the trigger, he stepped back into the shelter of a tree four feet in diameter. Her pulse snapped a branch from a sapling beyond where he'd stood a moment before.

Rebecca stood up, so focused on dropping the revisionist that she forgot the guards she'd dismissed as a diversion for the real assassination attempt. They *were* a diversion, but their weapons were quite lethal nonetheless. The one named Osric saw the motion and leaped for her with a shout. He swung a club like a baseball bat with iron bands around the meaty end.

She dodged back and shot him. Weapons training hadn't been one of the skills at which Rebecca excelled. She could hit a target the size of Osric when he was within spitting distance, but the microwave pulse hammered the German's shoulder rather than his forehead. The club flew from his hand.

At point-blank range the pistol delivered a heavier shock than a projectile weapon of manageable size, but sheer inertia kept Osric coming at her. Rebecca tripped on a stone hidden in the pine straw. The German tried to pull her head off but his right arm didn't work. His groping left hand clouted her across the temple. She managed to shoot him again, this time in the face.

Osric's head jerked back with a startled expression. His legs buckled and he toppled onto his face. Blood ran from his nose and ears.

Rebecca stepped over the body. Her faceshield was skewed. Her left eye got false-color images from the infrared spectrum that her brain tried to merge with the palette of grays and blacks her right eye saw in the twilit forest. Together they created blinding dissonance and a headache. She swept the headband off instead of trying to adjust it. She had Istvan in the sights of her pistol when Pauli shot and knocked the revisionist down.

Rebecca turned. The roadway was a blur of movement and glittering metal. Blades sparked on one another. Half the horses were riderless. She couldn't tell one fighter from another.

She knelt, patting the ground for the headband with her free hand. It was caught on the bark of a cedar sapling a dozen feet away, gleaming in white innocence. Rebecca didn't know how she'd managed to throw it that far. As she scrambled to it, a horse screamed louder than all the rest of the battle.

With her faceshield on, figures stood out in bold thermal contrast against the forest background. The bare skin of men and horses glowed yellow and yellow-green as they struggled. Pauli's steel armor was a cool blue; the microwave pistol flared red-orange in his hand. The weapon's mechanism heated up with use.

Rebecca couldn't get through the ruck; a horse would trample her and in the confusion anyone on foot was fair game for the Germans still mounted. She pushed into the lesser growth beside the roadway, ignoring the bite of thorns.

Rebecca's guts were tight with worry about what had happened to Gerd and what might happen to Pauli, but the first order of business was to take down the second revisionist. Nurses learn to prioritize.

A blackberry vine caught her cape and right elbow. She pulled free, leaving the garment behind when the tie string broke.

A German ran from the fight, looking over his shoulder and bawling with fear. He saw Rebecca in front of him and thrust up to disembowel her with the iron-pointed Roman javelin in his left hand. She shot, kicking his head sideways with an audible snap. He fell but she had to grab the javelin's shaft to keep him from spiking her as he thrashed.

The submachine gun fired from a clump of brush on the other side of the road. The muzzle flash was a white core in a bright orange shroud. Hannes was a green mass behind the gun, clearly visible on infrared but shielded against effective use of the microwave pistol. Rebecca fired anyway, holding the trigger down till the plastic receiver seared the inside of her gunhand.

Pauli rode in front of Arminius, blocking the revisionist's aim. Bullets raked his chest, sparkling and winking. The horse leaped convulsively as Pauli slid off its back.

Rebecca felt her heart die. She dropped the useless pistol and balanced the javelin on her right palm. Part of ARC training covered primitive weapons. She didn't have an aptitude for fencing, but she'd played darts often enough in her former life to take naturally to the javelin.

The revisionist sighted again from the elderberry copse. Rebecca cocked her arm, took a step forward onto the roadway, and hurled the javelin.

The instructors at ARC Central would have been pleased. The iron blade *ting*ed as it clipped a thin stem, but momentum kept it straight till it struck Hannes' chest with the sound of a cleaver splitting a joint. He fell backward, deeper into the clump.

Pauli lay faceup on the road. His lips moved, but they didn't form words for Rebecca to hear through her headband. His horse spasmed nearby. Other wounded animals pitched and screamed in the twilight.

Rebecca ran to her teammate. A German whose cut cheek bled across half his beard tried to grab her. The pistol lay in the undergrowth but Rebecca had reflexes honed in too many bars and military camps. She kicked the man in the crotch.

She closed the faceshield back into her headband as she bent over Pauli. His carotid pulse was strong but he breathed with difficulty and obvious pain. His mail shirt was of high-strength alloy rather than the mild steel available to the armorers of this time horizon, but a bullet's impact was still a hammer blow even if it didn't penetrate.

Pauli'd been hit several times. He'd be very lucky if he didn't have cracked ribs.

But he was alive.

"Did you get Hannes?" he said, more mouthing than speaking the words.

"Oh, yes," Rebecca said. "But he's not in shape to be interrogated about his buddies, I'm afraid."

Gerd Barthuli knelt beside the two of them. He pressed his left palm to his temple. "I'm very sorry," he said in a puzzled voice. "He was behind me and I didn't see him until too late. Istvan has gotten away, but I can track him easily."

He raised the scanner in his right hand, smiled oddly, and would have fallen onto Pauli if Rebecca hadn't caught him in time. Gerd's hand and his thin gray hair were caked with blood.

The Closed City of Obninsk, Kaluga Region, Russia

March 10, 1992

In the back of Matsak's long black Mercedes limousine, Grainger and the Ministry Deputy were chauffeured out of Moscow on a broad divided highway rutted like a goat track. Matsak confided wryly, "Obviously, we have not yet fixed this road from the damage the *tonk*—tanks—did rolling into Moscow to support Yeltsin."

Until that moment, Grainger had assumed that the pavement humps had been either the Russian version of speed bumps, because of their regular placement, or frost heaves. Once beyond the city limits, roads became wider. Divided highways were unmarred by billboards or roadside businesses, except for occasional unadvertised petrol dispensaries comprised of little more than a couple of pumps on broadened shoulders. Tall, rectangular high-rises in Bauhaus style could be seen from the highway. Lights in balcony windows revealed glimpses of the lives being lived within. Plywood lean-tos and blankets enclosed sagging summer porches. Old mattresses were propped against exterior walls. Plastic and wood had been conjured into makeshift greenhouses. Patched curtains provided privacy or replacements for missing glass patio doors. Clustered near the road in the shadows of the unremittingly Soviet architecture, tiny huts and sheds with curved roofs remained as reminders of a pastoral past. Even these antique peasant cottages occasionally showed lights flickering between boards or through paneless windows.

Once another Mercedes passed them. It was shiny, a recent vintage car making close to one hundred kph, if Matsak's own speedometer was correct. As the big car passed them, Grainger noticed that it had no license plate.

Matsak saw Grainger's questioning look and shrugged. *"Nomenclatura."*

Literally, Grainger thought the word translated as "list of names." In reality, he understood precisely what Matsak meant when he used it: the privileged class, the hereditary elite, those for whom rules were merely suggestions.

A Russian police car's blue light shattered the dark in hot pursuit of the speeding Mercedes. The Mercedes pulled over. The other traffic, Matsak's car included, slowed nearly to a crawl to watch the show.

The traffic cop got out and stalked over to the car with that threatening demeanor of cops everywhere, his hand hovering over his sidearm. The sight took Grainger back to Sunrise Terrace.

As the cop reached the unlicensed Mercedes, the window of the car glided smoothly down. A well-manicured head poked out. The cop bent down to hear.

Matsak's driver drove slowly by. Grainger saw the policeman laugh, nod, and wave the driver of the unlicensed car on his way.

"You see," Matsak said in sardonic triumph, *"nomenclatura."*

"The more things change, the more they stay the same," Grainger commiserated. The hours he'd spent with Matsak so far had been part political talk, part testing of Grainger's technological depth, and part bonding.

"Ah, as in Romania, you mean? Or in my Ministry. Our change in government and ideology has produced almost exclusively the same leaders. Of course, this is true only below the level where faces must look different for the international press. So you may not have noticed. I appreciate this American expression. In Russia we have a similar saying: 'The new is the well-forgotten old.' " The Ministry official opened the limousine's bar. "Vodka," he said. "From my home region. Very pure. Made with water from spring. Like velvet." The bottle was tall, green, and had no label. Home brew.

The Ministry official filled two glasses and handed one to Grainger. Matsak took a deep gulp from his glass. Grainger must drink or lose all the rapport he'd been building. So he drank, losing his chance to pursue any relationship between Matsak's well-chosen aphorism and the technology they were going to evaluate.

The vodka took his breath away. It burned less brightly than his recent antiradiation shot, but not much. Grainger leaned his head back against the Mercedes' padded leather and said, "I thought you'd have a Zil limousine. Or at least a Lada. I wanted to ride in a Lada."

"Ah, a connoisseur of *Ruskie* automobiles? My Ministry will put a Lada and driver at your disposal for the rest of your stay here. You will like this? *Would* like this," Matsak corrected himself. "So sorry, Tim. You must excuse my English. It is worst when I am tired."

Or drunk. *"Da, da.* I'd like that a lot. Look, before I get so drunk I can't think at all, tell me who we're going to see and what you think I should know."

"Oh, okay. You are saying you wish the prebrief?"

"Ah yeah, something like that."

"We each have our missions, I think. It is well that they coincide."

"You got that right," Grainger muttered, wondering if the vodka had made his voice sound as scratchy to Matsak as it did to his own ears.

"So, then, as I said you in hotel, we are going to the closed city, Obninsk. Obninsk is in the Kaluga region. The mayor and deputy mayor have extended you an official invitation. They arrange a small celebration in your honor for when we arrive."

"Isn't it going to be a little late for celebrations?"

"Please, you will be their honored guest. Many brilliant scientists will be present. I suppose you are now their excuse for big celebration—for food, for drink, for music. Dancing. You like pretty girls? The closed city girls are the prettiest. Daughters of brilliant scientists, each one."

"And the technology? I'd rather see hardware than mayors and girls, any day. I was hoping for a little open discussion."

"You say you wish it, you will have it. You will have all you need. But I must have what I need. Show my scientists there is interest in their work, possibilities for joint cooperation from Americans. The Tim Grainger visit is now an official Obninsk affair. This is well. We must work together to keep these scientists from selling their know-how to Arabs who use it against peaceful nations. To Koreans who come and take photographs and tell lies and pay nothing. To Japanese who pay small roubles for reports and begin right away the reverse engineering. Obninsk is at your disposal, as long as its scientists believe you are truly interested in their know-how. Each scientist hopes to make a contract with the Americans. Become rich in dollars. They need money to continue their work. But do not provide dollars directly. Tell me which scientists interest you and my Ministry will make the contract."

"You got a deal," Grainger agreed.

Once the protocol was established, Matsak seemed genuinely to relax.

"If they think you are truly interested in the joint cooperation, the city will be yours. They have all new forms of beginning businesses: joint stock companies, joint ventures, enterprises. If you can pay even small sums to anyone, even one person, they all will be encouraged. A few dollars is better than many promises."

"I got it," Grainger said. "I'll be happy to give you some dollars for whoever seems to have what I need." *And sort out the promising technologies from the hopeless ones for you.* Now Grainger understood what Matsak wanted out of this. Matsak wanted an American to handicap the players for the Ministry—find out how to triage the line, which scientists to support and whom to let starve. "I'm not the greatest all-around technology evaluator," Grainger said. Better to get this issue on the table now. "I know my area. I don't know everything." He didn't want to see everything Obninsk had to offer. He wouldn't know what to do with it. He only wanted to find the revisionists. Finding the right technology would lead him to them. "I don't want to get your scientists' hopes up for nothing."

"Hopes are not nothing to those who have so little. So sorry, but we must be gentle with these scientists. The man you want will be among them, absolutely. In my opinion, you will like Obninsk. There is hunting, if you wish it. The best hunting in the east. The big games . . . deers . . . bears . . . others, I don't know the names."

"Wonderful. I love hunting." Technology hunting. "How long are we staying?"

"Is up to you. Overnight, certainly. Tomorrow, you will say me what is interesting. Then we will decide."

"Tonight, I want to say what is interesting. I'll work straight through, all night long if your people are willing. Tomorrow night, I've got a dinner . . ." And then he realized he didn't. Couldn't. Had promised this man he wouldn't. Goddamn, it had slipped his mind. "I've got to call my friends when we get to Obninsk. Can you arrange it?"

"Of course. This will be possible. Now, I must say you about the scientist, Academician Igor Zotov, who has the know-how you will find most interesting."

For the rest of the trip, Matsak gave Grainger background on Zotov and the city officials they were going to meet.

Zotov was an academician, a rank of scientist that had no US equivalent, one with multiple doctorates and professorships. Zotov was also state science prize winner, a prima donna, and someone whose continued financial support by the Ministry was not in doubt, according to Matsak. However, it would help Matsak continue Zotov's funding if the US expressed interest in cooperating on some aspect of his work. Dollars were salvation to some of these project managers.

As they turned off the highway onto a forested access road and entered the closed city, Matsak refilled their glasses from the vodka bottle, drank deeply, and wiped his mouth with the back of his hand. "As you now see, I can arrange *any*thing. This is my great skill," he declared expansively.

By then, Grainger thought he knew what to expect at Obninsk.

But he didn't. First he saw lit high-rises. Then they were gone. Into view came an operational-sized rocket, painted red and spotlighted, poised in a central square. Then he noticed the buildings around it—yellow with white trim, columned in the classical style, and with lit windows. Then he saw what looked like an ancient football scoreboard on stilts. It was displaying lit numbers that changed as he watched.

"What's that, Sasha?" he asked, leaning forward to look closer. His shoulders rubbed the other man's as Matsak looked, too.

"Oh, this?" Matsak said with a wave of his hand. "This is nothing. This is readout, metering the background radiation outside at this time. Obninsk is, after all, a closed city which does much *Voyenna—soyuz*—much space technology. Here too is being done all the research into the aftereffects of Chernobyl. Obninsk is the center of post-Chernobyl international commission—Russian delegation, of course."

Grainger was shocked wide awake and nearly sober by Matsak's flat admission of meaningful levels of radioactive contamination. Suddenly his antiradiation shot didn't hurt at all. As a matter of fact, it felt good, warm, comforting.

Matsak's driver headed straight for the most imposing of the columned buildings. There, under a portico, several men in suits and women in dresses were waiting in the irradiated cold to greet them. One man was short, stocky, with wild white hair and thick glasses. He wore an old wool coat with leather patches and mismatched shoes.

Before Matsak had made the introductions, Grainger already knew that this man had to be Academician Igor Zotov. The other two men were too smooth, too well dressed and well formed, to be intellectual dynamos or groundbreaking scientists. The women towered over Zotov on spiked heels. Their stockings had seams running up the backs of their calves.

Grainger bowed his head with each handshake the way his hosts did. "Mayor. Deputy. Thank you so much for inviting me. Academician Zotov, I've heard great things about your work."

The little man took Grainger's hand with a surprising strength and held on to it. There were several growths on Zotov's face, round protrusions of fleshy tissue that were asymmetrically arranged: above his left eyebrow, in the crease to the right of his nose, under the left corner of his mouth. In Grainger's time, such growths, whether caused by environmental, hereditary, or viral agents, would have been immediately removed. He tried to look Zotov in the eyes but the growths kept claiming his attention. They made it hard to look squarely at the little scientist. Uncomfortable, Grainger looked away.

Horny nails bit into his wrist. "Dr. Grainger, I am so happy to meet you," said Zotov in painstakingly rehearsed English.

Nobody bothered to introduce the women formally. One was Marina and one was Tanya and one was Rita. Good enough. He couldn't tell one from another.

The mayor, Kokoshin, was a Rasputin of a man. "Come this way, Dr. Grainger. We have prepared a small welcome in your honor." Mayor Kokoshin, having assumed that Grainger was a doctor and exhausted his rote greeting, began talking to Matsak in Russian.

Beyond imposing carved doors, Grainger's sneakers squeaked on parquet wooden floors. He was becoming used to the vast expanses of open space in Russian public buildings, the dim lights, the huge light fixtures, the intricate flooring, the low leather furniture, the mass-produced patterned runners that seemed to be everywhere. Double doors opened before them as if by magic, spilling out laughter, light, and music.

There must have been a hundred people in the banquet hall. White linen tablecloths were everywhere except on the head table, which sported a green baize cover. Bottles were set before every few plates. Glasses beside them held pinkish squares of slightly waxed paper to use as napkins. Food was laid out family style. And young girls were everywhere, in red tunics that came only to the tops of their thighs. Beneath the tunics were fishnet hose and knee-high boots. On their heads were tall Russian furred hats.

"You see," Matsak said in his ear, "beautiful Russian dancers."

The girls were huddled in a group, giggling, staring at Grainger, the alien being from the capitalist world.

Grainger was grateful when Mayor Kokoshin guided him through a massing crowd of scientists and local officials to the green-covered table. He was immedietely seated among those who'd greeted him. Zotov sat on Grainger's right. Matsak claimed the seat on his left by putting his gift Marlboros on his plate. Loudspeakers played music, probably to make conversation safer.

Once seated, Grainger could see the far wall. It was decorated with latticed metalwork that at first looked merely decorative, but on examination revealed its nuclear theme. Atoms were described in artistic metal orbits, intertwining among hammered stars. The nuclear art wall was clearly to be used as a backdrop for tonight's entertainment. Chairs and musical instruments were already in place before it.

Scientists began to file by, holding visit cards for him, claiming their precious introductions. Zotov gave Grainger a running commentary, whispering each name in turn and giving an opinion of each scientist's value.

"Interesting," he would say. "Not interesting." "Perhaps you will think this work is of value." "This one is a show scientist."

Grainger was overwhelmed in the first five minutes.

Then the girls began to dance, kicking their long legs high to the music of a classical balalaika band that entered from the next room. Grainger had never before seen a bass balalaika. He'd never before seen fourteen-year-old girls dance, as if for their lives, with such manic energy. He began to feel helpless. These people needed a real visit from a real US government official who could open some doors for them. Not from him. He was here to close doors on them. Forever, if he could.

By the time the dancing was done, he'd drunk some of each wine handed him, plus vodka, cognac, and he didn't know what else.

Zotov tapped Grainger's knee to get his attention as the girls did their final splits on the floor and people started clapping.

The little scientist's face was lined and wrinkled everywhere but around the three growths, which were smooth and pink as baby's flesh. He grinned widely, showing teeth capped and filled with white metal. "So, American scientist, you are one of the first to visit our city of Obninsk. This is great privilege. Only those who qualify can obtain visit here, yes? Interested in my work, this is why you are coming here?" All Russian scientists might have some English by now, but Zotov was struggling to pronounce words he might never have heard, only read.

"Yes. I'm very interested in your work, Academician Zotov."

"Since my work is of such international interest, you will call me Igor." The Russian thrust his face so close that their foreheads nearly touched. A piece of octopus from the salad was caught between two of his metal-capped teeth. He'd eaten some of the pickled raw garlic that garnished it and his breath reeked.

"And I'm Tim."

"Ummmm . . . Tim. We say in my field that the true boundary conditions of the universe are that the universe has *nyet*—no—boundary conditions. You understand this in so poor English?" Zotov's eyes wrinkled in delight at sharing his joke. If it was a joke.

Grainger tried to think of an appropriate response. He would not move away from this old man, no matter how bad he smelled. "In my field we say that the universe ordered itself as it did in the first moments of creation in order to produce physicists."

After Mayor Kokoshin had been called to translate this, Zotov roared with delight and pounded Grainger on the back. "So we do understand each other. Good. Tim Grainger, come close." Zotov's voice dropped to a whisper.

"What?" Grainger asked the scientist softly.

"Do you believe the traveling from other . . . dimensions is possible?"

"Da, da," Grainger assured Zotov.

Now their foreheads were touching. Zotov said, "I have proofs. What would such proofs be worth in dollars?"

Damn, where was Matsak? "They are worth a great deal, if what I see is both convincing and . . . useful."

"Then you will see what is useful," said Zotov. "You believe in the unidentified object from . . . another . . . world . . . place?"

"UFOs?" Grainger's heart sank. If this was a wild goose chase . . .

"I have the real proof. I have myself seen these things."

"Up close and personal?" Grainger asked, straight-faced.

"I have films I take myself. I have the piece . . . the physical . . . evidences. And I am making the science of this traveling. The experiments. The improvements. The discoveries. The adding of Russian know-how. This is interesting for you?"

Before Grainger could answer, Zotov sat back, drained a small glass of vodka, and cracked it down on the table. His eyes were full of challenge.

"This is very interesting. I hope I can see it as soon as possible." Grainger too sat back and drained a similar glass in front of him. He couldn't believe any primitive, clear drink could pack such power. But he might as well get as drunk as his hosts. UFOs, yet. Alien encounters. Was this why he'd left Moscow? But still, what if Zotov had found something? Not a UFO that traveled through space, but one that traveled through time?

One of the scantily clad girls came around behind them, handing out full champagne glasses. She put a bottle of Georgian champagne in front of Zotov. Zotov lumbered to his feet, a glass of champagne raised high.

"To our guest, the Dr. Tim Grainger, senior science bureaucrat of the USA. May he see here the . . . brilliance . . . of Obninsk." He repeated his toast in Russian, and everyone raised their glasses and drank deeply. Zotov's English was getting better by the moment.

Then Mayor Kokoshin got to his feet and raised his glass in a second toast, entirely in Russian.

Soon enough, Grainger had been the subject of a half-dozen rounds. Now he must propose his own toast.

Before he knew it, he was on his feet, glass raised, saying, "To Russian scientists, the most hospitable in the world. May their hard-won freedom serve them well in their quest for knowledge. And to their daughters, most beautiful of all women." He turned to the gaggle of teenage girls. "May all my grandchildren be Russians." He couldn't believe he'd said that. He'd better go somewhere out of sight and use his pharmakit to sober up.

Every fourteen-year-old temptress in the room preened as Zotov translated the toast into Russian. The crowd broke into guffaws from the men and giggles from the women.

Somehow, Matsak reappeared abruptly, as if he'd always been sitting in the chair on Grainger's left. "So sorry, a few phone calls. Ministry never sleeps. Now, if you would like it, you may make your phone call."

It was clear he was supposed to get up and go with Matsak. He managed it, shouldering his gearbag with elaborate care. "I need the toilet, too."

"This too I can arrange," Matsak said dryly, "as I arranged your invitation here." He seemed very pleased with himself, but there was tension underlying his approving smile.

The phone was behind a desk in the dimly lit anteroom. "I need that bathroom first."

In the Russian bathroom, he was completely dumbfounded. He didn't understand how to flush the toilet at first. He couldn't find any toilet paper. He decided he was too drunk and dialed a dose on his pharmakit to sober himself up. Couldn't talk to Nan Roebeck if he couldn't find toilet paper in a bathroom. When he'd finished using the pharmakit, he still couldn't find any toilet paper.

Outside, Matsak waited, his lanky frame full of suppressed

energy. "So, the phone now. I have found the operator. Say me the number."

A Russian woman had to put the call through for him. Matsak served as translator.

Eventually, the phone was handed to him. "Nan, how's Chun?" he asked, using the code they'd devised.

"Doing fine. What's up?" Roebeck's voice was so immersed in static that it was hard to discern her words.

"I'm going to stay here overnight. I don't think I can make dinner tomorrow after all. Remember the agreement we made in order to get this visit?"

There was a pause on the other end of the line. For a moment he thought the connection was broken. Then her voice came to him amid even more static: "Of course. I should have realized. Well, do the best you can."

"How about you? How's it going?"

"About as expected. The same sort of thing you're doing there, we're doing here. I'm glad you called. I have to go out."

Out. Predawn visits in secret to laboratories, no doubt. He doubted the women were getting the same treatment as he. But maybe that was just as well.

"Have fun," he said.

"You, too," Roebeck replied. *"Das Vedanya."*

"Das Vedanya."

When he handed the handset back to the woman, the little scientist Zotov had joined them in the anteroom. Zotov was talking to Matsak earnestly. The tall Ministry functionary and the small, disheveled scientist didn't see Grainger approach until he was nearly upon them.

The two Russians noticed Grainger at the same time. Matsak held out a forestalling hand and continued talking to Zotov in rapid-fire Russian that Grainger couldn't decipher. The tone was argumentative. Zotov was giving Matsak some sort of problem. The Russians went on arguing for long minutes. Grainger shifted from foot to foot. Good thing he'd sobered up. From the meeting room beyond, light and music spilled out under closed double doors.

While he waited, Grainger vainly tried to identify the muted music he could barely hear. Maybe Haydn. Maybe some Russian composer.

Finally, the argument ceased. Matsak turned on his heel, straight as the flag officer he'd been or still was. He said to Grainger, "Zotov says okay. You can see the technology right now. The others will not notice we have gone. They will be celebrating until they go to sleep. We must go quickly. Hurry."

Zotov stomped away down a darkened hallway, not waiting to see if they'd follow.

Matsak motioned Grainger ahead of him. They followed Zotov through two corridors and down a flight of stairs. They hurried through an ill-lit, musty basement. At last they came to more stairs, leading to a subbasement. There Zotov fumbled for keys in his pocket. The scientist unlocked a door covered with chipped, peeling white paint.

Inside was a working laboratory. In that laboratory were three men in threadbare lab coats. Grainger had not met any of these men at the party upstairs. They were hunched over a rack of equipment such as Grainger had never seen before.

Huge dials, exposed wiring, makeshift housings. None of it seemed promising. Meters had German manufacturers' names on them. Beyond the rude console was a wall with homely curtains drawn across its upper half.

Grainger moved around the console.

Zotov barked something at Matsak.

Matsak said, "So sorry. The Tim must sit here and the technology will be presented."

Matsak tapped a plastic chair near the console.

Grainger said, "That's fine with me."

Matsak stood over him like a bodyguard.

Zotov muttered to his staff.

At last the little scientist seemed satisfied. A small black and white monitor was brought and set down on top of the console. The three technicians chattered, *"Mouschka! Mouschka!"* Eventually, the problem they were having with their computer mouse was solved and the display flickered alight.

The small monitor displayed a videotape, not a computer program. The tape was of an ongoing event in a town square. Above the square, something flickered into substantiality.

That something was oval, glowing with lights, and it settled onto the grassy square with an easy grace.

Grainger said, "What's this?" A chill ran over him that probably wasn't due to the mixture of alcohol, nicotine, and antitoxins in his body.

"Watch," Matsak said.

Grainger wished the monitor was better. But he could see what was happening on the tape well enough. The door of the capsule opened and six hardsuited men carrying long tubes came out. Russian peasants were crowding around. The men pointed their tubes at several of the people: a young man, a teenage boy, a pregnant girl. The locals surged forward as the youngsters crumpled. The hardsuits weren't from any time or place that Grainger was familiar with. Neither were the tube-shaped implements. Or the craft, although he was sure from the way it moved that it was a temporal capsule.

The men with the tubes aimed at the crowd. Broad, visible beams from their tubes swept over the frightened, angry people. More folk dropped to the ground. Three of the intruders from the craft ported their weapons and grabbed the youngsters they'd originally targeted. Slinging the inert bodies of the three Russians over their shoulders, the men disappeared inside the craft while their comrades covered them. Once those three were inside, the men providing cover began reentering the ship, one at a time. All very professional.

The last man was moving backward into the craft when a Soviet missile entered the picture, its trajectory enhanced by a computer graphic of linked oblongs. The missile struck the craft.

A rolling blossom of white engulfed the scene. The screen went blank.

Zotov barked commands in Russian. The technicians ran the tape again, this time using their mouse pointer to freeze frames and show the approach of the Soviet missile in slow-motion.

"What was that you used?" Grainger asked. His tongue seemed swollen. Those men with the strange weapons weren't ARC Riders. Wrong uniforms. Wrong technology. That wasn't a TC of any manufacture familiar to Grainger. It was bigger, for one thing. Clearly more advanced, for another. And yet it had been taken out by a Soviet missile . . .

"Missile? Was . . . a Tsyklon-class missile."

"I mean, what was the explosive?"

"Nuclear," Matsak said flatly.

"Christ . . ." It had never occurred to him that the Soviets would use a nuke on one of their own towns. "So nothing's left? Of the craft, I mean?"

"So sorry, say me again?" Matsak asked.

Zotov was watching him closely, a triumphant smile on his face that Grainger didn't understand at first.

"I asked if you destroyed the craft totally."

Now Zotov spoke, first in a barrage of Russian, then in slow English: "This is evidence. I have . . . pieces. Artifacts. I have my . . . group. We have engineered from this . . . piece . . . some interesting technology."

"I bet you have," Grainger muttered. "Can I see what you've got? What you've done?" He was on his feet now.

No Russian said anything immediately. Zotov was staring at Matsak and Matsak was appraising Grainger's reaction.

Grainger said slowly, "Sasha, you were right. This is very exciting. Please begin an arrangement with Academician Zotov on our behalf. Let's go to contract. Whatever it takes to get on with our evaluation."

The two senior Russians went off into a corner.

Grainger called out to them, "Can I see the tape again?"

From their huddle, both Zotov and Matsak gave obviously conflicting orders to the technicians. Eventually, an agreement was struck and the tape rolled again.

This time, Grainger saw many small details that indicated differences between this craft and the TCs of his era. By the time the tape had spooled through, he was sure he was looking at a vehicle from Up The Line—from the far future, not from any distant planet.

Damn.

And the Russians had the wreckage. Obviously, Barthuli had intuited something. But what had the guys from Up The Line been doing? Their mission had obviously been to take three youngsters, kids too young and powerless to be revisionists. Why abduct youngsters?

He wasn't allowed to see the tape a fourth time.

"Later," Matsak told him when he asked. "A copy will be made for you. Now, you and Academician Zotov will examine the equipment—both what has been found and what has been created. I will need your small payment. You will come with me outside now . . ."

Outside the room, Grainger leaned against the rough plastered wall. "You knew exactly what I wanted, didn't you? Where it was."

"Then it is interesting for you?" Matsak wanted to negotiate.

Grainger unshouldered his gearbag. "How much do we need to give Zotov to get to the next level?"

"How much do you have with you?"

No use playing games. "About nine thousand. This isn't my money. I can't just give it to you without getting something in return."

"So you will give me one thousand. I will give the small amount to Zotov now, but not where the *robotniki*"—workers—"can see. We will proceed to the next phase. When we give you the tape copy, you will give one more thousand of dollars."

"If I need more cash than what I brought, I've got to go back to Moscow—involve the others. If we make a deal, the whole thing's yours as a good faith payment."

"For now, this much dollars is adequate."

If the money had been real, Grainger might have been more cautious. Maybe not. He needed to use the greed factor as motivation. He had to see what lay behind the curtain that no one had wanted him to get near.

When Zotov joined them in the hallway, Matsak gave him the money. It was as slick a transfer as Grainger had ever seen. "I want that tape. I need to see it again."

Too bad the tape quality wasn't better. But then, considering that the whole area had been nuked, the Soviet-era Russians who'd put that surveillance equipment in that town square were lucky they had anything at all.

"Soon enough. But first, you will see our science. And our . . . artifacts." Zotov's infusion of dollars seemed to have further improved his English.

"Great. When did this event happen?"

"On fifth of August, 1989," Matsak said, guiding Grainger back into the lab. Zotov had disappeared, probably to hide his dollars.

Grainger hadn't expected to get a date that specific from Matsak. It shocked him into silence. Did Matsak know why he'd asked? What he was? Why he was here?

They had to wait for Zotov to return before the curtain was pulled back.

Matsak's disturbing eyes stayed on him the whole time. The technicians smoked. Matsak smoked. Even Grainger smoked. Several times, Grainger tried to make conversation. Matsak would just shake his head. The tape remained frozen at the point of the nuclear explosion, no matter how he tried to convince Matsak to let him see it again. He was beginning to wonder if it might be a fake, since they wouldn't let him look at it closely.

When Zotov returned, the academician clapped his hands and one of the technicians pulled back the curtains manually.

Nearly half of the craft from Up The Line was shoehorned into the workbay beyond the glass. It was shiny in places, black and charred in others. Whole sections were slagged, incomprehensible, melted and fused. In front of it, Russian-style workbenches sat, filled with rudimentary test equipment.

"You would like to see this more closely? Then you will need to wear protective clothing."

Getting revisionists out of Moscow to 50K was one thing.

Getting better than half of a temporal capsule from Up The Line out of here was going to be much harder. Maybe impossible.

"I believe it's real," Grainger said flatly. He wasn't looking forward to examining the radioactive wreckage in 20th-century protective clothing, antiradiation shot or no antiradiation shot. It was bad enough that he'd ingested food and drink prepared in this building and served directly above their heads. "I'll examine it closely later. I'm more interested in what you learned from it. What you made from what you learned." He looked first at Matsak and then at Zotov. "Can I see your own setup? I need to know what you're doing and how you're doing it." And for whom. He already knew why. "That's why I'm here," he said softly. "And that's why Matsak is here with me—to make sure I see it."

Tim Grainger was nearly faint. His hands were shaking with adrenaline he had no way to use. Nobody from the ARC Riders had ever gotten even this close to what lay Up The Line. Radiation sickness makes you feel faint at first. He had to limit his exposure here to the really critical elements of what he needed to know.

How had those guys Up The Line failed to realize that the Soviet Union, circa 1989, would nuke any encroaching threat?

And who was in control of this technology that the Russians had cobbled together out of the capsule's wreckage, besides Zotov? Who knew, besides Matsak? How the hell did three young, powerless Russian peasants fit into the picture?

And why had Matsak decided to show any of this to Grainger?

Zotov said, "Do not be impatient. We have all the proper authority." His eyes flicked to Matsak.

Matsak said, "The Tim is ready to see your genius, Igor. Let us agree that we have the good basis for cooperation and go to the next phase now."

Grainger would have agreed to anything about then, in order to see whatever it was the Russians had created from this wreckage—whatever allowed them to send people through time in a whole new way. Especially if doing so got him out of such close proximity to the radioactive proof before him that the Wise Ones from Up The Line were capable of making mistakes just like anyone else.

Bad mistakes.

He had to find out everything he could in Obninsk and get back to Moscow, fast.

Seven Kilometers East of the Hase River, Free Germany

G erd mumbled.

"Pauli, I think he's coming out of it!" Rebecca Carnes said. She pressed a transparent patch to the side of the analyst's neck. Gerd grimaced. He tried to raise his hand, probably to brush away the contact, though his eyes remained closed.

"Want us to stop, girlie?" Flaccus asked from just behind Rebecca. She walked beside the litter, and he was on the back end of the nearer pole.

"We'll be at the campsite anytime now," said Hordius, clerk of the 1st Company, 3d Cohort, 17th Legion. "We may as well keep going."

He looked at the sky and added with a scowl, "We're going to have a bitch of a storm soon. If not tonight, then tomorrow. And fucking early in the year for it, too."

Hordius had been noncom of the guard when the ARC Riders entered Aliso. A palmful of gold coins had made Hordius and the squad he'd commanded that day more than willing to improvise a litter for Gerd. The legionaries believed the 'slave' had been injured saving his master's life; otherwise they'd have been amazed at Pauli's extravagance.

Gerd lay on half the squad's leather tent, unloaded from a baggage wagon and wrapped around the tent poles. The combination made a better stretcher than the poncho liner and pair of rifles Rebecca was used to. With eight legionaries on the poles, the analyst was as safe and probably as comfortable as Varus in his ornate litter.

Pauli Weigand reined back the horse he'd bought from a tribune. He rode slightly ahead of the litter bearers, regularly stepping into the forest. There he pulled down his faceshield to scan for dangers the army ignored as Varus drove deeper into territory the governor—but not the Germans—thought had been conquered.

"I was starting to worry," Pauli said. He sat his mount with a certain stiffness himself. Despite Rebecca's protests, he'd done his usual set of flexibility exercises when he got up this morning. His face had been white and clammy when he finished them, but he *had* finished. Pauli believed against reason that pain was a challenge, not a warning, and he was afraid to back down from it.

"He's been doing fine," Rebecca said. She'd been worried, too, but on general principles. "Since I was able to sedate him, Gerd wasn't able to strain himself with manly nonsense."

"Home sweet home," Hordius said as the litter entered a natural clearing being expanded by the efforts of legionaries from the front of the column. Axes rang. Gangs of soldiers shouted in cadence as they dragged fallen trees deeper into the forest to get them out of the way.

As usual, there was no attempt to palisade the camp. Varus didn't give the orders, and soldiers tired from a hard march and roadcutting wouldn't volunteer for extra labor even if they thought their lives depended on it. Rebecca'd seen the result often, men who'd been wounded because they were too tired to dig in though they knew they'd be attacked during the night. Soldiering was a fatalistic profession.

And these legionaries didn't believe their enemy was any threat. They were more worried about the rain.

Rebecca leaned close to read the monitor she'd attached to the analyst's neck. Gerd's vital signs were all within normal range, and brain activity was rising quickly as the sedative wore off. She'd injected a twenty-four-hour dose metered to Gerd's body weight and metabolism, but it was always a marvel to her that 26th-century medicine worked with the regularity of a light switch.

The day before she'd applied first aid while the bellowing Germans checked their wounds and legionaries came up the road at the double, summoned by the clang of weapons. Nobody paid her any attention.

She'd covered the pressure cut in Gerd's scalp with first a topical knitting agent, then a liquid bandage that set like clear latex and would dissolve as the flesh beneath it healed. The sedative came next, followed by a transcutaneous patch at the back of Gerd's neck to dissolve the blood clots that'd be forming on the brain. He'd been slugged with either a club or the flat of a sword whose edge he'd managed to dodge. His skull wasn't fractured, but the blow had given him both a primary and a contra-cu concussion.

All in ninety seconds, working in near darkness. A 20th-century emergency room couldn't have done as much.

But neither could Pauli nor Gerd have done as much if they'd been working on Rebecca Carnes. Technology was wonderful, but it wasn't magic and it still left room for experience.

Dealing with Pauli had been more difficult simply because he wasn't unconscious. He kept insisting that he was fine and that he needed to go after the surviving revisionist immediately. He maybe could have walked—he was as tough as he was stubborn—but he couldn't ride and he certainly couldn't fight. Istvan still had his Skorpion. Another burst was likely to send splinters of weakened ribs through Pauli's lungs even if the bullets themselves didn't penetrate, and Istvan might go for a head shot anyway.

She'd gotten Pauli's mail shirt off him by saying she knew it would hurt him too much to raise his arms. Raising his arms *had* hurt, but he'd done it and Rebecca pulled the fabric of fine steel links off him like a sweater.

The mail had been driven almost through the leather undervest in three places. At those points the flesh was swollen and hot to the touch. She'd spread anticlotting agents, topical anesthetic, and—despite Pauli's objection— a general anal-gesic that left him too wobbly to walk without help.

She helped Pauli, and a gold piece brought Gerd back to the camp seated in the arms of a pair of legionaries bemused to be earning two weeks wages for walking a hundred yards.

They wouldn't have long to spend the money, but it'd keep them happy for a day or two.

Rebecca had examined her teammates in better light under the tent the army provided for the emperor's representative. She'd found and dealt with a cut Pauli'd gotten by falling onto his head. Only then did she go back to the scene of the ambush which the legionaries had put down to an argument between clans of Fritzes.

The German chiefs and their retainers had ridden away car-rying their dead even before the legionaries left. The corpses of the revisionists' thugs lay where they'd fallen.

Germans had found Osric alive though unconscious. Sigimer rammed the small end of the club down the man's throat and into the chest cavity. Rebecca didn't watch, but she had to pass the body when she searched for signs of Istvan.

There were none. Pauli hadn't gotten a clean hit on the man. The revisionist had taken himself and his equipment into the forest when he came to.

Hannes, the elderly Russian, was dead as Rebecca had ex-pected. No one had noticed his body in the elderberry thicket. There was a froth of blood on his lips. Both his hands were locked on the shaft of the javelin that had plunged in through the top of his breastbone.

She'd stripped the body of its 20th-century equipment. The radio might be helpful since Istvan and perhaps the unidenti-fied revisionists had similar units. The night-vision goggles weren't any use to the team, but she didn't want to leave something anachronistic for future archaeologists to find. The belt of gold coins would be simply weight. No finder on this or a later time horizon was going to learn anything critically important from even a detailed assay.

Rebecca Carnes belted the Skorpion and its pouch of spare

magazines on under her cape. She might not be as lucky the next time her microwave pistol failed her and a life was in the balance. Pauli knew she'd kept the weapon but he hadn't said anything about it.

Rebecca had never knowingly killed a human being before. She'd never even killed a warm-blooded animal. Her heart was cold and she'd see the Russian's face in nightmares for as long as she lived; but faced with the same choice, she'd make the same decision. She'd rather loathe herself for what she'd become than remember that she'd let a friend die because she was too squeamish to save him.

Gerd tried to sit up. Rebecca put a hand on his chest to keep him down. "A few minutes more, Gerd," she said. All they needed was for the analyst to fall off the litter now and break his neck. "You're still groggy."

They entered the clearing. Minutius, the centurion who commanded the 3rd Cohort, was assigning tasks. He saw the litter and nodded. Hordius had made sure the centurion got his share of the gold. 1st Squad was efficitively excused from ordinary tasks to serve the ARC Riders. Pauli's supposed rank might have gotten similar results, but hard cash cut through a lot of bureaucracy.

"Rebecca?" Gerd said in a rusty, frightened whisper. "My sensor pack? Do you have it?"

"I've got it safe," Rebecca said. Gerd had clamped so tight around the little device while he was unconscious that she'd injected a muscle relaxant to pry it from his fingers. "I'll give it back to you as soon as we're settled."

The team spoke Standard among themselves, completely unintelligible to everyone around them. That didn't concern the soldiers. A person who spoke Latin, Greek, and perhaps in the eastern provinces Aramaic could travel from one end of the empire to the other; but hundreds of separate languages survived beneath that common umbrella. Two members of the squad spoke Oscan between themselves, and they'd been born within sixty miles of Rome.

Hordius pushed through the mob to get direction from one of the surveyor's assistants laying out the campsite. "Right,

set it here!" he called, gesturing the litter bearers to a location
pegged in the natural clearing. The 17th led the column today;
its officers wouldn't have to contend with tree stumps in the
billeting area. "When Gaius Clovis releases you, report to
Minutius in fatigue kit."

"Pitch the tent," Pauli said to Flaccus, the senior legionary.
"We won't need anything more."

"To tell the truth, Clovis," Flaccus said, "I'd just as soon
hang around guarding you lot as clear fucking forest. But at
least you've kept us off road-building detail, so we won't
complain."

Rebecca helped Gerd sit up as Pauli dismounted nearby.
"I'm terribly sorry for the trouble I've caused," the analyst
said. Rebecca handed him a skin of water laced with dietary
supplements. He sucked greedily from it. He hadn't had anything to eat or drink while he was under sedation.

Gerd lowered the skin and paused, breathing deeply. "One
of Hannes' guards had gone off the roadway to relieve himself."

"A bad time for a barbarian to have a twinge of delicacy,"
Pauli said, obviously relieved that Gerd was alert again. The
big man's jaw muscles were no longer stiff.

"They were Germans, not French, Pauli," Rebecca said;
and realized that her making a joke meant that she'd relaxed
also.

"I was so absorbed with my sensor display that I almost
walked into him," Gerd said. He managed a wistful smile.
"Too close to the forest to see the trees, wasn't I?"

He looked at Carnes and said, "May I have my sensor pack
now, Rebecca?"

"Of course," she said in concern. Gerd was afraid she'd
refuse, afraid that she'd cut him off from all but his immediate
surroundings to punish him for his mistake. She wondered if
the analyst had been having a premonition of the dementia he
knew lay in his future.

Pauli glanced at them but said nothing. The packed confusion of the camp concealed the team's activities almost as
well as empty forest would have done. The sensor pack

looked like a plain gray tile, unremarkable to the natives of this time horizon. Its display was by air-projected holograms, visible from only one location in respect to the device. Nobody would care even if Gerd used the sensor in plain sight; which was unnecessary with the leather tent now raised.

The head of the column halted in early afternoon, but the tail wouldn't straggle into the encampment until well after sunset. Over twenty thousand people were marching into the dark interior of Germany. Little more than half were soldiers. Servants, wives, and whores made up the reaminder, with hundreds of merchants like those the revisionists had claimed to be come to buy loot or sell luxuries to the troops.

There were as many wagons carrying the personal effects of Varus and his retinue as there were for military baggage. With the addition of the train of civilians, the column included over a thousand vehicles.

The roadway was narrow. Every time an axle broke or a wheel came off, the damaged wagon halted everything behind it. On a surface of cross-logs and ax-hewn bridges, breakdowns were frequent.

"Have you been tracking the revisionists?" Gerd asked. His fingers played on an invisible control surface in front of his sensor pack.

"Gerd," Pauli said with the patience that Rebecca found remarkable in a man whose own actions were so crisply decisive, "neither of us could turn your sensor *on*. The only way we could have tracked Istvan was by sniffing the air."

"Oh, it's not really that complex," the analyst said, typing on nothing material. Rebecca couldn't tell whether his tone was one of embarrassment or pride. The air before him shimmered; to someone unfamiliar with the process, the holographic display could have been dust motes dancing in a sunbeam. "And the unit was on at all times, of course."

In a different, crisper voice the analyst continued, "Hannes is back at the point the attack occurred. I assume he's dead?" He raised an eyebrow.

"Yes," Rebecca said. "He's dead."

Gerd nodded, pleased to have his analysis confirmed. "Istvan is seventeen . . ." He frowned and manipulated the controls further. "Sixteen point seven kilometers from us on a heading of twenty-eight degrees. The likelihood is that he's on or near the military road since our general heading has been within ten degrees of that throughout the march, but I only state that as a probability. The course of the road isn't in Central's database."

He smiled at a private joke. "Though when we return, at least part of it will be," he added. "Istvan hasn't moved since last evening."

"How do you tell distances?" Pauli asked. "Is the strength of the rubidium signature that precise?"

He'd unbuckled his sword belt; now he tensed himself to lift off the mail shirt. Rebecca rose and stepped behind him. "Permit your faithful slave to aid you, master," she said mildly. She removed the fabric of linked steel, shockingly heavy for all its apparent delicacy.

"The pack recorded while we were moving," Gerd explained. "Even though I wasn't able to access the data." He smiled. "With Hannes as a control point, I can map both our track and Istvan's precisely."

"What's he doing out there?" Rebecca said, more to herself than for an answer. She looked at the dark vegetation surrounding the growing encampment. Like the jungles of Southeast Asia, this forest was neutral: hostile to men of all sorts. "Is he looking for his friends?"

"I'd guess he was running away, Beckie," Pauli Weigand said. He drank from the water skin, then offered it to her. "He couldn't get back to the camp when the attack failed, so he ran in the other direction. I don't think he's in any danger—he can't locate Arminius or have any significant effect on the massacre to come. But he's the only path I know to finding the other two revisionists."

Rebecca drank deeply of the fortified liquid. If you thought the container had merely water, it would taste sour but by no means as bad as much of what others in the column were drinking. Water purification for this army was a matter of mixing wine with the water—and the wine was acid besides.

"We'll go after him immediately," Gerd said. He rose to his feet. "I'm sorry to have delayed—"

His face changed. His knees buckled; he would have fallen on his face again if Rebecca hadn't caught him.

She looked at Pauli as she eased the mumbling analyst to the ground, pillowing his head on his rolled cape. "Tomorrow morning," she said. "I'll put fluids and food into him tonight. Although . . . we could go after Istvan ourselves?"

"And if Istvan moves?" Pauli said. "No, tomorrow morning."

He too looked at the forest, seeing not the trees but the German warriors gathering in glades and hamlets throughout them. "No matter what, we have to get away from the column by tomorrow morning. If we're caught with Varus, the best we can hope for is that Germanicus will give us proper Roman burial rites when he reaches the spot six years from now."

Between the Hase and Hunte Rivers, Free Germany

A cow bawled in pain nearby. Puli Weigand's nerves felt as if they'd been stretched between pegs. He'd switched his faceshield to thermal viewing, though light amplification gave him a better view of the trail for riding. Right at the moment he was more concerned with someone waiting in ambush than he was with his horse stumbling.

"We should dismount now," Gerd said in a voice thinned by pain. He actually managed to chuckle. "Not only are we close to our goal, I'm afraid that my body is about to imitate the wonderful one-horse shay and fail at all points simultaneously."

The analyst liked to borrow metaphors from time horizons he'd visited. Pauli didn't understand the particular reference—he didn't even know what a "shay" was—but he took Gerd's meaning loud and clear.

They'd left the camp in the morning with three horses, all of them purchased within the column. Pauli led while Gerd and Beckie rode double so that she could hold the analyst in the saddle. The pair traded mounts at short intervals to prevent overstraining either beast. It wasn't ideal, but it was the only way Gerd could cover the necessary distance.

The analyst was adequately fit, but he was neither a young man nor one to whom physical ability had ever been a major goal. These seventeen kilometers were proof that Gerd Barthuli could cut glass by willpower alone.

A good man. A good teammate. Pauli just wished the team leader were better at his job. . . .

He dismounted and stepped to help Gerd down while Beckie supported him from the saddle. His horse whickered. The cow continued to bawl.

"Her udder's full," Beckie said. "She wants to be milked."

"The revisionist is forty meters from the road," Gerd said. He clutched his chest as Pauli lowered his feet to the ground and his legs took the strain of his weight. "He's in a dwelling. I think I'd best kneel, Pauli. I'll display the layout."

Gerd and his sensor pack had been their protection on the ride. German warbands passed near the ARC Riders a dozen times during the day. Though the tribes massing to attack Varus didn't themselves use the old roadway, they knew that the Roman column would. Arminius and Sigimer were positioning their forces along the expected route.

Each time Gerd had given warning while the warriors were a full kilometer away. The team either broke a fresh trail to bypass the danger or waited for the Germans to move on. Evading enemies slowed the team's progress, but bands of hundreds of warriors together were too strong to fight.

"Not that we wouldn't have tried."

"What?" said Gerd.

"Sorry," Pauli said. "I didn't mean to speak."

Beckie stood on the horses' reins as she arranged feed bags to keep the animals quiet during the next minutes. The wind through the treetops was fierce. Occasionally a gust swept a billow of pine needles across the forest floor. The air was cold and the horses were restive because of the coming storm.

"Istvan is in a hut with another person, perhaps a female," Gerd said. He gestured to his controls. Pastel green light formed a rough oval in the air above the sensor with a blue and a pink figure within the frame. "There is a hearth in the center of the hut, though the fire is banked for now. There is a corral, a *cow byre,* here."

Pauli raised his faceshield. More green lines formed a rectangle with a half-dozen cow-shaped pink blobs beside the oval.

"There is a dead body here," Gerd continued with no emotional loading. Another pink figure, this time crosshatched and sprawled in front of the oval.

The analyst looked up. "I believe the woman is tied," he added. "She doesn't move for long periods of time."

"All right," Pauli said. He nodded twice as if he were pumping his thoughts to the surface. "Does the house have windows, Gerd?"

Beckie knelt beside them, her face lighted by the glow diffused from the holograms. Oats crunched between the horses' teeth.

"No," the analyst said. "The walls are posts set in the ground. The roof is turf over a supporting frame of branches, with a hole in the center for smoke. The door is a section of cowhide pegged to the outside wall at the top. The walls slope inward, and the doorway is only a meter high."

A branch tore loose in the wind and fell spinning, smashing other limbs. It hit the ground at last with a thud Pauli could feel through his boot soles. Soon it would be the weather against them along with the Germans and revisionists.

"Gerd lifts the flap and you and I both shoot?" Beckie suggested.

"You lift the flap, I go in and grab him," Pauli said. "Gerd keeps watch. I don't trust the pistols when I can't see the target. All it takes is a bunch of onions hanging from a roof beam to stop the pulse."

Beckie grimaced and nodded. She didn't refer to the submachine gun under her cape. They needed the revisionist alive for questioning.

This was a perfect opportunity to use a gas grenade. Pauli Weigand, team leader, hadn't brought one. If he'd tried to imagine everything he might need, he'd have wound up with more hardware than TC 779 could carry; but why hadn't he brought *one* gas grenade?

"I'm able to move, I believe," Gerd said simply.

Pauli forced a smile and drew his faceshield down again. "All right," he said.

He got up, massaged his calves to be sure that the muscles hadn't cramped as a result of the long ride, and took off his military cape. The doorway would be narrow as well as low.

"These'd be in the way, too," Pauli said. He unbuckled the belt and crossed baldrics supporting his sword, dagger, and metal purse.

Sliding the microwave pistol from the lining of his cape he stepped forward, walking lightly. His ribs no longer hurt, though they surely would when he came down off the adrenaline high in a few moments. Assuming Istvan hadn't learned from his failed ambush to be quicker on the trigger . . .

Pauli would have gone past the narrow trail connecting the isolated farmstead with the military road if Gerd hadn't pointed it out. The briers at the junction held tufts of short, coarse hair combed from passing cattle. There was no other visible marker. The analyst must be tracking variations in the infrared ambience at a level more subtle than a standard-issue faceshield could differentiate.

The scents might have alerted him: first wood smoke, a tingle at the back of Pauli's nostrils. It would have made him sneeze if he hadn't fought the urge. Then the cattle, warm bodies and warm manure with still as much the odor of vegetation as of waste.

Pauli had almost reached the dark hovel itself before he smelled the corpse. Even that was remarkable. The weather hadn't been exceptionally warm under the dark trees. The man lying at his own threshold must have been dead for most of a day to have ripened so far.

Pauli paused, aiming his pistol at the door. Beckie stepped past him and knelt to raise the dead man's torso. His upper chest was a mass of clotted blood through which insects already crawled. A dozen bullet holes pierced his cowhide jerkin.

He'd been a young man. His beard and mustache were full but had been neatly trimmed. Pauli wondered what he'd used for a mirror. Maybe his wife had groomed him.

Gerd raised his hand for attention and squatted, manipulating his sensor pack again. He projected a schematic of the hut's interior based on data refined at close range. Images hung in front of the cowhide door so that the team's attention was still directed toward the potential danger.

The pink shape of a woman lay to the left of the doorway. The revisionist, head to the back of the hut, was on the right. He lay on his side. Both figures were on the floor; there were no beds. The image of the submachine gun near the revisionist's hand throbbed twice, then became a white outline.

The image of the infant in the crib beside the woman was crosshatched, like that of its dead father outside. The body was too small to have shown up before.

Pauli pulled down his faceshield and nodded. He set the pistol on the ground beside him, then opened his mouth wide. He worked his jaws from side to side, loosening their tension. He smiled.

Beckie gripped the door flap's lower corner with her left hand. She bobbed the barrel of the pistol in her right hand once, twice, three times, and jerked backward. The cowhide tore away from its pegs as Pauli Weigand dived into the darkened hut.

Istvan couldn't have been sleeping well because he managed to lurch upright as Pauli hit him. The revisionist was ruthless but he hadn't been a trained shooter. He didn't reach for the Skorpion until the ARC Rider had flipped it across the hut with one hand while the other caught Istvan by the throat.

Istvan gabbled as he choked. Pauli grabbed his flailing right hand. The Russian was trying to kick. His feet tangled in the cowhide bedding.

The hut wasn't big enough for a fight. Pauli slammed the ceiling's lacework of branches with his armored shoulders. Dirt from the turf roof showered down. He backed toward the doorway, dragging his captive.

Istvan went suddenly as limp as a puddle of water.

"He'll be out for ten minutes," Beckie said, breathing heavily. "I gave him a white dose."

She dropped an empty injector cone back into her medical

kit. The casing was a long-chain starch that would fall to dust within a month, but ARC Riders were trained to leave nothing in an operational horizon if they could possibly avoid it.

"Good work," Pauli gasped. He hadn't noticed Beckie enter during the struggle. He backed through the doorway, pulling the revisionist behind him. "Get the gun, would you?"

"And I'll see to the woman," Beckie said. In a deceptively cool tone she added, "I believe the baby choked in its own vomit. Probably while the mother was tied and gagged."

"He's had a white dose, Gerd," Pauli said. Outside the hut he realized how thick the fug within had been. "How are you feeling? Want me to handle the interrogation?"

"Not at all," the analyst said. He'd already taken cranial pickups and a cone of hypnotic from his kit. The drug would erase the subject's volitional control for six hours without affecting his memory or the autonomic nervous system that kept him alive. "Have you considered what we're going to do with him after we've gained the information we need?"

"I've thought about it," Pauli said curtly.

A woman shrieked in wordless grief within the hut. Beckie came out ahead of the mother cradling the dead infant. When she saw her husband she threw herself across the body and cried even louder.

"We'll bury them in back," Beckie said as her strong, capable hands lifted the woman. She sounded calm. The women walked behind the hut, the widow wailing against Beckie's shoulder.

"All right," Pauli said. "I'll bring the horses here. Better to have them close by."

He felt light-headed; the short walk to the horses would settle him. He looked for the stars when he reached the military road, but the sky was solidly overcast. Lightning made the gray mass glow and sometimes gave a cloud visible edges, but Pauli heard no thunder over the wind's howl.

He unlooped the reins from the young birch to which Beckie had tethered the horses. His own mount tried to nuzzle him through the empty feedbag. The ARC Rider pressed his forehead against the coarse, dry-smelling trunk of a huge fir tree.

The dead baby made him sick to his stomach. He'd seen cruelty during his service with the Anti-Revision Command: cruel humans and cruel beasts; cruel fates. Most fates were cruel when viewed from a 26th-century vantage point.

The revisionist hadn't been cruel. He simply hadn't cared. A choking baby wasn't a reason to get out of bed.

Pauli drove the horses ahead of him down the narrow track. The cow had finally stopped bawling. One of the women must have milked some of the pressure out of the swollen udder. The corpse no longer lay beside the door.

Gerd had begun questioning their captive. In better light the pickups would have looked like brass beads; now they were vagrant gleams on Istvan's scalp. The drugged revisionist couldn't speak, but the pickups transmitted his mind's unshielded responses to the sensor pack where an AI converted them. The analyst listened to the processed data through an earpiece.

Pauli tethered the horses again. His pistol wasn't on the ground. Beckie must have picked up the weapon he'd forgotten. Leaving the analyst to his business, he walked around the hut.

The German woman was digging with a pointed stick in the small clearing. The corpses lay nearby. The corral's walls were branches woven around vertical posts every few feet. There were six cows within.

Beckie straightened into view behind the fence, holding a bucket made of bark bound with willow splits. "Have some?" she offered.

"Thanks," Pauli said as he took the bucket. The milk was still at body temperature. The cow's diet gave the drink a musky odor he didn't recognize. If the milk had been poisonous, the German family wouldn't have been around for Istvan to kill.

She handed him his microwave pistol. "Do you want the submachine gun?" she asked.

One of the guns. "I may as well carry it," Pauli said. He

slung the belt and holster over his shoulder, then drank more. The milk helped settle his stomach despite its odd taste. His eyes were on the woman digging.

"She was cooking dinner on the outside hearth yesterday evening," Beckie said. She nodded to a fire pit and clay oven under a bark roof. "Istvan must have smelled the smoke. She heard her husband speak and went to the front to see what he'd said. He was still standing. She saw a stranger, Istvan. Her husband was patting at his chest. Suddenly he fell down. There wasn't a fight. Istvan shot him without even speaking."

Beckie nodded toward the woman. "Her name's Grita. She ran but she'd left the baby beside the cooking fire. When she paused to get him the stranger caught her and hit her over the head. He tied her ankles but left her hands free to cook for him. Then he tied her hands as well."

The cow lowed and pushed Beckie with her broad forehead for attention. Beckie took the bucket and returned to her business.

"They're Cherusci but not from Hermann's clan," Beckie continued as her fingers stripped milk from the four teats in sequence. Pauli wondered where she'd learned the technique. It wasn't a common skill in the America of her day. "Her husband might have joined the attack, but the child was only three weeks old. He decided to stay with Grita. It was a boy."

"I have the information we need," Gerd announced. The analyst used the headband intercom to speak without shouting. There was a risk someone would stumble into the vicinity while the sensor pack was occupied with the interrogation.

"We're coming," Pauli said. Beckie brought the bucket out of the corral with her.

Grita was using a wooden shake to lift the loosened dirt. She didn't look up as the ARC Riders returned to the front of the dwelling.

The revisionist lay flaccid, but his chest rose and fell with the rhythm of normal breathing. Beckie walked over to him and closed his eyes. Her face was without expression.

"The remaining revisionists are in Xanten, that is Vetera, on the Rhine," Gerd said. He smiled vaguely as he manipulated a keyboard that existed only in his mind. "Istvan believes they are, at any rate. Their names are Boris Kiknadze—"

The pack projected the image of a heavyset man, then focused on his flat, swarthy face. Kiknadze had coarse black hair and a sparse beard. The puckered scars on his right cheek were probably the result of bullets. He looked as solid as a tank.

"Istvan considers Kiknadze a stupid Tatar," Gerd said. "Istvan doesn't respect him."

"I respect him," Pauli said. "When we hit Kiknadze, we'd better hit him with everything we have. I'd drop a building on him if I knew a way to do it."

"Yes," Gerd said, smiling as he typed. "I thought you'd say that. Istvan bases many of his judgments on class and race, and I'm afraid he also has an overly high opinion of the merits of raw intelligence."

The image shifted to that of a plump man with flowing white hair and beard, bright blue eyes, and the expression of a cheerful saint. "This is the leader of the revisionists, Dr. Kyril Svetlanov," the analyst continued. "He transported the group to this horizon. The others believe they must be with him to return—in physical contact with him. Istvan's plan was to hide here for a few days to avoid being caught up in the massacre he failed to prevent, then make his way to Xanten."

"You said, 'They believe,' " Pauli said.

Gerd nodded. "There's no way back. It's standard Soviet practice to sacrifice personnel when retrieval would be expensive, though of course the victims are told otherwise."

"Why Xanten?" Beckie asked. She knew Gerd would tell them eventually; knew also that "eventually" might be a long time coming.

The analyst smiled with pride. He didn't overrate intelligence as he'd accused Istvan of doing; he'd known that Kiknadze was a dangerous opponent. Every other member of Team 79 could outshoot Gerd, and there were circumstances where that skill alone was the margin of the team's survival.

But Gerd rated the value of his own intelligence and skills very high. Pauli Weigand would have been the last to say he was wrong.

"The revisionists' plan is more complex than Central and I had believed," Gerd said. "One team was tasked to prevent the destruction of Varus' army, the tool of expansion, by killing the revolt's leaders. That would allow the Romans to continue their drive eastward, but it wouldn't give them the will to do so. Augustus' successor, his stepson Tiberius, was a cautious man. He avoided military adventures after he became emperor, even though he'd made his name as the foremost general of his day."

"Even if the revolt fizzles, Augustus is going to send his top man to the region to take charge of operations," Pauli said. He drew on the background he'd sleep-learned for this mission—and on his personal experience with crisis management. "Tiberius is sure to arrive at Xanten because it was Varus' base camp. The revisionists are waiting there to kill him."

"If Tiberius dies, Augustus' grandson Germanicus will succeed," Gerd said. "A very popular, very *active* young man. Quite the sort for military heroics. He'll push a forward policy in Germany as sure as—"

He looked at Beckie. "As God made little green apples."

Beckie managed a smile. Her mind was obviously on the small corpse being buried behind the hut.

"All right," Pauli said. "We'll go to Xanten and neutralize the revisionists. Gerd, are you able to ride tonight? I'd like to get a little way away from here."

He didn't explain why. He didn't have to.

"Yes," the analyst said simply. That might have been macho posturing in another man. Gerd didn't give bad data.

"Pauli, what do we do with this one?" Beckie asked. She waved a finger toward the captive revisionist but didn't look at him.

"Istvan Korzybski," Gerd said. The analyst offered the name because he had it, not because there was any need. "He's actually of Polish extraction, though his family's lived in western Russia since the 19th century."

"He's practically harmless without his equipment," Pauli said. He rose to his feet. "We can't take him with us, so we'll leave him for now. When the operation's complete, we'll pick him up in TC 779."

The German woman came around the hut. She looked at the revisionist, helpless though fully aware of his surroundings.

Pauli Weigand began to don the equipment he'd hung across his horse's withers. "If we need to," he added quietly.

Moscow, Russia

March 10, 1992

The little girl begging beside the iron gates of the Kiev train station couldn't have been more than three years old. Her eyes were huge in a pinched, dirty face. Her hair had been shaved for lice no more than a month ago, giving her a pixie look. She wore an embroidered red dress, filthy and tattered, but clearly once her best. The matching ethnic cap was in her hand. She came toward Nan Roebeck timidly but with great determination, hopeful, silent, her empty cap outstretched.

Roebeck fumbled in her pockets for something—anything—to give the little girl. Between the gates and the train station were a number of small wooden and metal kiosks. The stalls displayed Russian cigarettes, trinkets, bottled drinks, and sweets this child could never afford.

Sergey Orlov, the Russian Foreign Ministry's Special Assistant for Proliferation, stayed her hand. "Please. This child is working for some gang—Russian Mafia. You will not help her. They will take her money and she will be out here again tomorrow." Orlov's face was flushed, his embarrassment obvious. "Do not encourage her. These organized beggars are new difficulty for us. We must find new ways to solve problems like her."

"I don't think she's a problem," Nan said. Among the swaddled poor lurking in the shadow of the train station, Nan had seen a worried woman watching the child carefully.

But Roebeck had no roubles. She was afraid to give the child dollars. It might be a reason to arrest her. Orlov's Foreign Ministry job was focused on showing foreigners only what it desired foreigners to see.

Clearly, this girl was not what Nan Roebeck should have seen. Roebeck had used her foreign visitor status to object to being whisked off by Ministry car to yet another controlled environment. She'd insisted that Orlov take her for a short walk, show her some of the real Moscow. He'd warned that streets in this city, as in any city, might be dangerous. Now those streets had proved dangerous to his agenda.

Roebeck knelt down, helpless. She wanted to touch the child, but dared not.

"Come, please!" Orlov was now thoroughly agitated. "I have roubles. Here." He handed her three one-hundred-rouble notes. When Nan didn't close her hand over the currency, he added a two-hundred-rouble note. "This is enough. This is more than enough."

Roebeck, rising to her feet, put the notes in the girl's cap.

"Now, please, madam, this way."

As Orlov hurried Roebeck away, Nan looked back over her shoulder. The child followed Roebeck for a few more steps, cap still outstretched.

Then the woman in the shadows called out.

The child fled to the woman.

Orlov determinedly demanded Roebeck's attention. As he escorted her to the waiting car, Roebeck looked over her shoulder a second time. The watchful woman had boosted the child onto an empty flatbed, enfolding the girl in her arms. She pulled up the girl's dress and began changing her clothes. If the girl was a pawn of some Russian Mafia group, then so be it. On the other hand, if she was a refugee fleeing from somewhere to anywhere with her mother, then perhaps those few hundred roubles would help the two of them on their way.

For the rest of her life, Nan Roebeck would remember the beautiful little beggar girl standing on the empty flatbed, a woman's hands changing her underpants in the cold shadows of the Kiev station.

Away from the station yard they went in Orlov's car. "Now perhaps we will skip the Arbat—the outdoor market, madam. We have spent enough time on trivial matters."

Orlov was overtly punishing his American visitor. The Foreign Ministry's proliferation specialist was still angry. Central had warned that when Russians were embarrassed, they became aggressive and hostile. She wished it could be otherwise, but the child's fate had touched her deeply. She even considered trying to take the child back with her.

That, of course, was impossible. Not to mention impolitic to consider.

As the car sped on its way in response to Orlov's orders, she couldn't help but ask about the fate of such children. "What if that woman was the girl's mother? Are they refugees? From where? Going where? What happens to children such as that?"

"The State once provided for them." Orlov shrugged. "Now, if they are from Ukraine, Kiev, a breakaway republic, the 'Stans, who knows? Perhaps they have come to Moscow to—what is the term?—throw in their lots with Mother Russia. The people want privatization. They wish to own, to dominate, to rule their own fates. They say they understand the risks. They have never known unemployment." Orlov's expression was haughty. "There is an old Soviet-era saying: 'We pretend to work and the State pretends to pay us.' Now many will have no work. They say they understand that unemployment may be the result of this great perestroika. They proclaim that if unemployment is what they need, then unemployment is what they will have. So they will. And we will take care of them the best we can. The Russian Federation is having some problems with Ukraine. Just this week, Ukraine tried to claim the Black Sea Fleet for its own. This lasted twenty-four hours, until we turned off the natural gas to their cities. Then their so-called government came to its senses."

Sergey Orlov was young. His hair was long and pomaded, curling over his collar. His beard was evenly clipped to a manicured shadow, pursuing some fashion of the times. Baby fat still rounded his features. His mouth was soft and petulant. Last evening he had taken Nan Roebeck on a whirlwind tour of privileged Russia. She had met a dozen young bureaucrats. They seemed to run in a pack, like wolves. There were a few women, but the women were treated as assistants or lovers. Or both. The young men had beautiful clothes, fine leather goods. Their women had fur coats that smelled strong but were clearly very expensive.

The pack had gathered her up and carried her with them, on the excuse of arranged meetings that all must attend. She knew she'd be their excuse for a night of carousing, so she'd insisted on seeing something relevant to her search. Orlov had sworn he could provide it. He and his pack had promised a real science meeting, and delivered. She had been taken to a place called FILI,where nuclear missiles were stored right in downtown Moscow behind high metal walls.

FILI had a guard house, armed guards, and a courtyard full of expensive Western cars. She saw soon enough why Grainger's man, Matsak, had warned about becoming embroiled with hard-liners. She'd been greeted in FILI by older bureaucrats, chiefs of divisions, heads of departments. Orlov's plans for her edification had been contravened by more powerful elders. She'd sat at green-covered tables. With old men she drank pineapple soda water, Czechoslovakian sparkling water, and Russian Pepsi that tasted like carbonated blood with a hint of cinnamon.

Orlov warned her off the sparkling water. "It tastes like piss—Czechoslovakian piss."

For hours, senior officials, including a chief of the Aviation Ministry, wasted her time with impossible plans for privatization, joint cooperation, and scientific exchange.

She drank tea in glasses set inside chased metal holders. She waited and listened patiently, playing the US government functionary. When finally asked, she explained as vaguely as possible her area of interest. But they weren't really interested in what she wanted to buy, only in making her buy what they wanted to sell. It soon became clear to her that the older Russians had intervened in Orlov's plan purposely to short-circuit it. Because they could do so, they dominated the agenda.

She was merely part of an object lesson those old boys were giving Orlov and his young wolf pack. The young wolves might be eager, but the old ones still controlled the territory.

It did not take long for the old bureaucrats to become frustrated. This American woman, who would not accede to their wishes or adopt their priorities, flouted their authority in front of Russian youths in need of object lessons.

A young sycophant of the hard-liners named Lipinsky nearly shouted at her. "Defense conversion," he lectured her, "so far as my region of military production is concerned, means converting excess defense capability to civilian use. Nothing more."

Lipinsky stared at her defiantly, as if she should counter this assertion. His glare dared her to accept his challenge. He wanted to further distinguish himself before his old masters. He had a hawk's face, a prominent Adam's apple, and English worthy of the US and Canada Institute's finest.

But Roebeck wasn't really representing the US or any time-localized interest. She reiterated that her only interest was in certain experimental geochronometric technology that might have potential for cooperation. Not missiles. Not space programs. Not modernizing the Russian air traffic control system.

Lipinsky was intent on showing his bosses how to keep Russia's military-industrial complex intact. He would give no strategic advantage to foreigners. She had a feeling that the young hard-liner's view of his country's future would turn out to be the prevailing reality. But then, she had the advantage of Central's hindsight.

And Central's clout. Lipinsky was so abrasive it was hard not to take his behavior personally. When the time came, it would be a pleasure to teach this nasty, perk-conscious young Russian a lesson. Offending people can have long-term consequences, not only for you, but for your faction. Perhaps even for your country. If this little bastard was as deeply involved as she suspected with efforts to revert control of Russia to its former masters, taking out the revisionists might mean taking out Lipinsky as well. Or at least could be construed to mean that.

Nan Roebeck would love to see Lipinsky's face if she deposited him in 50K.

Eventually, Orlov and his friends extricated her from the clutches of the aging elite and their fawning sycophants. Orlov apologized forthrightly for the evening's debacle. "We are so sad to have wasted your time. Sorry to say that your presence here has excited too much interest from the senior officials of the old regime. Their single hope is to use foreign pressure to reestablish themselves under Yeltsin. This is the only way they may continue just as they have done in the past."

She'd said, "I understand their need to send senior personnel to oversee such a visit. But it is not productive for me." If she'd wanted to, she wouldn't have been allowed to inspect any of the nuclear devices or large naval missiles she'd seen. During their tour of FILI, Orlov had leaned against one with a bad-boy smile and patted it, saying, "SS-N-25. The US does not yet know we have such a missile. So you can see, there is much of interest here." A tart rebuke by Lipinsky, who by then controlled the agenda, had followed.

She remembered Orlov introducing an old guard scientist sent to baby-sit her. "This is Dr. Nikolai Neat, Madam Roebeck." He'd pronounced it like the English word for tidy.

Dr. Neat had darted over, hand outstretched, back hunched so that he seemed like a gnome among the huge nuclear missiles. His bearded chin had jutted out in welcome. *"Privyet. Neat. Neat. Da. Da,"* he'd said.

She'd already resigned herself to a useless visit by then. Whatever Orlov's intent had been, this formalized exchange could include nothing of value. She'd had no choice but to continue going through the motions. She kept wondering how Chun was doing with Etkin, hoping Chun was having better luck. Tomorrow was another day.

Orlov, after he'd extricated her from FILI, had promised that the following day would be different.

So now, on the next morning, after four hours sleep and the disaster with the beggar girl, she reminded him of his promise. "Today we'll see something useful, I hope. Without too many of your senior officials present."

"Madam, these senior officials were informed by someone else of your impending visit. Well, who could this have been? Was it, do you think, Madam Chun's friend, Mr. Etkin?" He was still brooding over last night's embarrassing proof that he could not deliver all he promised.

"It could have been Mr. Etkin, I suppose. You did meet him. He is interested in helping us, of course." Orlov needed to be reminded that she knew he didn't run the only game in town.

"Well, madam, today we shall see what no one else can show you. And I will appreciate it if you tell no one what you see today. Otherwise, as you have seen, future access could be denied you. You will see what these scientists have to offer. You will tell me if it is interesting. If so, then we will discuss how to proceed. Privately. Not at the dinner with Professor Etkin tonight to which you have so kindly invited me."

The car was driving along a divided highway with trolley tracks in its center meridian. It paused to cross. On the other side of the street was a tall stone complex with the gatepost indicating a secure facility. Its whole block was enclosed within one metal wall of large diamond-patterned panels. Its green-painted gates were pulled back as their car nosed across lanes of traffic.

There was an interior guardhouse. Orlov's driver got out of the car and had a discussion with the guard inside.

Orlov's driver came to the car's rear doors, opened them, and stood there as Orlov, then Roebeck, got out. She was fumbling in her bag for ID when Orlov said, "No need. Come with me."

He walked her past uniformed guards without incident. He led her under a stone arch, through a side-set door in another stone wall, through an interior checkpoint. They received

Cyrillic-printed entry cards for the facility. "Keep your card at hand," Orlov advised.

Then they were allowed to continue into a broad stone room that seemed part secure facility, part hotel lobby.

Inside a Plexiglas and wooden booth there, a woman waited. Black leather jacketed men stood around talking very low in the cavernous reception area. Bright red leather divans were arranged on a broad granite and marble floor.

Two men sat on a divan. One had a dial phone in his lap. The other was smoking.

Orlov ignored the woman behind the Plexiglas and approached the two men. The three spoke together. Then all of them approached her. "Come," Orlov said. "We go upstairs."

The men in leather jackets didn't follow. She had the distinct impression that they were bodyguards, just looking her over.

A narrow Soviet-era elevator opened to Orlov's demanding jabs at a button. Into one fake wood wall was screwed a metal plaque with color engraving. One side of the plaque depicted a lit cigarette inside a red circle. The circle had a diagonal line through it: the international sign for *no smoking*. The other panel displayed the same diagonally bisected red circle around a bundle of dynamite: *no explosives*.

"What is this place?" Roebeck asked when she'd puzzled out the sign's meaning.

"This is the Gorbachev Foundation Socio-Economic Hotel," Orlov said gravely. "Provided to Mr. Gorbachev in thanks for valuable service. It is only semi State organization. Here we can meet without interruption. Without being overheard. Castro has stayed here. Arafat has stayed here. Very safe for discussions. Has Olympic swimming pool. Three cafes. Very good coffee bar. Only people who have done great service to the State may lodge here. Prominent Russians from out of the town stay here, as a prize or for important Moscow conference."

"Whatever you say. I'm sure it's fine." Roebeck was disappointed. She would see no technology in a hotel.

When the elevator opened on a large meeting area, two

more men awaited. These, also, spoke only to Orlov in Russian, then handed him a key attached to a large wooden ball.

Orlov motioned her to follow. "This way."

Orlov's key opened the door to a suite of high-ceilinged rooms. There, briefing materials and several samples of electronics were laid out on a long table. Four Russians were smoking acrid cigarettes and talking in a corner.

Orlov began introductions immediately. Nan Roebeck needed no prompting to recognize Dr. Nikolai Neat. Her heart sank. The show scientist cum baby-sitter from yesterday was here to make sure nothing interesting happened. And to report back to his masters. If Lipinsky slithered through the door to join the party, Nan resolved to leave.

Neat strode up to her, stared her right in the eye, and spoke in Russian, rapid-fire.

Before she could object that she didn't understand, Orlov translated verbatim.

"Dr. Neat says we meet today under different circumstances. He is here representing solely the interests of certain scientist you see. These scientists are from a *voyenna strategiya*—strategic military—organization. So Dr. Neat says this is a meeting which is not happening. You agree to these terms?"

"Certainly," she said. Whatever was on that table was important to these people. It might not look relevant to her, but at least the precautions seemed real enough.

Orlov turned to Neat: *"Da, da."*

Neat spoke again in Russian.

Orlov rephrased in English: "Dr. Neat says that these scientists are willing to show you the know-how. It is know-how for implanting in a person a device for moving that person from one—" Shaking his head, Orlov broke off. He questioned Neat. Neat responded. Orlov then said to her: "Is medical know-how for moving humans with implants back into the past." He shrugged. "I am just a translator. I am not sure this is technically correct description. But better translators are not trusted for this meeting. Please wait. I will ask more details."

Neat and Orlov began a long exchange.

Nan Roebeck needed the time. An implant technology? To send humans to the past? Could that be correct?

Neat began again to speak. Orlov translated, staying about a phrase behind Neat. "This technology is based on Russian know-how in very small devices and in human bone and tooth replacement material. It also involves very small—microscopic—technology machinery embedded in insulation. This is called silicon-on-insulator. These technologies are joined with special . . ."

Orlov stopped to question Neat again. Then he continued to translate, the English translation staying a few words behind Neat's Russian. Neat watched her closely as he spoke, as if suspecting that she understood every word of his Russian.

"The technologies are joined with special know-how to produce a remodulating—maybe 'transducing'?—system to tune human biostatic—electromagnetic—fields. This implant allows—causes—biological systems to become out of phase with current moment. Implant then allows biological system be moved. Remodulator attracts biological system to place in time where harmony with local fields can be reestablished," Orlov relayed.

It sounded like techno-bullshit to Roebeck. Neat, and then Orlov, stopped talking and waited expectantly. She had to say something.

"Go on," she encouraged. "Nanotechnology—small machines. Attuning biological systems to . . . home tones of epochs. I guess I understand that. Music of the spheres, and all. So tell me what you've got. . . ."

"Please, Madam Roebeck." Orlov held up his hand. "Say to me slower. Simpler. Not so many technical concepts before waiting for translation."

"Right. My apologies. I'm not used to working with a simultaneous translator so talented."

Orlov translated her request—she hoped. Central hadn't given them linguistic implants—most Russians spoke some English; most Americans didn't speak Russian, and the ones that did were assumed to be spies. Right now, she wished Central had decided they could sustain a fiction of not knowing Russian. But wishing didn't make it so.

Neat nodded very gravely.

If this was a joke, the punch line wasn't obvious.

Neat spoke once more in Russian, this time taking Roebeck by the elbow to guide her to the table as he was talking.

Orlov followed behind. "Dr. Neat says that you will see how this is working with animals very soon. Animal must be fairly young. Old animals so far have not had resiliency to accept surgical implant. Bodies must be young to survive implant and . . . initialization . . . process. Remodulation is easier procedure."

"I understand," Roebeck lied.

On the table were a series of Russian briefing charts, a few computer chips, some circuitry. She now recognized a primitive high-powered microscope, a bulky personal computer. One of the men then brought in a cage holding four white mice. He extracted one.

"Mouschka," the man said, stroking the white mouse in his hand.

The white mouse looked no different from the three others left behind in its cage.

The Russian holding the mouse pushed a clock timer much like a chess timer. Then he opened his hand. The mouse stayed docilely on his palm.

Neat spoke.

"Watch the rat," Orlov translated.

A second scientist or technician stepped forward. First he marked the mouse's spine with a red pen. Then he touched a handheld device against the mouse. The mouse disappeared from the first man's open palm.

"Now look at the cage," Orlov told her, once more translating Neat's words.

There were now four mice in the cage. One had a red mark down its spine.

It had to be a parlor trick. Yet the mouse on the first man's palm had never been obscured from her view.

"Do it again," Roebeck ordered, forgetting her manners.

"Nyet, nyet,nyet," Neat refused.

"Don't bother to translate that, Sergey," Roebeck told Orlov. "I know 'no' when I hear it."

Neat spoke again. Orlov translated, "Same rat, that is, mouse cannot do this twice the same. Mouse cannot occupy two places in same space-time at same time."

That explanation, more than anything else, convinced Roebeck that the Russians weren't playing an elaborate joke on her. "Then do it with a different mouse," she demanded.

Orlov translated. All the Russians conferred. Roebeck's head was spinning. How could these primitives *do* this? If they *had* done it.

Neat evaluated her speculatively. *"Roebecka,"* he said, adding a Russian suffix to her name, then jabbering at her in light-speed Russian. She hardly noticed Orlov translating. It seemed to her that Neat himself was speaking in English, so accustomed to the translation procedure had she become.

"We cannot go further until we know how you are involved with Etkin and the KGB. This is very secret technology. Not known to much of our government. Too dangerous for any single government to control. Our government might use this technology against the Russian people if the Politburo's inheritors knew of this. Do you understand?"

"Da, da," Roebeck said. These Russians understood at least some of what was at stake here. "What can I do to help?"

Orlov translated her words, then Neat's response. "Dr. Neat says we must have international commission to regulate use of know-how. We wish you to help arrange this? While protecting principals, of course. Before those you met yesterday do otherwise."

Otherwise?

"Certainly," Roebeck said. She'd do no such thing. But she still couldn't be absolutely sure if those at yesterday's meetings were the revisionists she was seeking. Neat and Orlov might be fingering their own enemies for their own reasons. If this Foreign Ministry clique were really the people who'd sent revisionists to 9AD, they couldn't have done so without

Neat. And Orlov was clearly involved up to his neck. Maybe Orlov was trying to feel her out, make her break cover. Roebeck must be very careful.

She chose her next words slowly, cautiously. Just because these particular Russians were giving her the party line didn't mean they had any interest in an international commission. Their work was still government supported, after all. "When I understand just how this technology works and what you have at risk, we'll discuss options. I have my own credibility to protect, you must realize. I'm sure you're aware how fanciful all this sounds. I must have proof. And we must be truthful with one another. Then I can act."

"Good," Neat said, not waiting for Orlov to translate. The bastard had better English than he'd been pretending. "Then you will tell us about what trouble we may expect from Director Etkin."

"No trouble. We've got a social dinner, at seven tonight." She'd better play the Etkin card herself, or they'd worry she was either stupid or holding back. "I haven't seen anything here worth troubling about. Some artifacts of experimentation with no viable theoretical underpinnings. And nothing's going to happen until I see something more concrete than a disappearing mouse."

A disappearing mouse on a one-way short-distance time trip with no geographical displacement—if that. The demonstration could have been rigged. She was on their turf. They controlled what she saw.

Orlov translated her words, probably to give Neat time to think. Nan was now positive that Neat understood every word she said.

"Yes, yes, yes," Neat agreed. "We will arrange further demonstrations."

"When will that be?" Roebeck asked. "I don't have much time."

Neat laughed as if she'd made a great joke. "Right now, this day. Time is what this know-how is concerning, yes? So, we shall make time obey us. Then you will be convinced."

Do that, old fox, and you bet I'll be convinced.

"I'll want to speak with the scientists—all the principals." Roebeck wondered if she could get Chun over here without causing these Russians to get terminal constipation. Probably not.

"We have arranged all things," said Nikolai Neat. "We will show you much more before your dinner with Etkin, our friend from the Academy of Sciences. You will know everything you must know."

At least these Russians were consistent about distrusting one another. Factions will be factions.

Orlov added, "And since you have invited me to this dinner, perhaps afterward we may continue our work?"

"You bet. We'll get out of the Etkin dinner as early as possible without being impolite. Then I'm all yours. We can work all night long if you wish. I'd cancel the dinner, but it might insult our host."

There were still four mice in a cage in front of her. She went over and lifted the cage to examine it. "To get you money and support for new work, I need to evaluate this research and its value to us. I need to know enough to write a proposal. I need to know where the real work is centered, who's involved. How many people. I need to project a cost estimate for any ongoing joint effort. On the other hand, I can buy existing reports or prototypes out of hand. However, to safeguard any work or contact with us in future, I need to know who else in your government knows about this technology. What use others are making of it. Can you trust me enough to let me help you?"

Without waiting for Orlov's translation, Neat spoke. "We are capable of rectifying small errors in judgment, using this technology. So it is not a matter of trust. It is a matter of mutual interests. We can help you. If we wish."

The bastard was threatening her. And in doing so, he was letting his facade slip. Neat was now sounding exactly like a homegrown revisionist in need of a one-way trip to 50K.

All that remained was to find out how many others were directly involved, where the technology was kept. Once that was done, she could bring the ARC Riders' considerable resources to bear.

This Foreign Ministry clique couldn't be allowed to turn the world into a Russian nightmare of a Fourth Rome, with Dictator for Life Nikolai Neat and his boy Lipinsky running the show.

Above all, one thing bothered Roebeck. In the mouse demonstration, nothing had been said about retrieving the mouse from its past. Of course, a mouse couldn't implement plans or utilize technology. But she'd been shown only the capability for a one-way trip.

She remembered what Grainger had said about technology in Russia. When one group was working on something, the assumption had to be made that others were working independently. So did she have the right group? Was there another, independent effort that was farther along? Or was Neat's group, hungry for dollars, nevertheless unwilling to show the real extent to which they'd developed their technology?

Roebeck needed Chun to evaluate what she'd seen. Now that she had formulated what seemed like an answer to her primary question of who was messing with the timeline from this horizon, secondary questions were popping up like weeds.

The most difficult data to accept was the information about implants. How did the traveler get back? Did the effect wear off, and the person automatically revert to his native space-time after an interval? Not very practical. Was there some way of calibrating and reprogramming the implants on the fly? Did the handheld control all travel parameters?

If the Russian handheld could replace the whole TC in which the ARC Riders had come here, then the base technology had to be from Up The Line. *Had* to be.

There was no other explanation. Such miniaturization of power sources was still impossible in Roebeck's epoch. Nobody in his right mind would take a one-way trip to 9 AD. Or to anywhere else for that matter. So that wasn't a possibility. Therefore, somebody from Up The Line was running a mission in which this timeline was a secondary staging area. And that somebody was going to great pains to have the technology look homegrown.

The science community here flat didn't have the skill to produce a handheld with even the rudimentary capabilities demonstrated by Neat's group. The mouse, which had traveled minutes into the past when touched with that handheld, was proof that the handheld and the implant worked just fine.

Now all she had to find out was who controlled the technology, where it was centered, how many key people were involved, and how to eradicate all knowledge of it from this horizon. For starters.

If the ARC Riders were up against operators from Up The Line, people from the ARC Riders' own future with better equipment and superior knowledge, then they might be in over their heads on this mission. She'd never heard of an ARC mission Up The Line, past the 26th, past Central's locus. She was pretty sure there couldn't be one. Safeguards against that very eventuality had been put in place before the Up The Line folks gave their technology to the savages who comprised the ARC Riders. So if this technology was from farther Up The Line than the ARC Riders could reach, then what?

You heard stories about adult supervision for the ARC Riders coming from Up The Line. Maybe somebody way above Roebeck's pay grade could send a message to those adult supervisors. But more help than that probably wasn't going to be forthcoming from beyond the 26th century. Whatever this furball was made up of in this century, Nan Roebeck's team of ARC Riders was going to have to spit it out on their own.

The more she thought about it, the surer she became that Central wasn't going to be able to do much for them. But that didn't mean she wasn't required to seek additional guidance in such an unusual situation. Damn quick, too.

Roebeck resolved to get back to the TC as soon as she could and take Chun with her. Maybe Chun could get some guidance from Central's download. Maybe they all ought to displace out of here, get some new orders, and then come back. They could reenter this horizon mere minutes, even seconds after they'd left it, if that kind of risk was warranted.

Maybe Chun and Grainger had done better than she. Maybe the other ARC Riders knew for certain by now just where, what, and who they needed to strike.

Too many "maybes."

Grainger had warned her that Russia was like dogs fighting under a blanket. Well, now Nan Roebeck was under the blanket, too, and she couldn't tell one Russian dog from another in the dark.

Three Kilometers East of the Hase River, Free Germany

A Roman soldier lay dead beside Rebecca Carnes with a javelin projecting from his armpit. It was a crude weapon, four feet long and made entirely of wood. The tip was shaved to a point and seared to brittle hardness.

It did the job, though. The legionary had lurched some distance before he collapsed, but the best surgeons of this day couldn't have repaired the artery that splinters had perforated. The man had died alone in the brush, unnoticed by friend or foe.

The thunder was almost continuous. Rebecca staggered from a gust so fierce that the rain it hurled in her face might almost have been hail. The horse she led shied. She didn't let go of the reins, so the beast dragged her off her feet. She slid on her hip for a moment, her head butting that of the desperate horse as she tried to rise.

The team had been trying to avoid the battle ever since the morning of the previous day. The Roman column had fragmented when the Germans attacked. Lines of wagons blocked the narrow roadway, separating units of troops and forcing them to act independently.

Some had continued forward, some held in place; many

had attempted to retreat. The nearby corpse had probably been one of those who'd counterattacked, charging into the trees that made Roman close-order tactics impossible. Light-armed Germans faded into the forest. Hidden warriors flung javelins into a pursuer's back or thrust iron-pointed stabbing spears from the cover of the dense undergrowth.

The marching column, miles long when Varus broke camp, had spread into an amorphous blob that thrashed and died in the Teutoburg Forest. The team had to get clear of the battle before they could safely leave the depths of the forest and head for the Rhine. Despite Gerd's skill and equipment, that was proving extremely difficult.

They'd lost one of the horses the previous night. Even hobbled the mare had managed to break her tie rope and flee farther than the team could search when they realized she was gone. Rebecca had lived through seven Asian monsoons and had been in a Tennessee trailer park while a tornado ripped it. She didn't remember ever seeing worse weather.

Lightning ripped the whole sky. Gerd Barthuli sat cross-legged beside a huge basswood tree. You couldn't say he was sheltering there because the wind came from too many directions. The air above his sensor pack spluttered with light like the corona discharge around a high-voltage switch.

Gerd's display depended on coherent light projected from two sources to interact precisely, forming a hologram. Raindrops and even blown spray interfered with the light beams, blurring their meaning. Rebecca didn't know how the analyst could use the device; but he said he could, and there wasn't any choice.

She'd briefly shielded the display with an ARC sleeping bag: a sock of impervious, microns-thin fabric that transferred heat in either direction to hold a constant temperature. The wind was too strong and variable. She and Pauli together might have held it, but they'd have lost the remaining horses if they tried.

The rain would interfere with the microwave pistols as sure as it did Gerd's holograms. The submachine gun holstered on her belt was a cold weight and no comfort. Beckie Carnes was no willing killer.

But the forest was full of killers tonight.

Pauli Weigand stood like a tree himself. His left arm was around his gelding's neck. He murmured to the animal as he turned, viewing each quadrant of the team's surroundings as he waited.

There wasn't much to see. They'd had to avoid the roadway. Sight distances within the old-growth forest were a matter of feet or inches. The storm didn't make things significantly worse.

Rebecca's horse stopped fighting her for the moment. It stood with its legs spread and head bowed, shivering violently. She didn't know if it was cold or just afraid. She patted its neck and said something pointlessly reassuring, the sort of thing she'd said often enough to a boy on a stretcher with guts poking out of his torn abdomen.

Pauli's wet mail gleamed in each flash. The steel links would be a good ground. Rebecca wondered what would happen if a bolt hit him.

If lightning killed Pauli Weigand . . .

If lightning killed Team Leader Weigand, Riders Carnes and Barthuli would make their way to Xanten, neutralize the two revisionists remaining, and wait for pickup by TC 779.

Unless Rebecca was standing close enough that the stroke killed her also, instead of just killing the part of her that would die with Pauli.

He saw her looking at him and smiled. His faceshield was transparent from the outside, but rain streaked its slick surface.

Gerd stood up with care born of stiff muscles and the slick leaves underfoot. "I believe we can cross now," Gerd said via their headbands, safer than trying to talk over the storm. "There isn't a way around the fighting for farther than I can view, even extrapolating beyond the sensors' real range."

"Then we go through," said Pauli. "Just give me a vector. I'll lead from here on."

Rebecca saw the analyst's nose wrinkle, though the *tsk* his tongue made against the roof of his mouth didn't transmit. "I may wander off occasionally, Pauli," he said, "but I hope I can usually be trusted to carry out my duties when I'm present. I will continue to lead."

Gerd set off through the brush, holding the sensor pack in front of him in both hands. Pauli slid his left hand down to the reins and followed. He held his pistol in the other hand, ready to act if a band of howling Germans came out of the night onto them. He didn't like putting the analyst in front when they knew there were warriors nearby, but Gerd was right: the sensors should be in the lead.

"Come on, horse," Rebecca said to her shivering animal. She stroked its neck. "I know, none of this was your idea, but life isn't fair."

Four Kilometers West of the Hase River, Free Germany

Twenty meters to the right, Pauli Weigand saw a score of Roman soldiers and civilians stand circled, trying to defend themselves against hundreds of capering Germans. This part of the forest was sandy bog. The trees were cypress, spaced more widely than the oaks and larches of firmer ground, and the undergrowth grew only waist high. Rain and darkness hid the team from the fighters, but it was still closer contact than Pauli would have chosen.

Thermal vision gave Pauli a good view of the fighting; he could have done without that also.

Most of the Romans had shields: thick, leather-covered ovals of cross-laminated birch. They knelt so that the curved bottom edge could rest on the ground. Two male civilians, wagon drivers by the broad leather hats both wore, huddled behind military shields they'd picked up.

The only woman among the defenders had a dazed expression and a short German spear whose tip was bloody. The merchant beside her held a small brass-faced buckler in his left hand and a leaf-shaped sword of Greek pattern in his right. He looked as if he knew how to use his weapons and the legionaries certainly knew how to use theirs; but it wasn't going to matter, and everybody knew that also.

The defensive circle had contracted as victims fell. A dozen

Roman bodies lay outside it, sinking noticeably into the wet soil. There were two Germans as well. More warriors lay against tree roots where their fellows had dragged them wounded or dead.

A dozen Germans charged, shouting and waving spears. They were commoners. None had a sword, body armor, or a metal helmet, though a few wore cone-shaped leather caps that would be some protection against a blow from above. Their round bucklers were made of wicker covered with cowhide worn hair side out to give each shield a distinctive pattern. Most of them were barefoot and bare-chested, their only garments breechclouts and sometimes a short fur cape.

Legionaries rose, lifting their heavy shields with difficulty from the ground. Two days of driving rain had soaked the wood and leather, doubling the shields' weight and making them hard to move, much less handle in combat.

The Germans fenced, staying just out of contact. Mud squished between their toes. The Romans held their places.

Several warriors stepped back, butted their stabbing spears in the ground, and began throwing the all-wood javelins they carried in sets of three or four in their shield hands. Even at such short range the darts couldn't penetrate Roman shields, but one stuck a legionary beneath his helmet's cheekpiece.

Bawling with pain and frustration, the Roman lurched forward. The missile flopped from his face. He thrust his own long javelin into a warrior's shield.

The German hopped nimbly away. Other warriors attacked the legionary from both sides. A spear pierced the Roman's thigh. He shouted and staggered back, dropping his javelin.

Two legionaries stepped out to cover him. One chopped overhand at a German who didn't dodge swiftly enough to avoid a shearing scalp wound. It bled like a waterfall. The Roman shouted in fierce joy and sloshed forward to finish the job. A javelin from the other side of the circle caught him in the neck. He pitched forward on his face.

The legionary with the leg wound stumbled. A warrior thrust the third of the advanced Romans through the face because the victim couldn't shift his waterlogged shield in time to block the spear. Germans surged through the gap in the circle before the tired defenders could back closer together for mutual support.

Romans turned to meet the warriors leaping onto them from behind, but fatigue and their heavy equipment slowed them. Warriors rushed the defenders from all sides. The Germans' own numbers worked against them for a moment, but only a moment.

The merchant broke free of the crush. His intestines dragged behind him in coils. He took three steps forward and fell. A warrior bellowed in guttural triumph, brandishing a bloody Roman sword in one hand and the woman's head in the other.

Pauli Weigand followed Gerd through the muck, drawing his horse along behind him. The smell of blood terrified the animal. A hell of a trait in a warhorse. The cavalry troop leader who'd sold Pauli the mount wouldn't be spending the money he'd bilked from the emperor's envoy, though.

Gerd pushed into a clump of willows that would screen the ARC Riders from the nearby Germans. Pauli felt the hair on the back of his neck prickle. Lightning struck a cypress a dozen meters to the team's left, knocking all of them off their feet. The thunderclap lifted waves from the brilliantly lighted puddles, but the shock—mental and electrical—was so great that Pauli didn't hear the sound.

He struggled to his feet. The horse had stumbled also; by the time it was up, Pauli had both arms around the beast's neck to prevent it from bolting. Beckie's horse charged blindly into the haunches of Pauli's, staggering both animals long enough for the ARC Riders to regain control.

The top of the cypress burned briefly. The flames decayed from sulphurous yellow through red to blackness, leaving the air sharp with the smell of smoke and ozone. A strip of bark three fingers wide had peeled from the peak to the ground. Willows near the base of the big tree were withered, and a branch broken by the flash now twisted loose in the wind.

The Germans turned from where they were looting the bodies of those they'd slaughtered moments before. The sky god's finger had pointed directly at the three ARC Riders.

"Pick up Gerd and ride!" Pauli shouted to Beckie Carnes. She might have argued, but the practical aspect was obvious: the team leader was much heavier than either of the other two, and the horses were little more than ponies. Beckie dragged herself into the military saddle, cursing the rain-soaked leather and the lack of stirrups.

Screaming like furies, hundreds of warriors charged their fresh prey.

Pauli aimed over the gelding's withers and swept his microwave pistol across the Germans. The pulses atomized raindrops. Fog filled the air between muzzle and target. Beyond the gray wall a few warriors fell, but the rain absorbed most of the weapon's output. Steam crackled from the pistol's receiver as droplets hit plastic heated by continuous use.

Pauli tried to mount with the pistol in one hand. The horse shied. Shouting in frustration, Pauli thrust the weapon under his sword belt and prayed it'd stay there. Using brute strength and a roll of skin gripped from the screaming animal's barrel, the ARC Rider hauled himself aboard. In a battle, they don't give points for gracefulness.

The sudden fog stopped the German rush for a moment. The leaders hurled javelins. Somebody'd picked up a heavy Roman missile that might have penetrated, but only a native weapon hit Pauli. The wooden point shattered on his mail coat.

He let his horse follow its head for a moment as he turned and tried his pistol on the Germans. A few more tumbled; the central wooden boss of a shield shattered like a gunshot. The main result was a gush of fog to replace what was dissipating. Some of the shouts were fearful.

Pauli kicked his mount forward. The horse with Gerd and Beckie astride splashed on just ahead of him.

Pauli didn't know whether his teammates were riding in a direction Gerd had chosen or just *away,* clearly a good choice with warriors whooping behind for another orgy of slaughter. He waved his gun blindly to the rear, holding the trigger down. Continuous operation wasn't supposed to overstress the mechanism, though he wasn't sure Central's technical staff had tested the weapon with rain spattering the hot receiver.

The microwave pistol operated with no sound or flash to betray its use. Normally that was an advantage. An ARC Rider could drop an opponent in his tracks without warning those nearby that anything had occurred.

Right now the lack of spectacular effects might get the team killed. There were too many Germans to fight even if conditions hadn't seriously degraded the pistol's performance. A huge flash and bang might have frightened the warband into searching for safer prey. Warriors with their blood up simply didn't notice when a few of their neighbors fell down silently.

The revisionist submachine gun was in one of the satchels balanced across his horse's withers. It was even more useless than the ARC pistols. The silencer throttled the weapon's flash and muzzle blast, and the light bullets didn't have nearly the authority of a microwave pulse. An adrenaline-charged warrior would ignore a body shot, though he might bleed to death internally five or ten minutes later.

The lead horse trampled through a screen of ferns. Pauli's mount was nose to tail. Beckie shouted. They'd ridden into a cleared strip.

In preparation for the ambush, Hermann and his allies had built ramparts of logs and earth along the expected Roman line of march. The team had blundered into this one from the rear, where the Germans had camped and waited.

High-stoked bonfires lit the scene. The flames overwhelmed rain that tried to quench them. A band of Germans, many of them nobles whose horses were tethered nearby, busied themselves with prisoners they'd taken during the fighting.

"Ride on!" Pauli said.

"To the left!" Gerd directed, swaying as he tried to stay on the saddle. Beckie tugged her reins with one hand and gripped the analyst's waist with the other.

The Germans had overrun part of Varus' train. Lawyers traveling with the governor had been stripped and tied to frames of bent saplings. Slaves and servants were roped together nearby, weeping and terrified but not under immediate threat from their captors.

Pauli kicked his mount to better speed in the clearing. He saw Silius Gallus, the lawyer who'd been speaking the day the team arrived in Aliso. The Germans Gallus had milked dry through his advocacy encircled him now.

The lawyer's lips were sewn shut with a thong. Blood seeped from the corners of his mouth. One of the Germans waggled Gallus' ripped-out tongue in his face.

A warrior stepped in front of the ARC Riders and shouted at them to halt. Beckie's horse shied. Neither she nor Gerd had a hand free to use their pistols. Pauli shot past his horse's neck. He rode over the German fallen in a gush of fog.

More Germans sprinted toward the team. Pauli dropped a pair only a few meters from his mount's flank. Mud from the hooves of the leading animal splashed back at him. In this rear area most of the warriors had butted their spears in the mud and leaned their shields against them in miniature A-frames.

A noble wearing checked woolen trousers and a Roman mail coat ran for his horse instead. Others followed, shouting to one another. Half the Germans present had at least some piece of Roman equipment. Several were dressed in complete legionary garb with the exception of the waterlogged shield.

Beckie guided her horse into the unbroken forest. They crossed a game trail. A branch slapped Pauli's forehead even though he'd tried to duck away from it. The pull-down faceshield smeared away from his left eye. He slid the headband back in place with the thumb of his gunhand.

The ARC Riders' mounts were tired and overburdened; the German nobles were better horsemen besides. The team was going to be ridden down with absolute certainty, even if they managed not to blunder into another of the scattered warbands.

The analyst was looking for a route clear even as he and Beckie staggered through the forest. Specks of light twinkled in the air over the horse's neck: raindrops scattering the scanner pack's display.

Pauli risked a glance over his shoulder. The leading German was barely a horse's length behind, riding with the reins in his teeth as he guided his mount with his knees. The German carried a lance more than three meters long and an oblong shield with a prominent boss. The shield's face was painted with star bursts and red crescents; glittering brass studs circled the rim.

When Pauli turned, the German noble snarled around his reins and thrust with his lance. The steel point quivered a handsbreadth from Pauli's ribs. He swept the pistol around more like a man swatting a fly than a marksman.

The German's shield was made of boards dovetailed together and braced across the back. The pulse hammered them apart with a loud *whack!* The German's horse shied, startled by the report next to his left ear. He brushed a fir tree and rubbed the rider off his back for all the German's skill. The lance stuck an overhanging branch and broke.

Undergrowth twenty meters to the rear thrashed. A pair of horsemen, one mounted on a striking gray, were following fast. There'd been scores of horsemen in the band torturing the lawyers; they were probably in pursuit.

The rain had paused. Now it returned with a roar like an aircraft passing low over the forest. The upper foliage caught the drops for a few moments, but the downpour was delayed from ground level, not stopped. When it began in earnest, German lances would have greater effective range than the team's pistols.

Pauli's mount shouldered a tree hard enough to stagger himself. Pauli caught a handful of mane. The horse was going to collapse within a few minutes—if the pursuers didn't overwhelm the team down before then.

He thought about the way his pulse blew apart a German's shield. He couldn't count on that again with the rain picking up, but if he unscrewed the Skorpion's silencer—

No. The weapon's muzzle blast still wouldn't be enough to spook the Germans' horses. The light cartridge, intended for a pocket pistol, didn't have enough authority to impress anybody. Certainly not in the midst of a storm like this.

The hologram display silhouetted Gerd and Beckie with a ghostly nimbus. Their horse was struggling, too.

"Gerd, can you throw a bar of light ten or twenty meters behind us?" Pauli asked, speaking even as the thought formed. "It doesn't have to be bright, just visible."

"Yes," the analyst said. Gerd would talk your ear off in a background briefing, but he never got in the way in a crisis.

"Beckie, we'll dismount and use the submachine guns," Pauli said. He transferred the microwave pistol to his left hand with the reins and rummaged in the right satchel for the Skorpion. The spare magazines were on the other side. They could wait. "When the Germans touch the light, not before. And aim for the horses. The horses'll notice the pain."

"Yes," Beckie said tersely. A moment later, "I'm ready, Pauli."

He knew that shooting horses would bother her even more than killing the riders, but there wasn't any choice. The sting of a light bullet wouldn't even slow a warrior seething with blood lust. Horses were herbivores whose reflex was to run from danger. They could be trained to obey human commands, but a jab of unexpected pain penetrated to the instinctive level.

It wasn't fair to the horses, but the majority of the civilians with Varus were suffering for no better reason. Hard times had hard remedies.

The rain came down in full blinding earnest. If the team's mounts had been in better shape, Pauli'd have tried to escape pursuit in the darkness. Wind twisted branches already strained by the weight of rain-soaked needles. They hurtled down as widowmakers.

"Gerd, start the light close and advance it if it works," Pauli said. "Now!"

He reined his horse to a halt. The animal wobbled, almost falling as its rider's weight came off.

Pauli stood, the Skorpion in his right hand and the microwave pistol in his left. The leading German yipped and raised his long-bladed sword as he came on.

A wedge rather than a band of pale canary light filled the air. Trees, leaves—Pauli's own poised body—cut sharp-edged shadows from the ambience. The sensor pack's output was only a few candlepower, but it had a shocking presence in the storm-wracked gloom.

The gray horse drove into the lighted air. The Skorpion stuttered in Pauli's hand as he shot the beast in the nose. It reared, screaming. The startled rider came off its back.

The second German swerved clear of the leader's mount, turning his horse's head broadside to the ARC Rider. Pauli gave it a short burst. The horse corkscrewed in pain. The German sawed his reins. He was wearing a mail coat. Pauli chanced a pulse with the microwave pistol. Fog bloomed in a spreading cone, but the rider pitched over his horse's neck.

Another horse twisted and bucked before Pauli could get his own weapon on. Germans were spreading to either side of the leaders, crashing through undergrowth to avoid the sudden pileup. One of them threw a lance as if it were a javelin. He must have been aiming at the glow itself. The missile didn't come anywhere close to the ARC Riders.

Gerd walked calmly up behind Pauli. He held the scanner pack over his head to maximize the volume of coverage. The lighted area became a hemisphere rather than a wedge. The color segued to pale red.

Pauli shot another horse. It skidded forward on its nose and knees, killed instantly by a lucky round through the eye. Lucky for the animal, at least; and luckier than the lawyers back in the German camp had been.

Pauli stunned the sprawling rider with the microwave pistol. Mud sprayed in a circle as the German's head reflected the point-blank pulse.

A riderless horse ran past, white sweat on its breast and its bulging eyes reflecting the glow. Pauli jumped aside. Gerd touched his pistol to the horse's skull and knocked the beast down in the mud with its legs thrashing.

Pauli tried to open the satchel where the ammo was packed without putting down the microwave pistol. His horse stood trembling, too tired or too terrified to bolt.

A German with bull horns riveted to his helmet rode forward, slashing at the light itself and shouting, "Wotan! Wotan!"

Before Pauli could aim the gutshot horse crawfished, fell, and rose in a spray of blood and water. Pauli, Gerd, and Beckie Carnes all fired. The horse collapsed again on its stunned rider. The fog of atomized rain made the glow richer and more angry.

Gerd manipulated the pack's controls with two fingers while holding his pistol. The glowing hemisphere expanded, engulfing more of the forest. The diffused light was scarcely a shimmer but it sent Germans bellowing away in terror.

They weren't afraid to die, these warriors, but they were terrified of the unknown. The team couldn't have defeated them, but harmless light provided a symbol for the Germans to fear.

Gerd lowered his sensor pack. The glow vanished.

"Oh, God," Beckie said. She stared at the submachine gun in her hand. The bolt was locked back, meaning the weapon had fired the last round in its magazine.

"There're some riderless horses nearby," said Gerd Barthuli. "I wonder if we can catch them to supplement our own."

"That's a good idea," Pauli said in a dull voice.

A horse nearby gurgled as it tried to rise. Bloody froth gurgled from its nostrils. Pauli walked to it and put a mercy shot into the back of its big skull.

He wondered what mercy there would be for a man who'd done this to innocent animals.

Moscow, Russia

March 10, 1992

Grainger had ditched Matsak as soon as they got back to Moscow. He'd worked all night and all day long with Zotov's team in Obninsk, getting every bit of information possible. Then he got Matsak to drive him back to the city as fast as he could, but by then night was already falling.

The rest of the ARC team wasn't in the Metropole. What Grainger had to say couldn't wait. When he finally found the private club where Etkin was hosting the ARC Rider women and Orlov, the club bouncer wouldn't let him in the door.

He considered using a tranquilizer dart to subdue the muscular doorman. Then he thought about shooting the doorman with his issue acoustic pistol and stepping over the body. But there were clearly more big boys inside.

Finally he stood on the sidewalk cursing and arguing loudly in English. Eventually, he'd made enough fuss that an English speaker poked a head out the door of this sanctum of the *nomenclatura*.

He bawled for Roebeck and Chun as loud as he could, invoking American Embassy privilege that he didn't have. If his luck was bad, some Embassy honcho was a guest inside and his cover would be summarily blown.

But it wasn't an angry US official who came down the stairs. It was Roebeck, Chun right behind her.

The ARC Riders' team leader didn't look pleased with him. "What *is* your problem, Tim? What kind of Embassy crisis could provoke this level of urgency?" What she meant was, *Make this look good, sucker.*

He said, still playing up his agitation, "I need to talk to both of you, alone."

As they came down the steps and huddled with him on the pavement near the riverbank, Chun scolded him, "Pull yourself together, cowboy. Your behavior is despicable. You, too, Nan, with all due respect. I'm making good progress with Etkin and the scalars—"

Both Roebeck and Grainger spoke at once:

"I found the technology," Grainger murmured urgently. "It's in Obninsk. Some of it's from Up The Line. We've got to get back to the TC."

"I've found the technology *and* the revisionists!" Roebeck exclaimed sotto voce. "It's the Foreign Ministry crowd. Lipinsky. Neat. Orlov led me straight to them. We need to consult the database, maybe Central direct."

Chun looked from one to the other. "Impossible," she said. "You can't both have found it."

Grainger was so pumped that he glared. "The boss is mistaken. I saw enough to scare the hell out of me."

Roebeck's eyebrows raised. "Oh, really? I'm mistaken? I agree with you about one point, Tim. This involves technology, maybe people, from Up The Line somehow. I found an implant—"

"Ssh! Be quiet," Chun pleaded. "Here comes Etkin. That means Orlov's alone inside. This is just great, guys. We're blowing this . . . Uh, Viktor Ivanovitch, you know our prodigal son, Tim Grainger."

Grainger had no choice but to shake hands with Etkin and smile.

"Dr. Grainger, we had not expected you. We thought you were detained on business." Etkin was cool, in control.

Okay, you bastard. So I'll apologize. "Yes, I'm sorry I was late. And if I'm too late, I'll leave. I just needed to speak to my team leader for a minute. Please, don't disturb yourselves . . ." He was backing away from Etkin. This was going too wrong, too fast.

Etkin said, "Our hospitality is boundless. But we mustn't leave Special Assistant Orlov alone too long. Special assistants have been known to become very worried when left suddenly sitting alone at tables in this club. Please, come inside with us. Eat. Drink. Enjoy our Russian form of entertainment."

One more endless meeting with strange food and constrained conversation. "No, no. *Spacebo,* but *nyet.*" Grainger refused outright. "I just needed some operating instructions. They're expecting me back at the Embassy."

"Surely not," Etkin purred, having caught Grainger in a far-fetched statement that might be verifiable. "We will call your Embassy and make your excuses for you . . ."

Grainger had known better than to try that. Caught, he smiled sheepishly at Etkin. Then he raised his hands to his chest, palms out, in the international sign for surrender. "I give up. I'm yours."

"It won't be necessary to bother the Embassy." Nan threw Grainger a lethal glare. "Tim can make time to join us for this important meeting, now that he's broken away. You know how bureaucracies can take up your time with useless paperwork. You got all your work done, didn't you, Tim?"

"Yes, sir," he said. "Ma'am." He corrected the gender, realizing that Etkin probably knew that "sir" wasn't gender-free in the 1990s.

And in they went. Up dark stairs into a tiny reception area hung with photos of famous visiting foreigners and infamous rulers of the Soviet state, all smiling in public-affairs-office style.

Once seated next to Orlov at their table, Grainger started sweating almost immediately. It was hot, that was all, he decided. And he hadn't expected scantily clad female contortionists doing splits on people's dinner tables. Orlov was introduced to him. The young Russian was frosted from having been left alone. Grainger was having trouble concentrating on the conversation. Fire-eaters, magicians, long-legged girls in strings and pasties . . .

He realized dimly that he was probably having an honest-to-God physical reaction from the combination of shots, radiation, weird food, no sleep, nicotine, alcohol, and excitement. If he'd been able to pull up his comm membrane, he could have dialed himself a physio check and some bio stabilizers. As it was, he had to sit there making insipid noises while the clock was ticking.

He never should have come here. He'd promised Matsak he wouldn't come. But he'd made a command decision that briefing the boss overrode everything else. Now he hadn't accomplished his mission. Worse, he was on display to anybody here who might know Matsak or Matsak's cronies.

If this stunt lost him his access to Obninsk, the alternatives were going to be much harder on everyone.

Etkin was watching him surreptitiously. Grainger caught his eye. The KGB officer leaned over his plate of borscht and smiled fraternally, showing perfect white teeth. "You are not enjoying yourself, Dr. Grainger? You are ill?"

"No—that is, yeah. Too much celebrating." He realized that his upper lip was beaded with sweat. Perspiration was running down his jaw, his neck. It wasn't going to do his comm membrane much good to get soaked. Suddenly Grainger's stomach started to feel as if it was about to heave its contents onto the table, whether he liked it or not. He took deep breaths. He said to Etkin, still watching him, "I think I'm going to spill my guts. Here or in the loo. Your choice." Then he pushed his chair back and put his head between his knees, trying every technique he knew to stave off a wave of dizziness.

He felt a hand under his armpit, an arm around his shoulders. "Come. Come this way. Quickly." Etkin half lifted Grainger from his chair, nearly dragging him toward the men's room.

They reached it just in time. When Grainger stopped retching and got to his feet, Etkin was waiting, watching.

The KGB officer handed Grainger a wet linen towel.

Grainger wiped his face, then scrubbed his mouth. "That's better." He lifted the knob on top of the Russian toilet to flush it. "Sorry. Too much exotic food, I guess."

"We will take you back to your hotel." The handsome KGB agent seemed genuinely concerned. "You should rest. Perhaps we have all had enough of the celebration this evening." Etkin's cultured voice echoed from irregularly set bathroom tile.

Great. Now he'd blown off Chun's meeting. Worse, he'd been so sick that he'd forgotten all about his gearbag, left unguarded under the table. Momentarily he panicked. He wasn't even sure where they'd been sitting or how to get back there on his own.

"Thanks for understanding, Professor Etkin," Grainger told the KGB man sheepishly. "I'm sorry to have ruined everyone's evening."

"*Nyet problema.* It is nothing. Tomorrow, we will begin anew with your friends. And perhaps without our Assistant Secretary's assistance." There was something about Etkin, standing there without even wrinkling his nose in a Russian men's room still smelling of vomit, that felt wrong to Grainger.

But help was where you found it. The Academy of Sciences cum KGB honcho helped him solicitously back to their table, where Etkin pulled the plug on the evening's celebration.

Nan Roebeck had found Grainger's unattended gearbag and set it ostentatiously on the tabletop. Terrific. He was really going to catch hell from Roebeck for this stunt.

Grainger was still feeling sick enough that he didn't argue when Etkin summoned one of the big beefy boys to escort him to Etkin's car to wait for the others. He just grabbed his gearbag from the table without a word to Roebeck and left. Sitting there in the black Zil limousine, he watched as his team and their Russian dinner partners came out.

Etkin and Orlov circled each other on the steps. Seeing them together that way was like watching a film of two claymation dinosaurs getting ready for a fight to the death. Body language never lied the way mouths did. Nan Roebeck's body language was telling Grainger loud and clear that he was in big trouble for blowing off their evening meeting like this.

He really had been sick. Although now, with an empty stomach, he was beginning to think he might live.

Orlov waved good-bye and went to a government-issue Lada that had pulled up behind the Zil.

Etkin and the women got in the limo. Etkin sat beside Grainger. The women took the rear-facing seats. The big car pulled away.

He heard the others chatting about the schedule of events for the next day. His head still ached. The car sped through city streets without regard to traffic regulations.

Nan asked him how he felt as the limo pulled up to the Metropole.

"I'll be okay." His voice was hoarse. "Just need some sleep."

"For somebody with green skin and purple lips, you don't look too bad. Maybe not trying to set the Moscow record for vodka drunk in one day by a foreign guest would be a good idea in future," she advised icily. Etkin looked away, out the window at the brightly lit hotel entrance.

When they got out of the limo, Etkin followed. He kissed Chun gallantly on both cheeks. "Tomorrow, then. Not so early, because of your friend. Say, ten o'clock, here. We will have preparations in order for your fruitful visit."

Chun promised Etkin that everybody would be shipshape. The KGB man shook hands with Roebeck and Grainger before he got back in his limo and it pulled away.

Grainger went straight to the front desk in the hotel lobby to collect his room key. The night girl handed him the key and a small package in a glazed tan envelope. He took the package. It had only his name on it, no return address. He hadn't been expecting anything. He'd open it in his room, where he could check to see it wasn't a letter bomb. Something hard and flat, about the length of his index finger and twice as deep, was inside.

Roebeck stepped in front of him as he turned and shoved him backward with a spread hand. "No. Don't go upstairs. Not yet. Can you make it to the TC, mister shrinking violet?"

"I guess," he said. "It's not like I'm gutshot or anything." He hitched his gearbag up on his shoulder. She was the boss.

He'd screwed up. It was going to be a rough haul for the next few hours.

They couldn't get into the TC through the Kremlin this late at night. They had to go down to the river and find the bolt-hole entrance. It took a lot out of him, but that was what Roebeck had in mind. Once they'd scrambled down the bank and into the tunnel behind some brush, he began really feeling the strain. Climbing around through underground tunnels was a fitting climax to his day. At least he was now free to pull his field-issue membrane over his face, use his pharmakit, and generally get his blood chemistries together.

By the time they'd reached the catacomb where they'd stashed the TC, they'd rubbed the worst of their rough edges smooth. The other ARC Riders had let him off the hook pretty easy. They were a team, after all, and no team benefits from dysfunctional members. But Roebeck ordered them to discuss no specifics en route, not about their recon, not even results of their fact-finding efforts.

They had lots of data to exchange, lots of ground to cover, no time for regrets. The boss had something up her sleeve.

Waiting for the TC to phase into view, Roebeck spoke through the com: "As soon as we get inside, Chun, get us out of here."

"Nan," Grainger began. "I want to explain what I—"

"No discussion of anything salient, I'm telling you, we can't assume that there's no technology here capable of monitoring or tracking us." The boss was really tense. She reiterated her standing orders, despite the arguably secure environment instituted when each ARC Rider was wearing an ARC-issue multi-function command, control, and communications membrane.

"Just come on back, TC," he heard her mutter.

She was counting the seconds aloud, waiting for TC 779 to reappear. It almost seemed as if she was worried it wouldn't show up.

But that couldn't be.

As the shimmer and shiver of air preceded the temporal capsule into being, Grainger could have sworn he heard Roebeck mutter, "Thank the stars."

Whatever she'd found, or thought she'd found, had really scared her. When she found out what Grainger had seen and learned, she was going to be even more scared.

"In, in. Let's go! Move," Roebeck ordered, sprinting for the capsule as its hatch cracked open.

Grainger was right behind her, running for the TC with Chun as if for salvation.

As soon as they were buttoned-up in the TC, he remembered the package. Around him, the TC hummed comfortingly, all power and protection. Outside, in the immediate vicinity of TC 779's outer hull, time was effectively stopped in its passage.

Inside, Chun was tapping her wands furiously, mining Central's download. The bow screen was quadranted. Three quarters of the wraparound view screen was filled with streaming data. One quarter displayed the time-locked catacombs around them.

Roebeck was pecking out information requests as fast as she could. "Got to get some relevant data," she said tersely. "Not this useless crap."

Grainger scanned the Russian envelope with his handheld. No explosives. Some composite. Some metal. Okay. He opened the package. It was from Zotov. There was no note, but a copy of Zotov's visit card was taped to a small, flat box with wire tabs for closures.

In the box were two chips, and a bit of metal in a clear housing too small to hold anything but nanotechnology.

"What the hell is this?" Grainger wondered out loud.

Roebeck said, "Let me see."

The team leader was silent too long after he handed her the box and she examined its contents. Roebeck turned the box cover and studied the card taped to it. "Zotov? Who's Zotov?" she finally asked.

"Obninsk scientist. When you're ready, maybe I'd better give you a whole after-action report, not bits and pieces."

"We don't have time for after-action reports. What we need is a hot wash."

You did a hot wash every time the work you'd done in the field went wrong.

"How come?" he asked.

"Because I know what this stuff of Zotov's is. It's an implant. Up The Line technology modified for Russian production," Roebeck said tightly. "Except *I* saw implants like this with Orlov, through the Foreign Ministry. It's supposed to be the work of Academican Nikolai Neat."

"A Russian invention? Nanotech?" Chun scoffed. "Everything Russians do is twice the size it needs to be, even for this time horizon. Etkin says—"

Roebeck shook her head despairingly. "I know what I saw. Let's leave the issue of how they did it, for the moment. Concentrate on what they can do. The implants are put into living tissue in order to transport mammals certainly, people by implication, through time without needing temporal capsules. But you have to do the implanting when the animal, or person, is young. Give the biological system time to accept the implant. Get it? Then all you need is a handheld, and they've got that, too."

Chun objected, "Just a handheld? That's impossible. What's the power source?"

Grainger said softly, "Implants weren't any part of what Zotov showed me in Obninsk." Then he stopped. Maybe Zotov had shown him pieces of a puzzle. Maybe these were more pieces. Puzzles were very Russian. On the tape that Grainger had seen, three *young* people were being abducted by the occupants of a TC from Up The Line. "On the other hand, maybe it's all connected."

"What's connected?" Chun wanted to know.

Neither Roebeck nor Grainger answered Chun's question. They were looking at each other.

Maybe Zotov had been trying to warn him. Zotov leaving hardware at Grainger's hotel like that was a clear signal that the Obninski academician believed he had to transmit this information through unofficial channels, or not at all.

Roebeck said, "Chun, we're out of here. Back to base. Forget the static download. Central obviously didn't anticipate the kind of data we're going to need now. I want the highest- level meeting you can get me as soon as we reach Central. Tell them we've run into proliferating Up The Line technology from beyond the 26th. Tell them we need better data, and we need it *now.* Whether or not we get any utilizable support from the ARC, I want to be out of Central and back in Moscow within six hours elapsed time from . . . now."

For a moment, Nan Roebeck's team literally stopped breathing.

What was the team leader saying?

Then Chun said, "Yes, sir," and her wands flew so fast they blurred.

Grainger was stunned at first. Then he understood. Roebeck didn't want to spend enough real time at Central to get bogged down in red tape. Or to get pulled off the mission entirely.

"Before the wheels start coming off Central's cover story for this mission, I want to be back in Moscow, March 11, 1992. Nine hundred hours sharp. Same coordinates."

Chun said, "Nan?"

"Do it, Chun. You'll understand after we've been through the hot wash. Get off this horizon. Hold us out of phase until we're up to speed internally. Take all the TC's running log systems off-line while we're talking, as well. Backtrack them ten elapsed minutes from my hack." She paused. She hacked the time. Then she added softly, "Ain't no telling just how nasty this mission's going to get."

"God, you two. You're scaring me," Chun said. Her wands had fallen silent. The TC under them was responding to commands that phased it out of space-time and held it in limbo.

Grainger's sore stomach threatened to buck as Chun stabilized TC 779 out of phase. Here he was again, cosmic hash with delusions of personality.

He stretched his arms above his head, cracking his intertwined fingers' joints. "Come on, Chun, don't be scared." His arm still hurt where serum made a lump under his skin. "Same war, different day, is all."

But he didn't believe his own pep talk. Not this time. Not with Central ahead and Russia acting as a staging area for some breakaway faction Up The Line.

If the other two ARC Riders were scared now, wait until they heard what Grainger had to tell them. When all else was said and done, you still had the nearly insolvable problem of a radioactive, wrecked TC from Up The Line, sitting big as life in a subbasement in Obninsk.

Fourteen Kilometers West of the Rhine River, Free Germany

September 2, 9 AD

Gerd sat cross-legged on a ledge of shale and manipulated his sensor pack at its full sensitivity. "There's a group of people, ten or a dozen, approximately a klick ahead of us," he said without looking up. "I believe they're refugees from the battle."

Pauli Weigand held a handful of grain to his horse in one hand while with the other he lifted one shoulder strap, then the other, of his mail coat. The weight of the steel links ground his collarbone despite the leather underlayer.

He wasn't about to take the armor off. His ribs ached where the revisionist's bullets had punched him, and he remembered vividly the sight of the merchant tripping on coils of his own guts. Pauli's teammates weren't strong enough to wear mail during this grueling trek. He was, and he wanted to have it on when he stepped between his friends and danger.

Beckie grinned wanly at him. Nearby her horse and the mule they'd caught for Gerd browsed young leaves from shrubs on the knoll. The beasts were drop-reined. They were too tired to bolt.

"I shouldn't have dismounted," Beckie said. "My legs're so

stiff that I'm not sure I'll be able to get back up unless you lift me."

Pauli shurgged. "So I lift you," he said. "We'll reach the river in a few hours."

"I rode from Memphis to Las Vegas on the back of my husband's Harley once," she said, bending backward as she massaged her thighs. "God, I was stupid when I was young."

Pauli didn't know if she meant about the motorcycle trip or about the husband. Maybe both, given some of the other things she'd said about the marriage.

"There's a German warband following us," Gerd said. "I can't be sure of numbers because they're six kilometers distant"—in the face of present danger he no longer played with jargon—"but there are probably more than a hundred. There are fifty or more horses with the band, though a percentage are certain to be remounts."

Pauli rubbed his face with his knuckles. It hadn't rained in almost a day but the sun was staying out of sight. Astronomical sundown wasn't for three hours, but it was already dark enough for twilight.

"Chasing us or also going toward the Rhine?" Pauli asked. He'd made the decision to ride directly to the river rather than head for Varus' summer camp even though the road east from there would make the rest of the journey much easier. He'd crossed his fingers that Gerd's sensors and database would prevent the team from riding into a bog or being blocked by a swollen stream.

"I can't tell unless we turn to the side and they follow us," the analyst said. "I believe there are larger numbers of Germans at a greater distance, moving in this direction. The amount of refined steel is consistent with thousands of men in armor. I doubt that many legionaries escaped the ambush with their equipment."

"I doubt it, too," Pauli said. His mistake in judgment was a cold mass in his stomach. He hadn't expected the Germans to move so quickly after slaughtering the Roman field army. "Barbarian" wasn't the equivalent of "stupid," at least not if you were talking about Arminius.

"All right," he said. "We'll ride and hope for the best."

He wiped his left palm on his thigh. "Gerd, Beckie," he said. "Do you need help mounting?"

"I'm all right," she said, smiling faintly.

"If we ride through the group of refugees," Gerd said as he rose to his feet with the stiff articulations of a scarecrow, "they'll occupy the Germans while we reach the Rhine. Getting across will still be a problem. Though we can—"

He pursed his lips.

"—cross that bridge when we come to it."

"Yes," said Pauli Weigand. "Sacrifice the refugees to save our mission."

The cold weight almost choked him. He was the wrong man for the job. He couldn't be trusted to make decisions. "All right, that's what we'll do."

He waited for Gerd to grab the mule's saddle, then boosted him aboard.

Though Pauli Weigand knew he was the wrong man for the job, he'd keep on going till he died in the midst of his mission's crashing failure.

Twelve Kilometers West of the Rhine River, Free Germany

September 2, 9 AD

Rebecca Carnes was in the lead because Pauli insisted on riding at the back, the direction the Germans would be coming from. She saw the refugees fifty yards ahead when she came through a patch of bracken growing tall from the well-watered soil.

"We've found them," she called over her shoulder. Her heels prodded the horse to a slight increase in speed, all she thought either of them could survive. Days of the horse's rocking motion made the muscles at the small of her back so stiff she was afraid they'd crack.

There were ten of them, all on foot except the pregnant girl riding a very expensive bay horse. The refugees were so exhausted that it was the horse who noticed the approaching riders and whinnied. Gerd's mule blatted an ill-tempered response. Only then did the humans turn.

Three of the six legionaries had javelins. The others and two civilians drew swords, while the third male civilian lowered a twelve-foot German lance. They might have captured the horse as well from a German noble in the vicious fighting.

The girl was dark, fifteen, and eight months pregnant if Rebecca was any judge. How she rode bareback was as much a wonder as how the refugees had come so far from the scene of the massacre.

"Castor and Pollux!" a legionary cried hoarsely. "It's Gaius Clovis and his household! Well, you've got a report for Augustus now, don't you!"

"Flaccus?" Rebecca said. It hadn't occurred to her that the refugees might include somebody she knew. The sight of the legionary's face beaming beneath a freshly dented helmet made her heart sink.

"It's all right, boys," Flaccus said to his fellows. Rebecca didn't recognize any of them. "Clovis here's one of the emperor's horse guards. Glad to see you, Clovis. We thought you were another batch of Fritzes wanting to nail our heads to trees!"

Pauli rode up beside Rebecca. He looked at the refugees with hard eyes. A bandaged thigh kept one of the legionaries from walking without the help of his fellows. He stood with his legs braced, trying to fit his short sword back into the scabbard without falling over.

Half the others had wounds; all were on the tottering edge of collapse from hunger and exhaustion. They'd thrown away their shields, though the legionaries wore full body armor and the civilians had picked up helmets. They must have been marching with only the briefest halts for sleep. They knew what to expect if the Germans caught them before they reached the Rhine.

"There's a German warband close behind," Pauli said expressionlessly. "They'll be up with us in an hour."

He glanced back at Gerd and raised his eyebrow. The analyst nodded. "Sooner," he said. Under his breath he added, "Although a Roman hour considered as one twelfth of daylight is a flexible concept to begin with."

"Oh, Mithras," Flaccus said. His weather-beaten features sagged, softened. "Then we're screwed for sure. It can't be less than five miles to the river."

"About eight Roman miles," Gerd said calmly.

One of the legionaries knelt and started to unbuckle his sword belt. The girl wiped her face with a hand. Her expression hadn't changed, but there were tears at the corners of her eyes.

The kneeling legionary tugged up the front of his mail shirt. He placed the pommel of his reversed sword on the ground.

"No!" Rebecca said. She kicked her horse. It lurched forward with an angry neigh. The would-be suicide scrambled clear of the hoofs, dropping the sword in his haste.

Rebecca dismounted awkwardly. "Pauli," she said. "We can't—"

"I'll decide what we can do," Pauli Weigand said in a voice like steel. "This is *my* responsibility."

Rebecca stiffened. She swallowed from a dry throat. "Yes, Pauli," she said; because he was right. What could the team do anyway, besides add more bodies to the toll?

Pauli dismounted. He handed the reins of his horse to the legionary with the leg wound. "Here," he said. "Can you ride bareback?"

"Gerd, you'd better stay on the mule," Rebecca said. Her relief was as bright as the sun breaking out after a storm. "You there"—to a legionary with his right arm splinted with a javelin shaft; his legs were uninjured, but his face was gray with pain—"mount this horse. And move it or we'll have the Germans arrive before we've got our thumbs out."

The Roman looked startled but obediently shifted to the animal's flank. Beckie Carnes had a lot of experience sounding like she meant it when she gave orders to wounded soldiers. She made a stirrup of her hands to boost him into the saddle.

"The leaders are two miles behind us," Gerd said in his usual tones of disinterested helpfulness. "The remainder of the band stretches back almost another half mile. They number about seventy all told."

"If there's that many, it's all over," another legionary said. "Urso's right—we may as well fall on our swords."

He looked from Rebecca to the pregnant girl. "The women might be all right," he added doubtfully.

"*First,*" Pauli said in a crackling voice. "I'm in charge from now till we get across the river. Second, the three of us are magicians from the east and the chances are pretty decent that we're going to pull this off. Third and most important—we don't quit. *None* of us quits. Do all you men understand me?"

He looked fiercely around the band of refugees. His left hand was on the pommel of his long horseman's sword. His knuckles were mottled with the tension of his grip.

"Mithras, I'm a believer," Flaccus said. "I didn't much like the idea of being cheated out of my pension by some fucking Fritz." He turned to the others and said, "All right, you scuts! You heard the man. We got eight miles to go. Anybody who doesn't keep moving's going to have my boot up his bum before the Fritzes get around to putting a spear there. Move out!"

Gerd prodded the mule with his heels. It ignored him. The analyst did something with his sensor pack. The animal skipped forward with a disbelieving bleat. Gerd had generated a spark—low amperage, but obviously placed where it did the most good. "To the left at the fork," he announced, his eyes on the projected display.

"I'll take the rear, Beckie," Pauli Weigand said. He sounded embarrassed for the way he'd taken charge. "They'll probably surround us when they see what's going on. I'll need you up front."

"Right," she said. She handed him the submachine gun she carried with her last nineteen rounds in the magazine. "At the range I can hit anything with this, the microwave does a better job anyway."

"All right," Pauli said, nodding.

Rebecca started forward, then looked back over her shoulder. "Pauli?" she said. "About the horses we had to kill back there?"

"What about them?" he said.

"People are more important than horses."

He grinned. "Yeah, I think so, too," he said. "And if the folks at Central don't see it that way, well, they can come here and tell me."

ARC Central

Out of the Temporal Universe

You've got fifteen minutes with the Chief, TL Roebeck. This is the seating plan," said the ARC Chief of Staff's aide. The aide had helmet-cut red hair and a dusting of freckles. Scrubbed and polished, stiff as a board, he held out the seating plan to her as if it, and not the meeting requiring it, were the most important issue at hand. "Sirs, if you'll just let me walk through this so you'll understand it . . . TL Roebeck, you sit opposite the Chief. Specialist Chun, you sit on your TL's left; Specialist Grainger, on the right."

The Chief's office was the size of a TC bay. To reach its threshold, the team had walked two miles of corridor. To get in here, the ARC Riders had passed by two guards in dress uniforms of the sort that Roebeck hadn't worn since her graduation. Each guard stood at unblinking attention beside a pole of battle standards on either side of the hallowed portal. Nan Roebeck had hoped to complete her career and never set foot in such an office. Now she was here with only her recon staff for support.

The Chief's aide was terrified that these field operators were going to blow some bit of protocol and get him in trouble. His lips were white with strain.

Roebeck knew exactly how he felt. She bit her own lips under the cover of one hand to make sure they weren't bloodless when she walked into the Chief's conference room.

Grainger couldn't resist the opportunity to tweak the kid's

tail. "So, team, I figure we do this fifteen-minute parade drill, and we're out of here. When we get back downrange, we'll have the comfort of knowing we got an official blessing."

The kid ignored Grainger pointedly. "Team Leader Roebeck, if you haven't any questions, please sit down and make yourself comfortable."

Nan had been looking at the seating chart. Four other places would be occupied at the long briefing table. "Who are these other guys indicated?"

"Senior Steering Committee officials, sir."

"Got an attendee list?"

"List?" said the youngster.

"Yeah, list. I want to see the list. Names. Office symbols. Contact numbers. The regular sort of thing." Roebeck was beginning to regret she'd asked for this meeting at all. She hadn't really expected to get it. But she and her ARC Riders had been briefing up the chain at the speed of infection ever since they'd displaced back to ARC Central.

"I'll see, sir. Coffee, anyone?" asked the kid weakly. "Tea? Soft drinks?"

"List," Nan Roebeck insisted.

She was hoping that her direct superior was on that list, or at least his boss. When you got a meeting like this, way above your pay grade, it meant somebody asked for that meeting who could get it—and you—on the Chief's schedule. That sure wasn't her.

They sat down on a soft blue couch with gold cord trim. Grainger said, "Lay this plan out for the Chief in fifteen minutes? Not possible."

Chun said, "Want to bet? I could do it in my sleep." She pulled out her handheld and brought up a text screen. Then she tapped for a bit. "Here, Nan. How's this?"

Nan looked at the text screen. Chun had reduced everything that had happened to four bullet points. Below the bulletspeak were three action items and one recommendation in three parts.

It would have to do.

She gave Grainger the handheld. "Make it better." Grainger was their area specialist, after all.

The kid came back with a tray holding china cups emblazoned with the Chief's office symbol in gold. His face was arranged in a determinedly polite smile.

"Fancy, fancy," Chun breathed.

The kid had the attendee list with him.

By then Roebeck didn't need it. The others were filing in. She could tell their offices by their outfits. A horse-faced lawyer from ARC CENTCOM sauntered in lazily, wearing plainclothes and a holographic entry badge that proclaimed his status as SES—Senior Executive Service. SES pay grade was four times the rate of equally ranked military personnel. Following him came a joint staffer, the J-3 himself, with three gold braid strips encircling his cuffs, who nodded his dark curly head to them stiffly. Then came the Assistant Deputy Chief of Staff for Ops and Plans, in operational dress greens. The ADCSOPS planted himself squarely in front of the coffee table, regarding the operations team with a proprietary air. Only the last to join them, Dr. Bill, the ARC Riders' Chief Scientific Advisor in ARC Science blues, was familiar to Roebeck. The scientist's shock of white hair above a bumper crop of liver spots wasn't a sight Roebeck was likely to forget. Neither was the nervous way Dr. Bill twisted his big Citadel class ring on his finger when he was about to speak. Among the officials her team had briefed during the last two hours, he'd given her ARC Riders the hardest time, the most resistance.

If Dr. Bill had set up this meeting, it wasn't to help them make their case. Nevertheless, the chief scientist was the only man here who'd taken a briefing from them. So he must have been the one to arrange this meeting. He glowered at Roebeck like a disapproving patriarch.

Hard to know what to do when you're in the second meeting on the same day with someone who has obviously decided you're the enemy. She stood up and greeted the chief scientist. She couldn't let him intimidate her. "Thank you for arranging this meeting, Dr. Bill."

"Don't thank me, Team Leader," Dr. Bill replied. "Bad

news always has a way of getting people's attention. You're not exactly in line for a commendation. Simply tell your story as you told it to me, no matter how silly it sounds. Then leave. Stick to the timetable. Don't ask for anything you're not offered."

Grainger, behind Nan, stood up, too. She was afraid for a moment that Tim was going to say something stupid to Bill. It wouldn't help their case if their team logged an open dispute with the ARC Riders' Chief Scientist. But Grainger didn't do that. Instead, he introduced himself to the strangers, shaking hands with everyone he hadn't met before.

She heard a snatch of conversation between Grainger and the ADCSOPS in greens. ". . . congratulations for cracking this nut, mister," the ADCSOPS told Grainger. "We're lucky it was somebody in an ops unit who brought this little dust-up to the Chief's attention."

Well, that was better than worse. Parochialism had its place.

Then the kid ushered them into the meeting room where the Chief waited, a spider in his web. The Chief was about six feet six, all gangly arms and legs and a balding, capacious cranium shining from the end of a long white conference table.

"Sit down, people."

Everybody but Grainger found their assigned seat without a hitch. Grainger had decided to sit beside the ADCSOPS. There was nothing to do about it now.

"You people are on a short stroke, I'm told. Give me the overview, Team Leader . . . Roebeck." The Chief had to look at his copy of the seating plan to find her name.

"Yes, sir." Roebeck looked at the text display on Chun's handheld. "Situation: Recon identified Up The Line technology in 1992 Russia. Technology includes one crashed Up The Line temporal capsule, partly nuked; an implant technology for moving biological systems temporally; a potentiating handheld controller for the implant which effectively replaces the need for a TC. A sample implant is provided."

The ARC Riders had withheld the sample so far. It was their hole card. Roebeck put Zotov's box on the table before the Chief.

Angry mutters came from the J-3 and Dr. Bill, who scowled at her. The Chief Scientist started to speak. Both the J-3 and Bill clearly wanted to object on the record to Roebeck's team withholding the technology sample until now.

The Chief raised his hand and stopped them cold. "Continue, TL Roebeck." Then he reached out with those long arms to Zotov's box, making the box disappear in his big hands.

"Yes, sir. Background: unidentified parties from Up The Line are proliferating this technology to 1992 Russia. Using Up The Line technology, Russian revisionists are emplacing agents in 9 AD to establish a Fourth Rome. Preemption was Central's original target on this mission and remains critical."

"And what do you think the ARC Riders should do, TL Roebeck?" asked the Chief.

Thank God and her team that she was ready to answer that question.

"Go back and finish what we started. Actionable Items. Number one: destroy the remains of the temporal capsule as well as Russian ability to create implants and related technology. Number two: identify and neutralize Up The Line actors on site. Number three: remove privy parties to 50K."

"Recommendations on how those can be accomplished?"

"Our three recommendations are linked, Chief," she said softly. This was the tricky part. It was also clearly why the lawyer and the Chief Scientist were here: to try to block or nay-say this plan on the grounds that the issue should be handled by more senior people.

Roebeck was suddenly overwhelmingly afraid that the mission would be scrubbed or pulled from her team and given to somebody else. "Our recommendations are predicated on the assumption that action isn't possible UTL."

UTL—Up The Line.

She waited one heartbeat to see if the Chief would stop her. He didn't. Her next words would decide her career and her team's fate. Maybe the whole Command's fate, if her ARC Riders tried and failed. Or weren't allowed to try and somebody else failed. Or failed to try.

Roebeck said, "Recommendation one. Return the 1992 operating segment downrange with expanded force projection capability and emended Rules of Engagement allowing for broader collateral damage tolerance in accordance with emerging operating requirements. Do this before the advantage of surprise is lost to our enemies UTL." She was asking for a free hand to use lethal and highly destructive force.

She paused to give those in the room time to react. No one said a word.

"Recommendation two. Because Up The Line technology beyond our current abilities is involved and ARC security may be compromised, suspend further command oversight and limit the privy parties to those in the venue." In other words, don't run this operation from your hip pocket. No telling whom you could trust. Give the field commander full operational flexibility. Once more, she waited for comments. None were forthcoming. That could be good, or bad.

Sometimes you could tell how you were doing by who took what notes when. In this meeting nobody was taking notes. The Chief's long fingers were interlaced over the Russian sample on the white tabletop.

Roebeck made the remainder of her case. "Recommendation three. Since UTL penetration must be assumed to exist at Central, until proven otherwise we request that Central clean house here—simultaneously." Finished, Roebeck sat back.

The Chief unlaced his fingers and stared at the box they'd brought back from 1992.

The lawyer said, "Sir, if I may . . . ?"

"Not now, Sid," said the Chief. "TL Roebeck, it's obvious you're a zealot for this mission." He paused. "We'll work out the kinks here. And we'll respect your security. You'll need to download a complete report before you go—no distribution beyond myself. Make it comprehensive enough that another team can pick up the pieces if you fail to attain your entire objective. Under the circumstances, I'll accept all your recommendations—that includes the one about security here at Central." The Chief turned to the ADCSOPS. "You've got the action, Jerry. Go do it. Give them whatever they need."

"Yes, sir."

"You four are dismissed. The rest of you, stay behind."

The lawyer and the Chief Scientist were already in a huddle as Roebeck's team and the ADCSOPS shook hands with the Chief on the way out.

Once through the outer office and in the hall, the ADC-SOPS gave Nan a high-five, then set off down the first mile of corridors at a sturdy dogtrot. "Let's go, ARC Riders," he called back over his shoulder. "Move it! You heard the Chief."

They had to hustle to keep up.

Grainger jogged up beside her. "You *trying* to get us raped and left for dead on the road, boss, or do you just have a talent for it?"

Roebeck ignored Grainger's comment. This was neither the time nor the palce for loose talk.

Chun joined them, pushing between them until the team trotted three abreast. "Oh, shut up, Grainger. You're just afraid you'll have to wear your hardsuit."

"You're wrong this time, Chun," Grainger said. "I wish I had my armor on this minute, to protect me from those EARS"—Echelons Above Reality—"in there who're right now planning their move once we're reported Missing In Action. You know this is a sacrifice play."

The ADCSOPS, who'd stopped to let them catch up, had heard what Grainger said. He tuned up Grainger with a practiced stare. "You have it wrong, mister. This is no sacrifice play. It's a long overdue wake-up call." He shifted bleakly sparkling eyes to Roebeck. "TL Roebeck, I've waited a long time for somebody to come into The Building and ask these guys the basic question they didn't want to hear."

"What question is that, sir?" Chun asked the ADCSOPS.

"Question? The only question: 'Is my war ready yet?' And thanks to your team, TL Roebeck, the answer finally was *'yes.'* "

So the ADCSOPS had known, maybe all of the flag officers had known, that there'd been more than a philanthropic interest at work Up The Line in the creation of the ARC Riders.

"Roebeck, let's talk about what kind of support you figure

you're going to need," said the ADCSOPS, as if he'd known her for a thousand years.

So the threat from Up The Line was real. And the flag officers of the Anti-Revision Command had known all along that someday it was going to come to something like this. Otherwise there'd have been more questions. Disbelief. Argument. Otherwise she'd never have gotten that meeting. Not with the Chief of Staff. Not in a million years.

Roebeck was reeling from the shock of not being laughed out of the Chief's office and summarily disciplined. She couldn't believe it. When her team was finally back in the launch bay, overseeing the on-loading of additional hardware, she still didn't believe it.

But Grainger believed it. He was sure they were dead meat, a lure to flush the bad guys out of hiding.

"You don't send three people to stop a threat to an entire way of life," he grunted to her. Grainger was personally working the yellow loader lifting cases into the TC's hold. He wanted to make sure he got exactly the weapons he'd requisitioned—and nothing he hadn't.

"Why the hell not?" Chun puffed. She was guiding the crates into the TC's hold. Roebeck was checking the manifest. "The ARC was formed to capitalize on force multiplication through superior technology. It's our stock in trade."

"It *was* our stock in trade, when we thought we had superior technology," Grainger corrected.

Thanks to the Chief's blessing, they'd been able to get the ADCSOPS to enforce the ruling about privy parties. So they were on their own, isolated, operating in a sanitized environment even in the TC bay. But that meant they had to load on their own. Roebeck checked her timetable.

"Let's hurry this up. I want to lift and strike in twenty minutes."

They made the elapsed-time deadline that Roebeck had set, but only barely.

When they were locked down inside TC 779, going through their systems' checks, somebody opened the bay's doors. It shouldn't have happened. The ADCSOPS had promised it wouldn't happen. But it was happening.

"Ignore him," Grainger begged Roebeck. "Just go. *Go!*"

Whoever was out there would be dead in seconds if that someone came too close to the TC as it displaced out of here.

"Can you tell who it is?"

"That's the Chief's job, not ours. We don't *care* who it is. Nobody's supposed to be in here but us," Grainger pleaded.

Chun was looking at Roebeck, not saying a word, her control wands poised and ready.

Grainger, although clearly paranoid, might be right this time. Maybe there *were* forces from Up The Line loose in Central.

"Okay, Chun. Do it. *Now. Go!*" Roebeck ordered.

The TC bay sparkled out of existence around them like so much confetti blown on a wild wind.

Six Kilometers West of the Rhine River, Free Germany

September 2, 9 AD

You know . . ." said Flaccus as he saw a dozen German horsemen top the hill and begin to spread out. "I'd got to hoping the Fritzes'd dick around watering their horses long enough that we'd come home free."

He spat. "Well, it wouldn't be much of a pension anyway."

"Beckie, keep the group moving," Pauli Weigand ordered as he checked one, then the other, Skorpion. "I'll send these off and then catch up with you."

He flipped the submachine gun's sights to the 150-meter notch. That was an optimistic range for the light bullets to do any real damage, but he was going for psychological effect.

The leading Germans dismounted two hundred meters from the refugees. For a moment Pauli didn't understand what they were doing. Footmen leading more horses reached the knoll. The nobles mounted the fresh animals and shook their lances.

Pauli glanced over his shoulder. Flaccus stood just behind him, balancing his javelin on his right palm.

"I told you to move on!" Pauli said.

"I heard you," Flaccus said. "I'm bucking for a field promotion. Seems simpler than learning to read and getting one the usual way."

The refugees continued forward at a steady pace. They'd be able to see the Rhine over the next rise, but it was too far for people so tired to run. Beckie'd keep them in hand.

Pauli grimaced. "I'm just going to hurt a few of them to give them something to think about," he said. "Then I'll run up with the rest of our people."

Flaccus nodded. "And I'll run along with you," he said equably.

The Germans came on shrieking a war song. Retainers ran alongside the mounted men, each placing a hand on a noble's horse. The horsemen were armed with a mixture of lances and long swords. The commoners waved stabbing spears, though some wore Roman swords as well.

Pauli took a deep breath. As he let it out slowly he put the front post of his sight under the face of the German noble and fired a three-shot burst.

The German flung his arms up and went over the back of his horse. The animal swerved, tangled with a footman, and rode the man down. The riders to either side slowed unconsciously as they looked in surprise at their fellow.

The man on the left end of the German line wore a gilded helmet with flaring wings. His short cape fluffed out with the wind of his charge. He bellowed as bullets hit him, slashed his sword through the empty air, and kicked his mount into a full gallop. Blood streamed from his neck.

Pauli shot him again. A tooth flew from the warrior's jaw, sparkling in the wan air. The man at last slid sideways from his horse.

The Germans reined up. Two horsemen shouted a challenge and resumed their charge. A pair of footmen accompanied each noble. Pauli stuck the submachine gun into its holster and drew the microwave pistol.

As the Germans came within fifty meters, Pauli shot the red-haired horseman in the face. The man's beard and mustache flared; he did a backward somersault. He hadn't hit the ground before Pauli dropped his blond fellow the same way.

To the ARC Rider's astonishment the retainers continued to

stride forward, brandishing their spears. Pauli stunned them each in turn.

The other Germans remained where they'd halted. Several of the nobles had dismounted to examine their fallen fellows. More warriors reached the knoll. One raised a brass-mounted cow horn to his lips and blew a staccato summons to those behind.

"Let's go," Pauli muttered, sliding the pistol back into the loops on the lining of his cape. "They'll probably follow, but I'll drop another and maybe they'll keep back."

Maybe. Pauli drew a submachine gun as he jogged on. He wished he had a proper holster for the microwave pistol, but when the operation started the team had been concerned not to display advanced technology on this timeline. More recently the problem had been to stay alive; niceties had gone out the window.

The group ahead plodded into a stretch of mixed forest and disappeared. Beckie shepherded out of sight the last of the refugees, a legionary using his javelin as a staff to support his injured foot.

"Pauli," Gerd's voice warned. "Nine of them are riding after you."

Pauli turned and fell into a squat. Flaccus halted well out of the way. He held the javelin at the balance in his right hand and supported the long point with two fingers of his left. The Roman breathed through his open mouth. He was pretty near his limit. Well, so was Pauli Weigand, truth to tell . . .

He tried to settle his breathing as he aimed. The Germans, five mounted nobles and four accompanying footmen, charged down the slope. They passed the men Pauli'd dropped with his microwave pistol moments before. Their horses kicked up clods of soft earth.

The Germans held their lances over their heads with the shafts parallel to the ground. The technique looked odd to eyes who'd seen the heavy cavalry of later ages, but without stirrups to anchor a horseman there was no way to put the whole weight of horse and rider behind the attack. A stroke with the lance firmly couched between the rider's arm and body would scoot him off his mount's bare back at the moment of contact.

The man half a length in front of the others had shoulder-length blond hair and a short beard in which gray mixed with the red. He wore no armor. Six broad bronze disks jounced on his chest. They were medals that had been awarded to some Roman soldier—or just possibly to the German who now wore them, while in Roman service.

Pauli squeezed. The Skorpion stuttered three shots before the bolt locked back over an empty magazine. The lacquered steel cases bounced into the bushes. There was no time to retrieve them.

A little smoke drifted from the silencer and the open chamber. The muzzle blast was softer than the thump of the horses' hoofs, but the breech rang against the barrel like a steel ball. Pauli thrust the submachine gun into its holster and stood up, drawing the microwave pistol. Twelve rounds remained in the other Skorpion, but if the Germans didn't halt now Pauli was going to have to nail eight men with a microwave pistol before a lance opened him up.

The warrior he'd shot through the upper chest rolled gracefully forward over the shoulder of his mount. The horse neighed and swerved aside to keep from trampling its fallen rider. The German charge milled to a halt. Men shouted in frightened anger. Pauli bowed to them, then turned and started after Beckie and the refugees.

Flaccus tramped along with him. The Roman's javelin pistoned. He breathed a little more easily.

"I'd just about say that was a crossbow you've got," Flaccus said. "Only I don't see any arrow. Or any bow either."

"I told you, we're magicians," Pauli said, trying not to pant. "I cursed them."

"They'll likely be coming along in a few minutes," Flaccus said. "Hard to get anything through a Fritz's head without you knock it off. Though I guess you'd know that."

"I know it," Pauli said. He didn't *like* it, but Flaccus was certainly right. In daylight, in the forest, the Germans would come from all sides at once. There wasn't a chance of stopping them.

Beckie looked back and forced a smile to greet their return. She couldn't wave because she supported the injured legionary with the arm that didn't hold a pistol ready.

"Well, maybe I get to curse a couple more Fritzes myself," Flaccus said judiciously. He whacked the javelin's shaft against his left palm.

Four Kilometers West of the Rhine, Free Germany

September 2, 9 AD

It struck Rebecca Carnes that most of what she'd seen on this mission was the ground in front of either her feet or her horse's. When you're slogging ahead that's all there was; and this one had been a slog.

It was going to continue that way for at least a while longer. If they got away from the pursuing Germans, a longer while than otherwise.

"Shit!" said Arnobius under his breath as his right foot came down. Rebecca took part of his weight on her shoulder as he strode forward. The blister on the ball of the legionary's right foot was infected and by now the size of a teacup.

"Shit!" It was the only thing Arnobius had said for the past three hours she'd been helping him, and perhaps the only thing for days.

He kept going. They all kept going.

Gerd was leading them along a track that meandered with the slope. It was used by merchants and by herdsmen driving cattle to markets across the Rhine. The undergrowth was trampled clear broadly enough for two people to walk abreast; the footing was packed hard.

"Gerd?" Rebecca said. "All those Germans we killed back at the ambush site—are we causing a revision ourselves?"

"Probably not," the analyst said. "Low-order changes like a

few more deaths among tens of thousands get subsumed into the temporal ambiance within a year or two."

He turned to look back with a smile. "Of course, if we had the misfortune of killing a critical figure, then Central won't exist when we try to return to it."

Rebecca's face froze. Gerd noted her expression and added apologetically. "But that's extremely unlikely in an ahistoric wilderness like this."

He nodded at the trees around them.

They didn't know if there was a boat on this side of the river, and it didn't look as though they were going to reach the river anyway. Rebecca's job for the moment was to make sure nobody fell out of line and to help Arnobius keep up. *First stop the bleeding; only then do you worry about the patient's internal injuries.*

"Coming through!" Pauli shouted, his words blurred between air and the headband intercom. He was afraid somebody'd shoot or chuck a spear through him when he burst into sight. "Coming through!"

Rebecca hadn't heard Pauli and Flaccus crashing up the trail behind her. They could have been an army of German warriors and she wouldn't have heard them either. She was so completely focused on the ground and one foot going in front of the other foot.

She glanced over her shoulder as the armored men appeared up the zigzag track. They panted like distance runners, pumping as much oxygen as possible into their lungs to support their exertions.

The holstered submachine guns jounced against Pauli's waist along with the sword that was part of his disguise. The guns were probably empty, but he'd kept them out of habit against leaving advanced technology on an early horizon.

Rebecca guessed he'd kept the sword because he thought he might need it.

"Pauli and Rebecca, the Germans are within a hundred meters of you," Gerd's voice warned. "They're spreading to either side of the trail."

Pauli looked back. Sight distances in the woods ranged

from ten yards down to arm's length; the trail up the back of the low bluffs wasn't straight for more than twenty feet at a time. Rebecca concentrated again on moving forward.

"I've told the refugees to circle on the rock knob we've reached," Gerd said. "I'm going to separate from the rest of you. I've an idea that might help."

"What?" Rebecca blurted. Flaccus looked at her in surprise since he couldn't hear Gerd.

"Gerd, don't—" Pauli said. He stopped there because he knew from experience that giving the analyst orders was a waste of time. Gerd would do pretty much whatever he thought was best.

"Besides," Rebecca said, half to herself, "he's right more often than he's wrong."

"Shit!" said Arnobius. His stride was as steady as the tick of a pendulum. "Shit!"

"All right," Pauli said for the benefit of the two legionaries. "We're going to take a defensive position up ahead. The Germans will be on us at any moment."

"My sword arm's—*shit,*" Arnobius said, "in a damned sight better shape than—*shit*—my foot."

The knoll was slate jutting out in the midst of a stand of birches. The slim trunks and brush would interfere with the microwave pistols, but at least the defenders could see each other and the attacking Germans some distance away.

The hill beyond rose higher than the back of the knob. A sixty-degree slope faced the trail, notched into steps by weathering between the layers of stone. Rebecca paused to brace Arnobius to climb it. Behind her hooves thudded and a voice cried, "Here the worms are!" in German.

"Beckie, get to the top for when they come around!" Pauli shouted. "Flaccus, get her up there!"

Callused hands grabbed Rebecca's thighs from behind and lifted her straight up. A civilian on top of the knob grabbed her left shoulder and pulled, nearly slashing her with the sword he carried in his other hand.

The *WHACK!* an instant later wasn't generated by Pauli's pistol directly. The low-frequency difference tone reflected from the flat surface of a German's shield. The warrior went over with a crash of equipment.

Rebecca got her feet down and turned. Arnobius climbed while Flaccus supported his right heel with one hand and held both javelins with the other. A dappled horse clattered on the stony trail. It leaped away when Pauli tried to grab its dangling reins.

Ten feet back the rider lay supine. Two boards of his shattered shield were still strapped to his left arm. Rebecca fired over Pauli's head, slamming the warrior's chest against the ground as he tried to rise.

Pauli dismounted a second German riding toward them. The horse neighed and turned, blocking the trail.

"Watch it!" a legionary warned. A German flung a javelin from above the group on the knoll. It glanced harmlessly from a birch tree.

The legionaries and armed civilians formed a wall across the neck of the knob. Arnobius pushed himself into the line, panting and swearing. He'd drawn his sword because Flaccus hadn't had time to pass the javelin to him. The team's three horses stood nearby, snorting and shivering but too blown to run.

Rebecca got only fleeting glimpses of Germans past the line of men. A warrior approached on the side slope, poising his spear to hamstring the legionary on the end. Rebecca shot him in the stomach. When the warrior doubled up, his head was clear of the leaves that had shielded him. She hit him again and knocked him cold.

A dozen javelins flew from the brush. One hit a civilian driver in the chest. He staggered and dropped his sword to pull the missile out with both hands. He continued to stand, holding the wooden javelin, but he didn't pick up his sword.

Rebecca needed a better vantage point if she was going to do any good. A birch spread into two stems four feet above the ground. She tried to pull herself up far enough that she could get her foot into the tight crotch. She couldn't manage it, not as wrung out as she was. "Help me!" she ordered the pregnant girl.

The girl held a ten-pound lump of quartz in one hand and a dagger with a silvered three-inch blade in the other. She looked at Rebecca with an expression as stupid as a sheep's. Nonetheless she dropped the stone and waddled to Rebecca, ignoring another flight of javelins.

The girl's grip was remarkably strong. With her help Rebecca scrambled up to where she could see more than the defenders' backs.

A score of Germans rushed the refugee line with swords and stabbing spears. The long lances were too awkward to use in this brush; the Roman driver who'd carried one now held a legionary's dagger instead. The Germans had shields but the tightly grown birches knocked them askew at unexpected moments.

Rebecca was ten feet behind the defensive line. She aimed with care before she squeezed the trigger; the refugees were at more risk than their attackers if she hosed pulses wildly.

White bark sprayed from a tree beside a rushing warrior. He ignored the slap of sound, but when his uplifted sword flew from his hand with a *clang* he looked at his empty hand in amazement. A legionary let his guts out with an upward stab and twist. Rebecca chose another target.

Usually when a warrior joined in combat with a Roman they were too close for Rebecca to trust her aim, but if the German stepped back to consider his tactics she had a shot. Repeatedly she knocked a warrior down, slammed his breath out, or spun him sideways with a broken shield.

The captured mail many of the Germans wore was no protection against microwave pulses that hit like sandbags. Defenders finished the job with steel.

But refugees were down also. One legionary lay on his back with a spear sticking up from the bridge of his nose. The civilian with the chest wound had fallen, and Arnobius knelt stoically while the pregnant girl bandaged his right forearm with the hem of her silk tunic.

The attack paused. Rebecca glanced over her shoulder to the base of the knob. There were a dozen bodies on the trail or close off it; one of them had a Roman javelin through the chest.

She couldn't see Pauli or Flaccus; they stood or lay too close to the rock. At least one of them must be alive or warriors would have swarmed up the knob. She was afraid to call Pauli to be sure.

The Germans regrouped on the surrounding slopes, visible through the undergrowth as movement though not as figures. One began to chant a guttural war song that a dozen of his fellows took up. Warriors called orders or challenges to one another. Several lancers worked their way carefully toward the edges of the defensive line.

Arnobius stood, muttered a curse, and took his place again. He held his bloody sword in his left hand.

A trumpet called from the near distance. Three curved horns answered raucously in succession, the notes subtly different.

"It's Asprenas come with his legions!" a legionary shouted. "By the mothering Venus, we're saved!"

"Double-time you whoresons!" Flaccus called from the base of the knob. "Double-time or we won't have any of these fucking Fritzes for your lot to finish!"

A second set of calls sounded, louder and nearer than the first. The refugees began to cheer, those who could speak.

The Germans stampeded. They'd been bloodied attacking a handful of refugees; they weren't about to face three cohorts of fresh legionaries. Warriors shouted to each other and to horses who'd caught the odor of sudden panic.

"Eagles to me!" Flaccus said as he clambered to the top of the knob. He'd lost his helmet and the left side of his face was streaked with dried blood. "Eagles to me!"

Pauli Weigand stepped into sight. He didn't try to climb because he still held both the microwave pistol and his sword. Heat waves shimmered from the pistol's receiver.

"Beckie?" he croaked. "Are you all right?"

"I'm all right," she said. She carefully lifted her foot from the crevice where she'd wedged it, then let herself down from

the tree. She hurt, particularly her foot, and her throat was dry
enough to use for sandpaper.

A rosy warmth of relief had filled her surroundings as soon
as she saw Pauli.

Gerd Barthuli rode cautiously down the trail on his mule.
The sensor pack in his hand synthesized another trumpet call.
Refugees stared at him in amazement.

"I'm afraid I made the signals myself," he said. "But there
are friendly troops on top of the bluff. They've heard the calls
and are coming toward us at their best speed."

"How does he know that?" the uninjured civilian said. He
looked up from removing the gold armlet of a German noble.
"How did you *know* that?"

"They said they were magicians, didn't they?" Flaccus
said. "Bugger me if I believed it, but I sure do now."

Rebecca tucked the pistol away in her cape. The receiver
was still hot enough to startle her when it touched her bare
forearm.

"Hold still," she ordered, stepping to Flaccus to see what
had bled on his face. There was nobody to fight for the moment, so she could get back to what she was best at: patching
damaged soldiers.

Pauli joined them, but he came the long way around instead
of climbing the face of the knob. He walked stiffly and there
was a tear in his alloy steel mail under his left arm. No blood,
though; she'd checked him after she cleaned the ragged tear
over Flaccus' left eye. A spearpoint had glanced from underlying bone instead of piercing it.

The girl had cut open the tunic of the civilian who'd taken
a javelin in the chest. The wound sucked when he breathed.
She put her left palm over the hole to close it while she ripped
more fabric from her tunic with the other hand.

"Is she married to one of you?" Rebecca asked. "The girl, I
mean."

"Ain't she a nice piece?" said Flaccus. "But she's none of
ours. We found her wandering the same direction in the
night . . . and she had a nice horse, but we guessed she needed
it worse'n we did. You know, I don't recall she ever said a

word in a language I heard of. Wouldn't it be a bitch if she turned out to be some Fritz's doxy?"

Rebecca tied a bandage over the wound when she'd sponged it. The flap of skin needed proper closure, but she didn't have a needle to stitch it and she wasn't about to use spray sealant. Central would have enough questions about the blithe way the team handled advanced weaponry in front of locals, though the refugees didn't appear to care about anything except that they were unexpectedly alive.

"The troops from Lucius Asprenas' forces are about to arrive," Gerd announced. The analyst still sat on his mule's uncomfortable saddle. Rebecca realized that he might be unable to dismount without falling. She moved toward him. Pauli got there first and lifted Gerd down as if his own pains were nothing.

"Rome forever!" Flaccus shouted. "This way the legions!"

Twenty men came down the trail. To Rebecca's surprise they were German horsemen, though they wore Roman helmets and mail shirts. Arnobius swore and gripped the pommel of the sword he'd been cleaning.

"They're friendly Ubians!" Gerd said. "They're operating with Asprenas!"

Legionary infantry followed the band of horsemen. Additional troops moved through the woods in battle order. Brass, steel, and their vermilion leather shield facings gleamed between tree trunks before the men had visible form.

Pauli murmured something to Flaccus. The veteran nodded and elbowed his way toward the newcomers. "Marcus Patius Flaccus, senior man here and late of 1st Company, 3d Cohort, 17th Legion. And by all the gods in Rome, are we glad to see you lot!"

A centurion, the only legionary present who'd mounted the horsehair crest on his helmet, strode over to Flaccus. More troops appeared from the woods. There was at least a full cohort and a similar number—five or six hundred—of Ubian horsemen.

The centurion looked at the bodies and raised his eyebrow. There were more than a dozen Germans sprawled where the refugees had made their stand and an equal number in the woods or along the trail in the immediate vicinity. "Not bad," he said to Flaccus. "We heard Varus had bit the big one. Any truth in that?"

"I sure hope the stupid bastard bought it," Flaccus said. More horsemen were arriving. "I told you I'm senior here. I figure I'm the senior survivor in my company and likely in the whole fucking cohort. Maybe some guys headed for Aliso instead of straight to the Rhine."

The centurion toed a German body. "Shit, I hoped it was all rumor, you know? Guess it's not."

Pauli moved to Rebecca's side. "You covered for me," he said quietly. "I got caught down below and couldn't get up to where I was needed."

"You and Flaccus covered our backs," Rebecca said. "You did more than all the rest of us together!"

She hugged him fiercely, then stepped away embarrassed. He had cracked ribs, maybe worse; besides . . .

"Well, we'll get you back to camp," said the centurion. "Word is we're not going any distance into this side of the river because the CO thinks all Gaul's going to revolt if we're not here to keep a lid on it."

A group of Ubians with gilt and silvered equipment moved through the crowd on big horses.

"That one!" said the broad, older man in the middle. He lowered his lance to point; the tip almost touched Pauli Weigand's chest. "He's a traitor! He'll come with me to meet Tiberius in Vetera!"

"Well, I wondered how we were going to get to Xanten," Pauli murmured calmly. "But for all the convenience, I'd as soon that King Segestes hadn't accompanied his troops this afternoon."

Obninsk, Russia

March 11, 1992

Tim Grainger felt bad about what was about to happen to the people of Obninsk, especially Zotov and those fourteen-year-old girls. But there was no other way.

At least Obninsk was a closed city—word might never leak of what was going to happen here. You had to think positively, this far into an operation.

Grainger had already put on one of the exo-skeletal servo-powered hardsuits they'd loaded at Central. He hated this bigger, heavier hardsuit even more than the standard issue TCs normally carried. It was the heaviest duty armor in ARC inventory.

Suited up, he was ready, willing, and able to stomp out the hatch when Chun displaced the TC into the Obninsk subbasement where the Up The Line capsule was stored. Too bad they couldn't find a way to take the UTL capsule back with them. It would have advanced the state of the art.

But you could only do what you could do. And, although getting into the exo-powered suit was a claustrophobic's nightmare, you couldn't do this mission without one. The big, bulky, self-powered exo-skeletal suit would protect Tim Grainger from the hell he was about to unleash in Obninsk. He had no way of knowing whether the Obninsk residents would be so lucky.

Zotov's Obninski scientists must have some kind of rudimentary shielding in the subbasement installation, to protect them from the wreckage of the nuked TC. And the scientists had the additional protection of the subbasement itself, dug into the ground. The placement of the installation below ground would protect inhabitants above from the havoc Grainger's HPM—high-power microwave—weapon was about to unleash.

In the lock, he ran a systems check on the big HPM gun. He couldn't even have lifted the gun without the exo-powered suit. He had to get into the suit before he could deal with the gun. Now he had the 40mm gun securely mated to the right arm of his suit, tight in its housing along the whole length of his servo-powered, armored forearm. So it was a point and shoot situation, so far as Grainger was concerned.

Point your arm and depress your trigger finger in its armored glove. Then watch all hell break loose through a fully polarized and multisignature suppressing helmet visor.

All Grainger had to worry about was running out of power or falling down. If he did, he couldn't get up by himself. Roebeck, in her hardsuit and waiting behind him, would have to come help him. Only one exo-powered suit—or the loader/charger they'd brought along—could reactivate another.

But for any Obninskis unlucky enough to be in the bay, things weren't going to be so easy. Orders were to slag the UTL capsule completely. Destroy all the Russian equipment around it. Trash their computer system irretrievably. Make the bay itself unusable through a methodology euphemistically called "denial of service." In this case, that meant making the bay a smoking mass of fused matter that couldn't be reconstituted into its constituent parts for a few thousand years.

This culture had no defense against head-on attack by the HPM weapon that Grainger was about to deploy.

Maybe the Russians really did have the mythical shielding paste to protect them and their equipment from ninety-nine percent of electromagnetic emissions. Maybe not. The paste, if it existed, was part of the Unobtanium category. Nobody from the West had ever gotten a sample while the inventors lived, or after. If the Obninsk scientists really had the paste sandwiched into their wallboards, they'd be partially protected from some effects of Nan Roebeck's servo-weapon, which was going to EM-pulse the whole of Obninsk while Grainger HPM'd the main target.

Proportional force was the name of the game today.

As soon as she deployed out the capsule door behind him, Roebeck in her hardsuit was going to back through the doors, up two flights to the surface level where Russian girls had danced before a mural of atomic symbols two nights ago. Using her servo-slaved grenade launcher, she'd fire out the door three times. The result would be three explosively driven electromagnetic airbursts. Conventional shielding, paste, and kill switches might protect from one or two bursts, but three would take down every piece of equipment that was operating, attached to an antenna or battery, or connected to a power source.

Lots of property and information damage, but maybe not too many casualties if people were lucky. EM airbursts packed a hell of a wallop in blast overpressure. Blast overpressure could kill you all by itself, if it was your day to die. If that overpressure was driving shrapnel, broken glass, or any object before it, you were in the lap of the gods.

Roebeck had gone to extraordinary lengths to keep innocents in Obninsk from becoming part of the collateral damage estimate. But nothing was going to protect anybody luckless enough to be in the path of Grainger's high-power microwave gun.

Which was why Grainger had insisted on deploying with the microwave weapon. Nan Roebeck didn't need any ghosts of fourteen-year-old Russian girls to carry around with her. Roebeck's psyche, like her native culture, was nonlethal by catechism. In Grainger's psyche, at least the ghosts he made today would have lots of company. Grainger had enough kills on his soul that a few more weren't going to send him to any deeper hell.

"Lock and load," came Roebeck's voice through his helmet's shielded com system.

"Roger that," he said absently. He'd already done it. Checked his weapon and his power backpack twice. Just to be

sure, he lit a red glow on the far bulkhead, a spot the size of
his 40mm barrel.

"Jesus Christ," Roebeck exclaimed in his ear. "I didn't say
turn the bulkhead into Swiss cheese."

He shut the HPM gun down. HPM just made things hot. It
left no environmental pollution behind. It was relatively
clean. "Sorry, boss. Just making sure this equipment ain't
lying."

Sometimes, you got a green light that said everything was
working, but the business end of the equipment didn't tell you
the same story when you asked for firepower.

This time, his HPM gun was working fine.

Chun's voice said, "Thirty seconds to displacement. On my
hack . . . Hack."

The world inside Grainger's suit shivered as if reality had a
sudden chill.

Even in his hardsuit, he felt the dimensional shudder that
meant they'd displaced to Obninsk before he heard Chun's
calm voice saying, "Displacement complete."

The lock deployed into a ramp. Grainger was already
stomping downward before the ramp contacted the floor,
moving as fast as the heavy suit could react.

His helmet visor adjusted to ambient darkness, giving him
multispectral scans. In multispectral, the Up The Line capsule
looked like the aurora borealis.

He hit it with everything he had, laying on the HPM gun's
trigger.

It was a surreal experience. He heard only his own breathing and Roebeck's occasional mutter as she passed him
encased in two tons of armor and weapon. Meanwhile, everything in the broad aim-point of his HPM gun blossomed into
flame. Melted. Puddled. Began to boil.

He felt something—a distant shudder—come up through
his armored boots.

It was the first shock wave of blast overpressure from
Nan's air-bursts, upstairs.

Only then did he realize that nobody had been in the subbasement lab when they'd hit it. No Zotov. No Kokoshin. No fourteen-year-old girls. Yet.

A second shudder realigned the floor. He was backing up, still firing for good measure: around the bay, at the window between the bay and the control room.

The window shattered. His visor showed him a flashing red indicator, telling him he was half through his power pack's available juice. Still firing, he walked with a giant's tread toward the blown-out window.

When he reached the window wall, he just kept going, spraying HPM fire as he advanced. What was left of the wall crumbled before the onslaught of his exo-powered suit. He slagged the control panels, the rack of antique equipment. The table holding them buckled and collapsed with a silent crash. And then he realized he'd been wrong.

There was somebody else down here. There'd been people in the control room. Those people were here still: hunched figures, hands over their heads, slumped in a heap in one corner of the room. A filing cabinet had melted on them. He didn't take one step closer. He'd seen death before. He didn't need to verify the obvious.

He felt the third concussion from Roebeck's weapon as he was backing up. Through the hole he'd made in the window wall, he retreated carefully. One slip, a wrong step, and he'd be helpless like a beetle on its back when Nan returned in need of covering fire.

He relaxed his pressure on the HPM gun's trigger. Better save whatever juice he had. You always wanted something left—in case you had to face the unexpected. He could hear Nan's increasingly labored breathing in his helmet as she beat her retreat.

A muttered curse, a grunt, and he could see her, striding through the far door with her grenade launcher ported.

You couldn't move fast in the exo-powered suits. Nan was moving toward him as quickly as her suit could safely go.

He had to face Nan's position to cover her as she came. Grainger took more slow, careful steps backward. His visor showed him a rearward-facing view as soon as he asked for it.

He enhanced the magnification. He wanted to see the relationship of his heel to the lip of the ramp. Watching carefully, he raised his powered heel onto the ramp and began climbing, still facing Roebeck.

He dumped the rearward-facing view to a left quarter screen window and took real-time forward view with the rest of his visor display. He needed to watch over his team leader. They were almost home free.

Come on, Nan! Move! To his combat-heightened awareness, it was excruciatingly slow going in an exo-powered suit. And by now, everybody in Obninsk knew the closed city was under attack.

Come on! Come on! "Come *on*!" he finally said aloud, almost prayerfully. "Team Leader, can we—"

Then he saw the first terrified, white face appear behind her, carrying an AK and shooting.

"Bandit! Six o'clock! Move out of the way!" He didn't want to shoot Nan's suit, point-blank, with his HPM gun. Fratricide was always a threat.

He really didn't want to shoot the unarmored local, either. But a lucky bullet could foul a servo, hit a critical part of Nan's suit.

"Moving right," Roebeck's voice told him. She stepped sideways.

Grainger fired his HPM weapon point-blank at Kokoshin, the mayor of Obninsk. The target dropped so fast Grainger didn't have to watch Kokoshin cook.

He had two more backward steps to take, then he was safe. He took one. Then he stepped carefully aside. From left of the lock, he covered Roebeck's slow, heavy approach.

The concussive thumps of her suit's heavy tread shook the ramp. *Hrrumph! Hrrumph! Hrrumph!*

Finally she was on the ramp. In two more steps she was beside him. In three, beyond.

"Now, Grainger! *O-kay,* you can *stop shooting*! Get *in* here! We've got to seal up and displace out!"

Until Roebeck said that, Grainger wasn't aware that he *was* shooting. He was reflexively emptying the rest of his weapon's power pack into the doorway where Kokoshin, and now several other armed Obninskis, lay sprawled.

He'd remember every detail, later, of the people who'd died trying to stop alien invaders in huge robotlike spacesuits.

Now, his mind was protecting him. He took one last step to safety, and the lock started to close.

A bullet streaked through the narrowing aperture, bounced off his helmet, and ricocheted around the lock before falling to the deck. The lock closed up tight.

"Sealed," came Chun's triumphant, relieved voice. "We're outta here . . . *now*!" The deck under him shivered as the ARC Riders' TC displaced out of Obninsk.

Grainger slumped in his hardsuit. It held him complacently. For a minute he didn't have the strength to move. They'd hoped to leave no witnesses, no tale-tellers. That last shooter had gotten himself an eyeful and lived to tell about it.

Not good.

Nan was out of her suit before he was.

She showed him the deformed slug from a Russian AK, holding it up, turning it in her fingers. "Not perfect," she said. "Somebody's going to have a story to tell their grandchildren."

Grainger craned his neck to look down through his visor at her and the slug she held. "Couldn't be helped," he said raggedly, not bothering to toggle-on his exterior speaker so that she could hear his words.

Then he continued stripping off his armor. You had to rack the 40mm before you took off your helmet. Then you could get out of your sarcophagus one more time. For a little while, at least.

Phase One was over, anyhow. Moscow, next stop. Grainger didn't bother going forward. He stayed aft, checking his gear, refilling the power pack on his HPM weapon, making sure that any minor damage to his equipment didn't slip by him.

He was going to need all his hardware again real soon now. Chun's displacement heads-up sounded through the TC's intercom. When a second shiver of reality and Chun's terse, "Displacement complete," told him the TC was back in its hidey-hole in the catacombs, he pounded the interlock release with his fist and went forward.

Both of his teammates looked at him soulfully.

"How're you doing, Grainger?" Chun asked.

He shrugged, leaning his head against the bulkhead. "Hope you got pictures of that UTL capsule while it existed."

"I did," Chun assured him. "But those people . . . are you sure you're okay?"

"Why?" he snapped in a furious rush. "Because I had to fry some indigs? Don't I look okay to you? Anybody tell you this was going to be a nonlethal mission, Chun? You got guilt by association? Or are you just trying to 'share my pain.' Don't bother. It don't mean squat. Where I come from, we would have said those Ruskies got off easy."

"Grainger, that's enough. Chun, let him alone." Roebeck returned her attention to the Phase Two strike plan for Moscow.

Live people whining about other folks' dead people always pissed him off. He whacked the bulkhead release and stalked aft to sulk. His equipment could use some attention. He'd cleaned everything he might be using in Moscow one more time. You couldn't be too careful.

The strike on FILI was going to be harder than the operation in Obninsk, because nukes were stored in the downtown Moscow facility. That was the real reason that Roebeck had gone back to Central. For one thing, you needed suits armored for operating in what might be a severely hot LZ. For another, you didn't want to irradiate the main timeline, make gross changes that might impact your own future, if you could help it. If you screwed up, you were doing an unintended revision, with all the consequences. And those consequences could be as damaging to the future the ARC Riders were trying to protect as the revision they were trying to prevent.

So Chun had huddled with the Extrapolation analysts, and they had a plan of sorts. But what they really had—what counted—was a risk analysis of the consequences of making a radioactive mess of downtown Moscow. If they had no alternative, even radioactive consequences beat letting this revision proceed unchecked.

No ARC Rider liked the thought of it. But downtown Moscow was no place to store nuclear weapons, either. Normally, the missiles would have been moved out to silos, submarines, various other delivery systems. But the privatization decree of July, 1991, had the weapons producers and the military providers at each other's throats about who owned what. So warheads and the missiles they rode in were sitting around in odd places. FILI was just one unfortunate place to choose to keep your nukes.

Since Roebeck had secured New Rules of Engagement with relaxed collateral damage parameters, they'd do what they damned well had to do. Central said maybe one more nuclear accident in Russia would be survivable so far as the timeline was concerned. As for the Muskovites, that was another matter.

Chun had ascertained that there'd been at least thirteen nuclear "events" before '92 that had never been publicly admitted or documented outside the USSR. Although none of those nuclear accidents had been in Moscow, Central had run the simulations and was pretty sure the local hot quotient wasn't going to get upped all that much—if the nuclear event was an emission. If the nuclear event was an explosion, all bets were off: They were just as likely to create a revision as to forestall one.

Still, getting Moscow hot was only a risk with Plan B. Plan A was for the ARC Riders to nab themselves some revisionists and do this mission the old-fashioned way. Do it nice and quiet and with as little fuss and muss as possible.

Grainger didn't mind trying Plan A. He just didn't think it would work.

It took long enough to stash the TC and scramble through the tunnels that he'd calmed down some by the time they'd gotten to the Metropole. After the hardsuit, the tunnels didn't make him feel shut in this time. They were downright spacious. The team just made it to the hotel by their ETA of 0900 hours local time.

Reobeck was emphatic about keeping her appointment with Orlov and having Chun keep hers with Etkin, planned the night before for 1000, local time. Bundling up the revisionists for their trip to 50K would be easiest that way, during scheduled meetings. If they could pull it off.

On this horizon, you could see no sign that, nearby, a closed city had been invaded, sacked, and left to mourn its dead. Russians didn't freak easy. Of course, Obninsk communications and transportation capabilites were pretty well nil right now. That might account for the absent signs of heightened alert status. No troop carriers were prowling. Police weren't doubled up in their cars. Ad hoc checkpoints hadn't blossomed on bridges and at intersections. At least, not yet.

It was also possible that so few knew of what happened— or would ever know—that the Obninsk strike was—and would stay—in the noise level. After all, the strike was on a secret city, accessible by invitation only.

Or so Chun insisted.

Here in Moscow, whatever happened was going to have visible repercussions. Grainger didn't bother to make the point. Everybody understood what was happening here. The two women just weren't as pumped as he was.

Roebeck wanted to get coffee, of all things. So off they went, repacked operational gearbags in hand, into the main dining room with its gold pillars and stained-glass ceiling. He left them to it. "I'll wait at the front door for Etkin," he told them.

The sight of all that good food and greedy, privileged people alive to eat it nearly made him sick.

"Grainger, you should eat," Roebeck criticized.

"Is that an order?"

"No, it's not. Go on then."

She and Chun had their heads together, whispering about him as he left.

Grainger didn't wait at the front door. He went outside, into the air. Polluted or not, it didn't smell like people and food. So he saw Etkin's car pull up, with Orlov's right behind it.

Damn.

Etkin had a bodyguard with him today. He recognized Grainger, waiting on the front steps. *"Privyet,"* he called, and spoke to the bodyguard.

"*Privyet,*" Grainger called back, shifting his gearbag on his shoulder. Like "yo" or "hello," it didn't mean much more than a basic mammalian acknowledgment.

Etkin came to meet him. The bodyguard went straight to Orlov's car and held the door open for Orlov as the Foreign Ministry official got out.

Etkin said, "Oh, I so regret arriving late. Let us hurry and find your friends." Etkin touched Grainger's arm to move him along. These senior Russians liked to touch you. Grainger was in no mood for physical contact. He shook off the touch. Over Etkin's shoulder, he could see Orlov, arguing with the bodyguard. Something was going to happen back there.

He wanted to watch it. But Etkin was insistent. As Grainger went inside with Etkin, he caught a glimpse of Orlov's frightened face, pale beneath its scrawny beard. The bodyguard was pushing Orlov into Etkin's car with a hand on Orlov's head in a practiced police procedure.

So Etkin had heard something about Obninsk. Or else he was coincidentally moving to preempt the competition.

Grainger paced Etkin, walking rapidly through the Metropole while telling him about today's schedule. When Etkin stopped for breath, Grainger said, "That was Mr. Orlov, wasn't it? Nan was supposed to see him today. Do you know where he's going?"

"Oh, yes. We will produce him later. We have a meeting he must attend." Etkin showed those perfect teeth.

Orlov was on Nan's list of candidates for 50K. Not having him available would be a real stumbling block in the path of Plan A: he was Nan's key to FILI. Without him, she might not be able to get back in there peacefully.

They found Nan and Chun in the dining room. Etkin and Grainger pulled up chairs. Once pleasantries were exchanged, Etkin said, "Mr. Orlov has been detained. He will meet us at FILI at approximately eleven o'clock, if it is satisfactory. I have his apologies for you."

Grainger couldn't believe his ears. Etkin knew Grainger had seen what happened. And then, slowly, it all fell into place. The perfect teeth. Even the best-looking, KGB-groomed, ready-for-export Russian didn't have teeth like that. Gold fillings, maybe. Caps, sure. But those teeth were the result of flawless nutrition over a lifetime. It all made sense to him: the calculated Russian English, the KGB gloss. The preemptive move all of a sudden on Orlov, so soon after the Obninsk strike.

Etkin wasn't after Orlov. Etkin was after the ARC Riders. He was getting a valuable asset, Orlov, out of his field of fire.

Etkin was the local agent from Up The Line. Grainger would have bet his life on that assessment. Probably was betting it right now. Etkin had stones, Grainger had to give him that.

Grainger didn't hear much of what Etkin was telling the women. Instead, his attention was drawn again to the pale skin on Etkin's ring finger. Not a circle, as a wedding ring might have left. But an oversize oval—class ring. A KGB ring, he'd thought when first he'd seen Etkin. Now he kept remembering the Citadel class ring that Dr. Bill had continually twisted back in Central. The white skin on Etkin's finger was that very size and shape.

Then he heard Etkin say, "Come with me to FILI, now. All of you," and Grainger focused in on the moment at hand.

The ARC Riders had a standing hand sign for "fall back and regroup."

Grainger gave that hand signal to his team. Maybe it looked to Etkin as if he was brushing away a fly. If there were flies in here, they would have to be *nomenclatura* flies.

Chun saw the hand sign. Nan didn't. Chun touched Nan under the table and shook her head. Nan's eyes flicked across the faces of her team. "Maybe we'd better pass. Tim has another meeting scheduled. We're all tired. We could take this time to rest up . . ."

"Oh; oh, no. I must insist," Etkin said. "We would not want to offend our hosts who are busy arranging the scalar technology meeting that Quo has so urgently requested. They must meet with all your team to set ground rules. I have gone to great trouble to arrange this."

"I bet you have," Grainger said. Nan's eyes widened.

"Then let's do this, Professor Etkin. You come with us up-stairs while we rearrange our schedule. Or wait for us here. Or in the lobby. Your choice."

Etkin sat back in his seat. His pale shooter's eyes appraised Grainger. Then he nodded. "All right. We will go to your rooms."

Okay, buddy, if that's the way you want it.

Chun and Roebeck were whispering together. Roebeck wanted to know what the hell was going on. Chun couldn't tell her. But they were going to back him. It was the best he could expect.

They paid the check, leaving a rouble tip written on the bill instead of dollars, since Etkin was watching. No use getting the wait staff in trouble. They might never get the tip, but they wouldn't get arrested for holding dollars, either.

Etkin moved in on Chun, deftly cutting her out of the group as the four made their way to the elevators. Nan whispered to Grainger, "What is it?"

"UTL." He indicated Etkin with a quick jab of his finger. "We've got to talk privately."

"Maybe he'll go with Chun and we can join them after we talk," Nan murmured.

Etkin and Chun turned to wait for them to catch up. Chun said, "Viktor says we really need to meet this group he has convened for us as soon as we can."

"We are due at FILI right now," Etkin said, scowling.

"Yeah, well. I can't offend my visitor, either. And Nan needs to get her things." Grainger crossed his arms.

Roebeck said, "You two go on. Go to Chun's room. We'll make a couple quick calls and meet you there in five minutes. I promise, it won't take longer than that."

Etkin seemed immediately mollified, almost jovial. "This is very acceptable. Quo and I have much to discuss, protocols for this meeting."

A big Russian in a raincoat joined them as they waited for an upward-traveling car. Maybe the guy in the raincoat was an innocent stranger. Maybe he was Etkin's boy. He acknowledged no one and pushed no floor indicator when he crowded into the small Russian elevator with them. Nobody said a word until the door opened at their floor.

The stranger got out, and headed down one corridor. Chun and Etkin took another. Grainger and Roebeck followed Chun and Etkin, then turned a corner, going toward Nan's room, not Chun's.

As soon as they heard Chun's door opening and closing, Roebeck said, "UTL? How do you know?"

"I was waiting outside, remember. Orlov pulled up right behind Etkin. Etkin's bodyguard just about arrested Orlov in front of me, muscled him into Etkin's car, and drove away with him. So Etkin's making his move. Why? He knows about Obninsk. How? Not from local channels. Not yet."

"You can't be sure, Tim. You're overreacting. Reaching."

"You want to talk about this *here*, in *this* hallway? You're the boss. Okay. It's those teeth. Too good for this century, let alone this culture. I should have realized it before. And his ring finger's missing a Citadel class ring like Dr. Bill's." If you were active-duty KGB and you had a ring saying so, you wouldn't be wearing it routinely enough to keep the skin under it from tanning.

"Sure, Tim. Fine. You call Matsak, cancel your appointment or postpone it. I want to see what Etkin's got up his sleeve. You've got your gearbag. What are you worried about?"

"Oh, nothing. Just ending up in a Fourth Rome, that's all. But if you don't mind returning to an altered future, who am I to quibble?" He stalked off to his room, keyed the lock, and slammed the door. Then he called Matsak and asked a secretary to make certain the Ministry of Science Deputy joined Grainger at the Metropole as soon as possible. He wasn't going to Etkin's meeting. He'd say he'd come later. They shouldn't all walk into the same trap.

When he was done, he half ran through the halls to join Roebeck and Etkin in Chun's room.

Nan was standing outside in the hall waiting for him. The door to Chun's room was open. He knew they'd fucked up by the look on Roebeck's face, before he saw any more than those basic situation parameters.

"What?" he called. "What is it?" He ran those last few steps flat out.

Roebeck, hands on hips, was standing in the doorway, shaking her head.

"They're not here," she said calmly and motioned him inside. "They're gone. Chun would never leave without us. It's against every procedure—"

"He's got her."

Grainger let his gearbag slip to the floor. The room looked just like his. It was completely empty of personal effects. Chun and her gearbag were gone as if they'd never been. The two remaining ARC Riders searched thoroughly, not saying a word where surveillance was a certainty.

Soon it was clear Chun had been able to leave no sign, message, or clue behind. She'd either been taken by surprise or . . . Grainger didn't want to think about the alternate scenarios.

Roebeck phoned the desk to see if either Etkin or Chun had left a message there for them.

"Nothing from Chun or Etkin," Roebeck told him in an emotionless voice. "Your Matsak's down there waiting, though."

Grainger ignored her last words. "Etkin's not worried about maintaining any fiction of cooperation at this point. I should have known," he said. He couldn't think what to do. He just stood there in the middle of the room, his own gearbag at his feet. "Of course, Etkin would try this stunt. *I* would have. Same mission parameters. Remove the opposing force from play on this horizon. We've got the same game plan, don't you see? And now he's got one of us . . ." If he went near any physical thing, a wall, a piece of furniture, he'd wreak havoc on whatever came to hand. "How stupid can you get?"

"Stop this. You've got a Russian waiting for you. I'm going back to get the TC. I want Chun back. Everything else is on hold."

"Bullshit. We'll get her back. Everything gets done. Plan B." He put a finger to his lips and grabbed a Metropole notepad. He wrote quickly, under cover of his left hand: *We can track her if she's still got her gear.* He tore the top three

·sheets from the pad, folded the notepaper, and handed the sheets to Roebeck.

Then he checked the pad to make sure there was no impression of the handwriting on the remaining paper before he threw the pad in the wastebasket.

She nodded. "All right. Plan B, with a little improvisation. But the TC's location is at risk. I've got to move it stat." As she talked, she walked out of Chun's empty room.

Grainger hefted his gearbag and followed her. They had to move fast. Or Chun would be irretrievably lost to them. You couldn't step twice into the same venue. Matsak was waiting downstairs. Roebeck had to relocate the TC or they'd all be lost—here or in a changed future Up The Line didn't matter.

"Hey, boss. Wait up." Roebeck was moving so fast Grainger had to run to keep up. Same war, different day.

When they got downstairs, not only Matsak but Zotov were waiting for them.

Matsak strode right up to Grainger, Zotov in tow. The Ministry official said, "The Tim! Oh, this is well! We have *bolshoi problema.*"

"*Bolshoi problema!*" Zotov echoed, his face working so that every fleshy growth on it wriggled.

Grainger said, "*Yop t'voyu problema.*" *Fuck your big problem.* "I've got a *bolshoi problema* of my own, Sasha."

"So sorry, Tim," said Matsak, stroking his beard. "In my opinion, these problems may be one and the same. Or at least connected."

Grainger was aware of Roebeck brushing by them, rushing off to secure the TC. Plan B was under way.

"*Da, da, da,*" agreed Zotov. "The one and the same."

"Okay, I'll accept that hypothesis—for now," Grainger said. "Then we'd all better pile into that Science Ministry car of yours or go somewhere we can talk openly. I don't have much time." *Ball in your court, Matsak.* It was time to find out where Matsak stood. With Grainger, against Matsak's local enemies. On the fence. Or in Etkin's pocket. "Chun's gone. Your KGB buddy's got her. And I want her back. Now."

It was a risk, here in the lobby. But less in the open space than elsewhere, including Matsak's car. *Put your cards on the table, Matsak. Are you a player or what?*

Matsak was all fire and ice, a smithy gauging the temper of a blade in the forge. "You know where they have gone?"

Grainger nodded. "I think so. FILI."

"In my opinion," the Ministry of Science general said with an almost sensual slowness, "it will be *ahb-so-lute-ly* my pleasure to help you with this problem. My *bolshoi* pleasure." He squinted out the door through which Roebeck had gone. "To be successful, we must avoid awaking the entire sleeping US Embassy bureaucracy to this situation, *da*?"

Matsak didn't miss a trick. He was more interested in what Roebeck, who was out of his sight, might do than what Grainger, who was offering to cooperate, might do.

"It's your country, *tovarisch*. But I accept your condition. We'll keep the US out of it—not a problem." Calling a Russian "comrade" wasn't quite the same as calling him "friend." Not here. Not now. Not ever.

Vetera, Lower Germany

S orry, soldier," Pauli Weigand heard the warder say. "Nobody sees this prisoner without authorization."

Pauli's cell had sidewalls of concrete, the material at the core of most Roman building projects. The bars at either end were placed too close together for him to get his head through the gap, so he couldn't see anything but the empty cell directly across the corridor.

"So I got authorization," a familiar voice replied. Coins clinked.

"Look, buddy," the warder said in obvious distress. "I'd like to take your money, but this guy's special. Why don't we just forget you came down here, all right?"

"Look, I'll tell you how it is," the other voice explained. "I was with Varus in the 17th, you see? I hear this guy was one of the Fritzes who planned us getting the chop. I want to talk to him."

"You want to kill him, you mean?" the warder said. "Buddy, I sympathize, I really do, but he's going to be the star turn in the games tomorrow. If anything goes wrong with him, I'll be his replacement."

"Nothing like that," the soldier said. "I just want to talk. Anyway, he'll be on the other side of the bars, right?"

"I don't get it," the warder said.

"You don't have to get it," the soldier said. Coins clinked again. He went on, "Look, if your buddy gets killed, you get mad about it. If everybody in Vetera but you got killed tomorrow—you wouldn't get mad. It's too big. But you'd want to understand what the fuck happened. Trust me. And drink a better grade of wine for the next week on me, right?"

"You got a few minutes," the warder muttered. Sandals shuffled away. "But for Hermes' sake, don't let anything happen to him or my ghost'll ride your shoulder till you die!"

Pauli stood up carefully as hobnails clashed in his direction. The cells beneath the amphitheater weren't meant for men his height. They weren't meant for men at all, really: they were beast cages that could double as holding cells for humans when necessary. The animals were more valuable than human prisoners; and in neither case was the stay going to be longer than a day or two.

"Hello, Flaccus," Pauli said. "I wasn't expecting to see you."

"There's a problem with your buddies coming," the veteran said. "Somebody might remember that because they'd been your slaves, they belonged to the state when you were condemned. Now me, I don't belong to anybody but the emperor I swear an oath to at the first of each year, so I said I'd come talk to you."

Flaccus wore a tunic. Even without armor and his weapons belts, nobody could have doubted he was a soldier. His stance; the long, darkened dent on his forehead where for years a helmet had ridden; the scars on his scalp and all four limbs.

The fresh gouge over Flaccus' left eye was healing nicely. That could have been pure good luck, but Pauli suspected some of the luck might have come from a phial of antibiotics in Beckie's kit.

"Now, I don't know who you lot are," Flaccus continued judiciously, "but I know your buddies aren't slaves just like I know you didn't help the Fritzes scrag the lot of us. Thing is, nobody's going to listen to what a grunt knows; and anyhow, they needed somebody to blame the mess on who's still alive to execute."

Pauli Weigand looked at the soldier and felt ashamed of

himself. Marcus Flaccus was no saint: he'd killed and looted and probably raped without the least concern. He was a soldier of an autarchical government bent on world conquest.

But he was also a simple man who knew Pauli was innocent of aiding in the massacre of Varus and all Flaccus' tent mates. *Knew,* and was wrong; because the ARC Rider too was the agent of a power that condoned any imaginable brutality that gained its ends.

"You know what's really weird?" Flaccus said, playing with a dimple in his left forearm, a scar that must be more than a decade old. "What I told your keeper about not hating the Fritzes because it'd all been too big. It's true."

His weathered face shifted from musing to a hardness that was more frightening than anger if you knew what you were seeing. "Not that I don't look forward to going back across the river with a general who knows what he's doing. We'll teach the Fritzes what a *real* massacre looks like."

An ARC Rider couldn't allow himself to become emotionally involved . . . but Pauli remembered watching the Germans torture their prisoners and he couldn't help wondering what would have happened to him and his teammates if they'd been captured alive.

Of course, Flaccus' government was about to feed him to wild beasts in the arena.

"My friends are all right?" Pauli asked, in part to break the mood.

"Yeah, they sent this," Flaccus said. He handed Pauli a headband. Now he could communicate directly with his teammates.

When Asprenas' troops took Pauli prisoner they'd stripped him of everything but a single tunic and put a sack over his head. The headband had gone with the rest of his gear, though nobody'd realized it was more than a strip of cloth.

"They say they've got a line on the people you're looking for," Flaccus said, prodding at another old scar. "The thing is, they're wondering—"

He looked up to meet Pauli's eyes.

"—if it might not be better to get you out of here, seeing as

Tiberius arrives tonight and you're for the chop at the games in his honor tomorrow. That's what they wanted me to ask."

"No," Pauli said. "We'll all be compromised if I break out. The instant Tiberius arrives there's risk of events of the sort we're here to prevent. They've got to get on with the job first."

Flaccus put his right leg up on the bars and pinched the half moon of scar tissue over his kneecap. He stared at the mark morosely. "Thing is," he said, head lowered, "there might be some people in this town who'd help them if they did bust you out. Not everybody who came out of the ratfuck with you's fit, but some of us are."

"No," Pauli said. "No, but thank you."

Flaccus nodded. "Sure," he said. "I don't guess a magician like you needs a lot of help anyway. Well, anything you want to say to your buddies?"

"Carry on with the mission so that we can all go home," Pauli said. He'd repeat the orders over the headband communication shortly, but he wanted no doubt about his decision. "Just tell them that. And Flaccus?"

The veteran raised an eyebrow.

"Even a magician needs friends," said Pauli Weigand.

Vetera, Lower Germany

I believe I've found one of them," said Gerd Barhtuli. Then, "I've found one of them!"

The buildings of Vetera were timber with thatch roofs, but many of the streets had been graveled; proper stone paving was for the future. Rebecca Carnes found it an unexpected pleasure to be able to walk at night without squelching.

"Any notion whether it's Svetlanov or Kiknadze?" Rebecca asked. Gerd was facing a building on the other side of the street with the sensor in his hand. Still at this hour the shutters of both stories were open, spilling lamplight. The lower level was a tavern.

"I've located a submachine gun, Rebecca," Gerd said mildly. "It's only a probability that a revisionist is carrying the weapon."

The sensor pack duplicated a headband's many functions (though not in as accessible a fashion), so it was Gerd's headband they'd sent to Pauli. Rebecca pulled her faceshield down to see if light amplification or thermal viewing showed her anything her unaided eyes had missed. No; but the naked woman who leaned on a window ledge for a few moments of relaxation indicated that the building's upper story was a brothel.

"He's down below," Gerd added. "The gun is."

Rebecca checked to be sure her pistol was in the cape lining. The plastic weapon was so light you wouldn't notice the change if it fell out of the loops. "Let's take a look," she said.

Vetera was a big camp capable of holding three legions in a

pinch, though most of the troops had moved into Free Germany with Varus. A very Permanent Change of Station, to use the phrasing of Rebecca's own day.

The civil settlement served not only soldiers but the vast logistical tail that followed the troops up the Lippe River. It had a population of ten thousand. Since the team arrived in the city, she and Gerd had been searching street by street for a sign of the revisionists. Carefully metered drugs kept Rebecca alert, but they couldn't do anything for sheer muscle fatigue.

There were a dozen men and two middle-aged women in the tavern's lower room. The doorman was a hulking brute with a broken nose and scars on his sloping forehead; the bartender could have passed for his brother.

Boris Kiknadze was going up the narrow staircase behind a whore younger than the other two. She wore a shift of thin wool dyed rose and brass spirals around both forearms. The armlets had stained her skin a dingy green.

"We'll have some wine and wait," Rebecca murmured. Gerd nodded. As usual in a new environment, his expression was of sprightly cheerfulness.

"We've got a room open if you're looking for a place to spend a half hour," the bartender said as the ARC Riders approached. The other folk in the tavern were eyeing Rebecca speculatively; openly hostile speculation in the case of the women.

"Nothing like that," she said. "We'll each have a mug of whatever's cheap and local."

Gerd peered surreptitiously at the sensor pack in his palm. He shook his head minusculely when he caught Rebecca's eye: he still didn't have a fix on the other revisionist.

At some point they'd have to retrieve the advanced gear taken from Pauli. Rebecca wondered whether that pair of submachine guns would confuse their search for Svetlanov's weapon.

"That'll be three bronze," the bartender said. He placed his hands flat on the stone slab, pointedly refusing to lift the narrow wine-ladle until he'd seen the strangers' money.

Rebecca reached for her purse. A woman screamed upstairs.

The doorman and bartender both grabbed clubs. Before they could get to the stairs, the whore took two steps down. She wore the armlets but she'd lost her shift. There were toothmarks on her right breast.

Kiknadze appeared behind her and grabbed her by the hair. A switch of false hair pulled out in his hand with a few of the woman's own ringlets. Half bald, she screamed and pitched the rest of the way to the bracken-strewn floor.

The bartender started up. Kiknadze tried to kick him in the face. The local man had plenty of experience with both violent patrons and this staircase. He grabbed Kiknadze by the ankle and pulled down. Kiknadze wrapped his left arm around the railing.

The rail pulled loose. Kiknadze's right hand dipped under his cape and came out with the Skorpion. The bartender swung his club at the weapon—uncertain of exactly what it was but in no doubt as to what Kiknadze's general intentions were.

"Down!" Rebecca shouted to Gerd as she ducked beneath the stone bar.

The tavern's only light was a pair of three-wick oil lamps. The submachine gun's muzzle flashes were bright enough to cast a flickering shadow. One wild round hit a drinker in a booth across the room. He collapsed and slid under his table. The bartender grunted, then lost his grip on both the club and Kiknadze's leg.

The bartender fell back, tangling with the doorman. Kiknadze clubbed the latter twice with the Skorpion's butt and pushed past the two men. A regular patron stepped in front of the doorway, then jumped back when he saw Kiknadze's murderous fury.

The revisionist ran out of the tavern, waving his submachine gun. The bartender stood on all fours, shaking his head groggily and dripping blood on the floor. The doorman was upright again.

Rebecca waited for Kiknadze to clear the doorway, then

followed him. Gerd was only a step behind her. She tugged her faceshield down, brightening the night to apparent daylight levels. The scene had a certain flatness from the loss of the three-dimensional modeling that shadows provide.

"That's right, get the bastard!" the doorman cried. He and a half dozen of the tavern's patrons spilled out after the ARC Riders. "Let's hang him by the dick!"

Kiknadze was twenty yards down the street. He glanced over his shoulder. Rebecca flattened against the side of the building. Kiknadze waved his gun but didn't shoot. Either he couldn't see targets or he'd emptied the Skorpion inside the tavern. He lurched around a corner.

Rebecca had the microwave pistol in her hand. If she knocked Kiknadze down the mob would beat him to death. She and Gerd needed to interrogate the revisionist; that, or hope he led them to Svetlanov on his own. Best that Kiknadze run until the locals had lost interest.

Adjacent buildings had common sidewalls. Kiknadze couldn't flee down an alley between structures. There were no streetlights and the partial moon was dim help without the ARC faceshield's advanced technology.

Rebecca reached the corner, pointed the opposite way from the one Kiknadze had taken, and shouted, "There he goes! See him there?"

The trick might have worked, but the revisionist tripped in the darkness and whanged his submachine gun against a stone doorstep. It rang like a bell. The locals panting in the middle of the street spun to look for the source of the noise. Kiknadze stood up in front of the only lighted window on the block.

"There he is!" the doorman cried. He and the twenty-odd locals with him crashed down the street after their quarry. The whore whose cries had started the trouble was among them. She wore sequined sandals and a short cape that covered her to the waist.

Doors opened; still more people were joining the hunt. Rebecca felt her lips tighten as if she were sucking something sour. All she could do for now was keep up with the mob and hope for the best.

Kiknadze ran into a public square, an irregular trapezoid where five streets met. He dodged around the stone coping of the wall in the center. Residents aroused by the mob's cries peered from windows or out half-opened doors. Patches of light spilled past them, quivering on gravel and the opposite walls. Kiknadze's head turned in all directions as he looked for a way clear.

At the opposite side of the square was a six-hole public toilet raised several steps off the ground. A plaque on the chest-high stone screen commemorated the benefactor who'd built the convenience.

A handcart holding a large terra-cotta jar was parked in front of the structure. As Kiknadze paused, a slave holding a smaller jar by the rim stepped out. The municipal sanitation detail was emptying the urinal—at a profit; the urine was sold to stiffen woolen garments for cleaning.

"Get him! Get him!" the doorkeeper cried as he ran into the square. Rebecca was beside him. She was more afraid of losing the revisionist than that he might shoot her if cornered.

Kiknadze saw the slave behind him and pointed the Skorpion. The pot of waste shattered as the slave fell forward down the steps. Kiknadze jumped his body and entered the structure. He dropped the submachine gun and reached into the satchel hanging from his shoulder.

"Rebecca, he's got a grenade!" Gerd shouted.

The revisionist's arm drew back. He intended to shelter behind the stone screen as the blast cleared the square.

Rebecca shot Kiknadze from twenty feet away. The jolt of focused energy knocked him backward into the structure, still holding the bomb.

Rebecca crouched. A man ran into her from behind and tripped. A white flash and ground shock were simultaneous. Light gleamed through cracks in the screen. The echoing blast hurled chips of stone and burned flesh skyward. One of the stone panels fell over.

The doorman picked himself up. The structure had channeled part of the shock wave out the entrance. "Lightning?" he said. "Was that lightning?"

There was blood on his face. Grenade shrapnel had nicked him, not seriously.

Rebecca stepped into the open structure, fumbling for her medical kit. The revisionist didn't have to be healthy or even conscious for Gerd to comb his mind for the information they needed. There was a chance—

There was no chance at all.

Rebecca straightened and let her faceshield roll back into the headband. The stench of explosive and mangled bodies was so familiar to her that she didn't even feel disgusted.

Some locals had recovered enough to enter the structure. One of them ran his fingers over the shrapnel pocks on the inside of the screening panels.

"Rebecca?" Gerd asked.

Rebecca Carnes let the whore push her aside to get a better look.

"I'd hoped maybe a tourniquet . . ." she said to her teammate. "But he must have had the grenade under his right ear when it went off. We're going to have to find Svetlanov on our own."

Moscow, Russia

March 11, 1992

Roebeck didn't pilot the TC as much as she should. A life like Roebeck's offered one basic choice: you got to pilot, or you got to shoot. Mostly, Roebeck preferred to shoot. But to keep her competency rating, she had to requalify on the TC every six months.

Thank God.

She wasn't a wand wizard like Chun. But she could slide this temporal capsule into a volume a cubic foot greater than its own and not scrape hull.

Still, it was an eerie feeling being alone in the TC. She had her coms wide open, monitoring all the ambient message traffic. Simultaneously, she was listening to Grainger's com channel in case he had time to check in with her.

He would if he could. She knew Grainger as well as any specialist she'd ever had. When it came to action items, protocols, and checklists, you could set your watch by him. He'd go by the book if he could. And today's Plan B playbook required him to attempt contact via membrane comlink before setting foot in FILI.

So as she was taking the TC out of the catacombs, she kept one ear alert.

Roebeck had to do this mission in stages, if her altered plan was to work. The absence of Chun felt very different than the absence of Grainger. Grainger was running around out there, loose on the local horizon, armed and dangerous. Chun was . . .

. . . gone. Captured by the enemy. Out of play.

She didn't even want to sit in the seat where Chun should be sitting.

But Roebeck had to go through Chun's data, find the FILI coordinates, lay them into a macro on a preset. Everything must be preprogrammed, this time. All systems had to be capable of functioning remotely, automatically, perfectly calculated in time and space.

Once an ARC ops team had worked a particular duration of elapsed time coordinates, they were barred from those coordinates forever.

If they blew this mission totally, Central could always send another team back—if there was still a Central Up The Line that wanted to send another team back here.

Which there might not be, if the ARC Riders failed here and now. So her two loyalties—one to team, the other to corps—were merged into a single concentrated need to act.

To preempt, if she got lucky. Prevent, if at all possible. Interdict, if necessary. Or stop, if all else failed.

You weren't expected to need to pilot a temporal capsule from a hardsuit. They had, theoretically, redundant capabilities. The hardsuit could take her anywhere in time that a temporal capsule could take her. But no hardsuit or TC alone could do everything else she needed to do today.

So at last, having exhausted every other possible option, she displaced from the local horizon in TC 779. Had to keep the elapsed time to a minimum. She hung the capsule out of phase until she finished her preparations, no longer listening for Grainger's hail. He couldn't reach her, not where she was now.

Then she deserted the chair where Chun usually sat and got into her overpowered hardsuit. At Central, they'd swapped the standard suits for these, citing altered requirements and sufficient danger to their persons.

She'd done it over Grainger's objections. She was being overly cautious then. There were nuclear devices in FILI.

There was nuclear contamination at Obninsk. Now she was doubly glad she'd insisted on the exo-skeletal servo-powered suits.

The big suit was a pain to get ready. But in this mode she had all the prep time she needed.

Still, when she displaced back to 1992 and phased in FILI, she wasn't going to have much time at all.

The TC could be preprogrammed to perform a number of actions with a variable delay. She could control that delay from the big hardsuit. She couldn't have done that from a standard suit.

When she'd finished all her preparations, she ran through every check she could perform, short of a real-time systems burn-in, a live-fire field trial.

She couldn't afford to lock herself out of a single critical instant of the real time out there beyond the nothingness in which the TC now floated.

On the temporal horizon in which 1992 was real time, too many lives and fates still hung in the balance.

Fitted out in her massive armor, she trudged into the lock. Sealed it. Checked her event sequencer. Pulled down her entire set of display options and tucked them into the corners of her visor display. Double-checked once more what she'd redundantly checked before.

On her visor display at two o'clock she had a locator that would try to zero on Grainger. She enabled it. At ten o'clock she had a locator that might be able to zero on Chun. If, that is, the ARC Riders still had their gearbags, or if their C and C membranes were in contact with their skins and therefore could respond to an inquiry. All membranes had integral inquiry-driven IFF: Identify Friend or Foe.

Okay. If Grainger and/or Chun were operational, the system would find them eventually.

Next Roebeck enabled a virtual remote controller under her suit's left glove and tapped once. TC 779 displaced. Every signature reader in her helmet opened to a feed from the TC's bow screen.

FILI's nuclear weapons storage bay came into view around

her with a rush. The bay looked, and read in all signatures, empty of human life. She felt as if she'd already rephased outside the TC by suit.

She hadn't. She tapped a second preset. The lock opened, not laterally, but horizontally, becoming the ramp they'd retrofitted at Central to accommodate the larger hardsuits. She strolled manually down into the nuke bay, taking her leisure. She was eternally safe here and now. Around her, to the edges of the storage area and beyond, was a blue nimbus, an aura. Static from the active field producing the nimbus buzzed through her audio channel as if a thousand bees were massing.

Once she was physically clear of the ramp, she surveyed the TC's situation in the storage bay. Several of the nuclear weapons had been dislodged, perhaps damaged by TC 779's materialization. A tail fin was sticking out under the TC itself, as if the capsule was sitting on a missile. A sick feeling came over her. She shook it off. Oh, well. If there were to be problems from the disturbed nukes, they wouldn't occur until Nan allowed time in this compartment of the venue to proceed.

Blue sparks and static bursts crackled and crawled along the walls and ceilings of FILI's nuclear storage area, along the weapons themselves. Some of these crude rockets were big enough to take out a good chunk of city if they blew. If they blew, Nan Roebeck would have created one hell of a revision. A few of the smaller missiles had keys attached to them by crude wires, a pair of keys per missile. How did ancient nuclear weapons work, exactly? If she'd ever known, she'd forgotten. She was pretty sure that a nuclear warhead wouldn't produce a mushroom cloud unless its triggering mechanism was keyed. It could still kill you if it dropped on your head, but most anything with mass could do that. Fissionable materials from cracked warhead casings might leak radiation at dangerous levels, but that too was less catastrophic than a thermonuclear explosion.

Roebeck stomped among the missiles and rockets, safe and secure in her hardsuit from any possible radiation threat.

She took the keys, pair by pair, from the smaller birds. Each key looked like an antique door key with a hollow metal oval at one end. Through the hollow oval were threaded red rep cloth strips, each sewn to a single point. Thin, short metal tags with serial numbers hung from each key on a small loop of flimsy wire. She crushed each pair of keys in turn.

These nukes might still go bang by accident. She was too unfamiliar with the technology to know how to preclude unintended detonation. And there'd been nothing about preventing nuclear warhead detonation in Central's download. But no one would arm them purposely. Not today, anyhow. Three large pieces of equipment she examined were neither missiles nor booster rockets. They were space station modules, big enough to walk through even in Nan's hardsuit.

There was no hurry now. Everything in FILI had been temporally frozen the instant that the TC arrived. Except for Roebeck in her hardsuit, there was no threat abroad here.

If she'd come too late in the day and found she must leave and return at an earlier insertion point, she'd have to be out of here before the instant of her initial arrival. Or she'd cease to exist and her teammates would be stranded.

She hoped to hell she wasn't too late. Or too early. Damn, why hadn't Grainger checked in with her?

She knew the answer must be that he couldn't check in. She tried not to dwell on it.

Tim knew the risks. Knew the plan. They all did.

Chun did, too. And that was one of the problems. If Grainger was right, Etkin was a UTL agent of revisionists from a future farther than her native present. If he had UTL skills, he might have been able to extract the specifics of their plan from Chun.

In which case, the hardsuit was going to come in very handy. Roebeck intruder-locked TC 779 to recognize only her combined heartbeat and respiration. No one else could operate it now but she.

It was either that or leave the temporal capsule vulnerable

to Etkin in order to make it accessible to Chun or Grainger if
they survived her.

Having precluded both the theft of TC 779 and the chance
of a nuclear event in FILI while she was hunting for her team
and the revisionists, she enabled the tracker that should be
able to locate Grainger.

When her in-suit tracking system had a lock, the little display at two o'clock on her visor began to blink. Grainger! The
system had located him.

Roebeck phased out to the auto-targeted LZ containing Tim
Grainger with a tap on her virtual keypad.

The room in which she found herself was the same one
where she'd sat interminably while hard-liners strutted their
stuff. Only this time, it was Grainger who sat at the green-
clothed table, arms behind him on a straight chair, flanked by
pineapple sodas and hard-liners with bad suits. He was
trussed in the chair like a Christmas turkey. His gearbag was
open on the table.

Grainger couldn't see her. He was frozen in time, caught in
a distended instant. He didn't know she was there. Neither did
any of the others in the room.

But Grainger was the only person in the room she really
cared about.

Neat was there, leaning forward with his woodcutter's
hunch, finger pointing in midair. Lipinsky was there, with his
lizard's smirk, standing, arm raised, a truncheon in his hand
poised to strike their prisoner. So she had two prime revisionist targets in her sights, plus cohorts. But Chun wasn't there.
Etkin wasn't there. Nor was Zotov. Or Orlov. Or Matsak.
They *had* to be here somewhere. Grainger was here. Chun
had to be here. Etkin had been absolutely determined to bring
them here.

Roebeck stood very still and watched her locator display
out of the corner of her eye. Chun's position still hadn't been
identified. With the tiniest of finger taps, Roebeck banished
the locator function that was still telling her Grainger was
right in front of her.

The tap, the tiniest motion she could manage, had massive repercussions.

Blue sparks streamed from her fingertip. They rose in a cascade across the ceiling to the walls. They crawled down the walls and across the floor. The stasis field was beginning to stress. You really weren't supposed to move around in frozen time. It was against all regulations. You normally created an active bubble in which you worked, a center-punch in which time proceeded normally. Her hardsuit was providing an active bubble around its occupant, but any move the suit itself made was still movement through a temporal stasis field. Even the tiniest motion of her finger was still making eddies.

At ARC school they didn't tell you why you shouldn't do things, except very generally. They'd say this isn't survivable, or you'll get your head handed to you if you do that. Or there won't be enough left of you to bury if you try thus-and-so. Nobody'd ever said exactly what might happen if you went roaming around in a frozen time stasis field. They just said don't try it, you won't like it.

Well, she wouldn't be doing this if she didn't need to do it.

"Coming to get you, Grainger," she said softly inside her suit to the Rider who couldn't hear her.

Determined, she clomped over to the frozen tableau at the table. Once there, she was standing in a whirlwind of blue lightning. Through it, she reached carefully for Tim Grainger. His unarmored body was frail. Suddenly she was afraid to touch him with her armored hand, crawling with blue lightning. Instead, she carefully scooped his gear into his bag with her armored forearm. The gear didn't melt before her eyes. She smoothed the bag closed, then slid her arm through its straps. She lifted the bag. It didn't explode or disintegrate.

But she'd made too many motions. The stasis field where she'd been moving was all choppy waves, blue-frothed and angry. A breaker of energy crashed against her forearm. Spume flew. For an instant she couldn't see anything but a blue wall sluicing over her like a tidal wave.

Then through blue sparks like sleet running down her visor, she noticed that Grainger's face was bruised, starting to swell. So there'd been a scuffle before they tied him up like that. He had a scrape running from his temple into his hair.

She must be very careful as she snapped the bonds that kept him in his chair and lifted him. She had no idea what moving an unprotected human frozen in stasis was going to do to that person. The bag over her arm was filled with inanimate objects. The fact that she could fill the bag and lift it only proved that inanimates weren't destroyed out of hand by the field disturbances she was creating. The effect of such a disturbed field on Grainger, or the others near him, was anybody's guess.

She was risking everything, here and now. Beyond what might happen to Grainger and the revisionists held in frozen time, she had growing concerns for her own safety. What might be happening to the active field generated by her hardsuit? Or to the bubble of frozen time in which all of FILI now existed? Was she putting the entire mission at risk because she was unwilling to lose Tim Grainger?

Attrition of your force was a risk all ARC team leaders had to accept. It wasn't that she didn't accept the possibility that she might lose Grainger. He might die yet. He might die from her very effort to save him. She just wasn't willing to lose him without a fight.

Now or never, she told herself. *Pick him* up, *fool. You can stand here until you die of old age, safe in your private active bubble. It won't mean a thing to him. Or anybody else.*

If she waited much longer, she'd talk herself out of doing anything at all. Or Etkin would find her and preclude her options. She still had no idea what kind of technology her UTL enemy might be able to field.

First she noticed, as she lifted the ARC Rider from his chair, how stiff he was. Grainger's limbs stayed rigidly in the position they'd asumed when time froze here.

Then she saw a nonexistent wind whirl the sparking blue sleet into the empty space he'd left. The sleet became trails. The trails became comets' tails. The comets' tails became a bright, human-shaped cascade. Then she had to squint to see far enough to make sure she still held Grainger's body in her servo-powered arms. Her visor had automatically damped her incoming video to protect her eyes from a blue flash of sheet lightning that wrapped around Grainger's form as if she'd pulled him through a blanket of wet tissue paper.

Electrically charged wet tissue paper.

There was no turning back. If she was killing him, then it was probably already too late. She couldn't leave him there. Not with so much at stake and other temporal actors at work.

She stomped determinedly three steps back from the table, intent on returning to her entry coordinates in the conference room before she phased out with Grainger in her arms. Never mind that those coordinates were now seething with blue light.

She wasn't sure whether carrying Grainger in her suit's powerful arms had been such a good idea. But the only way to transport him when she phased was to hold him in contact with her suit. She certainly couldn't tromp through the whole of FILI, carrying Grainger, plowing holes in the stasis field as she went. She had no idea what happened when you altered the volumetrics of a stasis field, except that so far, it seemed survivable.

Roebeck still thought she should try to step back into the space she'd originally occupied. She asked for a rearward-facing view. Blue sparking chaos filled every bit of space behind her, every cubic inch she'd disturbed as she'd moved away from the table. The sight convinced her not to move any more than necessary.

Her track through frozen space-time looked as if she'd plowed blue snow angels in a drift, or fashioned cut-out figures of herself from a blue sun's corona. She'd created a palpable daisy chain of suited Roebecks, all carrying Graingers, all limned in blue lightning. The time-prints didn't fade. They were solid, like footprints in concrete. If Etkin was from farther Up The Line, he might be able to use those neon tracks to chart her movements through the stasis field.

She hit the return button on her virtual remote. She heard

an earsplitting snap. Either the noise came from inside her suit or else was loud enough to hear straight through all that armor. She told herself not to worry about it.

Then for a moment she saw nothing but blackness. She was in total darkness. Maybe that snap had been the last complaint of failing visor-controlled electronics. If so, her hardsuit might now be her coffin. She had no idea whether the servo-powered system could be operated safely without visor controls. If the servos froze up, she couldn't get out of the hardsuit. She'd die when her air was exhausted.

The suit she was wearing gave her no sense of whether she was still carrying Grainger or not. She didn't move a muscle. Maybe just her visor circuits had fried. Maybe she was back at the TC, inside the active bubble, and didn't know it because she couldn't see anything.

But it didn't feel as if she was standing on anything at all.

Time to try to move.

She hit the virtual remote's keypad again, this time jabbing her finger downward as hard as she could.

Blue sparks flashed around the edges of her vision. Her visor flashed white. The white light shrank to a tiny blazing dot and disappeared.

"Shit, this is weird," she muttered aloud.

And then she could see. She was standing in the active bubble, a few steps from the TC, with Grainger in her arms. And he was struggling to get free.

She held him tighter for a moment before she realized why he was writhing so desperately. He saw TC 779 and safety ahead. Then she enabled her exterior speaker. "Grainger, you okay? Don't go near the capsule yet. It's booby-trapped. Hold on . . ." To cancel the intruder lock on TC 779 using her virtual keypad she needed more than one finger. She had to shift Grainger's legs up on her right forearm to free her hand. The servos made her motion more abrupt than she intended.

"Put me the hell down, if you want me to take your orders!" said the startled man being jostled in her arms. "What the fuck happened? First I was about to be whacked in the head with a sock full of sand, then I was—" Grainger looked up, around, at the ceiling with its blue trails, at the walls where sparks crawled.

Then he murmured groggily, "Roebeck, you didn't? You wouldn't . . . Yeah, you did. You could have killed me. Yourself. Chun. Blown the system. Punched a fucking hole in the Dirac sea. Then what?"

"I did," she admitted through her exterior speaker. "And nothing went wrong. So it never happened, okay?" When he didn't respond immediately, she tightened grip on his body in her arms, oh so carefully. "Okay?"

"Okay! Put me down before you snap my spine."

She carefully put him down on the floor of the nuclear storage bay. But he couldn't stand. He collapsed and half sat, half lay, propped up on one stiff arm, his free hand to his head.

"Take it easy," she told him. "We have all the time we need."

"Figures you'd say that," she heard him mutter, and she began to giggle. If he was trying to tear her a new asshole, then how badly could he be hurt?

"Hot dog," he accused.

For the first time, she was sure that Grainger was going to be all right. She couldn't stop giggling. He looked so helpless.

Then he said, "Where's Chun? Matsak? Zotov? Orlov? Etkin?"

Her throat went dry and prickly. "Don't you know?"

"Hell no, I don't know. We had this little . . . discussion. There were too many of them. They split us up. Last I saw, Etkin, Zotov, and Matsak were together. Etkin calls the shots here, but Orlov was right with him, taking direction like a pro. Guess Orlov had a little tune-up." Grainger wiped his mouth, spit a froth of bloody foam onto the floor. "I didn't see Chun at all."

"Her gearbag? Her membrane?"

"Etkin's got her, so he's got them. He knew exactly what mine were. Probably knew from the moment he saw us. Don't assume that he's stupid enough not to take her membrane off her. Those revisionists who had me didn't have a clue what they were looking at when they went through my stuff. Etkin didn't tell them, either. So he doesn't trust them, he was using them and me for a diversion, or he's getting sloppy. Don't count on him making that mistake with Chun."

"He didn't. I can't get a fix on Chun. He's isolated her from her equipment," Roebeck told him. "All right, Grainger, you can go inside now. Suit up. We'll launch Phase Two by the book. When I get back. That is, unless you think you're not up to it?"

"I'm up to whatever it takes." Grainger pushed himself upward to demonstrate. He managed to get his knees under him. Then he shook his head, hard, as if to clear it. "But what's this 'get back' stuff? Where are you going? Phase Two calls for—"

"I know what Phase Two calls for. I defined it. I'm going to go round up those hard-liners first. They're easy pickings in that stasis field."

"Don't. No. Don't *do* that. You don't know what can happen phasing—"

"It won't kill them. Bringing you through proved that. If I don't take them now, we might have to kill them later. Or lose them altogether. Anyway, Neat and Lipinsky are in there. They're two of my prime targets for displacement." As she spoke, she was clumping away from the TC, toward the edge of the TC's active bubble. "You better scramble, Grainger. Get inside where you're safe. Who knows whether there's any back draft when somebody in a hardsuit phases out of an active bubble into frozen time? From what I saw, it's not as simple as displacing in time. You wouldn't want to get caught . . ."

Grainger was already stumbling toward the ramp, cursing her with enough enthusiasm that she was now sure he wasn't functionally impaired. Except, perhaps, for his pride.

She watched her rearward-facing view to make sure the TC accepted him and locked up tight. Then she phased back into the conference room to pick up the first of her revisionist prisoners.

Capturing people alive was always the most difficult part of these operations. She was going to make as many of those captures as easy as possible. The real threat had never been from the Russian revisionists, but from any Up The Line technology or actors involved on this time horizon.

Mankind had always believed it had the moral right to kill to defend itself. Mankind had always believed in God, too. Belief didn't confer anything but consensus. Belief didn't make it so. In Roebeck's native epoch, technology had progressed to the point that it wasn't patently necessary to kill to defend your own life or the lives of others.

But killing was still an option to the unscrupulous, the stupid, the primitive, the barbaric, the desperate—in any time, at any place.

Killing was always an option, even to the ARC Riders. The most rudimentary, unthinking forms of life killed. Single cells killed other cells. The urge and skill to kill were hard-wired into living things along with other traits necessary to survive. You didn't have to learn to kill, any more than you had to learn to piss. Killing was a given. In the face of a threat to personal survival, it was natural.

Killing was easy. Not killing was hard.

The enemy was always prepared to use lethal force. You learned to expect it. Counter it. Prevail over it nonlethally when possible. But prevail.

Roebeck wasn't religiously opposed to lethal force. Killing the enemy was always a way to defeat him—at least in the short term. She considered killing a failure of mind over instinct, a defeat of technology. A subhuman act. She wasn't a savage. She wasn't so afraid of her enemy's revenge that she had to wipe him from the face of the earth.

She was civilized. She was a result of millennia of tool making. She would use the tools her society had created to subdue her enemy and put him where he could do no more harm to her and that society.

Displace him but good. Dump him in 50,000 BC, along with the other animals. Put him where his primitive instincts were in harmony with the time. Let him live out his life among the other fossils. Let him commune with the spirit of his closest relative, the dinosaur.

Mankind had no tolerance for barbarians any longer. The barbarians had ruled the Earth for more than twenty millennia of recorded history. Then, like the Russian people realizing they could revolt against their totalitarian masters, humanity had finally realized it could refute a reign of terror instituted by leaders who drew their sole legitimacy from their ability to field lethal force.

Technology had forced that realization by providing the tools that made it possible to assure personal and societal security by other means than lethal force. The barbarians had fought hard against their obsolescence. The killer instinct could not be eradicated without altering humanity forever. So no one tried to reengineer a race whose success in the future was rooted in its triumph over its past.

Barbarians still existed. Would always exist. Killers would always long to break things and spill blood. But in Roebeck's time, killing was not state sanctioned as standard operating procedure to enforce policy. Killing created dead heroes and generations of enemies, which served to perpetuate the power of a warlike nationalist state. Such states feared most of all the effect on the war effort of disillusioned veterans returning home.

With the attrition of state-sponsored lethal force had come a cascade of new technologies for the military. A military must be able to enforce policy to justify the cost of its maintenance. Nonlethal technologies had provided new tools for a military tasked with projecting power in a highly constrained environment with a low tolerance for cost, destructiveness, and casualties.

The military, like every other successful organism, changed in order to survive. When temporal travel was introduced in the 26th century by a wiser society Up The Line, the insertion point in humanity's evolution was chosen carefully. Humanity had to be ready to police its barbarians. Its military had to be self-restraining. An agreement was reached, quid pro quo, between the technology givers and the technology receivers. Behavioral *quids* were established in exchange for the *quos* of new technologies, including temporal mobility.

The ARC Riders operated under a strategic doctrine of containment of barbarism initially enforced by technology native to their era. Containment of barbarism was their overriding guidance, not just for policy, but for strategy and tactics as well. And those tactics of containment were considerably enhanced by integration into the force mix of temporal displacement technology from Up The Line.

So Nan Roebeck had to be very, very careful operating against an enemy who, if Grainger was correct, had arguably better technology from farther Up The Line. What else had been devised by those who'd made temporal displacement a reality? She wanted to get as many Russian revisionists as possible out of her line of fire before she faced off with Etkin.

What had happened Up The Line? Had there been a palace coup in the main timeline's future? Was there even a palace? Or was it a revolution similar to the Russian one she was witnessing here? If that was so, did a revolution Up The Line bode ill for the ARC Riders?

The thought of being suddenly obsolete, cut adrift like the Russian scientists she'd met here, chilled her. Watching helplessly as your way of life dissolved. Losing everything you'd worked for, sacrificed to build. Scrambling for handouts. Struggling even to survive. Through no fault of your own, becoming a casualty of a societal sea change . . .

Nan Roebeck felt an unaccustomed twinge of empathy, an ephemeral kinship with the Russians she was about to displace, by unilateral decision and imposition of superior technology, to 50K.

The ARC Riders' native horizon was as yet unchanged. The main timeline was still intact as far as Central was concerned. Her team had made certain of that by returning to base. Central's nontemporal locus would alter instantly if the main timeline was successfully tweaked below the 26th century. Roebeck's ARC Riders had found that out firsthand on their last mission, when they'd faced a hostile Central created by a change downstream that affected their nontemporal headquarters.

ARC was barred, by a temporal excluder built into the black-boxed UTL technology powering their displacement systems, from traveling farther Up The Line than the 26th century. When she'd been at Central, she'd checked to make sure. So in this instance the problem stemmed from Up The Line beyond the 26th, from wherever upstream the advanced TC had been launched.

Roebeck tapped her virtual remote and the FILI conference room coalesced around her. The statis field was still holding. Good.

Her second insertion riled the blue sparks into chains of connect-a-dot lightning crawling the walls. Her targets were still sitting frozen, exactly as she'd left them.

Roebeck took Neat through first. The hunchback scientist with his woodcutter's beard beamed jovially at nothing. Neat kept smiling until he came to his senses in the nuclear weapons storage area, held high in the arms of Roebeck's hardsuit.

Grainger was suited up by then. The Russian scientist who'd perfected the transition of UTL temporal implants to Russian fabricators began to scream, flailing in Roebeck's arms.

Roebeck dropped him and stomped two steps back. She saw Tim Grainger's sticky capture net descend over Neat as she phased back to get the next revisionist.

Lipinsky, the upwardly mobile lounge lizard of the Russian Foreign Ministry, was her next target. She had to be very strict with herself when she took Lipinsky's rigid, unknowing body in her arms. He was still holding aloft the truncheon he'd used to beat Grainger. She really understood, at that moment, the urge to kill.

But she wasn't even going to break his arm.

Grainger would do as he saw fit with Lipinsky. Short of leaving the revisionist alive for deposit in 50K, Roebeck would ask no more restraint than that.

When Lipinsky came out of stasis in her arms, Grainger was waiting.

"Thanks, boss," said the huge armored figure with a capture gun in hand. Above his head, the blue sparks at the stressed boundary between the active and stasis fields were thickening.

When Lipinsky saw Grainger's suited form and opaqued helmet visor, he actually tried to grab Nan's armored neck.

"Nyet, nyet, nyet!" moaned Lipinsky.

"Da, da, da," Grainger boomed through his hardsuit's speakers like Judgment himself.

They had to pry Lipinsky off her manually. Quarters were too close for a capture net.

Grainger tranquilized the struggling Russian and Lipinsky slumped, senseless. Next stop for Lipinsky was the casket he'd ride into 50K.

She didn't stay to watch the fun. All this phasing between states was taking too great a toll on the stasis field that TC 779 was maintaining in here. If the stasis field failed, for all Nan Roebeck knew, one or more of those nuclear missiles would blow despite her precautions.

And she still had more revisionists to collect, three old men who'd never for one moment in their lives deserved better. Each time she phased into that FILI conference room, the stasis field there was getting wilder. Each time, it was harder to see. Each time, it seemed to be getting harder to move, as if the disturbed energy was beginning to offer resistance even to her exo-skeletal servo-powered hardsuit.

When she made her last pickup, she was sure her hardsuit couldn't take much more. Moving at all required every bit of her skill. It was as if she were walking deep under phosphorescent blue, electric water.

Some after-action report this was going to be. If she wrote it up straight, she'd be in debrief way too long, answering all sorts of boring questions from scientists fascinated by the effects of moving an active field through a stasis field. That is, after she got through her disciplinary hearing. If she did. When word leaked, which of course it would, the physio guys

THE FOURTH ROME   277

would pull every string at Central to get hold of her. They'd poke and prod her interminably to see what, if any, changes had occurred in her biosystem from doing the unthinkable. She'd be in real danger of becoming a lab specimen for weeks, months, maybe years.

She couldn't afford to be that popular. By the time she had the last old revisionist back in the nuclear weapons bay, she'd decided to fudge that part of her report.

Grainger would go along. In the ARC Riders, you had to go along to get along.

Vetera, Lower Germany

September 7, 9 AD

Rebecca Carnes paused, leaning against a panel shielding one of the amphitheater's midlevel entrances. A
sausage seller elbowed her to get past.

Rebecca's misplaced frustration flared in a fashion that
shocked her. She forced her hand to relax on the grip of the
microwave pistol. Hit with the full charge at this range, the
vendor would've had blood in his urine for a week—if he'd
been lucky. All he'd done was jostle somebody standing in the
way in a crowded aisle.

Vetera's wooden amphitheater might hold as many as ten
thousand spectators in a pinch, but the current six or seven
thousand were enough to fill the lower tiers fuller than comfort. She guessed as many people had come to see Tiberius as
for the games themselves. The region's civilian population included many retired soldiers. Whatever faults Tiberius would
have as emperor in his later years, he was a popular and successful commander throughout his military career.

"I can't be sure," said a machine voice through Rebecca's
headband, "but I don't believe Svetlanov is on the other side
of the amphitheater either. Not if he has any advanced equipment with him, at least."

Rebecca had searched for the revisionist outside the amphitheater as crowds climbed the outside steps to the upper
entrances. When Tiberius and his entourage arrived to enter
through the tunnel to the first tier reserved for dignitaries, Re-

becca went in by a public entrance and worked her way down as close to Tiberius as she could.

Tiberius, a senator as well as the emperor's stepson, sat on a folding ivory chair looking directly down through a railing to the arena. Fifty fully armed Germans from the imperial horse guards had escorted him to Vetera. Some blocked the tunnel entrance while others separated the general from spectators behind and to either side. Only a half-dozen officials sat in Tiberius' immediate presence; the guards watched them as well with no great affection.

"I don't think a submachine gun would be effective from so far away, Gerd," Rebecca said. Spactators continued to bump her but the fit of temper had passed.

"Istvan didn't know Kiknadze carried a grenade," the analyst replied. "Svetlanov may have a rifle or even a rocket launcher. Though of course a bulkier weapon will be easier to locate."

Gerd had gotten a space early to the left of the area reserved for dignitaries and from there scanned for Svetlanov. There'd been a risk the revisionist would attack while Tiberius rode to the amphitheater; the general didn't use a slave-born litter, one of the reasons his men loved him.

Svetlanov was alone, however, and the only place he could be sure of finding Tiberius was at the entrance to the amphitheater or seated inside. By watching those two points, she and Gerd maximized their chances. It wasn't perfect, but it was what they had.

Squads of regular troops were stationed at intervals on the first tier. An event like this drew spectators from local tribes. There was a serious chance of a riot.

The crowd cheered. The pair of beast-slayers in the arena were dressed as Parthian horse archers in embroidered trousers, terribly exotic on this opposite end of the empire. Wild bulls charged up the north ramp. The riders shot arrows over their horses' backs as the bulls chased them across the sand. Maybe they really were Parthians. They were certainly skillful enough.

Three bulls were down, blowing bloody froth from their nostrils. The riders played with the last animal. His flanks were a pincushion of arrows, their feathers brightly dyed to add to the gaiety of the occasion.

More cheers as another pair of arrows slapped home. The beast stumbled but managed to pick itself up again. *My God, what a civilization!*

Rebecca was ten rows above the bottom tier and about fifty feet to the right of Tiberius, a youthful-looking man of fifty-one. From this angle she would see only sparse hair and the gleam of his high forehead. The big guardsmen glared outward, a living iron barrier to any attack. The murder of Julius Caesar had taught his successors the basics of imperial survival.

"Pauli," she said. "Svetlanov knows his fellows failed to prevent the massacre of Varus' army. Now Kiknadze's dead as well. Mightn't he just give up?"

"If he does," Pauli Weigand said, "it's going to be more difficult to find him. We've still got to find him, though. He could do just as much harm even if he can't execute his plan."

He paused and added, "Besides, it's our job."

Pauli's voice was weak and crackly despite sharpening by the AI in Rebecca's receiver. The headbands were short-range devices and the mass of iron and stone over Pauli attenuated the signal even more.

"I believe Svetlanov must have known from the start that he couldn't return to his own time," Gerd said. "A fanatic intending to sacrifice himself is unlikely to be put off by the loss of his fellows."

Because he didn't have a headband himself, Gerd keyed his words into his sensor pack and transmitted them in voice-synthesized form to his teammates. The result sounded surprisingly like the analyst's normal speech.

The bull was tiring. It stood directly below Rebecca, legs braced and nose to the ground. The Partians capered close, trying to entice it into another charge. Blood streaked the beast's black hide and dripped onto the sand. The air reeked of death and the bull's frustrated anger.

She knew how the bull felt.

"I'm going to move closer to Tiberius," Rebecca said. It'd

be a way to release some of her tension. They *had* to find Svetlanov soon.

She began to work her way down. Spectators watched from the aisles in ever-thicker numbers nearer the arena. She squeezed between, ignoring curses and the occasional elbow.

Pauli was right. The team couldn't leave the revisionist loose on this horizon, but he'd be very, very hard to locate if he'd fled Vetera when he realized he was alone. Maybe Gerd could predict Svetlanov's movements, but she didn't see how.

Her real concern, the fear that Rebecca Carnes kept hidden as deep in her heart as she could, was the knowledge that TC 779 couldn't rescue the team until they'd eliminated Svetlanov. Unless the capsule arrived, she didn't see any way that Pauli Weigand was going to survive the next hour in the arena below.

A Parthian chose an arrow with red fletching from the quiver hanging from the left side of his belt of bronze openwork. He laid the shaft across the ivory ring on his left thumb and aimed with particular care. The bull stared at his tormentor twenty feet away but refused to be drawn. His tail flicked stiffly.

The Parthian loosed. The arrow hit with a *tock!* like a hammer on wood. The tuft of feather stuck out only a handsbreadth from the center of the bull's skull. The animal shuddered but didn't fall over.

Rebecca'd seen the effect before. Brain damage had brought not only death but rigor mortis instantaneously. The corpse froze in place like the statue of a bull. Blood still dripped from its wounds.

The whole crowd rose, shouting and stamping its thousands of feet. The amphitheater's timber floor boomed and quivered under the battering. The Parthian who'd made the final shot rode around the arena, waving his peaked cap to the adoring spectators.

God. God *damn*. And they'd do the same thing to Pauli if they could.

"Pauli," she said. "I think we'd better get you out while there's time and worry about Sve—"

"No," Pauli snapped. "I'm in charge of this team. He may be planning to hit when the guards're concentrating on the finale. Or he hopes they are. I'm in charge!"

The crowd seated itself again. A cleanup crew of a dozen slaves with teams of horses came from the south ramp and began dragging away the bulls. The animal that had died in a seizure baffled them for a moment. Two groups set their chain hooks on the bull's spine and pulled the corpse over on its side before they could haul it away.

To cover the interval, the officials providing the entertainment brought out a comedy turn: eight slaves connected to a central hub by ten-foot chains as though they were the spokes of a wheel. Each slave carried a spiked club. They were naked except for heavy black bags covering their heads to completely blindfold them. Attendants guided the grotesque assembly into the middle of the arena.

A municipal official beside Tiberius rose and waved a napkin hemmed with narrow red stripes. He was not only a Roman citizen but a knight—and very proud of his rank. An attendant on the sand below blew a command with his curved horn.

The blindfolded men began flailing wildly. Spectators cheered and cat-called. The last fighter standing would gain his freedom. The attendant waiting with a long-handled mallet would finish off the rest.

"Gerd," Rebecca ordered. "Get close to the railing on your side. I'll do the same. Pauli, when you enter the arena move toward the target. We'll use straight microwave sound to keep problems away from you."

She reached the bottom tier, a broad walkway circling the amphitheater, but spectators still blocked her from the three-foot-high railing. Wealthy citizens sat on chairs they'd brought with them. Attendants, both slaves and free persons who hung on the wealthy for their living, stood behind the chairs and kept their patrons from being jostled.

Rebecca raised her cape and reset the control dial on her pistol's receiver from impulse to continuous beam. Nobody paid any attention to her.

She couldn't see the sand past three burly slaves standing behind a woman wearing orange and blue silk garments with jeweled combs in her hair. Her serpentine armlets reminded Rebecca of the past night's whore, but these were made of gold and didn't leave smudges of verdigris.

Rebecca pointed the twin side-by-side muzzles of the microwave pistol from the opening of her cape and played the beam at kidney level across the slaves. Their bowels began to quiver as though they'd eaten something that was causing intestinal spasms.

One of the men shouted in wonder. He dropped his cudgel. Sudden diarrhea fouled his legs. His patroness turned in furious anger at the stench just as her other two attendants rushed up the stairs, trampling spectators as they went.

The crowd was too thick for Rebecca to get completely clear even though she'd expected the result. One of the slaves stepped hard enough on her left foot that she'd be lucky if he hadn't broken a metatarsal.

The wealthy woman was so nonplussed by what had happened to her attendants that she simply sat on her ornately carved chair. Her mouth opened and closed soundlessly. She didn't appear to notice when Rebecca slipped by.

The blindfold melee had ended with all the participants down. The attendant postured for the crowd, flexing his muscles before swinging the mallet the last time. The victim's head burst like a dropped melon within the bag. The cleanup crew was already attaching hooks to the bodies.

Trumpeters blew a long call for silence. Criers with megaphones faced the crowd from both sides of the arena. With their unison blurred by echoes from the oval walls, they announced, "And now, citizens of Rome, a captive will pay the penalty of German treachery. His fate will provide an omen of what will happen to all Germans when our armies under the ever-victorious command of Tiberius Claudius Nero exact retribution!"

The trumpets blew again. Up the north ramp from the cages came a tall figure carrying a stabbing spear and naked except for a breechclout. The barred gate clanged shut behind him.

Fully armed soldiers had been ready to prod him forward, but there was no need.

Pauli Weigand wasn't a man who needed to be pushed into danger.

Pauli paused and let his eyes adjust to the afternoon sunlight. It wasn't a bright day, but the illumination of the cells had been only what filtered through slits in the stone twenty feet above.

"Beckie," he said. "If anything happens to me, you're in charge. Carry on with the mission."

"Pauli, get over here close to the wall," Beckie said in tight anger instead of answering. Her voice was clear as glass. He was so used to the interference of iron and wet stone that he'd come to expect the crackling.

The surface of the sand was warm, but as Pauli walked his bare toes found the underlayer was clammy with trapped moisture. It stank as well. Attendants shoveled up patches of blood and spread fresh sand, but dung and body fluids spattered in all directions with every violent death. Those scraps of organic matter were trampled down, covered by fresh layers of sand but removed only by decay. Simply walking across the arena released a miasma and a prophecy.

Beckie'd heard him; he could trust her to obey. It was probably the last order he'd ever give.

Pauli Weigand had never doubted that he was going to die. The Anti-Revision Command dealt in crises; death was the most basic crisis of existence, so he'd seen a lot of it. Feeling, knowing, that he was about to die *now* was something new. He wasn't afraid, but his light-headedness had as much to do with foreboding as with fatigue and lack of sleep.

The arena's masonry walls were eight feet high with a simple grill of finger-thick wrought-iron rods above that. In the south and east of the empire the grill would have been higher and more substantial; in Rome herself the grill was topped with a rotating basket to hurl back any creature who managed to leap so high. No big cats were available for slaughter here on the Rhine, however, and the local fauna couldn't jump high enough to be a problem.

"The German traitor's" death was intended as an exercise in sympathetic magic as well as entertainment. Just as the criers had announced, Pauli represented Free Germany and by dying would foretell Germany's conquest. They'd given him a spear, a real weapon though crude. Most of Varus' army had been killed by spears just like this one.

The head was iron hammered out on a stump in a forest glade. The metal was soft, but Pauli'd honed it sharp on the stone ramp during the minutes he waited for the previous act to be cleared from the arena.

He hefted the weapon and found it was for stabbing only. The short shaft wasn't heavy enough to balance the head. Well, throwing the weapon would have left him unarmed anyway. He'd rather die with it in his hands.

"Pauli, get closer to us!" Beckie ordered.

He was fifty feet from Tiberius and his entourage. The hawk-featured general was bent in conversation with two of his aides. His attendance at games held in his honor was a necessary part of imperial politics, but the man himself was no great fan of the amphitheater. He'd seen his share of slaughter on the battlefield. The version packaged for civilians was contemptible by contrast.

"If I get too close . . ." Pauli said, scanning the front rows of the crowd. He couldn't see either of his teammates in the press of faces avid for his death. "Then one of Tiberius' guards is likely to put a javelin through me on the principle of better safe than sorry."

Pauli knew from the ARC Central briefing that when news of the disaster in the Teutoburg Forest reached Rome, Augustus in panic had dismissed his German bodyguards for fear that they'd kill him in support of their free brethren. Tiberius, who'd spent years campaigning in Germany, knew better.

The German warrior class was raised to give its loyalty to a particular chief, not to its own race or even tribe. The guards around Tiberius had pledged to defend their chieftain's life with their own. So long as he kept his part of the bargain with honor and high pay, they would do just that.

The Praetorian Guard of Roman citizens rebelled frequently, slaying some emperors and selling the throne to others. The foreigners of the horse guard never in the history of the empire failed to keep their pledged honor.

The gates closing the opposite ramp squealed open. The crowd bellowed in delight. They'd loosed the beasts on Pauli Weigand.

"Pauli, it's a pack of wolves," Beckie said.

A moment later Gerd's synthesized voice replied, "No, they're dogs."

Pauli'd wondered what they were going to send after him. Amphitheater officials in the west of the empire had problems finding mankilling animals unless they could afford the expense of imports from Africa. Bulls and boars killed a lot of hunters, but they were still herbivores who didn't look on human beings as dinner. They'd pretty much ignore people who stood still, and you couldn't count on a condemned prisoner waving his arms to draw the animal sent to kill him.

The only major carnivores in Europe were wolves and bears; wolves had a well-founded fear of humans and tended to get spooked in an arena. Dogs, though, had the contempt of familiarity for people. A pack of feral dogs, released hungry into the blood-reeking amphitheater, would be perfectly willing to pull down a lone human and devour as much as they could before attendants whipped them off the body. They didn't need pedigrees or training: the work came naturally to them.

There were a dozen animals in this pack; big ones for the day, averaging thirty kilos apiece. They sniffed the sand; several rolled delightedly in some foulness they'd sniffed beneath the surface. Then a great brindled bitch sighted Pauli Weigand. She led the pack down the arena toward him with a series of incongruously high-pitched yelps.

"Gerd," Pauli said, "remember the first priority is to locate the revisionist."

"Yes, Pauli," the analyst replied. Gerd really would do that;

not because he didn't care about Pauli Weigand, but because his conception of life and death differed from that of most people. Gerd wasn't a sociopath, but he was equally outside the norms of human society.

The leading animals in the pack spread out as they neared their quarry. They'd circle him, tear his hamstrings out from behind whichever way he turned, and then snatch mouthfuls of flesh as he thrashed on the sand. Slower dogs—one was limping on three legs—straggled on in line at their best speed.

Holding his spear in one hand, Pauli raised the other and shouted in Latin, "Halt or feel my power!"

The brindled bitch yelped and turned a somersault. An instant later the ruff of a brown cur flattened at a silent impact. He rolled sideways, snapping at the invisible club. Another of the leaders doubled up, then dragged itself away with a whine.

The crowd gave a startled roar and rose to its feet.

Though he knew it was risky, Pauli turned to face Tiberius. The dogs swarmed around him. He shooed a sharp-featured bitch with the butt of his spear. Faces stared down from the amphitheater with expressions of anger and fear.

From behind Pauli heard the meat-ax *whop* of a full-strength microwave pulse. A pair of dogs ran back across the arena with high-pitched yelps. Fear makes a mammal's bowels tremble. Microwaves that induced trembling tricked the dogs' minds into believing their own fear.

Teeth closed on Pauli's calf. They released with a startled gasp before Pauli could stab his spear butt down. A tan dog rolled away. Its eyes were glazed. Repeated pulses hammered the short fur of its skull.

The pack broke up in terror. The dogs still able to move slunk away, speeded by sprays of microwaves. Their tails curled under to protect their bellies from the teeth of invisible foes. Pauli felt his own guts tremble as a beam brushed him by accident. Warm blood trickled slowly down his calf.

The official giving the games held the grill in front of him and shouted in fury. Trumpeters blew a signal even louder than the crowd. Archers entered the arena and began to shoot the dogs. They were locals using all-wood bows and their aim was poor.

Alone in the amphitheater, Tiberius remained seated. He leaned forward, resting his pointed chin on one hand. His face was as unreadable as a pool of water.

The gates of the north ramp clanged. This time the officials would send a bear. Bears were normally placid if left alone, but this one would have been starved and goaded into a rage that only leopards among the big cats could equal.

A leopard might weigh fifty kilograms. A full-grown European brown bear would be five or six times as large. Microwave pistols wouldn't even slow it down. Pauli might be able to kill the beast with his stabbing spear, but by the time it died the creature would have chewed the top off his skull.

"Pauli, it's a bear," Beckie said in a calm voice. She didn't panic in a crisis. You couldn't ask for a better teammate when everything was falling apart.

He'd been so *sure* that Svetlanov would attack during the games. He'd been afraid to consider the idea that Gerd and Beckie should break him out of his cell in case that cost them the opportunity to stop the revisionist.

Pauli Weigand was less afraid of death than he was of surviving failure and having everyone in the Anti-Revision Command know what he'd always known about himself: he wasn't up to the job. Not fit to be an ARC Rider and certainly not able to lead a team.

Pauli ran his hands along the shaft of his stabbing spear, judging the best spots to grip it for the one stroke the bear would allow him. The mission might be a failure, but at least he wouldn't be around to answer for it.

"Pauli, I've found—" Gerd said. Before the analyst could get out the next word, an explosion told Pauli that Gerd's sensors had located the revisionist.

The tunnel acted as a wave guide, channeling the blast and feeding it on echoes. Tiberius turned. Gray smoke puffed from the archway behind his chair. An officer barked a command; the guards formed an impassable array between their general and the mouth of the tunnel.

A second grenade burst in the midst of them with a red flash and another puff of dirty smoke. The guards went down like bowling pins.

Spectators screamed, surging like the tide. Those nearest the blast tried to get away, some of them bleeding from shrapnel wounds. Those just beyond in the packed crowd pressed closer to see what was happening.

"Pauli," Beckie Carnes said in a tone of quiet desperation. "I can't get to the tunnel. There's too many people."

Pauli took off his breechclout. His mind was running as if it were on rails. He was headed directly at a result, oblivious of all else. The cloth was too heavy as is, so he ripped it in half the long way.

The shock wave had knocked Tiberius down. He got up, stumbling when he stepped on the chair that had folded under him. His two surviving guards tried to carry him out of the way. The shouting mob blocked them. The guards turned, putting their bodies between the tunnel and their chief.

Pauli stuck his spear point-down in the sand and knotted the cloth around the shaft a few inches from the end. He knew the bear would be coming for him, but there were more important things on his mind. He had a mission to complete.

One of the guards above on the first tier crumpled slowly to his knees, then toppled forward. The other man bellowed. He dropped his sword, clutched at his face, and collapsed onto the body of his fellow.

Pauli started running toward the wall. He cocked his spear over his shoulder into throwing position.

Kyril Svetlanov stepped out of the tunnel. He was reloading his small submachine gun. Svetlanov's face was cheerfully pink, framed by his flowing white hair and beard. He looked like a 19th-century Santa Claus as he pointed the Skorpion at the future emperor.

Pauli threw his spear. It wobbled slightly around the point, but the drag of the cloth stabilized the weapon's flight sufficiently.

The spearhead was as long and almost as broad as Pauli's big hand. It hit Svetlanov in the center of the chest so hard that none of the iron was showing when the revisionist's body toppled backward. The shaft waggled frantically in the air as Svetlanov convulsed in death.

"Pauli, the bear!" Beckie warned.

Pauli turned. The beast was only a dozen meters away, coming toward its prey at a deceptively quick amble. Its legs seemed to cross at each stride.

The bear's brown fur was mangy. Shackles had left running sores on each leg; patches of its hide looked as though it had also been tortured with hot irons. The beast's small eyes were pits of red fury for the first human being on which it had an opportunity to wreak the vengeance it deserved.

Pauli braced himself. He couldn't outrun the bear's rush, and he preferred to face his death.

A Roman javelin sailed over Pauli's head and struck the bear in the neck a handsbreadth from the spine. The beast staggered; the lead-weighted missile weighed several kilos.

The bear twisted its head, trying to grasp the shaft in its jaws. A second javelin slammed the other side of its neck. The great body relaxed, free at last from captivity and pain.

Pauli Weigand turned to scan the rows of seats above him. A Roman soldier, a member of one of the squads on duty in the amphitheater in case of a riot, had been grabbed by fellow legionaries after he threw both of his javelins. A centurion was shouting at him.

"Flaccus?" Pauli called. "You're an artist with those things!"

The veteran grinned and nodded since his arms were pinioned. Flaccus had been in the army long enough to know he was safe if he stuck to any halfway believable story. He'd be all right.

The crowd thundered in the bowl of the amphitheater. Attendants and some of the regular soldiers clustered around Tiberius. The corpses of his German bodyguards lay about him, faithful unto death.

Thirty or more archers rushed into the arena from the south ramp. A few gladiators followed, some of them buckling on their weapons and armor. It looked as though an arena official had mustered all the armed men under his control to end the embarrassing problem Pauli Weigand had become. Even if someone wanted to countermand the order, he couldn't be heard in the echoing chaos.

Beckie climbed over the railing and poised to jump to the sand. Gerd started to do the same from the other side of the carnage around Tiberius. A pair of microwave pistols wouldn't make any difference against so many opponents, but Pauli didn't waste his breath trying to order his teammates back.

He placed his hands on his hips and stood arms akimbo, facing the oncoming archers. He and his team might be going out, but they were going out on a win.

Moscow, Russia

March 11, 1992

" B oss," Grainger complained, stomping through FILI on a room-to-room search with blue lightning crawling all over him. "You know how I hate these hardsuits. Ain't there some other way? Chances are ten to one all these field effects are gonna make me sterile or something."

Clomp, clomp, clomp came the sound of his armored boots on the tiled floors. He was taking external audio for any advance warning or situational information it might provide. Sometimes the floor beneath the tile would give and he'd hear tiles cracking like glass breaking underfoot.

The hallway wasn't wide enough to proceed two abreast in the big hardsuits. He was walking point, a 200 dB acoustic gun mated to his suit's right arm. With it, he could crumble masonry if he had to. If he had to, he could thumb the virtual controller to lethal. As he passed each door, he tried to open it. If it didn't give to his touch, he kicked it in or bashed it with his armored elbow. Nice to have servo-power when you need it.

He kept trying to ignore the static crackling everywhere. Blue sparks. Flashes of forked lightning. He didn't like this moving through a stasis field one bit. The boss was crazy. He'd always known that. She had crazy eyes, if you looked deep enough.

Her voice came over his helmet com channel full of static he could actually see as whorls of additional blue sparks in the air. "Sterile? You? Now, come on, Grainger, no woman alive and in her right mind—in *any* time—would have your baby. We've been through all this. You worried about sterile? Worry about what's going to happen when we release the stasis field around those leaky nuclear weapons."

"I'm sorry I told you about that warhead that's gonna leak. Maybe I was wrong. Maybe it's a dummy. The Russians built lots of dummy warheads. Anyway, if you hadn't set TC 779 down smack on top of one of those SS-N-25s, we wouldn't have this problem. Where'd you learn to park, anyway? On a grass strip? A twelve-bin bay? A Central VIP garage? If one of those big birds blow, you think there'll be a Central left to go home to?"

Nan Roebeck didn't answer. She'd stepped inside one of the rooms on the left without warning him.

Damn her.

"Roebeck? Boss, you copy?" He was moving in on that room as fast as this slow hulk of a suit could go without toppling over.

He had his weapon ready.

He nearly shot her as she stepped out from a closet.

"Whoa! Don't shoot, cowboy. At ease. It's just me."

"Well why the hell didn't you say? Answer me? Your com working, or what? These suits look pretty much alike. It didn't have to be you. It could have been Etkin. We don't know what hardware he's got. You could have said," he finished lamely, embarrassed because he'd nearly trashed her in her suit.

She waved a gloved hand at him and blue trails followed her hand through the air. "Let's go. Move on, mister. We've got lots of rooms to cover."

Grainger hated room-to-room search and destroy in urban venues. Especially hated them in the ARC, when destroy was only a last resort. There was only one thing worse than a house-to-house search, and that was a room-to-room search.

So he was still looking for some way to short-cut this leg of the mission. Too many wrongs. Not enough rights. The hardsuits were wrong: he didn't need one for this operation. He could handle Etkin stripped buck naked. The revisionist had just caught him by surprise. The stasis field was wrong: Nan was taking too much risk for too long with all their lives. As for her materializing the TC on top of an armed SS-N-25 in a nuclear storage facility, well, that sort of limited their options.

"Grainger, you said yourself that if any of those big warheads go bang from unforseeable results of our stasis field effects, it won't matter about one SS-N-25 leaking. These Russians can kiss what's left of their downtown Evil Empire good-bye. We can kiss the future as we've come to know it good-bye. I don't want it on my conscience, that's all. Plan B. We hold steady, keep all our instituted fields operational. No changes," came her metallically cold voice.

"I still say we should get back in the TC. Displace the fuck out of this venue. Then you go get Chun while I hang out of phase in my hardsuit." If Nan agreed to his plan, Grainger couldn't be any part of the action to rescue Chun. You couldn't step twice on the same horizon. The only window for a preemptive strike that was available was during the time Nan had been out of phase with the TC. And only if she executed the strike solo. If so, she'd have maybe eight, nine minutes. Nan had refused the plan out of hand the first time, so they hadn't calculated the strike window yet. But he wasn't done trying. You could make a good argument that putting the TC down amid all that fissionable material was going to solve their revisionist problem for them. Forever. But she didn't want to hear that. She wanted to fix everything, go clean with their intended targets in hand and no collateral damage or unintended casualties left behind. Fat chance.

They came to a corner. The hallway extended in both directions. In one direction, a man was frozen in midstep. His hand was zipping his fly, the fly half open as he exited the bathroom.

"Signs of life," Roebeck's voice said. "We can get past him. Let's go that way."

It was a tight squeeze, past the man in stasis. Grainger's armor brushed the guy and a streak of blue lightning shot up from the contact.

The concussion, even through the mediating electronics of his hardsuit's ear-protecting audio, was impressive.

"Come on, Nan. You hear that shock wave? This is getting dicey. Let's phase out and let those nukes down there go critical or whatever they'll do. What do we care, really? We tried. We can't stop time here forever. Maybe they'll get away with just some radioactive cleanup. Maybe Central's right and it won't end life as we know it Up The Line. Let's displace out of here. I'll hang out in my suit." She ought to copy how serious he thought this was, if he was making an offer to hang in the netherworld in a less-than-optimum hardsuit. "You phase the TC back in for half a minute in front of the car that took Etkin and Chun to FILI. So you stop traffic. So what? So some Russians see a UFO. What's new? Zotov sees 'em all the time. Takes home movies. You want to throw a stasis field, throw one around that car then and there. Pull Chun and the others out of the car. They can't hurt you if they're frozen in stasis."

"I'm worried about leaving you in that hardsuit hanging out of phase. After what we've put these suits through, I'm not sure I trust it."

There was that. There sure as hell was that. Still, he didn't join the ARC Riders for the retirement benefits. "I'll meet you anywhen you say. You can pick me up at your leisure. What's the matter, you think Etkin's going to overpower you? That he can defeat a stasis field?"

He really hated getting this far into an op and having to pull a new game plan out of his ass. It wasn't the first time that Roebeck had led them into a blind canyon. If they got through this, it probably wouldn't be the last. Frustrated, he slammed his armored chassis through the next door they came to, not bothering to try to open it.

And there they were: Chun, Etkin, Matsak, Zotov, a couple of goons Grainger didn't recognize. All still as death, frozen in place.

But they were up to their eyeballs in blue field effects so thick you could hardly make out what they'd been doing when the stasis field froze them.

"Plan B," he said softly. "Just the way you called it, boss."

They took Chun and Etkin out together. Roebeck had phased out with Chun in her arms before Grainger was ready to go. He was doing a quick recon of the weird-ass equipment that Etkin obviously had been operating. Roebeck had just torn the spidery electrode-bearing headset off Chun's head and booked with her.

If there was damage done by disconnecting Chun from Etkin's nasty-looking little hard case too abruptly, then they'd find out soon enough.

Grainger had thought he was going to kill Etkin when he found him. It hadn't really been a conscious decision as much as a natural result of what Etkin had tried to do to him.

Now he couldn't do that, in case Etkin had to help undo whatever he'd been doing to Chun.

It was hard to see too much in the room, for all the blue light and static.

Matsak and Zotov were trussed up, either in line to be Etkin's next victims, or his last. Both men's eyes were closed. Orlov, on Etkin's far side, was about to make use of a hand-held device.

Just for safety's sake, Grainger grabbed all of the hardware on the table. It was harder to control his servos with each move he made, but he kept at it. He stuffed the strange hardware into Chun's gearbag, slipped his arm through the straps. He was about to pick up Etkin when he noticed that there was a thin line of blood coming out of little Zotov's left ear. Another, frozen in midstream, coming from the left corner of the Obninsk scientist's mouth.

Okay, he thought. So he's dead. So were those poor folks in Obninsk under the melted filling cabinet. The blood had detoured to avoid the growth below Zotov's mouth. Somehow, it really bothered Grainger to see that blood there.

He tried to wipe it away with his armored finger, but he'd forgotten about the static, and the stasis field. The blood was still there when he lifted Etkin in a fireman's carry and phased back to the nuclear weapons storage area.

Chun was nowhere in sight. Roebeck was by the ramp, weapon at the ready, waiting for him.

He said, as his vision cleared, "This bastard tortured old Zotov to death."

Roebeck said, "Chun's all right. She thinks. Watch this guy."

"I disarmed—"

But then Etkin was struggling like a madman in his grip, trying to get to the gearbag hanging from Grainger's arm.

Crazy to fight an exo-skeletal-powered suit. Unless—

"Watch it. He's going for something in—"

Roebeck shot point-blank at Grainger and the Up The Line operator struggling in his arms, who was yelling in Russian.

At least she'd shot tranks, Grainger thought prayerfully as Etkin went limp again.

They stripped Etkin, tearing his clothes off because they didn't have time to waste, and isolated him in a storage casket in the transfer hold. He was coming around. They left Chun in charge. Nan didn't think Chun was fit to suit up.

"You sure you're okay, Chun?" Grainger heard through his com. Roebeck had gone aft. Grainger was standing at the open lock, watching the blue lightning turn into a capture net, or a chain-link fence of energy, and worrying that he had no way to measure the danger parameters.

He heard Chun say, "Yes. I'll be fine, Team Leader."

Then Roebeck's tread shook the decking under him.

"Let's get the rest, living and dead."

They phased one more time. It better *be the last time*. Grainger's hardsuit electronics were getting really balky. When he potentiated the system to return to the logged coordinates, for a minute it seemed like his suit didn't have a destination logged.

He was hanging in nothingness. His worst nightmare. He tried to move. Nothing worked. He was imprisoned in that huge hardsuit, nowhere at all. It scared the shit out of him.

He actually said, "Please, God, no." Until then, he didn't think he believed in God. But getting hashed was no way to die.

God must have heard him. All of a sudden his balky suit popped out of phase right where it should have. Roebeck was lifting Orlov. She hadn't taken any chances this time. She'd bound Orlov before she tried to move him. The motions she'd made had stayed in the air around her as if she were spinning herself and Orlov an electric blue cocoon.

"Where were you?"

"Stuck. Nearly got hashed. I ain't doin' but this one more trip without a complete tear-down of this system."

"That's all I ask—just this one more trip," Roebeck's voice said, coming from a blue-laced helmet that was all he could see above her static cocoon.

Then he was alone with poor dead Zotov and Matsak, still frozen in time. He grabbed them both with as few motions as necessary, scooping up the living man atop the dead man in one servo-mechanical embrace.

Grainger hit the virtual keypad and closed his eyes against the aurora borealis in the conference room, which seemed to be catching on fire.

When he opened his eyes again, he was standing among nukes with blue fire crawling all over them. Static charges were shooting around like bullets of flame. Sure as shit, if any of those birds had a live triggering mechanism, one or more of those nukes was going to blow.

"Come on, Grainger. Board! We've got to displace *now*!"

Roebeck's command was so urgent he barreled up the ramp without worrying about what would happen if he fell.

If he fell backward on his ass, or forward on the two unprotected men in his grip, the result would be the same.

In six steps, he was up the ramp. Roebeck was retracting it before he even got clear. He stumbled, all two tons of him. Caught himself with one hand before he crushed Matsak, still alive, into Zotov, already dead.

He heard the lock close up. Roebeck yelled, "Power down, Grainger, *stat*! Or you're not going where we are. We'll get you out of the suit later."

Damn. He didn't have time to get out of this suit first. If he shut it down now, he didn't have enough power left to start it up again on his own. She was the boss. He had to trust her. Dying of asphyxiation in that hardsuit wasn't his first choice, but it probably beat whatever had started to happen out there when the static charge in the stasis field caught on fire.

He crouched a long time in darkness, unable to change position, before the other ARC Riders got around to him and gave him some auxiliary juice.

His systems came back on. He knew he was sweating and shaky. He didn't want them to see. So when they started to help him, he warned them off. "I got into this suit. I can get out of it. Go torture the prisoners or something."

By the time he had his systems running, the other ARC Riders had removed Matsak and Zotov from under him. He tapped into the main data bank and got a fix on FILI at the moment they'd displaced. There was no mushroom cloud. Dumb luck or good work on Roebeck's part, disarming the FILI nukes, he couldn't say. Maybe the static fire had dudded out the triggering mechanisms of any live warheads, fried the electronics. There'd been enough charge loose in that nuke storage bay to equal anything an EMP gun could deliver. Who the fuck knew what happened when Roebeck released a stasis field that had been riled up that way? Not him, that was for sure. The only unusual reading he could get from FILI was an elevated hot count from the crushed SS-N-25. *You can't have everything.*

When he'd stashed his gear and changed into standard issue, he went forward. He didn't ask what they'd done with the live prisoners and Zotov's body. They were in holding caskets, waiting for drop off in 50K.

Matsak was sitting in Grainger's accustomed seat. When the revisionist saw Grainger, he grinned through his beard. "The Tim! *Privyet, tovarisch.* Oh, it is well to see you!"

"What the fuck? We're letting revisionists ride forward, now?"

He had his acoustic pistol on his hip in its regular quick-draw holster. The pistol leaped into his hand. He pointed it at Matsak without hesitation. "Up, Matsak. You ride in the back."

Matsak's bearded face fell.

"No he doesn't, Tim. Sasha's going to help us out with a couple problems."

"Such as?" Grainger asked through gritted teeth. Sure, Matsak was a good guy. But he'd been on the wrong side. The rules were clear enough. What was Roebeck thinking of? He didn't take his eyes off the prisoner.

"Tim, holster your weapon. That's an order." Roebeck's tone was like a backhanded slap. He put the gun away reluctantly. But he didn't take his eyes off Matsak.

Then Roebeck said, "Like the nuclear emissions from FILI, for one."

"Absolutely," Matsak agreed, nodding his head vigorously. His burning eyes met Grainger's. "My poor country needs no more of these . . . dirty nuclear accidents. In my opinion, I can help arrange a quick and quiet cleanup. The most minimal damages. The least proliferation of sensitive information. This has always been part of my job."

"You're going to let him *go*?" Grainger was thunderstruck. He looked away at last, to Roebeck at her team leader's station. The bow screen didn't show anything. They were hanging out of phase again. Damn, didn't Roebeck ever get enough? Chun was ready, wands poised, to send them to their next stop.

"We *need* to minimize the damage. Control further proliferation of the temporal implant technology. Lots of the technical reports related to this implant weren't done on computer. They were typed by hand. Chun can't get to them to destroy them. Every hard copy has *got* to be tracked down and destroyed. That has to be done by someone who has plausible and continual access to sensitive scientific research files. And we don't have an agent in place anywhere in the Eastern European theater on this horizon. Chun's just confirmed that for me. So now we've got a volunteer."

"Shit, I thought for a minute you'd lost it completely, Roebeck." Grainger leaned back against the bulkhead. "Yeah, that'll work. If you trust him."

"Trust me?" Matsak grinned slyly. "I am Russian. This is my country you have just been saving. So sorry, Tim, but how can you not trust a man to do what is in his own national interest? There will be many files to destroy. It will take much effort on my part." Matsak sighed heavily. "I will be very busy."

Chun said from the bow, "He's been giving us a lot of data about Etkin and Orlov. He'll help with the interrogation. Then we'll put him back in place on his horizon in time to run the damage control operation for his ministry. Best we can do for those people. Remember, we caused this nuclear accident. It didn't *have* to happen this way."

It was a good thing that time wasn't as sensitive to warping from small changes as people of Matsak's era had thought. You really had to bash the past over the head to get the present to take a different road to a new future. Thank . . . God.

"So very sorry, yes. Many will be ill, or be dead. But it is better than the alternative. You know our history, Tim. It must be this way."

Grainger shrugged. He still didn't like it. Matsak had seen too much. He wasn't even sure if they were empowered to take on locals as agents in place.

"The Russian people," Matsak said, sensing Tim's hesitation, "believe that the Roman Empire gave to the Byzantines, and the Byzantines to the Russians, the secret knowledge of power technologies. They are technologies for controlling societies. Not hardware, but those power technologies you have seen for yourself—social technologies. This is why we are called socialists. Our society is a result of those power technologies, applied for many years to innocent people. I cannot be a part of bringing that weight down on Russian heads again. I will work with you because you work for freedom. Freedom is what the Russian people want. Freedom is what they shall have. Remember, Tim, the new is just the—"

"—well forgotten old. Yeah, Sasha. I remember. Okay. If it matters, you got my vote." He stood up straight. "Guess I'll go back and start interrogating our buddies Etkin and Orlov. Who knows how much I can learn before we dump them in 50K?" The technology captured from Etkin was going to be well received by Central. Roebeck would probably get a real enthusiastic "atta-boy" for a mission well done.

Maybe if the ARC Riders asked Command what to do with the Up The Line revisionist, they'd have been told to bring Etkin to Central. At Central, Command would have squeezed every bit of information about UTL technologies and break-away factions out of Etkin's brain. But that decision was way above all their pay grades. Grainger was pretty sure he didn't want to know any of the details he was about to find out. But his team was charged with taking that information back to Central. When the ARC had that data, this mission was going to be classified out of existence.

Etkin himself was one problem that Grainger felt perfectly competent to handle. Orlov and his hard-liner friends were only some poor fools who backed the wrong team and were just starting to pay the price. There was no reason not to leave Orlov, Neat, Lipinsky, and the old revisionists to the mercy of 50K's flora and fauna. However they died, it wouldn't be worse than being HPM'd and then trapped under a molten filing cabinet in Obninsk. But Etkin was a different animal. A potentially valuable one. Grainger would personally inject a locator into Etkin's scrotum. Not much chance, in 50K, that Etkin would try digging it out of there. If Command later wanted the revisionist back, all they had to do to retrieve Etkin for further interrogation was follow the bouncing ball.

He went back to see Etkin in his holding casket. The caskets had clear view windows so that you could check on the prisoners. There was a slot for food and water in case you had them long enough to feed them, and a two-way intercom enabled from outside only.

Just Etkin's handsome blond head and neck were visible through the window. The revisionist's eyes were closed.

Grainger tapped the intercom. *"Privyet, tovarisch."*

Etkin's eyes snapped open. "Where's Orlov?" Etkin demanded.

Grainger didn't see a good reason not to tell him. The sooner Etkin understood his situation, the better. Might as well establish what was what. "Next holding casket over. Don't worry, as soon as we dump you and your Russian revisionist buddies in 50,000 BC, you can all compare notes."

"Fuck you," Etkin snarled, and lunged against the casket window. The revisionist from Up The Line wasn't much of a threat stripped naked in a casket, but Etkin would figure that out soon enough.

"Easy there. I just came to see if you're comfortable."

"We're going to bury you, you know, Grainger! You think you're civilized. You're not. You're primitives playing with toys you don't understand. We will rise from the ashes of the 20th with an empire that will span the stars. Our Fourth Rome *will* live! You haven't the technology, the might, or the brains to stop us. You're only mongrels, our natural inferiors. We'll blot you out forever—"

"Seems to me I've heard that kind of talk before." Grainger interrupted Etkin and toggled off the intercom with a slap at the glass.

Tim Grainger headed forward without a backward look. Etkin wasn't ready to be reasonable yet. How come these guys always thought they invented the Superior Race? Among Etkin's cohorts Up The Line, everybody was probably just as blond and beautiful as he was. But nobody from a superior race was going to be waiting for Etkin where he was going. Grainger would give the revisionist a chance to calm down and try again before he turned Chun and her mind probes loose on him. Chun would extract from Etkin every name and location of Etkin's revisionist agents, as well as the scope and design of the conspiracy Up The Line. Etkin would name names. Grainger was going to bet Roebeck half his hazard pay that one of those names would be Dr. Bill.

The ARC Riders would make another pass to pick up the small fry, once the big fish had been delivered to 50K and Etkin had given up whatever secrets he held most dear.

You had to let Chun verify whatever you were told by a captive. Etkin, like anybody else, couldn't be trusted to tell the whole truth, even if he swore he was cooperating voluntarily. The ARC Riders had to be thorough. Their mission parameters included apprehending every principal and collaborator involved with this particular bad idea, and dumping the lot in 50K before heading back to ARC Central. Luckily, the pickings were easy when you had a couple of principals who just wouldn't be able to resist telling you whatever they knew.

Sasha Matsak met him in the corridor. In the narrow confines, Matsak pulled out a pack of Marlboros. "Cigarette?"

"Shit, not in here." He wished he could have one. "Can't smoke in the TC." Maybe when they stopped over in 50K, he and Matsak could step outside for a smoke "Sasha, I got a bunch more American cigarettes, and lots of dollars I don't need. When we drop you back in Moscow, be sure to remind me. You can take them with you."

"*Spacebo.*" Matsak smiled. "Perhaps you will have a chance to see more of my city one day. If not today, then when Roebecka comes to pick up the young girl she will adopt. In my opinion, it will take some time to find this girl, but my Ministry will make her a priority. On our side, I understand we must establish that the girl and her mother will die from the radiation . . . ah . . . accident. Or verify that the girl has no mother. This is a relatively simple matter. We still have our ways."

"You're kidding me. What girl?" It was out of the question to go around saving innocent indigs, kid or not, about to die or not. What was Roebeck thinking, adopting a Russian kid? Then again, maybe this whole question was above his pay grade. What Roebeck did in her spare time was not his business. "Never mind. Sasha, what do you know about the implant work that Orlov's scientists were doing? Zotov slipped me a sample." Zotov was dead. He wasn't betraying a confidence.

"Oh, well. The implants." Matsak shrugged. His hand waved as if gesturing with a lit cigarette. "This is . . . program to save endangered species."

"*What?*"

"Do not laugh, this is official Academy of Sciences program, funded through Foreign Ministry by KGB. Implant is put into member of species which is in danger of not existing. Specimen is sent . . . back through time to find others like itself and improve species chance for survival." Matsak's eyes were boring into him. "Orlov is such a specimen. The implant in his body will send him back in time to whatever place the operator of the program chooses. This is very secret technology, of course."

"Of course. And Zotov and his boys reverse engineered the control mechanism from the crashed capsule at Obninsk, right?"

"Umm . . . So sorry, Tim. Not precisely correct. My side has been studying Obninsk artifact for many years without *concretne* result until Etkin came on the scene. It is under Security Service direction that the Foreign Ministry's Academy scientists have achieved—had achieved, for now there is *nyet* program, *nyet* key scientists left—the ability to send an implanted specimen to the past."

"Came on the scene? Are you telling me that Etkin *survived* the nuclear explosion of the UTL capsule I saw on that tape?" It was possible, if Etkin had been wearing the right hardsuit. The suits on the tape were more like the new exo-suits that the ARC Riders requisitioned at Central than the standard ARC issue. But why hadn't Etkin displaced back Up The Line? Suit malfunction? Blast damage? Unless Etkin had been in an active bubble or hanging out phase, crippling suit damage was a real possibility anywhere near ground zero. The UTL capsule that had displaced to that Russian town was capturing young adult Russians to implant, probably for the 9 AD operation. . . . Grainger's mind was racing, picking up pieces and fitting them into the puzzle. A picture was beginning to emerge. *Don't jump to conclusions.*

"Tim, I am saying you only what I know for certain. Etkin was no one of importance before the UFO came to Obninsk. After this, he is *bolshoi* senior official with sweeping powers in Section 6, KGB. Boss of Orlov's scientists, Lipinsky, many others."

Then Grainger finally realized what he had been missing. "Those implants. Just the living organism goes, right? And what he's physically carrying. If I understand the methodology, you couldn't carry much, no significant hardware, with you through time that way. So how do you get back? The handheld enabler? Or is the implant a round-trip mechanism, set with some sort of elapsed-time delay. Or what?"

"You do not."

"You do not what?"

"You do not get back," Matsak said flatly. He shook his head sadly. "Still you think like an American. The agents in the past—so what if they stay there forever? They are agents. If their mission is in the past, then in the past is where they will be. *Ruskie* scientists have not yet perfected the travel to the future. Perhaps now, they will not."

Grainger was staggered. His mouth was hanging open. He shut it. He leaned back against the bulkhead wall. "My error," he said with a weak grin. "I forgot this was a *Ruskie* operation." It sounded like Etkin had been stranded in Russia, unable to get home in a damaged displacement suit when his temporal capsule was destroyed by a Russian nuke. MIA— Missing in Action. Presumed dead Up The Line. He'd continued his mission from the Russian staging area where he'd become a castaway. "I didn't really understand what you were trying to tell me until now. So where does Orlov fit in?"

"It is my fault. So sorry for my poor English. Orlov is next . . . traveler by implant, yes? He will go—would have gone, since you have interfered—to the past. To wherever Etkin is—was—sending KGB agents."

"And Orlov knows he can't get back?"

"Ha! I do not think Orlov knows this. Only real scientists know this. Boys and show scientists think that anything is possible, including travel to future. It would be amusing to tell Orlov this, if he will be free with Etkin and Lipinsky at the same time and place."

Once a Russian senior official, always a Russian senior official.

"I—Sasha, that implant doesn't automatically trigger a displacement, right? Orlov's not going to disappear into the past before our eyes, is he? You have an enabler—a piece of hardware, right, to trigger the system?" Grainger was poised on the balls of his feet, ready to push by Matsak and warn Roebeck that they'd better get that implant out of Orlov before they lost their captive.

Matsak said, "*Nyet problema.* The enabling technology is among the artifacts you captured."

So the ARC Riders had it all. The implant. The enabler. A bag full of advanced UTL technology. Etkin. Orlov. Neat. And Matsak, a bonus. Finally, Grainger relaxed. His whole body seemed heavy. Tired. His head hurt. His bruises throbbed. His ribs ached where Lipinsky had beaten him. But despite it all, he felt pretty good. Satisfied. "*Spacebo,* Sasha. Thanks for the overview. I owe you one."

"You are giving me one—a new hope for future. So sorry, my country is broken. We are fixing it. You will see. Someday Russia will be great once more."

"Yeah. I know," Grainger replied thickly. Luckily, that day wouldn't be hastened by Etkin, Orlov, Lipinsky, and a bunch of unwitting kamikaze revisionists. That day would come soon enough for a lucky Russian kid who Roebeck was adopting. And for Matsak, the ARC's new agent in place. "Guess I'd better start explaining how you file reports with the ARC. How to contact Roebeck about her kid when you're ready. Or us. Whenever you need us."

"This is very well," said Matsak with a smile. "Very well indeed."

Under Grainger's feet, the bulkhead shivered slightly as Chun took the TC out of phase, displacing to 50K.

Vetera, Lower Germany

Pauli braced one foot on the bear's shoulder and drew up on the javelin with all his considerable strength. The point was deep in a neck tendon. When it released, the iron came out kinked just as it was designed to do.

Archers walked skittishly toward the team, obviously nervous. Beckie eyed them and said, "Is there any chance the capsule will arrive in—"

She corrected herself. "Soon, that is?" Her voice was steady.

"No," Pauli said. "They'll arrive next week as we decided. They can't view the horizon without shifting the revisionists."

He threw down the useless javelin. The base of the blade was tempered soft so that it bent on impact. An enemy couldn't throw the javelin back or even pull its weight out of his shield.

What it meant at the moment was that Pauli Weigand couldn't threaten the oncoming archers with the javelin. It wouldn't have been much of a threat anyway, but you use what you have.

Gerd Barthuli seated himself on the sand. "Neither Nan nor the automatic systems could hold the capsule sufficiently far out of phase to view the horizon without displacing the revisionists," he said. "Quo on occasion has demonstrated quite remarkable delicacy with the controls, however."

"I didn't think I could get Svetlanov's gun," Beckie said. "I thought I'd be more use here."

The only thing she could do here in the arena was die with

her teammate. Pauli's conscious mind wanted that less than anything else in the world, but a part of his subconscious was glad of the company.

"I was creche-raised," said Gerd as he sat cross-legged, bending over his sensor pack. "I suppose you were also, Pauli. I've always found it interesting to view earlier time horizons in which family groupings are the norm."

"Trust me," Beckie said dryly. "This team works better than any family *I* knew when I was growing up."

"Gerd, let me have your pistol," Pauli said. "Can you make a hologram to draw their attention?"

"I've been trying," the analyst said. His right hand continued to key the air as he reached across with his left to give Pauli the microwave pistol. "In daylight I can't get sufficient contrast in an image large enough to be seen at a distance."

A waver at the corner of Pauli's eye hinted that a giant figure stood beside them. Except for Gerd's statement, even Pauli would have thought it was a heat shimmer.

"All right," he said. It was what he'd expected. He'd also expected that Gerd would be trying.

The archers halted a hundred meters from the team. They'd spread out just as the pack of dogs had done, facing the team in a broad arc.

Pauli raised his hand and called, "Halt or feel my power!"

A brawny, black-haired man in leather vest and breeches nocked an arrow and drew it back. From the look of him, he didn't even understand the Latin words. He probably couldn't hear Pauli's voice over the crowd noise anyway.

Pauli aimed with the grace of long practice and squeezed his pistol's trigger. The arrow twisted away from the bow and fell to the sand. The microwave pistols couldn't seriously affect a human being at this range, but a pulse *could* flick a few ounces of wood to the side.

The archer's mouth opened in amazement. He reached for another arrow, then dropped his bow and backed away from it.

A man on one end of the line drew and loosed with a convulsive jerk. The arrow flew so wildly that he must have closed his eyes at the moment of release, but his attempt broke the spell. The fact he *could* shoot without being struck down by magic encouraged a dozen more to raise their bows.

Pauli swept his pistol across the line; beside him, Beckie was doing the same thing. It didn't help. An arrow spiked so close in front of Gerd that it kicked sand onto the sensor in his lap.

A spot of vivid yellow light appeared in the middle of the arena and grew instantly into a ball ten meters in diameter. The archers ran back, stumbling and spilling arrows in their haste.

The ball became paler as it formed into a woman twenty meters high. You could vaguely see the seats on the other side of the amphitheater through her, as if the image was a sheet of colored glass.

"It's Nan!" Beckie cried.

"They're copying the apparition that came to Drusus just before he died on the Elbe seventeen years ago!" Gerd said in delight. "Brilliant! A brilliant thought!"

"Come on!" Pauli said. "Gerd, you were sure right about Quo being able to handle the capsule!"

He grabbed the analyst to help him up. TC 779 shimmered into phase beneath the giant image. Tim Grainger stood in the open hatchway with a fléchette gun ready to cover Pauli's team.

Pauli knew the giant figure was a hologram of Nan Roebeck, but he could still feel awe at its translucent majesty. The figure pointed its forefinger at Tiberius.

"Oh, rash man!" its voice thundered. "Know that if you attempt to conquer Germany, your life shall end there as surely as your brother's did!"

That would put paid to any chance of Rome mounting a major invasion of Germany for the next generation. After that Rome's opportunity would be lost forever. Nan wasn't one to do a job halfway.

None of them were. They'd done the job with minimal resources and by heaven! they'd done it.

Pauli Weigand shouted in triumph as his team sprang aboard TC 779. Behind them the emperor-to-be stared without expression at the team that had saved his life and their own future.

DAVID DRAKE was born in Dubuque, Iowa, in 1945. He graduated Phi Beta Kappa from the University of Iowa, majoring in history (with honors) and Latin. He was attending Duke University Law School when he was drafted. He served the next two years in the Army, spending 1970 as an enlisted interrogator with the 11th Armored Cavalry in Viet Nam and Cambodia.

Upon return he completed his law degree at Duke and was for eight years Assistant Town Attorney for Chapel Hill, North Carolina. He then drove a city bus for a year and, since 1981, has been a full-time freelance writer.

Drake has a wife, a son, and various pets. He lives in a new house on 22 acres in Chatham County, North Carolina, where he feeds sun-flower seeds to the birds.

JANET MORRIS is Vice President of Morris & Morris, a private consultancy specializing in new defense technology and non-lethal warfare. She is a Fellow at the Center for Strategic and International Studies in Washington, D.C. She has participated in several unprecedented U.S./Russian technology exchanges. in collaboration with David Drake, she has written *Active Measures* and *Kill Ratio*, among other novels. With her husband, Chris Morris, she has written *The American Warrior* and other titles. She is also the author of the *Tempus* series.